TRENT'S OWN CASE

Edmund Clerihew Bentley was born in London in 1875; he won a scholarship to Merton College, Oxford, and it was while studying Law in London that he began writing for various newspapers and magazines. Although he was called to the Bar in 1902, most of Bentley's working life was spent at the *Daily Telegraph*. He first retired from journalism in 1934, but the outbreak of the Second World War and the call-up of younger men saw him return as literary critic in 1939, eventually leaving for good in 1947. His reputation as a crime writer rests almost entirely on his first detective novel, *Trent's Last Case*, widely acknowledged as the book that inspired the Golden Age of detective fiction. Bentley died in London in March 1956.

Herbert Warner Allen was born in Godalming, Surrey in 1881; he won a scholarship to University College, Oxford, and, with a talent for modern languages, was appointed Paris correspondent of the *Morning Post* in 1908. In 1914 he was an official representative of the British press at the French front, accompanying the British in Italy in 1917 and the American expeditionary force in France, and as a result was responsible for publishing many of the early reports on the war. He wrote books on his wartime exploits, spirituality, and detective novels including *Mr Clerihew: Wine Merchant*, *The Uncounted Hour* and *Death Fungus*, but it was his highly respected books on wine for which Allen became best known. He died in Berkshire in January 1968.

By the same author

Trent's Last Case
Trent Intervenes

E. C. BENTLEY

AND

H. WARNER ALLEN

Trent's Own Case

WITH AN INTRODUCTION BY
MARTIN EDWARDS

COLLINS
CRIME
CLUB

COLLINS CRIME CLUB

An imprint of HarperCollins*Publishers*
1 London Bridge Street
London SE1 9GF
www.harpercollins.co.uk

This paperback edition 2020

First published in Great Britain by Constable & Co. Ltd 1936

This novel is entirely a work of fiction. It is presented in its original
form and may depict ethnic, racial and sexual prejudices
that were commonplace at the time it was written.

A catalogue record for this book is
available from the British Library

ISBN 978-0-00-833392-8

Typeset in Bulmer MT Std by
Palimpsest Book Production Ltd, Falkirk, Stirlingshire

Printed and bound in Great Britain by
CPI Group (UK) Ltd, Croydon CR0 4YY

MIX
Paper from
responsible sources
FSC C007454

This book is produced from independently certified FSC™ paper
to ensure responsible forest management.

For more information visit: www.harpercollins.co.uk/green

INTRODUCTION

FEW detective novels published during 'the Golden Age of Murder' between the two world wars were as eagerly anticipated by crime fiction enthusiasts as *Trent's Own Case*. The book first appeared in 1936, and within months its publishers Constable felt able to boast that it was the best crime novel of the year—quite a claim given that the competition included Agatha Christie's *The ABC Murders*, one of the enduring classics of the genre. Yet despite its initial success, the book has long been out of print.

Edmund Clerihew Bentley's first novel, *Trent's Last Case* (known as *The Woman in Black* in the US) had been published almost a quarter of a century earlier, in 1913. A journalist, Bentley (1875–1956) had been struck by the thought 'that it would be a good idea to write a detective story of a new sort'. Although he admired the Sherlock Holmes stories, he was sceptical about the concept of the Great Detective, and soon 'the most pleasing notion of all came to me: the notion of making the hero's hard-won and obviously correct solution of the mystery turn out to be completely wrong. Why not show up the infallibility of the Holmesian method?' The detective who proved all too human and error-prone was Philip Trent, a gentlemanly artist with a taste for amateur sleuthing. As the title of that first book suggests, Bentley had no thought of creating what is now known as a 'series character'.

But Fate often conspires to defeat an author's intentions. *Trent's Last Case* was so well-written, and its plot twists so appealing, that people took it at face value as a highly entertaining country house murder mystery rather than as a parody. It became a best-seller, and was filmed. The legendary thriller writer Edgar Wallace hailed the book as 'a masterpiece', while

v

Dean Inge, a prominent cleric and avid crime fiction fan, said it was 'the best detective story I ever read'. After the First World War, when ingenious mystery novels packed with suspects, clues, red herrings and twists became all the rage, Bentley's book inspired a new generation of writers, including Agatha Christie, Dorothy L. Sayers and Anthony Berkeley.

When Berkeley founded the Detection Club, a social network for leading detective writers, in 1930, Bentley's lifelong friend G.K. Chesterton became the Club's first President and Bentley was invited to become a founder member. Although he'd shown little appetite for building on the remarkable success of his debut, younger writers whom he'd influenced held him in high regard, and possibly it was encouragement from fellow Detection Club members that then helped to persuade Bentley to revive Philip Trent in a sequel.

Trent's Own Case was, however, a collaborative work, and the person who did most to urge Bentley to return to the fray was his co-author, Herbert Warner Allen (1881–1968), a wine expert and occasional crime writer. It seems likely that the majority of the writing was done by Bentley, although Trent was not the only recurring character. Warner Allen's own creation, the wine merchant William Clerihew, had appeared in 'Tokay of the Comet Year', a short story published in 1930, and also in the book *Mr Clerihew: Wine Merchant* three years later. Here a champagne cork supplies a clue which is discussed between Trent and Clerihew in one of the most appealing scenes in the book. The Clerihew name was a hat-tip to Bentley, who had, long before, devised the humorous four-line verse form known as the clerihew.

Trent's Own Case concerns Trent's investigation into the death of a philanthropist whose generosity towards charitable causes masks a deeply unattractive personality. The story is told in a leisurely, discursive style, but the writing offers a variety of incidental pleasures, and Trent's return to the detection game after an extended absence is deftly explained:

'It was long enough since he had resolved to have no more to do, in a quasi-professional way, with problems of crime. But the murder of a man whom he had known, and who had aroused his interest as a human curiosity, could not be disregarded; and the utterly unexpected appearance of an old friend in the character of the self-confessed criminal had given the keenest edge to Trent's reviving taste for that grimly fascinating business.'

Writing to 'Jack' Bentley (as he was known to his friends) on 17 April 1936, before the book was published, Dorothy L. Sayers was rhapsodic: 'I was just savouring the way the story was told and submitting to the spell of beautiful writing . . . nothing about a book is so unmistakeable and irreplaceable as the stamp of a cultured mind . . . all your figures get cheerfully up and walk out of the tapestry and talk and eat and move about in three dimensions, as if it was the simplest matter in the world. It's not, of course, but you have the enormous advantage . . . of knowing, in the fullest sense of the words, how to read and write.'

The book's publication, by Constable and Company, was celebrated at a private gathering, 'The Trent Dinner', on 21 May 1936. Most of the guests were members of the Detection Club: Sayers, Henry Wade, Freeman Wills Crofts, Milward Kennedy and Nicholas Blake. The novelist Frank Swinnerton, who was quoted on the back cover of the dust jacket as saying that *Trent's Last Case* was the finest long detective story ever written, was also present; so were the publisher Michael Sadleir and his secretary, Martha Smith. But Chesterton, whom Bentley had met when they were boys at St Paul's School, was missing; his health had given way, and he died on 14 June.

Bentley succeeded Chesterton as President of the Detection Club and, having written a handful of short stories about Trent more than two decades earlier, produced several more, which were gathered in *Trent Intervenes* and published by Thomas

Nelson in 1938; Constable meanwhile published Warner Allen's new murder story *The Uncounted Hour*. The Second World War put an end to Trent's career once and for all, and although Bentley published one post-war thriller, *Elephant's Work* (1950), it was not a success. His health declined, and he gave up the Presidency of the Detection Club in favour of Sayers. After the war, Warner Allen became a good friend of T.S. Eliot, despite Eliot's decision to reject one of his thrillers: 'The plot is extremely ingenious and involved, but I think that it moves too slowly, and especially that it is very slow indeed in starting.' In his later years, Warner Allen's publications mostly concerned wine.

The critics were kind to *Trent's Own Case*. Torquemada, the *Observer*'s influential crime reviewer, was lavish in his praise, as were Milward Kennedy in the *Sunday Times* and Anthony Berkeley (under the name Francis Iles) in the *Daily Telegraph*. Later, the often acerbic Jacques Barzun and Wendell Hertig Taylor said in *A Catalogue of Crime*: 'The problem is gripping and its solution good solid work', and reckoned that it did not fall too far short of its legendary predecessor. In time, however, a reaction set in, which perhaps explains why the book has been absent from the shelves for so long. Bentley's son Nicolas, a distinguished artist and himself an occasional crime writer, regretted that his father had allowed Warner Allen to talk him into producing the sequel. Inevitably, the story could hardly match *Trent's Last Case* for originality or impact—very few books could. However, republication in the Detective Story Club now gives twenty-first century readers a welcome chance to judge this novel on its own merits.

MARTIN EDWARDS
January 2017

CONTENTS

Ἔνθ᾽ αὖτ᾽ ἄλλ᾽ ἐνόησ᾽, Ἑλένη Διὸς ἐκγεγαυῖα·
αὐτίκ᾽ ἄρ᾽ εἰς οἶνον βάλε φάρμακον, ἔνθεν ἔπινον,
νηπενθές τ᾽ἄχολόν τε κακῶν ἐπίληθον ἁπάντων.
ὃς τὸ καταβρόξειεν, ἐπὴν κρητῆρι μιγείη,
οὔ κεν ἐφημέριός γε βάλοι κατὰ δάκρυ παρειῶν,
οὐδ᾽ εἴ οἱ προπάριθεν ἀδελφεὸν ἢ φίλον υἱὸν
χαλκῷ δηιόῳεν, ὃ δ᾽ὀφθαλμοῖσιν ὁρῷτο.

CHAPTER I

SOUTHWARD BOUND

'I OUGHT to be going,' Philip Trent said. 'I've got an appointment, as I told you, and I mustn't be late. You go on dining, Slick—have some of the *crevettes* Waldorf; they will bring the roses into your cheeks. If I come round with the car tomorrow about ten, will you be more or less ready?'

'Less, I expect,' Slick Patmore grumbled. 'That is, if this ghastly weather doesn't change in the night. A two-hours' run through drizzle and chill is not my idea of a morning's pleasure.'

'It's bound to change in the night,' Trent assured him. 'The only question is how many times it will change. That's the exciting thing about a variable climate like ours; and it is at its best in April, as everybody knows. Oh to be in England, now that April's there, and whoever wakes in England is entirely unaware whether it is going to rain cats and dogs or be gay with sunshine, birds and blossoms. Besides, it isn't a question of pleasure for you and me tomorrow. It is duty, Slick, duty whose stern behest impels us to the deed of going to see Julian Pickett married.'

'And drink his health in what old Blinky Fisher imagines to be champagne,' Patmore added, moodily helping himself to another glass of La Tour–Figeac.

'Why shouldn't he have an imagination, just because he is a Canon of Glasminster?' Trent asked. 'He'll need it, I should say, when he gives away his niece to Julian, and has to pretend that he has some sort of responsibility for a girl of the present time. Ha! I can see it now. "Who giveth this woman?" Come on, Blinky; to what green altar, O mysterious priest, lead'st thou

1

that heifer? Probably he will have mislaid his spectacles, and will try to give Julian away.'

'Didn't you say you had an appointment?' Patmore hinted.

Trent, descending the staircase of the Cactus Club, stood in the doorway and lighted a cigarette as he nerved himself to the task of going to see his favourite aunt off on the boat-train to Newhaven. It is a part of our island heritage, he mused, that at such times as we are on the point of leaving the country the weather is usually pretty beastly. As God tempers the wind to the shorn lamb, so the Briton about to uproot himself from the native soil is upheld and solaced by the thought that the climate he is going to cannot possibly be so objectionable. An erroneous thought, perhaps; but what thoughts (he asked himself) are not so? This particular evening, at least, was quite noxious enough to warrant the rosiest anticipations of what it was going to be like anywhere across the Channel. Fortunate indeed was Aunt Judith!

As he looked out across Piccadilly, the air was full of a yellowish drizzle that had not character enough to be a fog. Behind the Green Park railings the trees showed vague drab outlines suggesting the scenery of a hell where the ache of dull depression reigned rather than any pain. Everywhere was that thin and scanty slime which modern cities dignify by the noble name of mud.

Trent glanced at the clock in the porter's office. He had told Patmore the truth, and nothing but the truth; not the whole truth, which, after all, nobody ever tells, if only because there is not time. He had an appointment, and he must not be late, since the 8:20 from Victoria waited for no man; but the fact that he intended to be there a quarter of an hour beforehand, and the reasons for that decision, would not have interested his friend. Although Trent had, like most of us, a strong distaste for prolonged farewells, he knew that Aunt Judith expected the decent observance of any social rite; and fifteen minutes appeared to him to hit the happy mean between the over-assiduous and the perfunctory. During the brief drive to the station he might tax his brain—fond hope!—for some happy and original form of good-by.

As he buttoned his overcoat, the slamming of the door of a motor-car came from without. The swing-door of the entrance was pushed half open, and a tall man, roaring with laughter, paused with his foot on the threshold, and spoke over his shoulder. '*Gute Nacht, du alte gute Kerl,*' he called, '*und herzlichen Dank.*'

'*Ach Quatsch!*' a harsh voice barked in reply as the car rolled away. '*Wiederseh'n!*'

The new comer pushed through the doors and moved with long strides across the hall. Trent knew the man well enough; so well as to want no conversation with him. A completely unashamed and unscrupulous egotist is not as a rule the best of company, even if one has not, as Trent had, a personal reason for objecting to his existence. There was, too, always the strong possibility that Eugene Wetherill would not try to be the best of company. The habits of that brilliant man of letters included a tendency to be gratuitously offensive, and Trent had had more than one unpleasant encounter with him before.

Turning his head as he reached the stairway, Wetherill caught sight of Trent and raised a hand in recognition. 'You're looking damnably serious,' he observed with a wolfish grin. 'It isn't the sight of me, I hope, that has banished the winning smile. Forget your trouble, dear friend. All may yet be well. Forget our little disagreements in the past. Drown your sorrow with me at the bar—it's astonishing what a lot can be drowned in one small absinthe cocktail.'

'Thanks, but I've got to go,' Trent said. He added, 'You don't look as if you had anything much to drown. If I look serious, you look quite pleased.'

'So I am.' Wetherill laughed as he removed his broad-brimmed black hat and white scarf so that it could be seen he was in evening dress beneath his overcoat. 'Much pleased. Nothing to drown, as you remark with that infallible discernment of yours; so I shall have that drink purely as a matter of principle—not with any sordid utilitarian purpose. Pleased! I should think I am pleased. I did a good stroke of business yesterday, dear friend, and I haven't got over it yet.' He paused a moment, as if recollecting himself; then he went on: 'Whenever that happens, I have an unreasonable impulse to forgive the world for being what it is, and mankind for being what they are.'

'Including Eugene Wetherill, I hope,' Trent suggested sympathetically. 'You ought not to be too hard on yourself, you know—it's a fatal tendency. Fight it. Don't let it master you. I've got to tear myself away now, but remember my words.' He hurried through the doorway and down the greasy pavement in the direction of Piccadilly.

Wetherill, he thought, was certainly in a state of high satisfaction about something. The expression of contempt which he usually wore was probably, like all the rest of his external appearance, a carefully studied effect; but this evening it had yielded place to a look of genuine pleasure, and Trent wondered what might be the cause of it. Anything that pleased Wetherill would be quite likely to have a very different effect upon more normal minds; and Trent happened to know—as a good many people, unfortunately, knew—of one stroke of business done by Wetherill with which few men would have cared to soil their hands. But that had been months ago; this was evidently something recent, and it was curious that Wetherill had plainly hesitated to say what it was. He was anything but secretive as a rule about his own affairs, even the most discreditable; he liked posing as a paragon of immorality. It was difficult to reckon with a man who boasted of having destroyed his own self-respect.

A massive policeman loomed up at the corner of Charles Street.

'Not a nice night, Officer,' Trent remarked.

'That it isn't, sir,' rumbled the constable in a tone suggesting that the grimy mist had found its way beneath his heavy water-proofs and permeated all his being. 'There's some that seem to enjoy it, though. See those runners coming up the other side of the way? Gawd! Sooner them than me. Funny amusement, isn't it, sir, on a night like this?'

'Splendid for them, really,' Trent said. 'When they've had a rub down and a change they'll be as happy as so many kings of the Persians. It is youth, Officer—youth footing swift to the dawn, or to the Polytechnic, or somewhere delightful. We ought to envy them.'

Pushing on past the scattered procession of bedraggled lads in shorts and singlets who were jogging along in twos and threes at the edge of the pavement, Trent found the cab-rank he sought.

As he sat in the taxi, Trent's thoughts turned back to the inter-view with old James Randolph which had preceded his dinner at the Cactus Club. It had been, he reflected, shorter than he had anticipated; shorter and even more unpleasant. Nobody could be expected to enjoy the discovery that one of his secrets, and a decidedly humiliating one at that, was shared by another person not at all well disposed towards him. Still, Randolph's uncontrollable rage had seemed rather excessive for the occa-sion; he stood, after all, to lose nothing in either purse or repute so long as he behaved himself. And as to that there could be no doubt. Trent's threat of exposure had obviously been quite effective. Whether Randolph's denials of any dishonourable purpose were sincere or not, the man was certainly frightened now, and would conduct himself accordingly. Any scandal about the Tiara of Megabyzus would be a deadly blow to the old man's inflated self-esteem. In short, Aunt Judith could be fully reassured before she left. If she were to do so with any remaining uneasiness about Eunice, it would spoil the trip to which she had looked forward so eagerly.

All his life Trent had been strongly attached to his aunt, that unusual old lady. This was a great moment in the life of Miss Judith Yates. She was leaving England for the first time in nearly forty years. Brought up in the twilight of the Victorian era, she had seen in her youth not a little of the world abroad; but the time had come when an over-confident brother had flung away most of the family fortune in some concern floated by a yet more hopeful financier. Thenceforward she had lived in the country on very small means, uncomplaining—indeed, singularly happy. She kept in touch with a wide circle of friends, many of them moving in the midst of affairs; she heard all that was made public, and a good deal that was not, of the world's events, and the seamy side of high life and politics was pretty well known to her. Her prim appearance masked an exceedingly active, well-furnished and seasoned mind. Sometimes, to her amusement, modern young women imagined that they had shocked her; actually, Miss Yates in her time had contemplated with calm breaches of convention more startling than anything coming within their philosophy. She asked only that there should be something about the trespass that was worth considering; it was at pettiness and worthlessness that she drew the line. The closest bond of affection in her life, indeed, was a friendship, quite casually begun, with Eunice Faviell, the most brilliant of the younger generation of actresses, whose private history centred in a liaison that was no secret to the world she lived in.

A few months earlier she had come into a legacy, and had decided at once to see something, while health remained to her, of the European world again. 'I mean,' she had told Trent, 'to travel in luxury, and to go on travelling until the money is spent.' The journey now in prospect was a visit to friends in Rome, and she had declared herself as excited as when she went to her first dance, ready to savour every moment and every incident . . .

It was by a chance that she was taking the Dieppe route. She had meant to enjoy the comforts of the shorter crossing; but as it happened, a commission that she had given to her nephew Philip could not be carried out until the evening of her day of departure. So, with memories of having been a good sailor, she had decided to take the night service.

It was this errand that had taken Trent to his acrimonious interview with James Randolph; and he was reviewing now, as the taxi took him to Victoria, the grounds of his conviction that the job had been well and truly done. Aunt Judith, he knew, had eyes of the sharpest, and would guess only too readily that all was not well if he showed any sign of uncertainty.

Arrived at the terminus, with a little more margin of time than he had planned, he proceeded to the boat-train platform, stopping by the way to make a purchase at the flower-shop within the precincts. To his surprise, Aunt Judith was not to be seen. She had, of course, her place reserved; but Trent, knowing well her habits of mind, and knowing too that it was the first time in her life that she would be travelling in a first-class Pullman, had assumed that the longer she took over the preliminaries the greater her pleasure would be.

As he turned back, however, from his search for a non-existent Pullman in the forward end of the train, he saw his aunt supervising the transfer of hand luggage to a seat in a rearward section. She must have followed close upon his footsteps through the barrier. As he approached, she was conferring with the Pullman attendant, and that occupational optimist was giving a favourable view of the prospect for the Channel crossing. Trent presented his tribute of exuberant carnations.

'Oh! That is kind of you, Philip. My favourite flower! And exactly what was wanted for the finishing touch to this stage of the adventure. My dear, you cannot imagine how I feel about it. Everything is so different from what it used to be—I mean everything in the way of getting abroad.' Aunt Judith certainly appeared to be enjoying to the full the excitement that she had tasted in anticipation. Her eyes were bright, and her cheek had an unaccustomed flush.

Trent came at once to the point that was uppermost in his mind. 'You will be glad to hear that it is all settled about Eunice. I saw Randolph this evening, as I had arranged, and I made quite sure that he won't trouble her again. You know, Aunt Ju, I could see you didn't feel quite confident about it when I told you I knew how to get a really binding promise out of the old man. Well, that is what I've done; you can set your mind at rest. I couldn't explain to you how I was going to manage it, and I can't now. I told him, you see, that I would keep quiet about it, as long as he lived at least; it was a bargain. But it's all right.'

'It is such a relief to know that, Philip.' Miss Yates buried her nose in the carnations gratefully. 'You are quite right, I couldn't help being a little worried until it was quite certain.'

'All the same,' Trent went on, 'it looks as if I am booked for a bit of a row with Eunice about it. It seems you wrote to her saying you had told me what had been going on, and you were letting me loose on the old man. She doesn't like it. I got a note from her yesterday, and it wasn't a nice note, though knowing what she is it didn't altogether surprise me.'

There was a slight but perceptible elevation of Miss Yates's chin. 'What do you mean, Phil, by knowing what she is?'

'Now don't get up in arms, Aunt Ju. Of course I didn't mean . . .'

'My dear boy, I am not up in arms, but . . .'

'Well, call it a partial mobilization then. You can't bear to hear a hint of criticism of Eunice, everybody knows that. It's how I feel myself about her, for that matter. But there's no harm in saying I wasn't surprised to be told that her private affairs were none of my damned business, and that she would be obliged if I would keep my nose out of them, and that she was perfectly capable of looking after herself . . . with more to the same effect.'

Miss Yates, smiling, laid a neatly gloved hand on his arm. 'If that's all you mean, Phil, by saying you know what she is, why of course you do . . . it's common knowledge that Eunice has a good allowance of spirit. I dare say you have heard things in that tone of voice from her before. So have I, sometimes. So has your wife, though she is a much older friend than you are. None of us take it too tragically, I am sure. We all know . . .'

'What she is. Wasn't that what you were going to say, Aunt Ju? So there we are again at the starting-point of our misunderstanding, and we find ourselves in complete agreement—just like foreign ministers in an official communiqué.'

'Yes; only we really are, my dear. Now I will confess to you, Phil, that I thought it quite possible she might write you something like that, and I hoped that you would disregard it. She has always insisted on managing her own life just as she likes, and making a hash of it in any way she chooses—which she has done, goodness knows.'

Trent nodded. 'Goodness does know, indeed. Speaking of that,' he added, 'I saw Wetherill for a moment just before I started to come here. He was looking extremely well, I'm sorry to say. I never set eyes on that fellow without wanting to murder him.'

'I wish you would, I'm sure,' Miss Yates said with intense feeling. 'Though there's no way of doing it that wouldn't be too good for him.'

'Yes; and another thing against it is that it's a game two can play at. He could give me points at it. Wetherill is not the convenient sort of villain who will always take a licking from the hero without doing anything about it. He is fit to take care of himself in any sort of a scrap, he's afraid of nobody, and he loves a row. It's a fact, you know, that he killed a man in a duel at La Spezia, after being wounded twice.'

'I expect he cheated,' Miss Yates said. 'I never cared much for La Spezia, and now I shall like it less. Wetherill ought to have lived in Italy of the fifteenth century, along with the Sforzas and the other Renaissance wild animals.'

'So he ought,' Trent agreed. 'But he has always left undone the things that he ought to have done.'

'She has had nothing to do with him for some time now—she told me so. But that has happened before, and it never lasts. I do wish,' Miss Yates said fretfully, 'Eunice could have managed to take that sort of interest in any other man. There were enough for her to choose from, goodness knows! and a number of them very decent fellows, I have no doubt. There was that young doctor friend of yours, I forget his name—'

'Bryan Fairman, you mean.'

'Yes. I never met him, but I always thought it would be nice for her to be married to a friend of yours and Mabel's, and I knew from the way you both used to speak of him that he was the right sort. What makes it all the more irritating is, she has always been very fond of him in a way.'

'I don't know,' Trent said, 'how many times she has refused to marry him—both of them have lost count, I should think— but I dare say she always did it in the most affectionate terms. Poor Aunt Ju! You never realized what you were letting yourself in for when you decided to become a mother to a girl like Eunice Faviell.'

Miss Yates smiled whimsically. 'When *I* decided! It was Eunice who made up her mind to adopt me—you know it was. Why she did, I don't suppose she knows herself.' Miss Yates turned the discussion to her plans of travel, and to the changes wrought in Rome since the eighteen nineties. Trent's own arrangements for the immediate future came under review. Early next day he was going down to Glasminster to attend the wedding of Julian Pickett. Perhaps Aunt Judith remembered Julian. Of course Aunt Judith did. He was the young fellow who had had a limp ever since a tiger bit him somewhere in the Himalayas.

'In the *gluteus maximus*,' Trent murmured.

'I knew it was somewhere like that,' Aunt Judith said. 'Yes; and the day you brought him to see me he rolled up a sheet of music and made a noise like a panther through it, so that Elizabeth dropped the tea-tray in the pantry, and had to be given sal volatile.'

At 8:15 Miss Yates was installed in her place, continuing the conversation through the open window. At 8:19¾ a man carrying a kit-bag hurried past the barrier. He fled to the first-class Pullman, and leapt in just as the train began to move. He was standing in the doorway, with the attendant hauling in his bag, when he chanced to turn and look Trent straight in the face.

Trent, whose casual glance had seen in him only an unknown individual in a big coat over brown tweeds, and a soft hat well pulled down, uttered an exclamation. 'Bryan! By Jove, you nearly missed it!'

'Phil! You here!' With a wild gesture the man leaned from the receding coach. 'Why the devil . . .' The rest of his shout was drowned in the rumble as the train gathered speed. Trent, in his astonishment, barely remembered to reply to his aunt's wave from the window.

What could be the meaning of Bryan Fairman's state of agitation? Why had his friend, usually so strictly self-controlled, looked and acted like a demoralized and desperate man?

CHAPTER II

A LITTLE SHEET OF PAPER

Miss Yates, for her part, had not perceived this brief scene of recognition, and she applied herself now, very contentedly, to the taking of things as they came. She observed that, as the train drew out of the station and gathered speed, there was a change in the atmosphere of the carriage. Passengers who had been painfully absorbed by long-drawn-out farewells pulled themselves together. They became more jaunty and less self-conscious. They were on the threshold of something like another existence, in which for a time they would be freed from the conventions of their environment and from neighbourly inquisition. Consciously or unconsciously, they hoped to be really rather more themselves. Moreover, they were southward bound, leaving fog and drizzle behind them. There was the sense of relief which doctors have in mind when they use the tactful expression 'change of scene.'

With a smile, Miss Yates settled herself in her place and looked round the carriage. There was a slight touch of luxury about it all which she found extremely soothing. The menu did not look exceedingly inviting, but to her there was a certain sense of adventure about dining in the train. And the man was so delightfully polite, particularly after she had ordered herself half a bottle of burgundy.

As dinner was served, she began unobtrusively to take note of her fellow-travellers, and build up for herself an imaginary picture of their lives. For Miss Yates had a keen curiosity about all strangers with whom she came in contact, and it amused her to fit each of them with a personal history. Sometimes she enjoyed the additional pleasure of contrasting her guesses with the later-appearing facts.

She had little hesitation in measuring up the tall, straight-backed, distinguished man, carefully dressed and with well-tended grey moustache, who sat nearest to her, reading a magazine. Not quite military, she decided; a more thoughtful type. Something diplomatic, undoubtedly; perhaps a newly-appointed ambassador or minister. Her conjecture would not have pleased the object of it, who prided himself on looking every inch a soldier. He was in fact a very eminent professor of history, on his way to Tunis, where he hoped to establish new facts about the battle of Thapsus that would blast the reputation of another eminent historian, whom he had been after for years.

Miss Yates was not much nearer the mark in placing the well-groomed young man of magnificent physique who came next under her eye. She thought the slight crookedness of his nose rather added to his attractiveness; too regular features often went, she had found, with an undesirable vanity in men. Some people might think his chest and shoulders over-developed, but that was often the case with rowing men, who were usually very nice boys; and Miss Yates thought of this youth as a Cambridge undergraduate going to join his parents abroad. His clothes were certainly quite right. At dinner he displayed a very healthy appetite, and drank only a little mineral water, while he happily studied a letter which Miss Yates surmised to be from a girl. She wondered what the young man could have been doing to his left ear.

The state of that organ, alas! was none of the young man's doing. Miss Yates was looking at the beginnings of what is known as a cauliflower ear, the work of Baker Isaacs of Hoxton; and the youth himself was Gunner Brand, formerly heavy-weight champion of the army, holder of the Abingdon Belt, winner of a series of lucrative professional battles, and looking forward to a contest for the world title in three months' time. He was on the way to join his trainer at their camp in Cap d'Antibes, and was now reading and re-reading a long letter from his fiancée, whose equal the world did not, in his opinion, contain.

Miss Yates was less at fault in her judgment of the neighbouring couple. Her quick glance took in a multitude of details of expression and turnout. The very pretty girl she set down unhesitatingly, and quite correctly, as a vain, selfish and bad-hearted fool. Her manner to the waiters as the train dinner was served appealed to Miss Yates as the very acme of the sort of *hauteur* represented in American films of English high-life. The young man, evidently her lately married husband, was a weak but not unamiable fool. Their whole appearance bespoke considerable wealth; and Miss Yates reflected, not for the first time, on the dangerous extent to which complete worthlessness is represented among the rich.

She understood best of all, perhaps, the kind of man who had so narrowly escaped missing the train. She liked his face, with its clean-cut lines and cloven chin. About thirty, she said to herself; an earnest type; a trained mind and a worker; perhaps a doctor; normally well controlled, but now showing signs of illness and all but ungovernable agitation. There was something reckless and haunted about his appearance. The term 'Byronic' occurred to Miss Yates's unmodern mind. Was he, perhaps, suffering from a broken heart? Miss Judith believed in broken hearts, though she had learned that they can be broken in more ways than one. Certainly this man was desperately worried about something. He ate but little at dinner, and he drank a whole bottle of champagne without any visible improvement of his spirits. His hand shook as he raised his glass. Miss Yates wondered if he were flying from justice; but she could not think him an evil-doer.

As soon as he had finished his wine, he called on the waiter to clear the table at which he was sitting alone. The table clear, he planted on it his kit-bag and opened it. Miss Yates observed that on the top of its contents lay a number of paper packages, each secured with an elastic band; and of these the man proceeded to make one compact parcel, wrapped in a sheet of newspaper and tied with string. Replacing this in the bag, he next took from it a handful of sheets of paper, which he laid on the table before him.

Snapping the bag as if he was shutting up in it a guilty secret, he turned to writing busily in pencil. From where she sat Miss Judith could follow the ebb and flow of his inspiration. He would cover some sheets with a big scrawling hand, then suddenly shake his head critically, and seem to begin all over again.

'Can he be an author?' Miss Yates asked herself. 'But surely no one could compose at that rate. And he doesn't look like a literary man. A journalist, perhaps—but would a journalist be in such a dither over his work? He may be preparing a speech—but then he looks like the kind of man who would always know what he wanted to say, and would say it in plain words.'

As Miss Yates toyed with these speculations, the man wrote on. At length, rejecting yet another draft, he paused and considered; then scribbled what appeared to be a much briefer document. As he threw down his pencil, his glance met that of Miss Yates: and the blue eyes seemed to look right through her, focussed on something far beyond. So, at least, she hoped; for she saw him shudder violently before she turned her gaze away, with a sense as if she were spying on something that she had no right to see.

Vaguely she looked round the carriage, and remarked that the passengers were preparing for the arrival at Newhaven. Some with a half-furtive air were stowing cigarettes or tobacco from their bags in their pockets, with a view to the eluding of the French Customs. Others even more shamefaced were gulping down tablets and cachets of the drugs guaranteed to defy the demon of seasickness.

Miss Yates began to follow their example and prepare for transit to the boat. She had no fear of seasickness and no tobacco to conceal, but she got ready her tickets and passport. Her eyes wandered back to the agitated traveller. He had folded his final copy and placed it in a long envelope. The rest of his writing he folded into a wad, which he thrust beneath the fastenings of the newspaper-covered packet that Miss Yates had already observed.

As the train drew up at the platform he was the first to leave the Pullman; and Miss Yates noticed that as he started from his chair a piece of thin paper was wafted from it, unseen by him, to the floor of the carriage. It was unmistakably a leaf torn from an engagement-block, being headed by a printed date in thick capitals, with pencilled jottings below. So much Miss Yates could not but notice as she bent to pick it up; but the man was already heading a stream of travellers passing out, and she saw nothing of him as she stepped to the platform.

'But certainly,' she thought, 'he will be crossing to Dieppe, and I shall see him on the boat.'

There, indeed, he was, already striding rapidly up and down the upper deck on the starboard side. Miss Yates attended first to the stowing of her own hand luggage. The turmoil of cargo-shifting and the casting-off of moorings ended at length; the steamer began to plough its steady way towards France. It was then that Miss Yates approached the man who had so much engaged her sympathy.

'When you left the train, sir,' she said without any nervous preliminary, 'you left this little sheet of paper which had fallen from your seat to the floor. I thought it might be something of importance, so I had better return it to you.'

The man gazed at her a little wildly; then at the leaf which she was holding out to him. His eyes narrowed as he examined it in the half-light of the deck lamps; then he looked away, his face contorted as if with fear or keen anxiety.

Suddenly he turned to Miss Yates squarely. 'You have made a mistake, ma'am,' he said, in a shaking voice. 'Very kind indeed of you to take the trouble, but that paper is not mine. I never saw it before. Many thanks all the same.' He jerked a bow at her and immediately resumed his uneasy pacing of the deck.

Miss Yates was naturally taken aback. Why the man should

so reject her good offices she was unable to conceive. The paper had unquestionably fallen from his chair. More than that—she had seen him, with a perplexed and frowning brow, intently studying that very paper more than once during the progress of his writing. Indignation might have overcome her; but Miss Yates was one of those who will always find excuses for anyone seeming so distressed and overwrought as did this fellow-passenger. She felt the agreeable thrill of a mystery as she carefully tucked the disowned scrap of writing in a pocket of her handbag.

The voyagers, for the most part, settled themselves for the crossing in the saloons and cabins, for the night was wet and cold. Miss Yates, in a glow of freedom and adventure, was resolved to lose none of the sensations proper to travel; she preferred to seclude herself with a rug in the shelter of one of the boats. That end of the deck might well have appeared deserted to the man who had so aroused her interest, when next she saw him. Emerging from one of the deck-houses, he resumed his pacing to and fro; and she noted that he now carried the shapeless package under his arm. Soon he paused beside the rail; and he quitted it with a nervous start when one of the crew passed by on some errand.

A minute later, what Miss Yates was half-expecting happened. The mysterious traveller again approached the rail, and furtively dropped overboard whatever it was that he was carrying. That done, he disappeared below; and Miss Yates saw no more of him until the disembarkation at Dieppe. She noted that he was among the first to pass out of the Customs shed; but neither on the Paris train nor elsewhere did she again set eyes on the man who had so surprisingly disowned the little sheet of paper.

Not until half an hour later did Miss Yates, having savoured the pleasure of skimming the first French newspaper she had seen for many years, think again of the leaflet which she had tried to restore to its possessor. Turning from the lively polemics of the *Homme Trompé*, which she had found more than a little bewildering, she began to review the details of the puzzle which had so much intensified the happiness of her release from the daily round of life in Farnham. The scrap of paper, now! If its possessor chose to deny his right to it, it was surely for anybody's reading.

Miss Yates drew the paper from her handbag and noted at once that it was headed by that same day's date. But what she read next, in a firm and legible pencilling, gave her a surprise far more thrilling than she had yet known in the brief affair of the mysterious passenger to Dieppe.

Heads jerked round, and startled looks were turned upon the quiet little Englishwoman, as she exclaimed aloud: 'Good gracious!'

CHAPTER III

DEATH OF A PHILANTHROPIST

To Chief Inspector Gideon Bligh's experienced eye the scene explained itself—up to a point. That able officer stood in the centre of the late James Randolph's bedroom on the upper floor of No. 5, Newbury Place, known to a simpler age as Newbury Mews. This was a small enclosure, approached by archways from the streets at either end of it, in one of the purlieus of Park Lane; No. 5 being the nearest to Bullingdon Street of the neat row of stables and coach-houses, converted now to the uses of well-to-do human habitation.

Mr Bligh stroked with one great hand his prematurely bald cranium while he considered the position. His appearance always commanded respect. He was tall and loosely built. His clean-shaven face, with its massive, vigorous features, wore habitually a stern expression. His skin, slightly tanned, was otherwise colourless.

In the doorway stood a police-sergeant, closely attentive to the proceedings of the man from headquarters. He had already put his superior in possession of the facts learned since the police had been called to the place by telephone, just after midnight; he had mentioned the points of interest so far disclosed in examination of the bedroom, and what he regarded as 'a queer piece of evidence' in the sitting-room below it. The time now was half past eight in the morning.

The body had been left by the police-surgeon as he had found it, lying prone before the dressing-table. The old man had been shot from behind and killed instantly, the bullet entering below the left shoulder-blade. He had been at the time—whether it mattered or not—in a peculiarly defenceless posture; for, being fully dressed in day clothes, he had been in the act of taking off his coat. The left sleeve was half-way down the arm, and the right had just slipped from the shoulder, so that the arms were for the moment pinioned. Clearly he had not believed himself to be in danger of any sort of attack. He had placed the contents of his pockets on the table before the looking-glass. Assuming him to have been still facing the table at the moment of his death, the murderer would have been standing at or near the doorway of the room—possibly outside the open door.

The room, kept in a state of speckless neatness, was some-what scantily furnished; but Inspector Bligh knew enough of such matters to perceive that the few movables were articles of value—probably, seeing what had been the dead man's reputation as a connoisseur, of great value.

Randolph, it was evident, had been about to dress for dinner. His evening clothes were neatly set out on two chairs. What he had carried in his pockets lay in a small disorderly heap before the looking-glass—a case containing notes to the value of seven pounds; a handful of coins; a watch with its slender chain of gold and platinum links; an eye-glass case; a leather key-case; a few letters, being ordinary business communications; a pencil; and, incongruous among these other articles, a champagne cork.

The inspector examined this last with some interest. Certainly it was an odd thing for Randolph to have been carrying, as appearances suggested, on his person. Had it been used, perhaps, to sheathe the end of some sharp-pointed object? The officer satisfied himself that this was not so. The cork was flawless and compact, to all appearances in just that condition in which it had left the bottle; it was branded 'Felix Poubelle 1884.' The inspector rubbed his chin as he considered these facts; but he found himself unable to attach to them any significance at all.

Close to this pile of personal oddments lay the separated parts of a safety razor, lacking a blade. The other materials for shaving, as Mr Bligh soon ascertained, lay among the articles on a shelf in the bathroom adjoining. They had not been recently used. On the same shelf lay the little case belonging to the razor, and within it were two new blades in their unbroken envelopes. Curious, then, was the presence of the razor alone, unscrewed and bladeless, on the dressing-table.

The inspector turned now to a small chest of drawers against the wall hard by the door opening from the passage. On the embroidered blue linen 'runner' covering its top stood a water-bottle, half-empty, and a tumbler from which, it appeared, water had been drunk. A glance showed that the inevitable finger-prints had been left on both of these—probably Randolph's own prints, the inspector reflected sadly. Still, you couldn't be sure. Murderers were not—so ran Mr Bligh's train of thought—like criminals as a rule. All the regular crooks knew about fingerprints; and none of them were deliberate killers. Murderers were apt to be quite respectable; at least to know nothing of the ways of criminals or of the police either. But again, you couldn't be sure.

Leaving this point for later investigation, he turned next to the fireplace. Randolph, the police had learned, had always a good coal fire burning in this during the cold weather. Yesterday's fire had long burnt itself out, and the inspector raked through the ashes with the small poker that lay to hand. Nothing, however, rewarded his search.

His eye travelled now over the floor of the room, and came to rest where, beneath the window, there lay a quantity of crumpled brown paper and tangled string, marring the extreme tidiness of the surroundings. A moment's examination showed that several packets, fastened with sealed cord, had been opened, their contents removed, and the covers flung down carelessly. From the appearance of these relics Mr Bligh judged them to have been slim parcels containing letters or documents of some kind, each parcel conspicuously marked with a number in soft black pencil. The string in each case, the seals being unbroken, had been cut with an instrument of peculiar sharpness, as the perfectly clean division of the strands made plain.

The inspector's eyes narrowed as his deft fingers smoothed these crumpled wrappings into their original shapes—shells emptied, now, of so much perhaps explosive matter. Had Randolph been shot for the sake of what was in these packets? Was that the murderer's intended spoil? Letters, or papers? Not money or valuables, certainly; enough of those had been left on the dressing-table. And what kind of letters or papers were worth the taking of a man's life? Apart from secret treaties and other materials of thrilling fiction, which Mr Bligh did not take very seriously, he knew of one kind which had, not seldom, been considered worth that price of guilt and peril.

But surely old James Randolph, that busy architect of good works, could have had no interest in blackmail. Scotland Yard knew of some little peculiarities of his—it knows so much about so many public characters, little as they dream of it. But there was nothing savouring of illegality. Besides, the man had been for years immensely wealthy, and the sources of his wealth were no secret. There could have been no temptation to one of the most sordid of crimes.

Setting aside this difficulty for the time, Mr Bligh poked about diligently among the brown paper and string; and on the carpet beneath them he soon discovered a safety-razor blade. His lips pursed themselves in a silent whistle. Here, no doubt, was the instrument chosen hastily for the opening of the packets—a blade taken from the razor where it had been placed in readiness for use. Bending down, the inspector noted that this was a blade of the make that went with the unscrewed razor on the dressing-table; a duplicate of the two in unopened envelopes in the razor-case.

If, thought Mr Bligh, the man who cut strings with this blade has left no fingerprints, it can only have been because he was careful not to do so. The inspector used his own pocket-knife to raise the little slip of steel from the carpet, and place it beside the water-bottle and tumbler already destined for expert examination.

His eyes now began to search the wall at this part of the room, and he discovered at once the small keyhole of a built-in safe—a safe of a primitive type, as Mr Bligh's experience suggested.

It was as he noted this that heavy and hasty footsteps were heard on the stairs, and the excited red face of a young constable appeared over the shoulder of the sergeant in the doorway. The formula which Mr Bligh had employed so many hundreds of times in the earliest phase of his career rose again to his lips. 'Now then,' he said gruffly, 'what's all this?'

'This is the man posted at the street door,' the sergeant explained in the tone of one inured to the follies of inexperience. 'What is it, Clarkson?'

'I've just found this, sir, in the corner of the passage, just inside the entrance,' the young man said. 'I thought it might be important.' He held out a green tie-on luggage-label, the string of which had somehow been snapped. 'It's a dark spot just there, and this label is much the same shade as the carpet. The door opens into a narrow passage, as you know, sir, and it would be awkward going out in a hurry with a bag of any size. This label may have caught against something, and come off without it being noticed, if the man was a bit flurried—so I thought, sir.'

The inspector, who had listened to this with wooden impassivity, now took the label in his hand. It was inscribed, in a shaky but sufficiently legible script, 'Bryan Fairman, passenger to Dieppe.'

'Dieppe, eh?' Mr Bligh said thoughtfully. 'I wonder.' He spoke sharply to the attentive sergeant. 'Get me the Yard on the phone at once.' The apparatus stood on one of the two small tables flanking the bed; and the sergeant jumped to it.

'Very good, Clarkson,' the inspector said. 'This may very possibly have a bearing on the case. I am acting on it now. You can go back to your post.' He took the telephone instrument in hand.

In a few moments he was in touch with a colleague at head-quarters, and giving swift instructions that inquiry should be made whether a passenger giving the name of Bryan Fairman had travelled by the night-boat reaching Dieppe that morning. The French police, he said, should be asked to co-operate to the extent of keeping this man, if identified, under observation, supposing that he had remained in Dieppe. If not, it would be of great assistance if his movements could be traced, as a serious charge might be brought against him.

Mr Bligh rang off.

CHAPTER IV

NOT HARD OF HEARING

'AND now,' Inspector Bligh said to his subordinate, 'for a look at the sitting-room, and that queer piece of evidence, as you call it.'

He led the way downstairs to the room beneath the bedroom. It was an apartment of less bare appearance than the other, an effect of more luxurious comfort being produced at once by the deep-piled, patternless grey carpet which covered the whole extent of the floor from wall to wall. Two low-backed, thick-cushioned armchairs flanked an old-fashioned fireplace. One of these, the one having its back towards the window, had between it and the wall a table just large enough to hold a grey-enamelled telephone instrument, a London telephone directory, and an orderly pile of journals and printed documents. There were an oval centre table and, before the window, a small writing-table; both, as the inspector correctly guessed, 'pieces' of great price. At right angles to this last an inviting double-ended sofa stood backed against the wall; beside it, rising a modest two feet from the floor, was a narrow bookcase. In the bedroom there had not been a book to be seen. The bookcase here appeared to be occupied entirely by works of reference, from the austerity of Bradshaw, Baedeker and Whitaker to the more engaging appeal of a tall row of art-sales annuals.

Mr Bligh spent little time in examining the room and its contents as a whole. All appeared to be in precisely the state of undisturbed neatness that a man of rigidly orderly habits would require in his own establishment. It was the writing-table to which a gesture from the police-sergeant directed his special attention. Upon it was trimly laid out the usual array of writing materials, with a small open-fronted cabinet of Chinese lacquer, on the shelves of which were arranged in various sizes, note-paper, sheets of blank paper, cards and envelopes.

Upon the flat top of the cabinet stood an upright engage-ment-block. It had a separate leaf, with a sentence of Scripture at the foot, allotted to each day, and the leaves were set loosely so as to be turned over on metal rings as each day passed. On the leaf which now met the eye, two afternoon appointments at City addresses were noted, followed by the words, '5:30. T. Searle to call,' presumably referring to some visitor expected by Randolph at his own house. The leaf so exposed was that for the day which had just begun; not, as would have been natural, the leaf for the previous day, the day of the crime. That leaf was missing, and vestiges of paper showed that it had been torn roughly from the file. Handling the block delicately, the inspector satisfied himself that this was the only leaf that had been so removed.

The block, he knew, had not been touched during the first police examination of the premises some hours before, when the signs of a leaf having been torn away had been noted. He considered the fact with bent brows. Someone, before or after the murder, had been tampering with this record of Randolph's arrangements, and tampering to some purpose. The fingers of Mr Bligh's left hand drummed lightly on his hairless skull—an indication with him of restrained excitement.

'You were right,' he observed to the gratified sergeant. 'This is important. I don't know, though, that I should call it queer when a murderer destroys the only direct evidence of his having been on the spot. And now I want to see this man Raught. Send him to me in here.'

Randolph's manservant, who had been told to stay in his bedroom adjoining the sitting-room, soon presented himself—a lean, small, dark-visaged individual with a furtive eye. A shifty-looking character at the best of times, thought the inspector; and now looking sick and frightened. Mr Bligh stared hard at him for a few moments; then said with a quietness that seemed only to add to the man's discomfort: 'So your name is Simon Raught.'

'Yes, sir.'

'You were the late Mr Randolph's personal servant, and you always slept on the premises when he was staying here. That right?'

'Yes, sir.'

'Any other servants?'

'Not here, sir. Mr Randolph kept his establishment at his place in Yorkshire, where he lived most of the time. Besides me, there's only a woman, Mrs Barley, to look after this place. She has a door-key and her job is to keep the place tidy, all the year round. Mr Randolph liked to have it kept so that he could come to London any time without notice, and find it ready for occupation. So long as he did find it ready—which I must say he always did—Mrs Barley could arrange her time to suit herself. When we were here, I used always to get the breakfast and do the bedrooms myself.'

Mr Bligh, still bending on Raught a gaze which he continued to avoid meeting, said gently: 'It isn't exactly your place as valet, is it, to do that sort of thing?'

'I didn't consider that, sir—not in dealing with Mr Randolph,' Raught said. He swallowed nervously, and went on: 'I didn't mind what I did for him, owing everything to him, as you might say.'

The inspector grunted sceptically. 'What about this Mrs Barley?' he asked. 'Oughtn't she to be here this morning?'

'I don't know when she'll be coming in, sir,' Raught declared. 'She had been here when we got down from Yorkshire day before yesterday, and she was here yesterday morning for an hour. But as soon as she hears of what's happened, she'll be along quick enough, you may be sure of that.'

'What do you know about her?'

'She's a perfectly respectable woman, sir, I need 'ardly say.

Before her husband died—a carpenter, I believe he was—they rented one of Mr Randolph's cottages in Humberstone. I have 'eard that Barley got into bad company, sir, and got himself into some sort of trouble, which Mr Randolph 'elped him out of; but there was never anything against Mrs Barley. Since he died, she's been living with her sister, who keeps a boarding-house used by foreigners mostly, I've been told—in Bayswater it is, Oldbury Terrace, I forget the number.'

The inspector took down these particulars in his notebook; then referred to an earlier entry.

'When you were first questioned this morning, you mentioned a secretary.'

'Mr Verney; yes, sir. He's the gentleman that had the management of all Mr Randolph's charities and that—his good works, as you may say. When Mr Randolph was staying here—'

'When did he stay here? How much time did he spend here?'

'There was nothing regular about it, sir. Every few weeks—I couldn't put it any nearer than that; sometimes it was more frequent—we would come down for two or three days. Or we might go back to Brinton the next day. This time we came the day before yesterday, the Tuesday.'

'Well, now about Mr Verney.'

'He was often up at Brinton, sir, the place in Yorkshire; but he didn't live there. He had rooms here in London, in Purvis Crescent, No. 36—off Willesley Road; I believe he spends a lot of time running the Randolph Institute, sir, in Kilburn—a sort of club, that is, for young men and boys. Whenever we were here, Mr Verney would come in, having his own door-key, to talk business. I should have expected to see him here before this, sir.'

Mr Bligh took another note; then once more he fixed the man before him with an intimidating eye.

'And where do you say you were last night, when your employer was murdered?'

Raught repeated the account of his movements of which

the inspector had already learned the substance. It had been the valet's half day off, as it always was on Wednesdays. He had not gone out until a little before 6:30, when he had done so after laying out Mr Randolph's clothes for a dinner which he was to have attended. Raught, on leaving, had gone straight to the Three Tuns in Rowington Street, where he had spent some time, and had afterwards visited the Running Stag in Gooch Street. He had often 'used' both places while in London, and was well known. Miss Whicker at the Tuns and Archie at the Stag could bear out his statement. Raught had then joined his sister, Mrs Livings, and her husband at the Pilatus restaurant in Warsaw Street at 7:30. After dinner they had gone on to Battersea, where his relations lived, and had visited the Parthenon Cinema, where a film called 'The Two-Gun Terror' was being shown. After that he had had a drink at his brother-in-law's place, and come back to Newbury Place just before twelve o'clock. He was not expected to be back, he explained, before midnight, Mr Randolph being 'very human' in that respect.

'And then?' Mr Bligh inquired in his uncomfortably colour-less tone.

Raught had gone upstairs to see if his master had returned. He had found the bedroom door wide open, the lights on, and his master lying dead on the floor before the dressing-table; it had given him 'such a turn, sir, as I never had in my life.' He had 'felt' at once that Mr Randolph was dead. There couldn't be any mistake about it, the valet said, looking at him as he lay 'all of a heap.' He had, therefore, rung up the police immediately, being careful to leave everything just as it was. He had seen, when he came in, no signs of any stranger having been about the place. In reply to a question, Raught declared that he had not touched the body, or even examined it closely, his nerves being 'all to pieces.' Then how had he known that it was murder, and a case for calling in the police? Raught had not known; he had only 'supposed it must be that.'

Inspector Bligh now resumed his silent study of Raught's unprepossessing face. The valet, his eyes wandering in all directions, pulled out a handkerchief and squeezed it between his palms. Suddenly the question was shot at him:

'Weren't you in trouble a few years ago?'

'Well, sir,' Raught said with that shade of candour peculiar to those found out, 'there was a small matter of false pretences—'

'Blackmail, don't you mean?' the inspector asked grimly. 'I thought I remembered your face—it's a kind I see a lot of.'

Raught licked his lips and took on an injured expression. 'Truly, sir, it wasn't blackmail. What would be the use of my telling you a lie? I was in a bit of a 'ole, sir—through betting, it was. I was in Mr Randolph's service at that time, and with your memory, sir, you may recollect he gave evidence of my good character while I was with him—no man could have acted kinder. I got six months, and when I came out he took me into his service again. Not many gentlemen would have done as much—saving me from drifting from bad to worse, as you may say. I would have given my life for him, sir.'

Raught's cry from the heart did not impress the inspector, to whose accustomed ear it had not a genuine ring. Nor did he think much of the man's alibi. The police surgeon had thought it probable that Randolph's death had taken place not earlier than seven o'clock and not later than ten. Unless both Miss Whicker and Archie should prove able to time their customer's coming and going with some accuracy, there was room enough in Raught's tale for him to move about in, before keeping his verifiable appointment in Warsaw Street.

Setting that matter aside for the time being, the inspector opened another line.

'Do you know anything about any person having an appointment to see your master yesterday evening, or any person who might have been coming here that evening for any reason?'

'Well, sir, the only appointment Mr Randolph had made—to my knowledge, that is—was at six o'clock, with Mr Trent, the artist, who had been at Brinton painting his portrait some time ago.'

The inspector smiled faintly. 'Ha! So Mr Trent, the artist, had an appointment at six. Why? Wasn't Mr Randolph satisfied with the portrait done by Mr Trent, the artist?'

'Oh! It wasn't that at all, sir—quite the contrary. Everyone thought highly of the portrait, and I believe Mr Randolph's intention in asking Mr Trent to call was to arrange about having another portrait done, or I should say a copy, like, of the first one. It was to be hung in the hall of the Institute, sir, the place I mentioned just now. Mr Verney was very keen about it, and though Mr Randolph was not so at first, he came to approve of the idea, sir.'

'Hm! Very natural he should.' Mr Bligh gazed thoughtfully out of the window. 'It was to be a copy, yes? For the Institute—I see. You're sure it was for the Institute?'

'Oh yes, sir. Mr Verney was very anxious they should have it. They were speaking of it when Mr Verney was at Brinton last week, sir, and Mr Randolph said he would write a note to Mr Trent at once.'

The inspector suddenly turned his eye on Raught once more. 'Not hard of hearing, are you?' he observed agreeably; and as the colour flooded the man's pale face he added: 'You're sure you haven't forgotten any other little details of this private conversation between your master and his secretary? No? All right. Then Mr Trent called at six?'

'It was just six, sir, when I opened the door to him,' Raught said subduedly. 'It was accidental, sir, as you may say, me being here when he called, because on Wednesdays my time is supposed to be my own after three o'clock. But you know, sir, what the weather was like all yesterday, and I hadn't anything to do with myself before meeting my sister and her husband at seven thirty, and so I had a bit of a sleep in the afternoon, and then there was my best suit wouldn't be none the worse for a pressing, and what with one thing—'

'Never mind all that,' Mr Bligh snapped. 'You were still here at six—is that it?'

'Yes, sir. And when I went to answer the bell, Mr Randolph was just coming out of the sitting-room to answer it himself; and he says: "Oh! You're here still," he says. "Well, if that's Mr Trent at the door," he says, "show him in here," he says. So I showed Mr Trent in.'

'And then what did they talk about?'

'I could not say, sir.'

'You didn't listen, I suppose,' Mr Bligh remarked dispassionately, 'because you knew all about it beforehand. Well; what next?'

'After about a quarter of an hour I heard the sitting-room door open, and Mr Randolph calls to me to show Mr Trent out again, which I did. And that's all I know, sir, about anyone calling on Mr Randolph yesterday, because I went out for the evening myself a little later, and never come back again till near twelve, like I told you.'

Mr Bligh considered for a few moments, still fixing the unhappy Raught with a baleful eye.

'You say you were out of here,' he summed up at last, 'by not later than 6:30. And your master had a dinner appointment in the City. You have told the sergeant here that the dinner was for eight o'clock, and that Mr Randolph would usually send for a taxi when keeping appointments of that kind. Is that right?'

'Quite right, sir. He never had his own car in London.'

'Hm! Time enough,' the inspector muttered; then: 'What do you know about a person called Bryan Fairman?'

Raught appeared sincerely surprised at the question. 'I suppose that would be Dr Fairman, sir?'

'I shouldn't wonder,' Mr Bligh grunted. 'Who is he?'

'I believe, sir, he is one of the doctors at the mental 'ospital at Claypoole, which is named after Mr Randolph, and kept up as you probably know, sir, entirely at his expense.' (Mr Bligh nodded.) 'I have seen Dr Fairman once, when he was dining at Brinton one evening. I think he had been asked over, sir, to speak about the work he was doing at the mental 'ospital.'

'You think!' Mr Bligh remarked with devastating emphasis. 'You heard what he and Mr Randolph were talking about—that's what you mean. Well, you've seen Dr Fairman. What kind of a man is he to look at? Tall or short? Dark or fair? Give me a description.'

Raught, in evident relief at the thought of some other person having attracted the notice of the police, took a moment for consideration. 'I saw him only the once, sir, and that would be about three months ago, as near as I can fix it. But I remember him as a gentleman of what you might call medium size, rather thin, with black hair and a little moustache, a bit pale in the face.'

'About what age? Does he wear glasses?'

'I should say somewhere in the thirties, sir. I didn't see him wearing glasses; he seemed to me like a keen-sighted man, his eye being sort of piercing, as they say, when he looked at you. I can't think of anything else special about him, except his acting a bit nervous-like—jerky in his movements, if you know what I mean, sir.'

'What about his expression? Pleasant?'

''Ardly that, sir. I should call it severe—not unpleasant I don't mean, not that at all, but as if he wouldn't laugh very easy. If I may say so,' Raught added with an air of cringing slyness, 'Dr Fairman's expression is a little bit like your own, sir.'

'Not unpleasant, eh?' Mr Bligh said. 'Well, you ought to know. Now then; apart from his appearance, what else do you know about Dr Fairman?'

'Nothing, sir, only what I've heard mentioned in talk some-times between Mr Randolph and other parties when—'

'When your ear happened to be in the neighbourhood of the keyhole,' Mr Bligh suggested pleasantly.

'No, sir,' the valet said, as one making patient allowance for the working of a suspicious temperament. 'In my position, sir, people's conversation often comes to my ears without me having to listen for it, even in a big 'ouse like Brinton. And as for a small place like this, you can see for yourself, sir, I'd be bound to hear a good deal of what was being talked about unless it was meant to be private—what with doors left open, or me going in and out about my work. And if I know anything about Mr Randolph,' Raught added with the first touch of genuine feeling that the inspector had noted in him, 'anything he wanted to be kept private *would* be kept private.'

'And no blooming error,' Mr Bligh prompted him with the ghost of a smile.

'You take the words out of my mouth, sir,' Raught said. 'But I only mean that the old man—Mr Randolph, I should say—was no fool, if he was kind-hearted to a fault, as the saying is. I do know this, sir—if he wanted to see anybody here without the chance of being overheard, it was his habit to make an appointment for the Wednesday evening, which has always been my time off, and open the door to them himself.'

'No fool, as you say,' the inspector observed drily.

Raught ignored this offensive interjection. 'As for what was said about Dr Fairman, his name has come up in conversation more than once between Mr Randolph and Mr Verney. Mr Verney seemed to think a lot of some special job Dr Fairman was doing at the mental 'ospital; what it was I can't say. I thought Mr Randolph didn't seem to think quite so much of it—spoke of it a bit short-like. Once, I remember, he said that the worst of these loony-doctors—'

'Did he say "loony-doctors"?' Mr Bligh cut in.

The valet hesitated. 'He did not, sir; but he used some expression which the meaning of it was obviously that. And he said that the worst of them was that when they often got a bee in their bonnets themselves—that he did say, I'll swear to it.'

The inspector smiled another wintry smile. 'I said you were not hard of hearing,' he commented. 'Did anything more about this Dr Fairman come to your ears?'

'Nothing that I can recall, sir.'

Mr Bligh sighed gently. At this hour the much-wanted Fairman, if he had caught the night-boat, as appearances suggested, might still be at his destination in Dieppe. On the other hand, his true destination was more than likely to be elsewhere, and he might be receding each moment farther beyond the reach of the English law's long arm. The inspector strode to the sitting-room telephone, and soon was in touch with the same official to whom he had spoken before. He repeated briefly, for transmission to Dieppe, Raught's description of the suspect, and asked that inquiries about him should be made immediately at the Randolph Mental Hospital at Claypoole, where he was one of the medical staff.

'Now then,' he resumed, turning to the valet who stood uneasily awaiting his attention, 'before you went out, you left your master's evening clothes ready for him?'

'Yes, sir.'

'Did you put out his razor?'

'No, sir. I never knew him need to shave in the evening. I had left the razor on the shelf in the bathroom, with the other shaving things.'

'Was there a blade in the razor?'

'I had put in a new blade ready for next morning, sir. Mr Randolph liked to have a new one every day.'

'And when you found his body, did you see the razor lying on the dressing-table?'

'No, sir. I was too much upset to notice anything of that sort.'

'You didn't even see that there was a lot of brown paper and string on the floor?'

Raught dropped his eyes. 'Now you mention it, sir, I did notice that—an untidy mess lying under the window, as if someone had been opening parcels. It slipped my memory sir—truly it did. And I never touched it.'

The inspector grunted. He had the impression that the valet was meeting all these inquiries with as much frankness as was in his nature. 'Do you know,' he asked, 'if your master kept any valuables in his bedroom?'

The man hesitated. 'None, sir, to my knowledge, except studs and links and that. But I—I fancy he had a safe set in the wall by the window.'

Mr Bligh's face hardened. 'Yah!' he said ungracefully. 'You fancy! Don't you know?'

'Well, sir,' Raught said unhappily, 'I *have* seen a keyhole.'

'Of course you have,' the inspector said brutally. 'And the edges of the door too. The question is whether you know what was behind it.'

'That I don't indeed, sir,' the valet protested. 'And it was never opened in my presence.'

Mr Bligh still surveyed him with a disparaging eye. 'Now, Raught,' he said, 'what can you tell me about this?' He indicated the engagement-block standing on the Chinese cabinet. 'Is that the usual place for it?'

The valet appeared genuinely startled. 'It certainly is not, sir,' he declared with emphasis. 'That thing—I never remember seeing it there before. I have seen it often enough, and anyone could tell what it was for, sir, of course. Mr Randolph would often jot down an appointment on it when I was about. But he wasn't ever communicative-like about his engagements—not that they were any business of mine. And this block, sir, was always treated like something specially private-like. He would always lock it away in a drawer of the writing-table—never once have I seen it left standing about like this. Most peculiar it is, to anyone knowing Mr Randolph's ways.' He shook his head portentously.

'Well, that's that,' the inspector remarked after a moment's rubbing of his chin. 'Now come upstairs,' he directed curtly. Raught's leaden complexion became visibly less healthy as he was shepherded into the room where the body still lay.

'Now, here's another peculiar thing I want your opinion about.' Mr Bligh pointed to the small heap of articles on the dressing-table. 'Did Mr Randolph usually put the contents of his pockets here?'

'Yes, sir. He always dressed here. There is no separate dressing-room.'

'And have you ever seen anything of this sort among his personal effects?' The inspector, watching the man's face, indicated the champagne cork. 'Can you think of any reason why he should have carried it about with him?'

Raught looked blankly at his questioner. 'In the five years I have been with Mr Randolph, sir, I have never seen a cork among his things. It's funny it should be that kind of a cork, too. He didn't seem ever to care for sparkling wines. At home—at the place in Yorkshire, that is—he never touched them, though he kept champagne for his guests.'

'Well,' the inspector said sharply, 'he might have had someone to lunch or dinner here, and given 'em champagne or something of the sort. You'd have known about that, I suppose.'

The valet shook his head decisively. 'He never had lunch or dinner here, sir; let alone entertaining. When in London, he would have his meals mostly at the Lansdowne Club—that was where I had to ring him up in case of anything pressing. An egg and a bit of toast and a cup of tea in the morning—that is all the food I have ever known him take here. It wasn't a 'ome, sir, not in any sense of the word. I had to cater for myself, that being allowed for in the wages—generous too. As for yesterday and the day before, he was out to lunch and dinner as usual. It's true I wasn't here at dinner-time being out for the evening; but I can answer for it there wasn't enough in the place for what you might call a proper meal. And the only drink ever kept here was some brandy and bottles of seltzer, which Mr Randolph would sometimes have a drop of before going to bed. Besides,' Raught went on after a brief pause, 'he certainly intended dining out last night, sir—the Tabarders' Company dinner it was to be—and he never missed anything to do with the Tabarders'.'

Mr Bligh looked interested. 'Didn't he?' he said. 'And why was that?'

'Why, you see, sir,' Raught explained, 'Mr Randolph was a very large contributor to the Company's charities—very munificent indeed, sir, I have heard; and he naturally liked the position it used to give him at their public occasions.'

Mr Bligh nodded. 'Of course,' he said. 'Anybody would. And so,' he added quickly, 'you knew all about it being the Tabarders' dinner-night, though you never saw what was written on the block, and Mr Randolph was never, I think you said, communicative-like about his engagements. Not only that; you knew all about how he felt on the subject of the Tabarders' dinner. You seem to know a lot more than you pretend, Raught.'

The valet's tottering self-control gave way at this. He wrung his hand together, and it was with a sobbing voice that he broke out in a suddenly degenerated speech: 'That's it! That's the way! Leading of a man on till you get 'im in a corner, and set 'im up against himself. I ain't told you nothing but what's gospel, and you come making me out a liar. Why shouldn't I know it was the Tabarders' dinner-night? I got ears, ain't I? Even if he didn't say nothing to me, I 'eard him talking about it to Mr Verney 'alf a dozen times, if you want to know; and as for 'im likin' to be made a fuss of, and to be told 'e was a-runnin' over with the milk of 'uman kindness—ain't we got a reg'lar staff of servants down at Brinton, and don't they talk over the guvnor and his little ways? Not 'alf!' Raught exclaimed with lachrymose fervour. 'Crool, that's what it is, a-badgerin' a man what ain't done nothing but his dooty about this 'ere business—sendin' for the pleece as I did, and a-dealin' with 'em honest and truthful. A chap what's once gone wrong ain't ever give a chance.' Here the valet's emotion overcame him, and he mopped his eyes in wordless misery.

'There, that's enough of that,' Mr Bligh said heartlessly. 'You've told me a lot more, my lad, than I'd have got out of you if I'd been soft with you. Now about this safe.' He took up the key-case, and held out its contents in silence.

'This 'ere's the key of the street door downstairs,' whimpered Raught. 'I know that because I've got one that's the same. I don't know nothing about any of the others, I wish I may—'

'That'll do,' the inspector snapped. He picked out without hesitation the key to fit the lock in the wall, and soon the interior of a small and shallow safe was exposed—completely empty. His eyes travelled to the small pile of wrappings still lying almost beneath the safe, and again his fingers caressed his hairless scalp.

CHAPTER V

TRENT IS TAKEN ABACK

TRENT stood at the sitting-room window of his small house in St John's Wood, gazing at the sky and meditating on the enviable life lived by such men as old Blinky Fisher, in such lovely and well-tended retreats as the Cathedral Close at Glasminster. It was the evening of the day after his leave-taking of Aunt. Judith at Victoria. He had driven down to Glasminster with his friend Patmore that morning, had surveyed the spectacle of Julian Pickett—looking rather more unnerved than a big-game hunter should—being married to a young woman who did not seem at all formidable; had foregathered with a number of old friends at the house of Canon Fisher, and had returned as he had gone.

The effect on his spirit had been, as he had known it would be, to discontent him with any way of life but that of the 'mild, monastic faces, in quiet collegiate cloisters.' Being not particularly pious, far from learned, and delighting in the society of his fellow men, Trent never came in contact with the life of piety, erudition and seclusion without yearning to be a part of it. It was, as he put it to himself in a familiar phrase of godliness and scholarship, too damned silly for words.

'What a wonderful sunset, Mrs McOmish!' Trent said.

His housekeeper, who was laying the table for his solitary dinner, glanced briefly at the flaming sky. 'I've seen waur,' she said. She was a person whose words, thought usually of the driest, were as usually highly charged with unspoken significance. In this case, Mrs McOmish contrived to convey the strongly held opinion that nothing was to be gained by encouraging either this sunset, or sunsets as a class.

Trent shook his head. 'Sophisticated!' he said sadly. 'To you, Mrs McOmish, all nature is old, outmoded stuff, I suppose. The sublime, unapproachable self-sufficiency of art—that is your whole creed.'

'No the whole,' Mrs McOmish replied guardedly. 'I dinna ken what a' that means aboot airt, and it may be pairt of the confession of the United Presbyterian Kirk, but there's a guid deal else forbye, I assure ye.'

'I shouldn't wonder,' Trent said absently. 'But a truce to theology, Mrs McOmish. We were talking animatedly about the sunset, and you were just going to recall to me those moving lines in which Sir Walter Scott describes a similar phenomenon in the neighbourhood of the Trossachs. But what says another poet, Mrs McOmish; the one who uttered nothing base, though occasionally something silly? It is, he observed, a beauteous evening, calm and free—'

'Weel, we a' ken there's nae chairge for it,' Mrs McOmish admitted.

'The holy time is quiet as a nun, breathless with adoration—'

'It's a peety,' Mrs McOmish commented with some severity, 'he couldna appreciate the weather without being popish aboot it. There's a gentleman turning in at the gate, Mr Trent. Is it a friend of yours? Is it like he'll be staying to dinner?'

Trent looked at the tall, quietly dressed young man who was approaching the house. 'I know who it is,' he said, 'though he is a good deal changed in his looks. He doesn't give me the idea that dinner would agree with him just now—had some kind of a shock, I should think. Now,'—Trent went nearer to the window—'what on earth can it be that he's picking up from the path?'

Mrs McOmish, an elbow clasped in either hand, also came to overlook the proceedings of the visitor. 'It might be a wee piece of coal,' she opined, with more display of interest than she usually permitted herself. 'We had the new coal in three days syne. It's terrible good luck to pick up a wee piece of coal—or what is better still, an auld rusty nail. Only the nail maun be crookit, ye ken. Oh ay, it's a nail; he's putting it in his inside pouch. Twenty years, and mair, I've keepit a rusty nail I found just by the Tammas Coats statue in Dunn Square—Oh preserve us! What a loup he gave, Mr Trent, seeing ye at the window!'

'His nerves must be in a shocking state,' Trent said. 'There's never been anything frightening about me, has there, Mrs McOmish? The beasts that roam over the plain my form with indifference see; let alone the private secretaries of Congregationalist millionaires. Well, if he wants to see me, will you show him into the studio? It isn't so maddeningly tidy in there.' And Trent walked to the door communicating with that scene of his labours.

'I wouldna wonder!' the housekeeper said grimly. 'Ye've been in it a full half hoor since ye came back.' She went out to admit the visitor.

'Mr Verney to see you, sir,' Mrs McOmish soon announced in what she would have described as an English voice.

Mr Verney, whose age might have been guessed at twenty-seven or thereabouts, was a person of somewhat damaged aspect, for he looked harassed and distraught to the last degree. But there was nothing weak in the essence of his appearance. His frame was spare and athletic, his carriage erect, and in his fresh-coloured eagle-featured face there was a pair of restless bright-blue eyes that did not give an impression of spiritual sloth.

It was he who spoke the first words as his hand met Trent's in a rather perfunctory salutation.

'What do you think,' he said earnestly, 'of this terrible news?'

'What do you mean?' Trent said. 'I haven't heard of any terrible news, believe me, my dear fellow. I only hope it's not too bad—for you.'

Verney stared at him intensely. 'How can you have missed it?' he demanded, with a puzzled look in his very expressive eyes. 'It's been in all the early afternoon papers—it's all over the town. Or do you mean that old James Randolph's death doesn't distress you at all?'

Trent was thoroughly taken aback, and for the best of reasons. Himself, at a little after six o'clock the evening before, he had left the same James Randolph not only alive but in a furiously bad temper, a picture of choleric vitality. 'Randolph dead!' he said blankly. 'Why, did he have a stroke or something?'

'A bullet was what killed him, Trent,' Verney said coldly. 'I can't conceive—'

'Oh! he was shot!' A light broke over Trent's mind. 'Now I understand. You see, Verney, I drove down to Glasminster to a wedding this morning, and I've only just got back after all the merrymaking. If anyone had heard of it down there, it wasn't mentioned in my hearing. But the early editions! They all had it, of course—I see that now. But you know how they like to keep you guessing. On the way back, I should think I saw a score of bills saying that a well-known millionaire had been found shot. I didn't care if fifty millionaires, each more well-known than the last, had been found shot. It never occurred to me that it was Randolph. My dear fellow, what a shocking thing! It must have been a bad blow for you, being what you were to him. Tell me what happened.'

'That's just what I can't tell you,' Verney said in a dull tone. He sat with hands clasped between his knees, and stared at the floor. 'All I know is he was shot by someone last night in his bedroom at Newbury Place, when nobody else was there— it's the evening his manservant always had free every week. The man found his master lying dead when he came home, and at once sent for the police. You cannot imagine the shock the news was to me—I didn't even know Randolph was in London. The first I heard of it was when a C.I.D. man called on me early this morning, to see if I knew anything that could give them a line. All I could say was that the old man hadn't an enemy in the world, as far as I knew. And I said the last I had seen of Randolph had been last week, when I was staying at Brinton Lodge, having various matters to talk over with him; and that then he had seemed quite at ease and free from any anxiety. Since I heard the news I've been living in a sort of bad dream. I had a very real feeling for the old man; more like veneration than anything else. And this means more of a chaotic smashup than you can very well imagine. At last I took to walking aimlessly about the streets, just to take the edge off my nerves; and when I found myself near your place, I thought I would look in for a talk. I suppose you had not seen Randolph lately?'

Trent looked at his visitor consideringly. What he had just been told by Verney made one thing clear: he, Trent, must have been one of the last persons to see Randolph before his being murdered. And he had strong reasons for wishing that interview of his with the old man to remain a private affair. It had concerned the reputation of a woman for whom he had a deep regard; and it had been of a decidedly unpleasant, not to say scandalous, nature. The less said about it the better, in Trent's judgment; above all, to those with whom Randolph had left an honourable memory. As for the police, of course they must be told; for one thing, the information would set a limit in one direction on the time during which the murder had been committed. But Trent saw no reason for taking Verney into his confidence.

'It is some time since I saw him,' Trent therefore replied, with more truth than candour. 'It's no use offering you a drink, is it?' he asked; and Verney shook his head. 'Very often a cigarette helps you to pull yourself together,' Trent went on. 'You look all to pieces. Try one of these.'

Verney looked up gratefully. 'Thanks, I will,' he said, extending a shaking hand towards the box held out to him, 'I know all about tobacco and what it can do to you, though it's long enough since I smoked any.' He lit a Virginia cigarette and inhaled deeply. 'You see, the first year at Oxford I used to smoke a lot too much, as so many freshers do. Then, when I began to have dreams of a Blue, I dropped it altogether.'

'And you got your reward, I dare say.'

Verney smiled, in momentary forgetfulness of the day's bad news. 'Do you take an interest in that sort of thing? Yes: three-mile; also cross-country running, since we are on the subject.'

'No, I know nothing about it,' Trent said; 'but as soon as you spoke of dreaming of a Blue, I could see that your dream had probably come true. You look like a Blue. When Nokes outdares Stokes in azure feats, you know, it often marks him for life.'

Verney's dejection again took possession of him. 'Well, it came in useful when I began working for Randolph,' he said. 'The boys' club part of the job was what always appealed to me most. You know about the Randolph Institute, I dare say. Nothing sectarian; just educational and social and athletic. I love it—in fact, I spend most of my time there, because there's a room I use as a sort of general office for all Randolph's charitable affairs. And of course, having a bit of a record in athletics gave me more influence with the lads than almost anything else could have done. Then my being a non-smoker was a good thing too, you see. You can hardly imagine the state that many of these young fellows get their respiratory tracts into with eternally smoking cheap fags. And as for running, there's simply nothing like it for our sort of lads, so long as they're sound physically—hard exercise in the open air, easy to fit in after the day's work, and costs next to nothing.'

'It's good for you,' Trent said. 'You get all the exercise you need, I expect.'

'All I need—yes. But to tell you the truth,' Verney said, rather in the manner of one confessing to a secret vice, 'since I began playing golf about five years ago, I prefer a round of that to any other open-air sport I know—and I have had a pretty good experience. Whenever I can manage it, I go off for a game to Matcham. It's not a good course, and you often can't get a caddy, but then I never want one; and it is the cheapest golf I know this side of London, which is what I have to consider. How I wish—but it is no use talking about that. As far as keeping fit goes, I have every opportunity, as you say. There's nothing like running, above all, for that.'

'There's a good deal, no doubt,' Trent said, 'in having that sort of thing managed by someone who knows all about it.'

'Yes,' Verney said simply, 'there is, of course. The boys have their committee; but they leave the whole show to me really, and I'm rather proud of the way our fellows have come forward since I took over. Last January the Randolph Athletic Club was runner-up in the Middlesex cross-country team championship, and challenged Southgate Harriers pretty closely. We provided the first two men home in that event, and we won the junior race easily. And now, I suppose'—he tossed the end of his cigarette into the fire—'the Kilburn Institute's all over and done with.'

Trent felt a moment of keen sympathy, for Verney's whole manner was that of a heartbroken man.

'Do you mean that his death really means the end of all that work?' he asked. 'Wasn't there any endowment? Or surely there would be some provision in his will for the keeping-up of the various organizations he had started—what was that phrase he was so fond of using?—for the benefit of the community. I should think, from what I've heard, that the shutting-up of that Institute would pretty well amount to a social disaster for that part of London. It ought not to be possible.'

'Well, it is,' Verney said, as he accepted another cigarette. 'You see, Trent, old Randolph had a rather strange side to his character as a public benefactor. He made a great fortune fairly early in life, and he devoted almost the whole of his income to charities and public objects. He continued to heap up more money; but I think it was because he could hardly help it. The real hobby of his life was to attend personally to all his enormous expenditure on charities and public objects. Sometimes he would give a great sum for some special purpose; but when he did that, it was always in the way of capital expenditure. He would build and equip a sanatorium, say, for some town or some big charitable institution; but he would never settle anything on it. He might, and usually did, put his name down year by year for a contribution to its upkeep; but he used to say he started a place like that as an opportunity for charity on the part of other people.'

Trent nodded. 'That's not unusual, I know,' he said. 'But how about places like the Institute? I always understood that was entirely his own private show, maintained by him exclusively. He surely can't have left it high and dry, so to speak.'

'That is just what I was coming to,' Verney said. 'The position of the Institute was just as you say—he held it in his own hands entirely, financing it as if it were a part of his own household. And he had other establishments on just the same footing, like the Randolph Infant Orphanage at Bishopsbridge, or the Randolph Mental Hospital at Claypoole. He was very proud of them, too, and saw to their being the best run places of their kind in the country. They cost him something, Trent; I'm telling you, and I know. But they never had a penny of funds of their own; and whatever Randolph parted with in any sort of way, he always would know what happened to it. He couldn't seem to bear the idea of anyone else controlling wealth that he had amassed—that was at the bottom of it. And I don't see that you could find fault with that, seeing that he did devote all those vast sums to other people, and put himself to a vast amount of trouble in looking after the spending of the money. But the unfortunate consequence is that now—' he raised a hand, palm-downwards, and brought it down sharply on the arm of his chair.

Trent stared at him. 'You don't mean to say he's made no bequests to these places that he created, and lavished money on, and that made up a large part of his reputation?'

Verney arose and crossed his arms. 'I mean this,' he said harshly. 'Randolph made no bequests at all. He left no will.'

CHAPTER VI

AN ARREST HAS BEEN MADE

THERE was a momentary silence as Trent took in this amazing statement and its implications.

'The man who murdered Randolph,' Verney said, 'has probably killed half a dozen invaluable charities and other good works stone dead with that same bullet. Besides that, he has dried up completely a great stream of benevolence that spread itself out in all directions. For I am convinced that there is no will; and if there is no will, what is to happen to the Randolph fortune, and to the causes that it supported, heaven alone knows. Somebody will inherit, I suppose; but there will be delay, and who can answer for what he will do with the money? He may prefer horse-racing, or yachting, or play-producing, or any other way of getting rid of money by the cartload. One thing is practically certain; he won't live on a few thousands a year, and devote the rest to well-directed benevolence.

'Another thing,' Verney went on, holding up an expository finger. 'There may be rival claimants, and a dispute dragging on indefinitely; for as far as I know Randolph had no near relations. You may have heard that he had a son, an only son, who disappeared from home when he was about sixteen, and has never been heard of since. The old man did everything possible to find out what had happened to him, but no trace of him was ever found and he was given up for dead long ago. But there may be other relatives. You see what a disaster the whole thing is likely to be, apart from the personal loss of such a man, and such an influence for good.

'There is one detail,' Verney went on after a moment's pause, 'of interest to you. Randolph was very anxious that you should paint a replica of the Tabarders' portrait of him, to be hung in the hall of the Institute. Did you hear about that?'

'I had a note from him about it,' Trent said, 'but nothing was settled.'

'Well, it never will be now,' Verney said; and then broke out desperately: 'I tell you, Trent, the shock and the horror of this business, and the prospect of so much wreckage, have driven me pretty nearly insane.' And Verney sunk his head between his hands, his fingers clutching his hair.

Trent, while his lips took a dubious twist, put a hand on the young man's shoulder. 'Better not meet trouble half-way,' he said. 'After all, the whole thing depends on your belief that Randolph had made no will. What grounds are there for thinking that he could have been guilty of such an amazing piece of imprudence as that? It's really hardly credible.'

Verney, without looking up, shrugged his shoulders. 'The grounds for thinking so are good enough, unfortunately. The fact is that, at the time of his death, he was really thinking, for the first time, about putting his affairs in order. His lawyers had been dropping hints for a long time that it was high time he made a will. I told him so myself, too, more than once—it was my obvious duty to do so, I thought, though a very unpleasant one. Whenever I did, he made it quite clear that there was no will as yet. He used to say there was time enough, that he was good for many years yet. But he hated the subject being mentioned—didn't like the idea of dying, I suppose, like many other people; though if any living being had a right to feel confident about his prospects in the next world, Randolph had. And then at last he did begin to consider the thing seriously. Several times he said things that showed me he was thinking about the disposal of his estate. And then, before he had got to the point of doing anything definite, he was struck down.'

Trent thought for a few moments before saying: 'Still, he may have made a will earlier in life—when he was married, for instance. Men usually do, I believe.'

Verney made a gesture of impatience. 'He may—yes; when he was a comparatively poor man with no great philanthropic interests to think about. But if he did, I think he would have mentioned it; and anyhow, it's not to be supposed that the terms of any such will would prevent everything getting into the sort of hopeless mess that I'm thinking about. Then, apart from his own foundations, there are all the causes that had expectations as regards Randolph's estate—had a right to have them, I mean, seeing that for years he had been a regular and generous supporter of them.'

'What sort of things do you mean?' Trent asked. 'Never having been a philanthropic millionaire, it would interest me to know how it all works—if you won't think I'm being irreverent to say so.'

Verney looked into vacancy, as one assembling his ideas. 'Why,' he said, 'to put it the simplest way, there must have been dozens of secretaries and chairmen of committees trying, at odd times, to sound me discreetly about what Randolph's testamentary dispositions were. There's the Humberstone General Infirmary; and the Humberstone Endowed Schools Foundation; and the Moss Lane Congregational Church of the same place; and the London Missionary Society; and the British and Foreign Bible Society; and the Yorkshire Congregational Union; and the Congregational Pastors Retiring Fund; and Leeds University; and the Scalbridge United Independent College; and the National Lifeboat Institution; and the Harrowby Seamen's Institute; and the Dewsby Deaf and Dumb Institute; and—oh! I could name another dozen or more that have a direct interest in what happens to Randolph's estate.'

'Thanks! Thanks!' Trent said smiling. 'You needn't go on, Verney, I see how it is. I'd no idea your field of work was such an extensive one. It's no business of mine, of course, but I'm afraid this is going to be a serious thing for you personally.'

Again Verney shrugged. 'It will send me hunting another job, after over two years of such a job as I shall never get again. But

I'm not worrying about that just now. I want,' he said savagely, 'to see the man who killed Randolph taken and hanged—the cowardly brute who shot a defenceless old man in the back, and cut short a life that was given up to works of mercy and humanity. I suppose they'll run the fellow down, Trent—you understand these things. It's not likely he'll escape, do you suppose?'

'No, not likely,' Trent said. 'It does happen of course, now and then. But you have to give the police a reasonable allowance of time when a murder has been undiscovered for a good many hours, as I gather from what you tell me.'

Verney nodded. 'Yes, naturally. I suppose it must depend on the traces left behind by the murderer—the weapon, footprints, fingerprints, the kind of thing one reads about.'

'If he was careful,' Trent pointed out, 'he need not have left any traces at all. Criminals often don't; but they may easily get found out all the same. Do you remember exactly what it was that was given out to the papers this morning?'

'I've got one here.' Verney produced a folded copy of the *Sun* from his coat pocket. 'There you are—it's little enough.'

Below an array of headlines, and a portrait of a clean-shaven, hard-looking old man, Trent read as follows:

At an early hour this morning the police were called to No. 5, Newbury Place, Mayfair, the London residence of Mr James Randolph, the millionaire whose long record of charitable activities and public beneficence has made his name honoured throughout the country.

He had been shot through the heart, the body lying on the floor of the bedroom, where he had, it is presumed, been dressing before attending the banquet of the Tabarders' Company.

His absence from the banquet caused surprise, as he was a member of the Court of the Company, and was to have spoken to the toast of the guest of honour on this occasion, the Home Secretary. On inquiry at Tabarders'

Hall this morning, we learn that several attempts were made during the evening to call Mr Randolph's house by telephone, but that the calls were unanswered.

Mr Randolph's valet, the only servant sleeping on the premises, was, in fact, out for the evening; and it was by him that the body was discovered on his returning to the house, when he immediately telephoned the police.

No. 5 Newbury Place is one of a row of mews converted into five small residences, all tenanted by persons of social position. Such a house was well adapted to the simple way of life preferred by the late Mr Randolph, for he spent but little time in London, and lived as a rule at Brinton Lodge, his country house in the neighbourhood of Humberstone, Yorks.

'So that's all,' Trent remarked. 'Most of that was written up in the *Sun* office, after they'd made their own inquiries. There's hardly anything at all about the crime itself, is there?'

'Hardly anything,' Verney agreed. 'But I suppose it's all that was given out. The other evening papers have just the same; not a syllable more. I've looked carefully.'

Trent considered the other's haggard face for a moment in silence. 'Well, the officer who saw you this morning,' he suggested, 'didn't he tell you anything more? By the way, it's the kind of case they would put Bligh onto, I should think, if his hands aren't too full already. Was your visitor a tall, powerful-looking sort of bloke with a head like a billiard-ball?'

'That was his name,' Verney said with a faint smile, 'and your description fits him nicely. No, he hadn't a word more to tell me than there is in that paper. It was I who was expected to do the telling—whether I knew of anyone who could conceivably have had any ill-will against Randolph, or whether he had seemed at all upset or unusual in his manner lately, or whether I knew what he kept in the safe in the bedroom; and so on. And to all of that my answer was no, and no, and no. The inspector also wanted to know how I had been spending my own time that evening.'

Trent laughed. 'Of course,' he said. 'That's the routine.'

'So he was good enough to assure me,' Verney said, with an answering gleam of grim amusement. 'Fortunately I was able to satisfy him that my time had been fully occupied, in the presence of other people. It was the Institute Athletic Club's weekly grind that evening, you see. I never miss running with the boys, and after changing, I stayed on with them in Kilburn, till half past ten, as I usually do. And now I must be off. It's been a relief to talk the thing over.'

Trent rang the bell. 'You might wait and see the latest edition,' he said. 'It's usually delivered here before this time.'

Mrs McOmish appeared at the door, a copy of the *Sun* in her outstretched hand. 'If it's the paper you want—' she said.

But her speech was cut short by an exclamation from Trent, who had already caught sight of the line of capitals strung along the top of the first page. He seized the paper from her and read aloud to Verney the brief paragraph which had been added, in heavy type, to the matter which he had already seen dealing with the Newbury Place murder.

'It is understood,' he read, 'that an arrest has already been made in connection with this abominable crime.'

CHAPTER VII

ON A PLATE WITH PARSLEY ROUND IT

VERNEY had taken his leave, and Trent had noted that he was properly impressed—not to say astounded—by the fact, if fact it were, of the swift success of the official hunt for Randolph's murderer. Trent had busied himself at once in procuring copies of all the latest editions and comparing their statements; then, after a meditative dinner, he had rung up a certain number in Bloomsbury, and proposed himself for a private and friendly call upon Chief Inspector Bligh, whom he was lucky enough to find at the other end of the wire.

The number of Trent's friends among the metropolitan police, in its various grades, was small, but his relation with them was entirely one of mutual liking; and there was none with whom he was on easier terms than Mr Bligh, an officer of unusual parts, whose range of interests went considerably beyond his notable equipment of expert professional knowledge. In particular, he had made a hobby, and owned a considerable library, of the history of the Civil War in the United States.

It was nine o'clock when Trent found the inspector deeply engaged with book and pipe in his comfortable bachelor quarters.

'Sorry to spoil your evening,' Trent said as he placed his hat on a chair.

'You won't,' Mr Bligh assured him. 'If I'd thought you were likely to, I'd have told them downstairs to set the dog on you, instead of bringing up the drinks for you. Help yourself.' And he waved a vast hand towards the tray with its convivial contents on the plush-covered table.

Trent took the armchair facing his host's, and began the filling of a pipe. 'Oh blessings on his kindly face and on his absent hair!' he said. 'I've interrupted your reading, anyhow. What is the book, I wonder? But need I ask? It is the Life, Campaigns, Letters, Opinions and Table-talk of General Joseph Eggleston Johnston, the Victor of Pumpkin Creek.'

'There's no such book,' Mr Bligh retorted positively; 'and,' he added after a moment's thought, 'there wasn't any such battle. What I was reading was Bernard Shaw—my favourite author.'

'Another bond between us!' Trent exclaimed. 'And what draws you so especially to Shaw?'

The inspector patted affectionately the volume lying on his knee. 'Shaw,' he declared, 'is the literature of escape. That isn't,' he added, in answer to Trent's bewildered gaze, 'my own expression.'

'You relieve my feelings,' Trent gasped, 'more than I can say.'

'No,' the inspector said reminiscently. 'That was the phrase used about Shaw by the man who first brought him to my notice. I had to interrogate a prisoner some years ago about a certain matter. A confirmed criminal, he was. They used to call him Pantomime Joe, on account of the cheek he used to give everybody from the dock. Why, if I've heard a judge say once that his court wasn't a music hall, when Joe was on his trial, I've heard it half a dozen times. Joe was an educated man, and it was no surprise to me, when I visited him in his cell, to find him reading a book from the prison library. He showed it to me—*Plays Pleasant*, by G. B. Shaw. "What's this?" I said. He grinned at me. "This is the literature of escape, Blighter," he says, using a silly nickname he and his sort have always had for me. I thought that sounded a funny sort of reading to be put in the hands of a man who spent half his time in gaol, but he explained his meaning.'

'And what can that have been?' Trent wondered.

'Why,' the inspector said, 'Joe meant, and I agree with him, that Shaw takes you right out of the beastly realities of life. I can tell you, after a hard day at our job, with all the spite, and greed, and cruelty, and filthy-mindedness that we get our noses rubbed in, it's like coming out into the fresh country air to sit down to one of Shaw's plays. Nobody half-witted, nobody brutal, nobody to make you sick. And if he ever does try to give you anybody who is a rotten bad lot, he doesn't come within miles of the real thing. And there's never a dull moment. Every dam' character has something to say; even the stupidest ones. Everybody scores off everybody else. Who ever had the luck to listen to anything like it in real life? I tell you, it's a different world.'

Trent nodded his appreciation of this. 'But,' he said, after a brief silence, 'it was the world we live in that I wanted to consult you about.'

'The Randolph murder,' Mr Bligh said. 'I know; you said so on the phone. And you have been painting his portrait, staying at Brinton to do it. And last week the man who runs the Randolph Institute said it would be a good idea to have a replica of it to hang up there. And Randolph was persuaded to agree, and wrote asking you to call at Newbury Place yesterday evening at six, which you did. And then he talked to you about doing the replica. And then you left, about six fifteen—so that you were one of the last persons to see the old man alive. Well! You've got something to tell me that I don't know, I hope.'

Trent gazed at him as if in awe. 'I don't think,' he said humbly, 'there can be anything you don't know. You have forgotten for the moment, perhaps, that he and I had a little disagreement, and I declined to do the job. Apart from that, I have nothing to add to your summary of the proceedings. How do you do it, Inspector? I may have an open countenance, but I hardly think you can have read all that in my face. Were you up the chimney listening to us, or what?'

Mr Bligh smiled grimly. 'Information received—that's what we usually call it,' he said. 'As for listening, Simon Raught, Randolph's man, does all of that that's required when he's on the premises. Most of what I've mentioned he happened to hear, quite accidentally, last week at Brinton; and as for your visit, of course, he told me all about that.'

'Of course,' Trent agreed. 'Be told, sweet Bligh, and let who will be clever; hear useful things, not deduce them, all day long. All the same, you will not persuade me that all that perfectly good information fell into your lap, as it were, when you were not noticing. I have seen Simon Raught only a few times—in fact, he never got as far as telling me his Christian name, as he evidently did with you—but he did not strike me as one who, when in trouble, would insist that all his secrets should be sung even into thine own soft-conchéd ear. I won't inquire how you got all that out of him—there are various ways and means, I know. The thing I really wanted to ask you when I came here appears not to be in any doubt. The case is in your hands, as I hoped it might be.'

'Good guess,' the inspector remarked sardonically.

'And you ask if I have anything to tell you—about Randolph as he was at our interview, I suppose you mean? No, I haven't. He said nothing about anyone coming to see him after I had gone. He didn't say anything about expecting to be shot, and he didn't look as if he was. He seemed just as usual, in excellent health, and perfectly satisfied with himself.'

'Hm! That doesn't help much,' Mr Bligh said. 'Well, why did you want to see me about the case, then? We all understood you had gone out of the amateur sleuthing business long ago.'

'Just because I happened to know Randolph, and to know some things about him that interested me—things I had heard before I made his acquaintance through painting his portrait, and things I have learnt since. And only this afternoon I was told a good deal by his secretary, Verney, whom I had met at

Randolph's house last January. He had already been giving you information, I gathered, earlier in the day.'

The inspector nodded. 'But not a lot that I didn't know. There was that about his having left no will, of course, which seems to be the case. But bless you! That's not an unheard-of thing, even with the general run of wealthy people; and old James Randolph was not exactly an ordinary character.'

'That's just it. I know how very far from ordinary he was, and that's why I'm interested. Besides, one of the reasons why I went out of business, as you call it, was that my wife has a morbid distaste for crime; but just now she is in the Cotswolds. I am alone and free, like the man in Chesterton; shameless, anarchic, infinite.'

'I don't know about anarchic and infinite,' Mr Bligh said pointedly. 'Well,' he added, assuming an expression of regretful sympathy, 'I'm more sorry than I can say, but there's no need to let the thing trouble your ingenious brain any further, my lad. We've got the man.'

'The papers have been told so—I saw that. And that is why I came to you; to hear more.'

'The papers have been told nothing of the sort,' Mr Bligh said testily. 'They've found out for themselves that an arrest has been made, and they may possibly have found out that the man arrested was connected with one of Randolph's concerns, and had just been sacked. But they've said nothing about its being the man who shot Randolph, because of course they daren't; and in fact he hasn't been charged with that. All the same, he's the man.'

'He is, is he?' Trent looked into the other's rugged face. 'Swift work, with a vengeance. You're certain about having got the man? Is the case really, so to speak, in the bag already?'

Mr Bligh's smile was grim. 'In closest confidence, as usual, I don't mind telling you that I have clear evidence of the man's having been in Randolph's house in the evening, when Randolph was there alone. I have also—'

'Yes,' Trent murmured. 'An "also" would seem to be in order.'

'Also,' the inspector went on, after blowing a couple of elaborate smoke-rings, 'I have the man's written and signed confession that he murdered Randolph.'

Trent fell back in his chair, while Mr Bligh resumed his pipe and gazed dreamily at a corner of the ceiling.

'That seems to have made you think a bit,' he remarked after a moment, cannily observant of a slight frown on his guest's usually untroubled countenance. 'I shouldn't wonder if you had been working up some valuable theory of your own about the case. If you have, let's hear it. A good laugh's the best tonic in the world. Come on! Am I right?'

'Very often, I dare say,' Trent said, with a swift return to his accustomed manner. 'Not now. I never had the slightest notion of a theory about the case. I only heard of it three hours ago. But I do take an interest in it as I told you, and I thought, with my well-known helpfulness, that you might like to have a talk about it, and even let me have a look at the scene of the crime; but now, perhaps, everything being as you tell me, you'd rather not.'

Mr Bligh rubbed his chin. 'I don't know about that,' he said slowly. Then, after a few moments' consideration, he added: 'It's like this. The evidence is all there. I've told you, roughly, what it is. But there are some queer things about the case all the same, and we might as well have a yarn about it.'

'Just what I should like. You know it's safe to talk to me.'

'If it wasn't, my lad, you wouldn't be here.' A chuckle agitated the crumpled expanse of Mr Bligh's waistcoat. 'Well, you've seen what little there is in the papers, of course.'

'Certainly; and it's very little indeed. Can you tell me one thing, for instance, that they don't mention—just how Randolph was shot?'

'He was shot through the heart from behind, probably from the direction of the door of the bedroom, when he was just taking his coat off. It looks as if it was done by someone who had come to see him by appointment, and whom he had let in himself, the valet being out for the evening. The bullet was fired from a Webley .455, probably fitted with a silencer.'

'Ah!' Trent received this information with a thoughtful brow. 'So that's how it was. And you're telling me that nobody knows this as yet but the police—and the surgeon, of course.'

'Well, the man who murdered him knows it, I suppose,' the inspector observed.

'Yes, I'm capable of supposing that myself,' Trent rejoined. 'And now that we have arrived at that point, who did murder him?'

'We haven't arrived at that point.' Mr Bligh, it was clear, was taking an innocent pleasure in saving up the climax of his tale. 'Let's take things in their order. First, there were the obvious possibilities to be thought of.'

'The servants, you mean.'

'You've read in the paper that there was only one, a manservant, sleeping in the place. He was out for the evening, and found the body when he came home; then informed the police by phone immediately. So he said.'

Trent nodded. 'Raught—yes, I know him. And you put him through it, of course.'

'I thought,' the inspector said dubiously, 'I had wrung him pretty dry; but one couldn't be certain. Still, he'd got a reasonable enough story about having left the place just after you left it, to spend his evening off with some relations; and he hadn't any motive that lay on the surface. He declared that when he found the body, he was in too much of a dither even to make out how Randolph had been killed. It might be true; but naturally I didn't set him aside. The only other servant is a charlady, Mrs Barley, who kept the place in order when Randolph wasn't staying there. I saw her too this morning—a simple soul, she is. I thought to myself, I miss my guess if she knows anything whatever about the crime—or about anything else worth mentioning. Then, as you know, I saw Verney, the secretary, who was always about the place when Randolph was in London; and he gave me a satisfactory account of his movements on the evening of the murder.'

'Movements,' Trent murmured. 'An admirable word. Bend against Primrose Hill thy breast, dash down like torrent from its crest, with short and springing footstep pass the Marble Arch and Hamilton Place. Not a very good rhyme, that.'

'The account he gave was rather more detailed,' Mr Bligh said coldly. 'After the run, which you appear to know about, he stayed at the Randolph Institute till ten thirty, and was in his rooms off Maida-vale five minutes later. All that's been checked. As for motive, all he seems to have got by the crime is the loss of a good job.'

'Like Raught—yes,' Trent said. 'And now, if I may ask a question—you know what weapon was used. You've got it, I suppose.'

'Why should you suppose anything of the kind?' the inspector retorted. 'It's not usual for murderers to leave the weapon lying about, is it?'

'It's not usual for them to confess,' Trent pointed out; and Mr Bligh grunted morosely. 'I only thought,' Trent went on, 'he might have led gently up to the confession, as it were, by not taking away the revolver.'

'Well, we haven't got it, that's all,' Mr Bligh snapped. 'But we know what make it was, and what calibre, by looking at the bullet and the breech-markings on it—nothing easier, as it happens, with that type. As for where it is, all I can say is that it's more likely than not to be lying somewhere on the floor of the Channel; but that's nothing better than a guess.'

'What I want to know,' Trent persisted, 'is *why* this Webley should be visiting the bottom of the monstrous world, since the murderer has confessed.'

The inspector rubbed his chin once more. 'Well, of course, so do I. But come! We're getting in advance of the story. If you do want to know what really happened, you must let me tell it my own way.'

He proceeded to give Trent a brief account of his investigation on the scene of the crime. He told of the empty safe; of the signs of documents having been stolen; of the fingerprints on the carafe and tumbler, and on the razor-blade found on the carpet; of the champagne cork; of the leaf missing from the engagement-block in the sitting-room.

Trent, who had listened in closely attentive silence, interposed at this point.

'An engagement-block!' he said. 'And was that in a position where it could easily be seen?'

'Anybody could see it. The cabinet it stood on was on top of the writing-table, just in front of the window. What about it?'

'Only that I feel certain that it wasn't there when I saw the old man in that room at six o'clock. I noticed that dwarf cabinet, too—it is a beautiful little thing.'

'Hm! Yes.' Mr Bligh again fingered his chin. 'That does happen to be one of the funny points. Because Raught, the manservant, says positively that it never was left lying about, that Randolph was always most careful to keep it locked away. Still, of course, he may have had it out to refer to, some time before he was shot.'

'So he may. And then, of course, the man who came to see him, and whose name was on the block as having an appointment with him, very cunningly tore off that leaf and took it away; thus destroying a piece of direct evidence that he had been there that evening.'

'Yes.'

'After which he rushed off and bunged in a confession of having been there, and having shot Randolph. Changeable sort of bloke!'

The inspector sighed wearily. 'I know, I know. And Randolph may have torn off the leaf himself, for some reason. But look here! There's one more thing I haven't mentioned yet. When I saw it, it looked to me like a fatal blunder; and so it would have been, if the damfool hadn't gone and—but never mind that just now, I am telling you things as they happened.' He went on to describe the last of the morning's finds, the luggage-label picked up in the hallway; and when he repeated the name written on the label, Trent made a movement of uncontrollable surprise.

'Bryan Fairman!' he exclaimed.

'That's what I said. He's the man who did it,' Mr Bligh added.

'Do you mean to say he is the man whom you know to have been at Randolph's place when he was shot, and who has confessed to the murder? Why, I know him!'

'Is there anybody in this blasted case that you don't know?' the inspector asked plaintively. 'Anyhow, if you know Bryan Fairman, you know a damned nuisance—him and his confession!'

'I suppose you might call a murderer that,' Trent admitted. 'But really, Inspector, this is incredible. Fairman is one of my oldest friends. Do you remember when we were talking about Eunice Faviell some time ago, and the way so many men go crazy about her? I mentioned to you that a great friend of mine was one of those victims. I was speaking of this same Fairman. I have known him half my life, and of all the men that I should call sound citizens, he is about the most blameless. Why, I saw him only last night—' and here Trent broke off, realizing suddenly the possible significance of that meeting.

The inspector's eyelids narrowed. 'Yes?' he said gently.

'He was catching the 8:20 at Victoria,' Trent said slowly. 'He very nearly missed it. And that's the boat-train for Dieppe—I was seeing somebody off by it. But good Lord! Bryan Fairman! You know, it's quite impossible to believe—'

'Wait till you hear all there is to believe,' Mr Bligh advised him. 'There's plenty. To begin with, "Passenger to Dieppe" was written on the label, as I was just going to tell you. Well, all that did for me was to give me someone to go after; which of course I did. If he was going to Dieppe by the night-boat, as seemed most likely, it was a thousand to one he was on his way to somewhere much further off, and had had a good many hours' start on his journey, whatever it was—because the boat gets there in the small hours. But on the off-chance of Dieppe being his real destination, I had him looked for there; and sure enough I soon got news of him—and a lot of it. The first information was that Dr Bryan Fairman, complete with passport, had come by the boat and taken a room at the Hôtel Beau-Rivage. He left there about nine thirty this morning, after taking nothing but a cup of coffee. Then it came through that an Englishman carrying a kit-bag had been seen hanging about in a place called the *Impasse de la Chimère*, in the outskirts of the town, looking as if he had lost something. What on earth he can have wanted there the French police haven't the least idea; they say they have made every possible inquiry—and they are pretty good at that, as you know—and they cannot imagine what he was after in that spot.'

'That is remarkable, too,' Trent said thoughtfully. 'If the French police could not get any information they were looking for from local householders or *concierges*, it should mean that there wasn't anything for them to get. And as for my friend Fairman being seen wandering about in the environs of Dieppe, it simply doesn't make sense to me. He studied for a year at the *Salpêtrière* in Paris, and as far as I know that is all the experience of France that he has. What else did you hear about him?'

'In the same place,' the inspector proceeded, 'there is an inn, and Fairman had some more coffee there before he went away. The man who keeps the place says that the Englishman looked sick, and a bit dotty.'

'Did he really say that?' Trent inquired with keen interest.

'His words were, as reported to us,' replied the inspector, who numbered a practical, working knowledge of French among his professional merits, 'that the man seemed to be *"souffrant"* and *"un peu toqué"* and, if you can make that mean anything but what I said, you're welcome. Well, as I was about to tell you when interrupted, the next thing seen of Fairman, he was booking a return passage by the afternoon boat back to Newhaven. One of our men on duty at the port recognized him by the description which we had phoned across; also by the initials on his kit-bag. So our chap took a passage too, to keep him under observation. And then, dammit! What do you suppose the crazy fool did? The boat hadn't much more than cleared the harbour when he walked to the rail, climbed over it, and was in the act of jumping overboard when Sergeant Hewett grabbed him by the jacket and pants, and hung onto him until the crew came and dragged him inboard again. Quite a scrap they had of it, Hewett says—he's got a lovely black eye, and a mouth like a pound of liver with a slit in it. Then Hewett took him in charge for attempting suicide; and that's what we're holding him for at the present moment.'

Trent looked his amazement. 'Fairman tried to drown himself! And then you say—'

'Wait a bit,' the inspector said. 'You must let me tell it my own way. Shortly after Fairman had been brought home and charged, a letter was received at the Yard which he had posted at Newhaven just before the boat left for Dieppe. It contained nothing but a confession of his having shot Randolph—short, but definite enough. I've got a copy of it here.'

Mr Bligh got to his feet, and opened a dispatch-case that lay on a side-table. He took from it a typewritten document.

'Before you look at this I may tell you the result of our inquiries at Claypoole, which had already been received in London. Fairman bore an excellent character, though he was rather reserved; didn't get on with people very easily I gather. He was said to be entirely devoted to his work at the mental hospital. He was carrying on some sort of research there in addition to his ordinary duties, and had been showing signs of overwork. Then a month ago he got influenza pretty badly; and he seems to have returned to his job when he was still rather the worse for wear.

'The next thing was that he was suddenly sacked from the hospital staff, with six months' salary in lieu of notice. He got a letter to that effect yesterday morning, which he showed to one of his colleagues. The letter gave no reason; and the writer of it, the medical superintendent, Dr Dallow, tells our people plainly that he is not obliged to explain his action, and will not do so, the hospital being a purely privately managed institution. That, of course, was this morning, when he had no idea of why the police were showing this sudden interest in Fairman—when we knew nothing ourselves, for the matter of that, except that Fairman's label had been found on the scene of the crime.

'We are informed that Fairman, after getting his notice, had an interview with Dallow, which didn't last long, and that he came away from it looking haggard and desperate. He left the hospital about three o'clock, carrying his kit-bag, not having said a word to anyone. He was seen by a porter at the station, who knew him, to take the 3:10 up-train, which is due to arrive at St Pancras at 7:30. I may say here that among the things found upon him, after his arrest, was a crumpled sheet of paper with Randolph's London address on it. Now then, how does all that look to you?'

'Bad,' Trent said, looking at the floor. 'I don't see how it could look very much worse.'

'Not any worse at all,' Mr Bligh rejoined, 'when you know that Randolph had absolute control of the entire management of the hospital.'

'Well, I did happen to know that, and that's why I agree about the badness. Dallow, of course, may talk about refusing to give his reasons; but he would have to sing a different tune if he was subpœnaed as a witness.'

Mr Bligh rubbed his hands. 'You're right there. There's another thing, too, that he would be asked to explain—what was the subject of the interview he had with Randolph at Brinton at 5 p.m. three days before the murder? I got that by looking back through the engagement-block. Well, we're agreed, I take it, that Randolph was responsible for the sacking. As a matter of fact, he had a bit of a down on Fairman for some reason or other—Raught, the valet, gave me that point. Well, now, to get on—all this I've been telling you is the result of inquiries made at the Claypoole end this morning. It was dictated to the Yard over the phone, and most of it was in my hands by lunch-time. As for what followed his arrival in London, we've only his own account—a bit sketchy, but definite enough as far as it goes. Here you are.'

Trent took the typescript that the inspector now held out to him. 'Pretty smart work,' he observed glumly. 'Activity on all fronts, London, Claypoole and Dieppe—with a naval engagement, so to speak, thrown in. You start on the job after an early breakfast, and it's all done up in a parcel just when it's getting to be time for a nice hot cup of tea.'

Mr Bligh emitted a depreciative grunt. 'I don't say the machine didn't run smoothly. It did—and a bit too slick for my taste, though you may think it a funny thing for me to say, perhaps. I don't care about it so much when things all come my way on the run, as if I was a bally magnet or something. Dammit! It's like having the case handed to me on a plate with parsley round it; and the more I've thought of it the less I like it.'

Trent nodded. 'I think I know what you mean. You feel that Destiny may have got a section of lead pipe concealed behind its back, ready to land you one unexpectedly on the cervical region.'

'Something like that,' the inspector grumbled. 'It's the sort of thing that's happened before. And yet—but you run your eye over that paper, and let's hear what you think of it.'

Trent turned his attention to the neatly-typed sheet in his hand, and read what follows:

In the train. London—Newhaven.
9:20 p.m.

This evening I shot and killed James Randolph. I went to his house in Newbury Place at about 7:45, as near as I can guess. There was no one else in the house. We had a violent quarrel, and it ended in my shooting him. I filled a glass with water from the carafe on the chest of drawers and drank the water. I then left the house and took a cab to Victoria, where I caught the 8:20 express to Newhaven, as I had intended. I am going to cross to Dieppe.

I prefer not to give my reasons for anything that I have done.

BRYAN FAIRMAN

After reading and re-reading this brief document Trent looked up with raised brows and met his host's expectant eye.

'Interesting, isn't it?' the inspector asked drily. 'Prefers not to give his reasons for murdering a man, but doesn't mind mentioning that he had a drink of water after doing him in. Tells us he had arranged to escape from the country after shooting his victim; then changes his mind, doubles back on his tracks, and tries to drown himself on the way home. What infernal sense can you make of it?'

Trent, thrusting his fingers through his hair, stared a few moments into vacancy. 'I suppose it's a silly suggestion,' he said at length, 'but have you considered the idea that he is trying to shield someone else?'

'Yes, of course. The confession, and the leaf missing from the block, and the care he takes to fix the thing on himself, suggested that to me at once. But it really doesn't hold water. To begin with, accusing yourself of a murder you didn't do is a pretty large order, however anxious you may be to do anybody a good turn. On the other hand, genuine confessions of murder are common enough. Then again, he had a motive of his own—resentment at the way he had been treated. Many a man has been bumped off for less than what had been done to Fairman. And besides all that, how are you going to fit the shielding idea in with this unaccountable flying visit to Dieppe, and his returning home again immediately afterwards, and his attempting suicide? No: I say again, what sense can you make of it?'

Trent glanced again through the paper in his hand. 'Certainly,' he said, 'it leaves a good deal to the imagination. But—' he paused a moment—'I haven't had time to consider it, of course, but I don't see how this confession, open to criticism as it may be, makes such a devil of a lot of difference.'

The cloud of chagrin on Mr Bligh's features grew heavier. 'In a way it makes very little difference. There's a strong enough case against him already. We know he had a motive. And we know he was there about the time when Randolph was shot. His fingerprints have been taken, and they correspond with those on the glass that he is so careful to mention.'

'And, of course, with those on the razor-blade too.'

'No, they don't,' the inspector said shortly. 'That's just one of those points that I was afraid, at the time, were going to give a lot of trouble. The fingerprint artist found a lot of Randolph's and the valet's marks, naturally, and he found some—not only on the water-bottle and glass—which have now been identified as Fairman's. But he found marks on that razor-blade that don't belong to any of the three; and he didn't find those marks on any other article in the whole place. Raught says it was a new blade, only taken out of its envelope that morning. If so, somebody else had been handling that blade; had taken it out of the razor, as the appearances suggest, to cut open those packages.'

'What does Fairman say about it?'

'Nothing. He refused to answer any questions, or say a word of any sort, from the moment he was arrested. Soon after he was charged, he had a complete nervous collapse—I don't think I told you that—and at present he is in the prison infirmary, quite unfit for interrogation or anything else. That's the doctor's report; and so the whole case is hung up until he is well enough for us to get on with it. We shall ask for an adjournment at the inquest, of course—we should have done in any case.'

Trent rose to his feet and began to pace the room. 'You can understand,' he said, 'that all this is very painful to me. To hear of his being in that state, after all the rest that has happened— well, I won't talk about it. Now look here. The case you've got against Fairman is a stiff one, even without his confession—I know that. But I could see from the start that you were not quite satisfied, and I suppose those unidentified fingerprints on the razor-blade are among the points that don't seem to you to fit in. They don't to me.'

'That's right,' the inspector said. 'They certainly don't seem to fit in—not at the first glance, that is. Like those missing papers. All the same, I have got an idea about those prints, and the papers too. Tell me, how much have you seen of Raught, old Randolph's servant?'

'I have stayed as a guest at Brinton three times, when Randolph was sitting to me for his portrait. Raught used to look after me, as he did after his master.'

'And how did he strike you?'

'You mean in the role of a gentleman's gentleman?'

Mr Bligh grinned assent.

'Well, of course, it was comic,' Trent said. 'Raught is an intelligent, clear-headed sort of fellow, I suppose you'd agree—' the inspector nodded assent—'but he's got the words "wrong 'un" written all over him in large capitals. There's a sort of greasiness about the man—I don't mean on the surface, but showing through from his soul.'

Mr Bligh grunted. 'Well, whatever that may mean, I

happened to spot him as a man who had done time; remembered his face the minute I set eyes on him. But without that, he's obviously a good many notches below the class of a gentleman's servant. I put him down as one of the old man's reclamation cases. Anyway, my notion is that when Raught came home last night he had a pal with him. Perhaps they were going to have a spot or two of the old man's brandy, if he'd gone to bed. Then Raught found him lying dead; and they may have decided to have a go at the safe before the police were sent for. Or perhaps it was his friend who insisted on doing it. I didn't like the way Raught answered when I questioned him about that safe—pretending he wasn't sure if there really was a safe. If that was what happened, or something like it, the strings on those packages may have been cut by the man who was with Raught, and the prints on that blade were his. Then he cleared off with all the papers, and anything else there may have been that looked useful, before Raught rang up the station.'

Trent leaned back and contemplated his friend with an admiring eye. 'It's no wonder that you've got on in your profession,' he said. 'All that might have happened, no doubt—or it mightn't.'

The inspector knocked his pipe out into a large ashtray presided over by a spotted china dog of melancholy appearance. 'Well,' he said, 'it fits the facts, and it's suggested by experience, that's all; and it doesn't really matter. As far as the murder goes, we had got Fairman nailed to a board. And then, when everything was going nicely, he pitches in this blasted confession.'

Trent rose, and made ready to take his leave. 'But I still don't see,' he said slowly, 'why Fairman's confession should have cast such a shadow over the smiling prospect.'

'You still don't see!' Mr Bligh's tone expressed weary resignation. 'Look at it again—look at the damfool thing again. And consider how the man has acted all through.'

Trent re-read the typescript in his hand, and then again met his friend's exasperated eye. 'You mean—?'

'I mean unsound mind,' the inspector rasped. 'Not just nervous breakdown, but lunacy—and a silly end to what I thought looked like being a respectable bit of work.'

CHAPTER VIII

THE WHITE FLOWER OF A BLAMELESS LIFE

TRENT, as he walked homewards that night after taking leave of Inspector Bligh, thought over all the pitifulness of the policial tragedy now being faced by that officer. All that keen directive energy, that rapid working of a high-powered routine, to end in the arrest of a lunatic! But much more was he distressed by this dreadful news of one between whom and himself an old and deep attachment existed. He was completely convinced that the Fairman whom he knew was incapable of such a crime. The shooting of the old man in the back was an added detail of incredibility. But all this could but make more inevitable the conclusion that Fairman, if guilty, must be mentally deranged. His conduct, as the inspector insisted so strongly, had not been that of a man in his right mind.

As for the facts that might account for such a collapse, they were not in much doubt. Randolph's capricious dislike of the young doctor must be, as Mr Bligh had suggested, at the bottom of it. Trent remembered well an evening, some months before, when both he and Fairman had been Randolph's guests at Brinton. It had been evident then that the two did not take any pleasure in each other's company. The old man had seemed to be merely amusing himself, in a strange way, by pretending to be unable to believe in, or even understand, the lines of research in mental disease to which Fairman had devoted himself at the Claypoole Hospital. It appeared to Trent quite understandable that Fairman, with body and brain still depressed by the poison of influenza, had completely lost his balance under the shock of sudden separation from the work he lived for. One thing more Trent remembered with a shade of discomfort. Fairman had known of the old man's unpleasant advances to Eunice Faviell; for Trent himself had mentioned this in a quite recent letter to Fairman, adding that he knew how to put a stop to it, and intended doing so.

It was while Trent was reviewing this situation over an early breakfast the next morning that he was called to the telephone, and a sepulchral voice, the voice of Inspector Bligh, came to his ear.

'Is that Monteagle 3474?'

'Nothing less,' Trent answered. 'And I know who it is speaking. Why is it, Inspector, that you always talk on the telephone as if life was dead and so was light?'

'I wish to God,' Mr Bligh retorted in accents yet more hollow, 'you could be serious for a few minutes.'

'I am not feeling particularly playful, as a matter of fact. Pure from the night and splendid for the day, of course, but not exactly frivolous. However, if I sound so, don't take it too much to heart,' Trent urged. 'Remember that if I appear untouched by solemn thought my nature is not therefore less divine. Besides, I can always be serious to oblige a friend. Let us see— it's just a quarter past eight. I can be perfectly serious most of the morning. At twelve o'clock Admiral Sir Densmore ffinch— you know, the man with two little effs and one leg—comes to sit for his portrait. He is one of the most amusing talkers I ever met. Until then, I can be as serious as an outbreak of cholera. What was it you were going to tell me?'

'You said last night,' Mr Bligh answered, 'you would like to have a look at the scene of the crime in Newbury Place. Well— there's nothing against your doing that if I'm responsible for you. But you will find that the only remaining bird has flown. I'm there now.'

Trent hesitated a moment. 'Do you mean Raught, the manservant?'

'Yes; he's gone.'

'Really? Like a summer-dried fountain, when our need was the sorest? Well, well! So Raught has hopped it.'

'If you prefer to use that low expression,' the inspector answered, 'he has. Another vulgar way of putting it is that he has beaten it while the beating was good; for I came here to arrest him this morning.'

'What for? Do you mean you've got evidence of that theory of yours about Raught and Charles, his friend, going through the safe?'

A cavernous chuckle came over the wire. 'Come along if you want to, and you can hear all the revolting details.'

When Trent arrived at the little abode in Newbury Place, a salute from the attendant constable showed him that he was expected. No signs of life appeared on the ground floor. He mounted the stairs to find Inspector Bligh, accompanied by a long-faced sergeant, engaged in measuring distances on the thick-carpeted floor of the bedroom.

'That'll do for the present, Mills,' the inspector said; and his subordinate, taking the hint, shut up his notebook and withdrew.

'Raught,' Mr Bligh began without preliminary, 'cleared out during the night. There was a constable posted at the door, of course; but it seems that our friend simply got out of the window of his bedroom, which is on the ground floor, crossed the small yard there, climbed over the wall into Torrington Alley, then walked down either to Wigram Street at the one end or Bullingdon Street at the other, and was off on his way through London to Lord knows where. He was lucky not to be seen coming out from the alley; but probably he listened in the yard for the passing of the constable who goes through the alley at intervals, and gave him time to get well away on his beat.'

'And why did Raught give you the slip?'

Mr Bligh drew from his breast pocket a long envelope. 'He had his reasons all right. This letter, addressed to the commissioner, was delivered at the Yard by the last post last night. It was forwarded by Randolph's solicitors, who ought to have known enough to send it by special messenger as soon as they heard of the murder. As it was, they took their time about posting it—probably a firm who know nothing about criminal business. This was what they sent.'

Trent took in hand the letter, which bore a date of three years earlier, and was written, as he saw at once, in Randolph's clear but somewhat crabbed hand. It ran as follows:

SIR,

Your attention should be directed to my valet, Simon Raught.

He is a man whom I have befriended by taking him into my service again after he had served a sentence of imprisonment. In addition to that, my silence has saved him from the consequences of a more serious crime. Attached to this letter is a confession, signed by him, of the part he played in the Maidstone bank-robbery in 19—, when a watchman and a policeman were seriously injured.

How the facts came to my knowledge is my own affair. I threatened Raught with the disclosure of them unless he signed this confession, but it is not my intention to make use of it personally. I have always been in favour of reclaiming by personal influence rather than punishing the criminal, but I do not—though I have done my best with Raught—conceal from myself that with men like him some deterrent influence cannot wisely be neglected. He is, I am afraid, still a dangerous man when exposed to temptation. I have told him that his confession is a security for his good behaviour, and will not be brought up against him so long as he remains faithful to me.

I have accordingly instructed my solicitors that this letter, with Raught's confession enclosed, is to be destroyed unopened at my death, unless I should die by violence or in suspicious circumstances, in which case it is to be forwarded to you.

Yours, etc.,

JAMES M. RANDOLPH

'And what,' the inspector asked grimly, 'do you think of that?'

'To begin with,' Trent said, 'there seems to be rather an over-plus of letters to Scotland Yard, and an unusual amount of confessing, in this simple little case.'

Mr Bligh snorted impatiently. 'You can see for yourself,' he snapped, 'that Randolph's letter was written long ago, and Raught's confession has nothing on earth to do with this murder.'

Trent sighed. 'I stand rebuked. I was only wondering at the ways of coincidence. And this confession, as you say, can have nothing to do with a murder committed by Bryan Fairman. Where is Raught's confession, by the way?'

'They're checking up on it at the Yard. It's quite plain and circumstantial, signed by Raught, and with the signature properly witnessed. But you see, of course, that if his confession has no bearing on the murder, it has all the bearing in the world on my suggestion that he, and probably a pal of his, went through the documents in the safe after finding Randolph's body. Raught hoped the confession would be found among them. Then when they realized it wasn't there, the friend walked off with the papers, whatever they were, and Raught, instead of walking off too, rang up the police.'

Trent frowned. 'I think I see. He knew his confession was hanging over him somewhere, and that if he ran off that night, leaving the murder to be discovered and reported by somebody else, everything would point to his having shot Randolph himself. He couldn't expect, of course, that the real murderer, after getting away, would proceed to inform against himself, as Fairman has done.'

'Exactly. He had the sense to see that if his confession reached the police, and he was arrested here without any trouble, and got a long sentence for the Maidstone crime, that would be more comfortable than being tracked down and tried for his master's murder, with an excellent chance of swinging for it. And then, you see, next day, he soon saw that no serious suspicion was attached to him; and he heard in the evening that an arrest had been made. That being so, it seemed to Raught that he had nothing to answer for but that old business at Maidstone, so he decided he might as well give us the slip if he could. A near thing it was, too.'

'And what chance has he of keeping out of your clutches?'

Mr Bligh laughed shortly. 'Not a great deal. We've had his photo and fingerprints since that false-pretences job that he did time for. We know where his relatives live. He'll be well looked out for everywhere. But never mind about him now. I wanted to show you over the ground here, and to have a little more talk with you about Randolph.'

Showing Trent over the ground involved a close examination of all the clues already picked up by the inspector, and described by him in the evening before. Trent, who knew that his friend had no superior in this kind of skill, followed his explanation with close interest and keen questioning. Despite Mr Bligh's conjectures, the razor-blade appeared to Trent as the strangest detail of the whole affair, with its finger-marks that were unmatched among all the numerous other prints brought out on the spot by the police expert. The champagne cork, too, he felt, had a mysterious fascination of its own, if it was true that Randolph had no taste for that beverage.

'All right,' said Mr Bligh, on hearing these comments. 'You can have the prints to turn over in your mind if you like.' He turned to his dispatch-case. 'Here's a duplicate enlargement of the photos of the finger and thumb that you can take, and if you make anything of them, I'll be glad to hear of it. What *we* make of them is that they aren't in the Criminal Record Office at Scotland Yard, and that the man who made them is probably not over ninety, and that he may not be an engineer's fitter, and that if he had anyone of a number of nasty skin diseases, it hadn't spread to that finger and thumb. Isn't that useful? And here's the cork. I can't part with that, but you can take an eyeful of it, and make a note of what's stamped on it; and if you find that Felix Poubelle 1884 made the marks on the razor-blade, we shall begin to know where we are, of course.'

Unmoved by this ponderous pleasantry, Trent carefully examined the cork, found it to be in perfect condition, and made a note of the brand, which, he reflected privately, was of a certain interest in itself.

'And now,' the inspector said, 'can we hit on any useful line by having a further talk about the old man, as you say you knew something about him? Suppose we go down to the sitting-room and make ourselves comfortable.'

He led the way to the room downstairs, and took his seat in the corner of the sofa by the bookcase, producing a pipe and pouch as he did so.

'There's the engagement-block, with the leaf torn off, as I told you,' he said with a wave of his pipe. Trent inspected the block with interest, carefully turning back the leaves with his fingertips; and he noted with surprise that the name of Wetherill was put down for an appointment at 4:30 on the day before that of the crime. There was, so far as he knew, only one Wetherill; and what he could have had to do with Randolph passed conjecture. But the fact seemed pointless; and he joined Mr Bligh on the sofa.

'Let's come back, to start with,' the inspector said, 'to this amazing letter of his about Raught.' He held the document out to Trent, who took and glanced through it once more.

'The character of Randolph seems to have been opening out like a flower in the sunbeams since his decease,' he remarked. 'Here's a piece of benevolence that nobody ever suspected. For once in a way, he did good by stealth and would have blushed to find it fame.'

'Blushing might have been one of the things that happened to him,' Mr Bligh allowed. 'But if this precious business had become known during his lifetime, he would have done his blushing in quod. "My silence has saved him," you observe. Randolph didn't mind compounding a felony.'

'Not if he was going to be dead when it came out. But there were a lot of things Randolph didn't mind, it seems. He didn't mind keeping a man about him who dreaded and hated him. He didn't intend to let him go—"so long as he remains faithful to me," the letter says. Then again, he didn't mind doing his best to smash a blameless young man of science merely because, as far as I can make out, he had taken a dislike to him. It may have been just that and nothing more. Fairman is one of those tight-lipped chaps—I mean that he has a physical habit of always keeping his mouth shut, unless he is using it for any purpose, and a moral habit of not talking unless he has got something to say. There are lots of people who don't like that—you may have noticed it. Especially people who are rather by way of getting themselves looked up to as little tin gods. They expect an ingratiating expression, or at least one of awed respect. Fairman, I should say, is quite incapable of either.'

'Well, so am I!' the inspector said, not without compla-cency, as he completed the filling of his pipe. 'I hope so, anyhow.'

'Yes, but it is your business to be feared rather than loved, don't you see? It isn't Fairman's. Still, perhaps I'm all wrong; it may be just my imagination extending itself. The point is that Fairman was fired, presumably by Randolph's orders, without any reason given. And Randolph being dead, and

Fairman out of his mind, as I agree he seems to be, it seems possible we shall never get at the whole inner history of the affair. But as regards Randolph's personality, which you wish that we should talk about, there surely must be very different opinions about that. Most people seem to have thought of him as an altruistic saint in the baffling disguise of a North-country business man. That I could understand in people who knew nothing about him except his record as a public benefactor; but that secretary of his, Verney, who I suppose was as close as anyone to him, talks about him in just the same way. Yet I didn't think he showed himself any more pleasant to Verney than to anyone else down at Brinton, during the times I was staying there to paint the old man's portrait.'

'How do you mean?'

'Well, to begin with,' Trent said, 'the first time I met Verney there, not realizing what his position in the establishment was, I asked him if I hadn't seen him a few years before in the *cercle privé* at Monte Carlo, where I was having a mild flutter at the tables. I said this in Randolph's hearing. Verney assured me that I was mistaken, that he had never been near Monaco in his life. All the same, it struck me Randolph was a little abrupt in his manner to Verney after that. Then again it struck me he probably always was like that—I'd never heard him speak to Verney before. And really he was unpleasant, more or less, to everyone about him. He wasn't what I should call very agreeable in his dealings with me. I don't believe he knew how to be.'

'Preferred to love his fellow men at a distance,' the inspector observed reflectively. 'No doubt it's easier. And you may say that, in a way, it flows a profit. Raught, the valet, told me the old man got a lot of satisfaction out of his reputation for benevolence all round. I'd heard that about him before; and after all, it's not very surprising.'

Trent smiled wryly. 'The charity that doesn't begin at home.

Still, it *was* charity—what people call charity, anyhow; and a solid article enough, in Randolph's case ... You know, I suppose, that he had an only son, who ran away from home when he was a lad.'

Mr Bligh gave a grunt of assent.

'Why he ran away,' Trent said, 'I don't know, and perhaps nobody does. But I heard that he had never turned up, though everything possible was done to find him.'

'Everything possible!' Mr Bligh exclaimed. 'Well, I can tell you one thing possible that wasn't done, because I happen to know. The police were never asked to take a hand in tracing him. They were never even informed that he was missing. Officially, they've never heard of it to this day. And that reminds me of a funny thing. About a year ago, I should say it was, we got to know, in a round-about sort of way—it doesn't matter how—'

'It came to your ears, say,' Trent suggested.

'Well, it did come to our ears,' the inspector said defiantly, 'that Randolph was employing a certain private inquiry agency—'

'Not the one that is run by ex-Chief Inspector Targett, I suppose?'

'Never you mind which it was. He was employing them to trace the whereabouts of any persons nearly related to him.'

'Was he? That's very interesting,' Trent said. 'It looks as if he really was thinking seriously about putting his affairs in order, as Verney believes. But I gather that they didn't find the long-lost son.'

'They did not. And no wonder, after more than twenty years. But they found another relative—however,' Mr Bligh broke off, with an oblique glance at Trent, 'all that is no business of mine or yours. We were talking of the disappearance of his son, which there never was any secret about. It caused a lot of talk, as you may suppose, because Randolph at that time was already getting to be a well-known man in the North, and when his servants began putting the story about, it soon became common knowledge. There wasn't any doubt about the fact. The lad's mother died when he was seventeen, working as an apprentice with an engineering firm; and soon after that he told his friends at the works that he had had enough of living at home, and was going to clear out. The next day he was gone; and Randolph would never say anything but that the boy had chosen to leave him, and no doubt would turn up again when he'd had enough of fending for himself. Well, he never did; and that's all I know about it.'

'It's a queer story,' Trent said thoughtfully. 'One could imagine that that home, where charity didn't begin, may have been a little difficult to endure; but the boy must have had hard stuff in him to go away like that and stay away, when he had a well-to-do parent who was bound to provide for him.'

The inspector nodded. 'Yes, a queer story, as you say. But all of Randolph's life was a queer story. You've heard, perhaps, that he laid the foundations of his fortune as an owner of slum property in Humberstone—yes, and used to collect the rents himself, long after he was well enough off to pay other people to do his dirty work. House property, shrewd speculation in land values, here, there and everywhere—that's how he became a wealthy man. He understood the business, and he had the reputation of never making a mistake. He was chairman of two big real estate companies. Then he took to laying out his money in other directions, and was always getting richer, they say—in spite of all his enormous outlay on charities and public objects. But we've got to remember, of course, that he spent precious little on his own comfort and tastes. Look at this little hutch for a London house, for instance. And though I suppose keeping up Brinton cost him something, it must have been a trifle out of an income like his.'

'Don't forget,' Trent said, 'his position as a donor to art collections and museums. That must have helped to keep the money moving, if you like. I know more about that than I do about his philanthropy, and I don't believe there has ever been anything quite like it. I don't know when he began to take an interest in pictures and art in general, but by the time I got the commission to paint his portrait he had come to know a lot more about the buying and selling end of it than I shall ever do. I don't believe, though, that he really had the stuff of a connoisseur in him. He had collected very little on his own account. Although what he had got at Brinton was all absolutely first-class—and in this midget of a place too, for that matter—he didn't give me the idea of being keen on it at all. What he certainly must have done was to get the best possible advice about his purchases.'

'I've heard, of course,' Mr Bligh said, 'about his fad of giving things to foreign art galleries. Some of us have got a pretty good notion of what lay behind it. But I don't know anything about how it was done—it isn't my line of country.'

'Well, I can tell you this much. There's hardly a national collection in Europe that he hasn't presented with something they were delighted to get hold of. Sometimes the gift would be cleverly selected for its particular interest to the nation concerned, like the Dante manuscript he gave to the Victor Emmanuel Library. Sometimes it would be a thing that any museum in the world would welcome, like that little Rembrandt, called *The Alchemist*, that he chose to present to the Pinakothek. He's been doing it for many years now, and all the curators and librarians and blokes of that description— why, their ears used to go up with a click when his name was mentioned.'

'Funny,' the inspector commented, absorbedly probing the bowl of his pipe with a penknife. 'Because of course he got nothing out of it.'

Trent scowled at him thoughtfully. 'What have you got in that pure mind of yours?' he demanded.

Mr Bligh reached back to the bookshelf that skirted the wall

at his right hand. 'Did you ever take a look at his record in
Who's Who?' he asked, turning the pages of that dropsical tome.
'Here we are. There's pretty near a column about him, consisting
mainly of—what do you think?'

Trent shook his head. 'I give it up.'

'Orders,' the inspector said. 'Decorations—all foreign ones.
Legion of Honour, Red Eagle, Crown of Italy, ditto Sweden,
Daneborg, Redeemer, Rising Sun, Star of Roumania, St
Vladimir, and lots more. He must have had a truckload of them.
The big swells, I've noticed, don't put down all these things,
as a rule; but Randolph was missing nothing.'

Trent took the volume, and glanced over the impressive
proofs of the regard in which James Mewburn Randolph had
been held by foreign governments.

'Rather like collecting stamps,' he remarked.

'But rather more costly,' Mr Bligh rejoined. 'You see the
meaning of it, don't you? Every one of those little tributes
represents a jolly expensive contribution to the art galleries
and museums of the civilized world—or those parts of it that
have official jewelry to hand out as a slight token of their
esteem. Also there had probably to be a little palm-oil, or a
lot, distributed here and there—you know how it is. Randolph
would have wanted to be sure of getting his *quid* before
parting with the *quo*. He was fond of recognition, as we've
heard already.'

'And yet,' Trent mused, 'he never had an English handle to
his name. He could have got it easily enough long ago. Perhaps
he thought it was rather a distinction for a man in his position
not to be a Sir Somebody Something.'

Mr Bligh laughed shortly. 'Not he! It was just his wanting
it so badly that started the whole of this chasing after foreign
distinctions. At least, that's what I've been told. Anyhow,
there's no doubt that he wanted a knighthood many years
ago. One of the assistant-commissioners knew all about it at
the time, and I heard it from him. The first time Randolph

let it be known that he thought a knighthood was about due, and that he was ready to stump up, there was a hitch some-where—possibly the list was a bit too long already. Or possibly one of the Prime Minister's private secretaries didn't like Randolph. You never know. Anyhow, he was told he'd have to wait till next time. Randolph was furious; and it didn't improve his temper when the list was made public, and he found in it two new knights that he'd had personal dealings with, and the best you could say of them was that they'd managed never to be caught with their hands in the till, so to speak.'

'And sometimes through the mirror blue the knights come riding two and two,' Trent murmured.

'I don't know anything,' the inspector said, 'about riding through mirrors—a dangerous amusement, I should say. Well, Randolph's idea was that if he wasn't good enough for the English order of knighthood, he would show them that he could get recognition enough in other quarters. And so he did.'

Trent nodded; then looked hard at his companion, who returned his gaze with professional stolidity. 'Well, what's on your mind?' he asked at length.

'All this about Randolph's deep interest in other people's art collections reminds me,' Trent said, 'of a rather quaint experience I had a few years ago. In a way, it led up to that bit of a row I had with Randolph, as I told you, shortly before he was murdered. I was going to mention the subject of this row in any case, because it raises a question that may be of interest to you. It's this. Did you ever hear of Randolph being—let me put it as delicately as possible—a bit of an old goat in his later years? My little trouble with him seemed to point to that; and isn't it just possible that his apparently aimless persecution of Fairman, and Fairman's very extreme method of resenting it, may have had behind them a quarrel of the same kind—a kind that Fairman wouldn't want to say anything about?'

The inspector pursed up his mouth dubiously. 'Hm! *Cherchez la femme*, eh?' he said slowly. 'Well, Randolph had been in the public eye, you know, for a good many years, and there was a lot of talk about him one way and another, but I never heard anything of what they call immoral mentioned about him; and you bet there would have been plenty, if there had ever been the slightest foundation for it, or even suspicion.'

'I suppose there would,' Trent agreed. 'And yet I happen to know that he had been making himself objectionable to a certain woman of my acquaintance.'

'How objectionable?'

'I'll tell you just as much as I know, and you will tell me, perhaps, that I jumped to a conclusion. I have an aunt who is a rather remarkable old lady, and she and my friend Miss Tanville-Tankerton, if you will allow me to call her so, are on very intimate terms. There's about thirty years' difference in age between them, and they've sort of adopted each other. Now she told my aunt that she had received from Randolph some notes which had very much distressed and upset her. I couldn't think why they should, because she is in a way a public character, and she gets lots of letters from unknown asses who admire her, and she is not a fool—'

'Are you talking about Miss Faviell?' Mr Bligh asked.

'How did you know?'

'You didn't wrap it up very much. I remember you telling me some time ago that she was an old friend of your wife's and that you knew her very well; and now you mention a lady who is a popular favourite, and has a fan mail, and has the pleasure of your acquaintance. Not so difficult! A good job for you, too, I should say, being a friend of Miss Faviell's. There has never been anyone like her in my time. And so,' the inspector went on, with another swift sidelong glance at Trent, 'she had been receiving letters that distressed her from old Randolph. I wonder what can have been in them.'

'When you look sideways like that,' Trent observed, 'it

means that you know something the other fellow doesn't know. You did it before, when we were talking about Randolph's missing relatives. I don't care about them; they can miss as much as they like; but I am interested in this odd business of the letters Eunice Faviell received from Randolph. I can't imagine how you could know anything about them, but perhaps you do, and it is something it wouldn't be good for me to hear.'

'I never even heard about them until this minute,' Mr Bligh said. 'As for me and my looks, don't you get fancying things. What *was* in the letters?'

'She wouldn't tell my aunt what was in them.'

Mr Bligh grunted several grunts, each grunt eloquent of a profundity of experience. 'Just so,' he remarked. 'So your aunt suspected the worst. Very natural.'

'I thought so. And when the old lady told me of this in confidence, asked me if I could do anything about it, I said to her: "Watch me!" or words to that effect. Because, you see, I happened to know something that I could use to choke him off that or any other game. So I saw him, and I did use it.'

The inspector, to all appearance quite unmoved, regarded him benevolently. 'You're a very fair blackmailer for your age, I must say,' he observed. 'But if I may ask, what did the old chap say?'

Trent frowned with a shade of annoyance. 'All that he said,' he admitted, 'goes to justify those admirably produced grunts of yours. He denied indignantly that he had ever had any evil designs on the lady, and said he had only wanted to do her a kindness. Also, that what he had written to her was none of my damned business. So all I could say was, of course, that if there was any more of his worrying her, I would tell the world the story of the Tiara of Megabyzus.'

'Of course,' the inspector agreed. 'No gentleman could say less. And what in suffering cats *is* the story of the Tiara of Megabyzus?'

'It's one,' Trent said, 'which, as you have not already heard it, I will now proceed to relate.'

He then recounted the experience which is described in the following chapter.

CHAPTER IX

THE TIARA OF MEGABYZUS

It happened in the course of a long tramp in France with which Trent was refreshing his spirit after a long spell of work extending through a breathless London summer. It was now mid-September, and for a fortnight he had carried his knapsack through Lorraine and Burgundy, keeping up our national reputation for lunacy by marching long distances without being compelled to do so, avoiding cities, and halting for food and sleep at small country inns where an Englishman was as unfamiliar a sight as a crocodile.

Trent did not mind being the object of a curiosity that was always friendly; and when his entertainers politely hinted, as they sometimes did, that his way of taking his pleasure was beyond all understanding, he would try to explain the method that was in his madness. He was storing up health in abundance. He delighted in the beauty of the land, which, as commonly happens, had escaped the notice of its inhabitants. Moreover, most of the inns where he stayed were adapted to the needs of the French commercial traveller; a being who is by no means easy to please in the matter of creature comforts, and at the same time prefers, like most of his nation, to get value for money. Everywhere there was excellent cooking, drinkable wine, and clean accommodation; good living at about one-third of the cost of bad living in England—a point which Trent would refrain from making, in defence of his sanity, until after he had received his bill.

The harvest of the grapes had begun, and Trent, as a wayfarer through the *Côte d'Or*, had more than once been allowed to assist in those beautifully simple preliminary processes, carried out at the side of the vineyard itself, which have their result in the noblest wines known to our civilization. He had stood with others round the open tub, rammer in hand, and taken his part in squashing down the sweet-smelling mixture of grapes, stalks, dust, spiders, '*et tout le bazar*'—as one of his *vigneron* friends had crisply put it—with which the great vessel had just been half-filled by the gatherers.

Now he was marching into higher altitudes and a keener air. It was the Jura. As he passed through its crowded folds of mountain land, two sounds were never out of his ears; the dull tinkling of the bells borne by the collared cattle, and the noise of the waterfalls. Trent knew his France, its people, their manners and language, very well; but this corner of the country was new to him. Wild of aspect as it was, he found that it was run upon business lines. The more dense grew the cow-population of the countryside, the more difficult it became to get the midday glass of milk that Trent considered to be due to him in the midst of a pastoral landscape. It had all been carted off, still warm, to the local cheese-and-butter factory.

So he came at length to Lons, the chief town of the Department, and decided in favour of a break of routine, and a few days' stay in that small capital among the mountains; for it was the ideal centre for expeditions into a new and fascinating kind of country. Like the habitat of the Snark, it 'consisted of chasms and crags' very largely, clothed with dark forests and filled with the music of cascades. Trent found the capital itself, however, when he explored it that afternoon, to be very much the type of such centres throughout the land of France. It possessed its *Hôtel de Ville*, *Palais de Justice*, Museum, Theatre, and main street flanked by arcades. In the middle of the *Place de la Liberté* was a fine statue of a general in a commanding attitude, who had been born in Lons. Trent was unable to recall the exploits, or even the name, of General Lecourbe; but it was evident that he had been one of the Napoleonic galaxy, and no part of France easily forgets a soldier of the Empire whom it can call a son. In the *Promenade de la Chevalerie* was a yet finer statue, in a yet more commanding attitude, of Rouget de Lisle, who had been born near Lons, represented in the act of declaiming the Marseillaise.

It was, Trent reflected, a general rule that the more eventless and humdrum the French provincial centre, the more flamboyant and exciting its statues were likely to be. He wished that the same principle of compensation could have been observed in the planning of English country towns; but reminded himself that it would be difficult to raise exciting statues to the memory of men who, however incontestably great, had not usually been very exciting characters. It was while these frivolities floated through his mind, as he stood contemplating the upflung right arm and impressive top-boots of Rouget de Lisle, that the capital of the Jura suddenly began to belie the reputation already attached to it by Trent as a place where nothing, excepting famous Frenchmen, ever happened.

The head of a column of marching infantry—of the 5th battalion of *Chasseurs*—turned into the Promenade, on the way to their quarters at the edge of the town. They looked workmanlike and formidable, though a little neglectful of their personal appearance. As they came on, dogs barked, pigeons fluttered up from the roadway, carts drew aside with drivers shouting inexcusable epithets at their horses, and the attention of some workmen at the top of a high building was momentarily distracted from their task.

It was before this building that Trent was standing. At the time of the enlivening appearance of the military, he had been watching the hoisting of bricks to the roof, by means of a pulley, from a dray beside the kerb. Now he was appreciating, with the eye of a painter, the intensely Gallic aspect of a plump gentleman with a fuzzy, forked beard, tinted eyeglasses, and a general appearance of vivacity combined with dignity, who had halted a few yards away at the first sound of the rhythmic marching of the troops.

As the column approached, the idle squeaking of the work-men's pulley overhead was suddenly changed to a strident scream of friction. Trent, glancing upward, had barely time to make one jump at the plump gentleman, thrust him violently backwards, and leap aside himself, before a great round basket full of bricks, with a length of chain attached to it, hurtled to the ground on the spot where the plump gentleman had been standing.

The plump gentleman, after a moment's whirling fandango on the pavement, came to rest in a sitting position against the wall of the building; and the young men in the ranks, it is regrettable to have to say, laughed very heartily at the incident as they swung by.

In spite of the shock which he had received, the plump gentleman took in the situation instantaneously. He bounded up like a football, and rushing at Trent, seized his hands and wrung them. '*Intrépide!*' he panted. 'You have saved my life at the risk of your own! Those cursed animals above there all but killed the two of us!'

The plump gentleman then replaced his tinted glasses, which were swinging from his right ear at the end of a little chain, and turned to the pressing business of hurling denunciations, pref-aced by the term 'Assassins!,' at the cursed animals on the roof. They in their turn could be seen to shrug copiously, with apologetic and explanatory gestures. A considerable crowd had already gathered, discussing the affair in loud voices; and then two policemen, cleaving the throng from opposite directions with shouts of '*Allô! Allô!*,' proceeded to take the names and addresses of all concerned. There was, in short, a scene.

When order had been restored, Trent's new friend passed an arm affectionately through his, and led the way to a neigh-bouring restaurant, the *Plat d'Argent*. In the forepart of this establishment a number of citizens had already entered on a prolonged preface to the evening meal with *apéritifs* and conver-sation; for it was by this time nearly six o'clock. Trent was delighted with the cordiality of the plump gentleman who, the moment they were installed behind the marble-topped table on the red plush settee, produced a formidable visiting-card with a self-introductory bow. 'The man who owes you his life,' he observed, touching himself on the chest with the fingertips of both hands, then slightly extending them palms upwards.

It appeared that the name of the man in question was M. Calixte Dupont, and that he resided at the *Villa du Puits* in the *Rue des Hirondelles*. Trent, with an apology, inscribed his own name and address on the back of the card; whereupon M. Dupont presented him with another. He read off aloud what Trent had written very much as an Englishman would have read it. 'Aha!' he exclaimed, beaming with satisfaction, 'I can read English, even speak English if I must. I have lived and worked two years in your colossal London. But you, my friend, you speak our tongue with such a facility! No English for me, if you permit.'

M. Dupont proceeded, after consulting Trent, to order two glasses of export-cassis and a packet of Maryland cigarettes. 'You dine here with me,' he insisted, 'at seven o'clock. One eats better nowhere in Lons, and I come here every Sunday. It would be a pity if the saver of my life could not swallow a morsel at my expense.'

In answer to his host's inquiries, Trent explained the reason of his presence in Lons. 'You are travelling on foot!' cried M. Dupont. 'That is England!' Trent remarked that it was, perhaps, even more characteristic of Germany as he had known it. 'It is quite possible,' M. Dupont said with an air of detachment. 'The Germans do not possess much interest for me.' What did interest him was to hear of Trent's wanderings through France on this and earlier occasions, and to know that he was familiar with the region where M. Dupont had done his military service.

When Trent revealed that he was an artist by calling, M. Dupont's pleasure in his company was redoubled. He also, he declared, was an artist. Who had a better right to the name than a designer and artificer in a craft more ancient even than the painter's—that of the jeweller? Jewellers of the first order, said M. Dupont—modestly leaving it to be implied that he was in that class—had something in common with the architects of past time; their work remained for the admiration and delight of mankind, but those works were without signature, the name of the artist was unknown. M. Dupont could not estimate, he said, the number of his own masterpieces in their kind that were now in the possession of rich people everywhere. For the world of the jeweller, he remarked, had no frontiers.

By this time, the hour named by M. Dupont for dinner was close at hand, and he led his guest into the spacious room set apart for more serious refreshment. Trent begged his host to do him the kindness of choosing both the food and the wine; and M. Dupont, not unwilling to prove his quality as a gourmet, did so. The dinner was excellent. The wine—*Château Châlon*, followed by an admirable *Vin d'Arbois*—*was* equal to it. As it proceeded, M. Dupont became more and more communicative. He spoke with animation of the jeweller's craft, and Trent, who liked nothing more than listening to other people's 'shop,' kept the flow going with question and comment.

It was when the stage of coffee and brandy had been reached that M. Dupont began to show signs of having something deeper to disclose, as well as of having enjoyed the lion's share of three bottles of wine. He looked carefully round, drew himself a little closer to his guest, and raised a forefinger with a glance of profound significance.

The restaurant was well-filled, and the conversation of those present was conducted in a key that favoured the imparting of confidences.

M. Dupont began by hinting that his present state of comfortable retirement in the place of his birth was not entirely due to his own thriftiness. He had always made his economies, he admitted—and Trent recognized that this was the utmost length to which a Frenchman could bring himself to go in speaking of his private means—but there was another source of income. It was due to the amiable generosity—here M. Dupont looked sideways at his guest with raised eyebrows—of one of Trent's own countrymen. On Trent confessing to a discreet interest in this statement, M. Dupont plunged into his story.

Some six years before, when he was at the height of his reputation as a craftsman, he had been approached privately by a certain archæologist, who had the reputation of being eccentric as well as wealthy. This client required, and was willing to pay well for, an original piece in the style of the earliest known examples of ancient Persian jewellery. It was, M. Dupont pointed out, a task for an artist par excellence. Any capable artificer, supplied with the very costly materials needed, could make a passable copy of some existing piece of the period. What was asked of M. Dupont's talent was something of entirely new design, in which the style, the very spirit, of that period of ornamental art had been captured. He had consulted long with his new client, and had spent many hours with him in examining the best examples, before the decision was made that the work should take the form of a tiara. One had designed then, and effectively created, a tiara—a beautiful and sumptuous piece, despite its archaic quality. For what purpose it was wanted M. Dupont was not told, nor was it for him to inquire. He was well enough paid.

It was at this time that M. Dupont had received an offer of engagement, on irresistibly tempting terms, in the service of a London firm. He had accepted it without hesitation, and for two years his more intimate contacts with the life of France had been broken. Then, while taking a brief holiday in Paris, he had visited the Louvre to refresh his memory of the triumphs of his craft housed there. What had been his amazement to find, in the place of honour among the objects of Persian art of the fifth century, B.C., his own *chef d'œuvre*! It had been expertly treated so as to reproduce the ravages of time; but its creator could swear to every least detail of the Tiara of

Megabyzus, as the piece was now officially entitled. It had been presented to the museum, as the inscription showed, by an English benefactor, Mr James M. Randolph.

M. Dupont had lost no time in making inquiries. He learnt that Mr Randolph's gift, when offered to the Louvre, had been simply described as what it appeared to be, without any account of how it came into the owner's possession. The museum authorities knew well enough that objects of art of this kind were often brought to market by persons who preferred not to say how they had been acquired; that the looting of ancient tombs, for example, had enriched many public as well as private collections in Europe. All that concerned the Louvre was the genuineness of the piece; and upon that the museum experts, after the closest examination, were in no doubt. It was assuredly authentic. It was accepted with gratitude; it was placed in the position in which M. Dupont had seen it; and the French government's sense of the donor's generosity was manifested by his investment with a commandership of the Legion of Honour.

'Is not that a pretty little history?' M. Dupont asked of his guest. 'But wait! Listen! That is only the beginning.'

M. Dupont's inquiries in Paris, he continued, had shown further that, at the time of his visit, a spirited squabble over the genuineness of the tiara had only just died down. A certain Dr von Rieseneck—whom M. Dupont described pithily as a *saligaud d'Allemand*—had raised his voice from the archæological recesses of the Kaiser Friedrich Museum, asserting that the tiara was a forgery; a marvellously clever piece of work, but a forgery. The details of the dispute, said M. Dupont, would not interest Trent. Enough to say that the Louvre experts, and other French archæologists as one man, had leapt to the defence of the Tiara of Megabyzus.

A furious controversy had raged for months, in the course of which Dr von Rieseneck's son, a lieutenant in the army, had fought an inconclusive duel with one French savant, and had assaulted another whom he did not consider socially competent to measure swords with him. The whole affair had ended— perhaps one might say fortunately—in the mental breakdown of Dr von Rieseneck. As an expert, he had been formidable. As a lunatic, he was harmless, and the champions of the tiara were left in possession of the field.

What was M. Dupont to do? As an honest man, he had thought it his duty to inform Mr Randolph that he had been imposed upon.

On his return to his work in London he had written to Mr Randolph asking, in discreet terms, for an interview. He had seen Mr Randolph, and had told him the plain facts. Mr Randolph had been overwhelmed. 'I told him, moreover,' said M. Dupont, again cocking a sideways eye at Trent, 'that I was not without the inquietude that this dispute over the tiara might be renewed; and I asked him to give me his advice as to the course which I should pursue.'

Mr Randolph had reflected for some little time. He had looked M. Dupont in the eyes, '*d'un regard indéchiffrable.*' He had then said that the fact of Dr von Rieseneck's affliction was not unknown to him; that he had, indeed, received from that personage a number of obviously insane letters, not only abusing him but threatening him in the most violent terms.

Mr Randolph had then gone on to say, with an appearance of choosing his words carefully, that in his own opinion no good purpose would be served by doing anything at the present time which might have humiliating results for France. That, however, was a view which he could not presume to urge upon M. Dupont, who was the best judge of his own responsibility. Apart from that, he had a proposition to make to M. Dupont. He had given such remarkable proofs, in this affair, of his talent and flair in his own department of art, that Mr Randolph would ask him to become his private adviser in all matters of that particular sort for the future. He hoped that M. Dupont's other engagements would permit of his acting in that capacity. If so, he would propose M. Dupont's acceptance of a retaining fee of a certain sum per annum, to be paid quarterly.

At this point in his narrative, M. Dupont made an artistic pause, and lighted a fresh cigarette.

'I hope,' Trent said, with a gravity to match that with which M. Dupont had described this dignified transaction, 'that the amount mentioned was such as you could consider.'

'Since I am still in receipt of it!' M. Dupont replied simply. 'It is paid regularly by Mr Randolph's bankers. So far, he has had no occasion to consult me; but I remain always at his disposal.'

'And the controversy?' Trent inquired. 'Has it arisen again as you were led to anticipate?'

'Circumstances intervened to prevent it,' M. Dupont answered gravely. 'Shortly after my interview with your amiable compatriot, an object of inestimable value was stolen from the Louvre. One might have imagined that the theft of da Vinci's superb masterpiece, a few years earlier, would have made the custodians more vigilant. But no! The Tiara of Megabyzus disappeared. Who knows,' M. Dupont said sadly, finishing his third glass of brandy, 'if it will ever again be restored to the world?'

By now the restaurant was nearly empty, and Trent hinted that it was time for a weary traveller's retirement to his hotel and to bed. M. Dupont vainly urged his guest to join him in taking another little glass; and he took one himself while checking his bill and counting the change. He walked to the door with elaborate steadiness; but once he was outside, the keen air of the mountains began to affect him slightly. 'I live quite near here, my friend,' he said, supporting himself with a hand on one of the *terrasse* tables.

Trent begged to be allowed the pleasure of accompanying him so far; and M. Dupont gratefully took his arm. '*Nous sortons,*' he remarked solemnly, '*des—des portes de Trézène.*' Taking up at that point the very long speech in *Phèdre* in which Theramenes describes the death of Hippolytus, M. Dupont went on to declaim, with thickening speech but unfailing memory, the noble lines of Racine, as they made their somewhat wavering way to the *Rue des Hirondelles*. He did not cease, nor let go of Trent's upholding arm, as they entered the front garden gate of an ugly little house painted dove-colour. Having now reached the couplet—

> *Excusez ma douleur; cette image cruelle*
> *Sera pour moi de pleurs une source éternelle*

—M. Dupont burst into tears. He produced his latch-key, not without difficulty, and Trent obligingly opened the door for him. M. Dupont embraced him, saluted him on either cheek, and stumbled into a lamp-lit passage smelling strongly of furniture polish.

Trent, as he went his way to the *Hôtel des Cascades*, wondered how much of the evening's talk M. Dupont would remember next morning; and how he would feel about what he did remember.

Such was the unusual story which Trent summarized for the benefit of Inspector Bligh as that officer smoked his pipe in attentive silence in the sitting-room at Newbury Place.

'I didn't give Randolph all of what I've told you,' he concluded. 'In fact, I merely mentioned that I happened to know the exact truth about the tiara and the origin of it. I said that if I saw fit to do so I could and would make it public. That was quite enough to shake him badly; I could see that. And what do you think of the pretty little history, as my French friend called it?'

Mr Bligh took the pipe from his mouth and stopped the tobacco with an outsize forefinger. 'It goes to show,' he observed, 'that I was right when I said the old man didn't mind compounding a felony. Very interesting! I've never come across anything in that line of forgery myself—it's not up my street at all. But of course I know there's a great deal of it done. I dare say if all the truth was known . . .'

At this point he was interrupted by a sharp knock at the door.

'Here!' shouted Mr Bligh.

Sergeant Mills appeared. 'There's a man at the door, sir,' he said, 'wanting to see the officer in charge of the case.'

'Well! Who is he?'

'He sent in this card, sir.' The sergeant held out a slip of pasteboard about the size of a post card.

'Joshua B. Waters,' the inspector read aloud. 'Private cars for hire. Chauffeur driven and self drive. Private ambulances with trained attendants. New car sales, all makes. 146, Kemble Street, Salisbury.' He looked at Trent. 'And who the devil is Waters, I wonder?'

'Waters on a starry night are beautiful and fair,' Trent remarked thoughtfully.

'I wouldn't say this Waters looked that way—not by daylight,' the sergeant said, with no trace of expression on his long face. 'But if you look at the back of the card, sir, you'll see he's pencilled another name.'

Mr Bligh looked at the back of the card.

'Well . . . I . . . am . . . damned!' he said slowly.

Trent, catching the card from his outstretched hand, read the name, 'James Randolph.'

CHAPTER X

A MATTER OF TEMPERAMENTS

TRENT and the inspector caught each other's eye in a glance of amazement on the entrance of the personage who, at Mr Bligh's brusque order, was now shown into the room. He was a vigorous man whose age might be guessed at forty, short and compact of figure, and well-dressed in the police rather than the Savile-row sense of that term. His whole appearance bespoke the sturdily independent provincial who had got on in life, and of whom the world was at liberty to think exactly what it chose. But it was the face that had so undisguisably astonished Trent and the police officer; a clean-shaven face, square, hard and ruddy, blunt-nosed, and with eyes glinting shrewdly between narrowed lids.

The newcomer took note of their surprise with grim amusement; then, glancing from one to the other, made the obvious choice. 'You are Inspector Bligh?' he asked; and received the curt reply: 'That is my name.'

'I carry my credentials in my looks—it's easy to see that,' the square-faced man remarked with a faint trace of Northern accent. 'Yes, gentlemen, I am the old man's son; the only son who ran away from home.'

Mr Bligh, his gaze still dwelling on the features of the claimant to the name of Randolph, took hold of the situation. 'I am very sorry, Mr Randolph,' he said, 'you should be returning under such tragic circumstances. When you speak of yourself as the son who ran away, I understand you to mean that you never have returned until now—never made it up with your father, in fact. That must make it all the more painful for you.'

The hard face betrayed no emotion. 'No man likes to hear

of his own flesh and blood being murdered. As for our not having made it up, that's right enough. Since I was a lad, my father and I never set eyes on each other, or took any notice of each other's existence. I heard no more about him than anybody might do who reads the papers, and for all he knew about me I might have been dead and buried years ago. I suppose it would sound well for me to say I never expected to return to his roof under such tragic circumstances, as you put it. But I am no hand at saying what I don't mean. I have always known there wasn't likely to be any going back while my father was alive. When I let him know I meant to leave home, he told me I could go if I wanted to, and come back when I had learned some sense, but I needn't think he would ever send for me. Both of us were pretty hard chaps, so that settled it.'

James Randolph, while offering this abridgement of a chapter of family history, had placed his hat on the table and serenely seated himself in one of the arm-chairs before the fireplace. Now, with a hand on either knee, he looked from one to the other of his hearers.

Trent's knowledge of his friend told him that, for all his expressionless face, Mr Bligh was not unfavourably impressed by the manner of this unusual self-introduction.

'Well, Mr Randolph,' he said with a trace of a smile, 'there can't be much doubt about who your father was, I should say; I never saw such a likeness. Barring a few lines in the face, which you'll get in time, you're his living image. Put on one of his square-topped bowlers, and carry that little bag he always took about with him, and anybody would think it was the old gentleman himself. But you say you are in favour of frankness, and you've shown that you are; so you won't object to me speaking frankly too. Your statement that you are the legitimate son of the late Mr Randolph will have to be legally made good, if you are counting on deriving any benefit from your claim. Of course you know that.'

'I do, of course,' Randolph said. 'There won't be any

difficulty about that, though. As for my getting any benefit from being my father's son, the Lord knows I haven't counted on it; but you never can tell what may happen, so I have always been in a position to prove my identity if I wanted to do so. And from what I hear now,' James Randolph added coolly, 'it seems there is a chance of something that you might call benefit coming my way. So here I am, and here I stay, until we've got it straightened out about how I stand. I've left my business in good hands, and I am in no hurry.'

Mr Bligh looked at him with pursed lips. 'What you should do first, Mr Randolph, is to get in touch with your father's solicitors. I can give you the name and address. Perhaps that was what was in your mind in calling here.'

'Oh no,' Randolph said, with some hint of a self-satisfied grin that made him for the first time seem quite human and very Yorkshire. 'That wasn't in my mind. I've learnt to know my way about the world a bit, Inspector. When I read the news in the paper yesterday afternoon, I saw my solicitor in Salisbury, who knows me by the name of Waters. I got him to telephone his London agents to find out who were the late Mr Randolph's solicitors in London; and I soon got the information. I came up by car yesterday evening, put up at the Woburn Hotel, and called on the firm first thing this morning. When I asked if they could see Mr James Randolph, I hadn't any difficulty in obtaining an interview.'

'No,' the inspector said with a grin, 'I suppose not. Then I take it you have come here to see me about the investigation of the crime, and possibly give me some help.'

James Randolph nodded briefly, 'Ay, that's it. I don't know about giving help, seeing that it's twenty-five years since I had anything to do with my father. But I would like to hear about the investigation, if you agree with me that I am entitled to do so; and what prospect there is of bringing the man who did this thing to justice. Any differences there may have been between my father and me were in the family, and nobody else's business. If I had cause for what I did, it didn't extend to wishing him any harm in his old age. As my father's son, I want to see the man who killed him taken, and made to pay the price.'

Mr Bligh stroked his knees thoughtfully. 'I should like,' he said, 'to know first of all just how we stand—or how you stand, to put it plainly, Mr Randolph. Have you any objection to telling me briefly what I suppose you have been telling Muirhead & Soames this morning? You could speak quite freely before this gentleman, Mr Trent, who is a friend of mine, and sometimes gives me his assistance as confidential adviser.'

Trent, hearing with suitable gravity this rather ambiguous account of his position, exchanged nods with James Randolph, who said: 'I don't mind if I do. I've nought to be ashamed of, according to my view, and I don't worry much about other people's views. Well, then—I'll say just this much about my father, that he was never an easy man to live with. He had very strict notions about conduct. He had some fault to find with pretty near everything that anybody did. It was part of his belief that those who did wrong ought to suffer for the good of their own souls, and that it was his Christian duty to see that they did suffer, if he was in a position to do so. Naturally, his own family got the full benefit of that.'

'And they were not grateful?' Trent suggested.

'They were weak, sir—that is how my father would have put it,' Randolph returned composedly. 'His sister, who lived with him until she made a marriage that he strongly disapproved of, must have been a bit like me; she went out of his life and stayed out, and her name was never mentioned in his household. My mother was the best of mothers to me, and it fair gives me the creeps to think what my boyhood would have been without her; but she couldn't please my father. Her health was not good, and she had a nurse to help look after me. After mother died, my old nurse stayed on, and she was always next door to a mother to me; but it wasn't long before she married, and then

I couldn't stick it any longer. So there you have the story of why I left home.

'I told nobody where I was going when I went away from Humberstone. What I did was go straight to Salisbury, where my old nurse and her husband were living, to see if they could give me a job. His name was Waters, the same as you've seen it on that card I sent in. He had started a small motor-car business, as I knew, and I was a pretty good mechanic after a couple of years in Townrow's works. Waters was a right good chap, and besides, he would have done anything to please his wife. He agreed to give me a trial, and to say nought about who I was. It was given out that I was a nephew of his, of the same name. I wouldn't take anything but my keep at the start, but after six months I was getting decent pay, and earning it. Between us, we built up that business. Waters took me into partnership, and when he died I carried on under the old name, as I am doing now.'

Mr Bligh glanced at Randolph's trade card. 'So I see. A fine business, I should think, Mr Randolph, in these times.' His tone expressed an amiable interest.

Randolph shot him a glance that was not quite so amiable. 'The business is all right,' he said bluffly.

'It means everything to a business,' Mr Bligh reflected, 'to have a man at the head of it who started at the foot of the ladder. You know how to pick your men, for one thing. And I expect you're a first-class driver yourself, Mr Randolph.'

'The name of Waters,' Randolph declared, 'used to be pretty well known on the track at one time. But I have given all that up long ago. No time for it.'

'Did you bring Mrs Randolph to London with you?'

'I have never married,' Randolph said. 'No time for that neither. Old Aggie—that's my partner's widow, my old nurse— she's living with me and looking after me still. There, gentlemen; now you know all about me, or as much as need be anyhow.'

Randolph, still seated squarely in his chair, now pulled out a large handkerchief and blew his nose sonorously, as if sounding a challenge to all incredulity and suspicion. Trent, observing the gesture, once more exchanged significant looks with the inspector, who proceeded at once to make the comment for which the speaker appeared to be waiting.

'And so that is the account you have given to the lawyers, Mr Randolph,' he said. 'A plain enough solution of the puzzle about your disappearance. Well, well! It's all very simple when you know. You said something about being able to prove your identity, I think, if anyone should raise the question of your legitimate parentage. I suppose you are relying on the testimony of your old nurse.'

'Ay! And there's more than that,' Randolph said. 'I brought several things away with me when I left home, in case they might be useful. There's the birth and baptism certificates that were taken out when I first went to Freyne Park School—my mother gave me them. And there's the silver mug I had when I was christened, with my name and the date engraved on it. And there's the Bible that was given me when I had learnt to read, with an inscription signed by my father—"from his attached father, James M. Randolph," it says. And there's a photograph of my mother and father, taken when they were first married, which she gave me—there's something written on it,' Randolph added after a moment's hesitation, 'and signed by her. All those things I brought with me when I drove up from Salisbury yesterday evening, and I left them with the solicitors this morning. Taken together with the family likeness I bear, they pretty well settled the matter, and I have asked Muirhead & Soames to go ahead and get my position legally established.'

The inspector nodded. 'I gather, Mr Randolph, you have heard your father is believed to have left no will.'

'So I have been told; and nobody more surprised about it than me. When I heard of his death, I thought he would have left a will of course, and if so there might or might not be something in my favour. 'Twasn't as if he had cast me off and disowned me, you see; none so bad as that. And you never know, anyhow. So I thought the sooner I came forward in my lawful name the better. I'm none so sure as yet, mind you, that there is no will, though the lawyers say they had often urged him to make one and he had always put off doing so. But however that may turn out, I mean to stand on my rights if I have got any.' Randolph closed his lips inflexibly; then added with a change to an easier manner, 'And now, if you're satisfied, Inspector, what do you say to letting me know what the police inquiries have led to, and what it means when the papers say an arrest has taken place?'

At this point Trent rose to go, for the hour of the appointment which he had mentioned to Mr Bligh was by this time not far off. James Randolph, who seemed now to be comfortably conscious of a certain mastery of the situation, gave him a curt but friendly farewell.

As a taxi took him homeward, Trent thought of Randolph with a sympathy which, to all appearances, was the last emotion that he desired to awaken in his fellow-men. The brief and trite intimations he had given of the sort of life lived in his father's household had developed in Trent's fertile fancy to a tragic history of watchful, self-righteous rigour and of spirits broken or stunted by unending frustration. It was curious—Trent had seen the same oddity before—how, despite a feeling in the child which must have been at best one of dogged resentment and rebellion, he had derived from his father not only a remarkable likeness in face and physique, but similarities of bearing, gait and gesture such as no merely conscious imitation could ever have produced. The inspector, as Trent had noted, had been as much struck as himself by the way that this was shown even in such trifles as the posture of sitting in a chair or the management of a handkerchief. The parentless and untaught kitten, crouched with twitching tail by the mouse-hole, did not give more telling proofs of heredity.

An hour of work at the portrait of Sir Densmore ffinch, and of drafts on that veteran's fund of scandalous recollection, drove Trent's thoughts away from the Randolph affair; but they returned to it refreshed as he sat at a solitary luncheon. It was long enough since he had resolved to have no more to do, in a quasi-professional way, with problems of crime. But the murder of a man whom he had known, and who had aroused his interest as a human curiosity, could not be disregarded; and the utterly unexpected appearance of an old friend in the character of the self-confessed criminal had given the keenest edge to Trent's reviving taste for that grimly fascinating business.

Bryan Fairman, he was still convinced, was quite incapable of deliberate homicide, to say nothing of shooting a man in the back. But there had always been—Trent now admitted it to himself—something in the make-up of Fairman not inconsistent with the idea that he might, in a state of extreme nervous tension, be guilty of fatal violence. The air of cool reserve that marked him in ordinary social relations, and made him a man of few friendships and no popularity, cloaked a nature of the most sensitive kind. He would have treated with disgust the sugges-tion of his being what is called temperamental; but he was, in his own way, nothing else. That was to be seen in the intensity of his devotion, quite hopeless as it had always been, to Eunice Faviell; but that was another aspect of the matter. Trent, as one of the few who knew Fairman thoroughly, could name some things that raised his temper to a white heat and strained his steely self-control to bursting-point. Cruelty was among those things; so was injustice; so, too, was the self-satisfied and, as it were, studied obtuseness that threw an ignorant contempt upon all pioneer work in the spacious world of scientific research. There could be little doubt that Randolph had been guilty of the first two—that the cutting off of Fairman from the research that he lived for had been his work; and the old man had, to Trent's own knowledge, made a deliberate display of the third. All this, taken along with the self-evident truth that Fairman's illness had told upon his mental condition, made it far from difficult to believe that he had called upon Randolph in a dangerous temper.

Trent, pacing up and down his studio as he turned these unacceptable thoughts over in his mind, felt in his pocket for a pipe; and along with it he turned out the thin cards on which were printed the enlarged photographs of the fingermarks found on the razor-blade in Randolph's bedroom. He looked at them with scant attention as he recalled the ingenious attempt of Inspector Bligh to fit these unidentified traces into his picture of what had happened on the night of the crime. It was long ago—Trent could not think how long, but certainly a number of years—that he had made a careful study of the system used by the police in the preserving and classifying of fingerprints. For practice in the use of it, he had for some time amused himself by taking impressions of the fingers of any of his friends who would submit to that rather messy operation. In this branch of knowledge, he told himself, he had grown decidedly rusty. Looking at these well-marked prints of a finger and thumb, he had no more than a vague recollection of the dactyloscopic terms to be used in describing them. He turned to rummage in one of the drawers of a tall cabinet, and soon pulled out a bundle of photographs fastened by an elastic band. He spread them on the table. Each consisted of a set of prints marked with a name, and with the characteristics of each print noted against it by his own hand in small but clear red-ink script. Neat work, he reflected; a waste of time, but neat enough. Ah! yes; that was the word for which he had been searching his memory—the word 'ulnar.' The forefingerprint on the blade showed an ulnar loop, with—he numbered the ridge-marks delicately with a fine pencil-point—seventeen counts. A very ordinary sort of pattern; there were many such, he could see, in his collection. But the unknown print had something else about it; a small white line dividing four of the ridges immediately to the left of the delta. The scar of a cut? No; there was no displacement or puckering of the ridges. What was the term for it? He shuffled through his own photographs rapidly. Yes; that was it! A crease.

And then Trent exploded in an oath, and the blood rushed to his head as he stared in consternation at the print from which he had read that harmless little word. He caught up the police photograph, and with shaking hands compared the two minutely. There could be no doubt or question. Here were two forefinger-prints exactly alike in every detail, even to the tiniest particulars brought out in each ridge by the process of enlargement. He turned to the thumbprint on his own card, and again compared the two. They were identically similar—of course!

Trent collapsed into a chair and wiped the beads of sweat from his forehead. He felt as if he were in the crisis of a nightmare. The thing was madness; it didn't make sense. But this was no dream; the cold facts were there. He strove to put a check on the racing tumult of his thoughts; the facts were there.

This, then, was the answer of experience to his resolve, so well kept until now, to have no more to do with mysteries of crime. His personal contacts with old James Randolph had tempted him to the extent of seeking information, at least, about the course of the official inquiry. Then the discovery of an old and close friend's incrimination in the affair had moved him to an absorbed and deeply distressful interest. And now this bewildering complication, this direct suggestion of something far worse than the revengeful act of a man mentally unhinged, had arisen as a challenge to the full exercise of such ingenuity and imagination as Trent had given formerly to problems of the sort. He could do no less than take that challenge up, and by his own way arrive at the truth, if possible, about this baffling case.

The most direct and swiftest approach would be by means of a personal appeal to Bryan Fairman, that he should consent to clothe with as much detail as he could the outline of what had happened, or been seen or heard, that night at Newbury Place.

His statement, it was clear, had been deliberately made as bare and uninforming as was consistent with his purpose. But the making of any such appeal, Trent saw at once, was out of the question. Even if Fairman had been in a condition to reply to questions, he had the right to keep his own counsel if he had so determined, and he was not a man who could easily be made to see better reasons than his own, even by the closest friend. But Fairman was ill and unapproachable; the police themselves could not question him, and leave to speak with him in such a state would never be given to anyone applying merely as a friend of the accused.

It seemed to Trent that there was one line of inquiry, not altogether without promise, lying open. He had been struck at once—more so than Inspector Bligh had appeared to be—by the statement of the Dieppe police, that they had been completely unable to discover any reason why a foreigner, '*souffrant et un peu toqué*,' should have betaken himself to a certain quarter of their town, and there appeared to be in search of something.

Trent knew his France, as has been said, pretty well. He had lived two years there, for the most part in Paris, and at other times had explored many of the towns and countrysides. He was well aware that some acquaintance with the private affairs of every household was an object which every local police headquarters, for the soundest of public motives, set before itself, and was usually able to attain to its own satisfaction; so that a hand could be laid on the recorded facts at need. Fairman, whatever his state of mind, must certainly have had some purpose in travelling straight to a particular neighbourhood in Dieppe when he left England—in going thither, and in looking about for something which, it was alleged, he had failed to find. The Dieppe police, so Mr Bligh had said, declared themselves absolutely at a loss to account for such actions on Fairman's part, although they had made every possible inquiry.

It might be true. The Dieppe police might, on the other

hand, have the soundest of public motives for being unable to find any clue to the proceedings of Fairman on this occasion. Trent could recall more than one case in which much more extraordinary facts had completely baffled the intelligence of officials who were certainly in a position to discover the truth if discovery had been their object. He reminded himself, indeed, that it was not an unheard-of thing for the French police to go to quite remarkable lengths with the purpose of making the truth undiscoverable by other people. On the whole, he was disposed to think that, as there was obviously more in Fairman's proceedings at Dieppe than met the eye, there might well be more than met the eye in the official inability to supply a clue to them.

At least there was something to be done in the way of search for the unguessable truth; and the next afternoon saw Trent setting foot on the quay in the old Avant Port of Dieppe.

CHAPTER XI

IMPASSE

'IMPASSE de la Chimère.' Trent said the words over to himself, relishing their hint of mystery, as he walked out of Dieppe harbour on his quest. Such a name, he thought, must lend some glamour of magic to the blindest of alleys.

Like all places worth finding, the Impasse de la Chimère was hard to find. Trent had to consult several passers-by before he discovered that the way to the Impasse ran down an old-fashioned narrow side street off a tram-bedevilled, motor-ridden road. From that side street another even narrower turned on the left.

He had the impression of walking into loneliness and the unknown. The grey houses were mute and mysterious; the streets were empty. At last 'Impasse de la Chimère' caught his eye, rudely carved and half defaced by time, at the corner of a narrow passage down which a cart might just be able to pass with hubs scraping the wall on either side. It was a place of emptiness, for the alley ran straight for fifty yards or so between high and formidable walls above which showed the branches of ancient trees. The uneven cobbles of the roadway might have been laid in the days of the Grand Monarque.

Suddenly the alley turned right and opened out with a sweep on either hand. On the right was a gate surmounted by a battered nondescript animal in stone, which might well be the Chimera that gave its name to the Impasse. The house that lay behind it, visible through the iron gateway, was evidently a place of dignity and tradition. Unhonoured by any name on the gate-post, it was distinguished, convict-like, by a number, 7A, on an ugly little enamelled plaque set crookedly on the wall by a careless workman. Why the authorities of the town should have bestowed on the largest house in the Impasse this number-letter combination, as though there were not enough whole numbers in the universe, was a riddle to which Trent saw no answer. There were, in fact, four houses, 1, 3, 5 and 7A, with no gaps to account for the even numbers or the missing 7.

Musing on the high degree of success with which the fundamental logic of the Latins is concealed from the inquiring stranger, Trent went forward. A little wind sighed in the burgeoning branches overhead. The sense of desertion became almost unbearable. He thought with a shiver of the words:

> Where no one comes
> Or hath come since the making of the world.

Further along from the gateway of the Chimera was another opening in the long containing wall, closed by a wooden gate. This was much the worse for wear, and through the chinks in it could be caught a glimpse of a smaller house, detached from its neighbour, but much resembling it in architectural style and in the traces of age. On the gate-post, below the official 5, was carved the curious name 'Pavillon de l'Ecstase,' and above the gate was a rough wooden notice daubed with whitewash, announcing 'Villa à Louer.'

As Trent stood gloomily considering the poetic contrast between these two inscriptions, a miracle happened; one of those miracles which so often pass unnoticed, though they change the whole face of nature. The sun coming out from behind a cloud shot a sudden shaft into the Impasse de la Chimère, and a great splotch of colour blazed up beyond the gates he had been studying. A huge round pumpkin, a *potiron*, all red and gold, with a chunk cut mathematically out of it, flamed like fire outside a modest shop that was No. 3 of the Impasse, and an adjacent pile of withered oranges, a few green apples and some miscellaneous vegetables became a scene of splendour.

Trent's depression vanished. He thought no more of the loneliness, the grey mouldering gates and walls, the atmosphere of decay and desolation which had chilled him for the moment. He turned away from the Pavillon de l'Ecstase. The glory of the pumpkin had opened his eyes to the truth that the end of the Impasse was as inviting as the approach to it had been dismal. An ancient inn, one wing of it adjoining the fruiterer's shop, was built right across the dead end of the alley and round its other side in the shape of an E without the centre stroke; and this alluring hostelry bore the name of Hôtel du Petit Univers et de la Chimère. 'Cuisine Bourgeoise, Vins de Touraine et d'Anjou, Quetsch de Lorraine, Armagnac Vieux,' were among its promised attractions, and Trent succeeded in deciphering a prehistoric notice—'*Ici on loge à pied et à cheval.*'

Here it was, no doubt, that Fairman had taken his cup of coffee as mentioned in the brief report from the Dieppe police, before returning to the steamboat quay. It was clearly the place for beginning his own inquiries, and surely they could have no pleasanter starting-point.

'Here goes,' he said to himself, 'for the Hotel of the Little Universe. And there is Gargantua himself to welcome me! What more could the god of travellers have done for me?'

Gargantua had, in fact, appeared at the door in the shape of an enormous man wearing a cook's cap. His face was round and red and merry, and the leather belt around his middle would have girt two men of average corpulence.

Trent, taking off his hat, addressed this being courteously in the being's own language. 'Sir,' he said, 'I have come from across the sea to greet you in the name of the Curé de Meudon. For surely you are a Tourangeau of the country of Rabelais.' As he spoke, he pointed to the notice 'Vins de Touraine.'

Gargantua was quite unmoved by the extravagance of this greeting. With a gesture of his great arms he bade Trent enter, saying simply, 'Welcome. Monsieur is right, I am of Chinon. We have good wine.'

The Hotel of the Little Universe and of the Chimera was such an inn as wise men hope to find at the end of the world. Its rooms were long and low, shaped by an eccentric magician with a sense of humour and a taste for complicated geometry. Here and there the darkness of old oak was lightened by the gleam of burnished copper.

Trent found himself in a room half dining-room, half café. A tall fair woman with handsome impassive features and dark eyes was sitting behind the *caisse*. Trent had resolved that for that night at any rate he would be 'lodged on foot' at this fantastic inn, and when he made his intention known, the lady, whom Gargantua addressed as Louise, laid aside her knitting and led him up a crazy zigzag staircase to the chief bedroom. This was a chamber with a matrimonial four-poster, an uneven floor and walls broken by a variety of unexpected bulges and angles. The air was stuffy, but pleasantly burdened with the scent of *pot-pourri*. He opened the window and looked out into a wilderness of trees and shrubs, surrounding a grey villa that must have been gay and smiling in the days of the Pompadour, though now in the abandonment of its shuttered windows it looked desolate enough.

'*Tiens!*' exclaimed Trent, 'is that the Pavillon de l'Ecstase?'

There was no reply. Surprised at the silence, he turned round to find Louise already leaving the room, forgetful of the busy politeness with which she had dwelt upon the qualities of her best bedchamber. Had she made this sudden retreat to avoid his question? He repeated it as he followed her down the headlong stairs, and she mumbled something that sounded like '*Mais oui, Monsieur*.' She made it clear that the Pavillon de l'Ecstase was not a subject that she intended to discuss. Her attention was absorbed first in sending the maid to prepare Trent's room for his occupation, then in despatching the boot-boy to bring his bag from the station *consigne*.

Trent fell into talk with Gargantua in the café. It soon appeared that his name in this incarnation was Alphonse Legros, known to his intimates as '*Le Joufflu*' from his cherubic cheeks. His wife was a Lorrainer and responsible for the Quetsch, the liqueur made from her father's plums. Trent called for a Pernod, and had no difficulty in persuading his host to take thought for the good of the house.

'Welcome to the Hotel of the Little Universe,' said Gargantua, raising his glass, when a merry, black-eyed maid had busied herself about them.

Trent banished for the moment his natural curiosity about the oddly-named Pavillon, and his deeper concern with the events that had brought him to Dieppe. He addressed himself to the immediate and pleasing mystery of the name of this inn, the Hotel of the Little Universe and of the Chimera. Certainly the Chimera—a fabulous mongrel of lion, goat and dragon, if Trent remembered rightly—might reasonably adorn the escutcheon of some noble family; and the name, no doubt, was taken from that unidentifiable monster in weathered stone which stood above the gateway of the neighbouring *château*. But the Petit Univers! On the sign, he recalled, these words were painted in above 'de la Chimère' as though they were a later addition. Gargantua could never have thought for himself of anything so philosophically satisfying and cosy.

'Monsieur Garg . . . ,' he began, 'I mean Monsieur Legros, your very good health; and would you mind telling me, in the name of Rabelais and all other livers of the good life, what fly had bitten you when you named your inn the Little Universe?'

Gargantua scratched his head. 'It was an idea,' he said. 'An idea of Monsieur le Comte. In the old times it was just the Hôtel de la Chimère, like the Impasse and like the Maison de la Chimère, the great house that belongs to the count. That was good enough for me and my father. But one day—perhaps it was five years ago, or seven . . . when was it, Louise?'

Louise was back behind the *caisse*, silent and inscrutable, her knitting-needles flying with incredible speed.

'It was the year of the great storm,' she said calmly, 'when your brother's vintage was ruined by the hail.'

Gargantua nodded. 'That was it. Not a drop of decent wine did they make on the Loire that year. Happily the next year made up for it. I still have some bottles of Chinon and Rochecorbon of that year behind the faggots. It was a good year both for red and white. Perhaps Monsieur will like to taste them.'

Monsieur certainly would, but for the moment his interest was monopolized by the Little Universe.

With an effort Gargantua resumed his tale.

'One day in 19— . . . now was it in the spring or summer?'

Trent mildly suggested that perhaps it didn't matter.

'Well, anyhow, Monsieur le Comte came to me and said "*Eh, le Joufflu*"—it is like that he calls me—"I am going to diminish your rent." I was all taken aback; not but what it had been hard enough to make both ends meet, what with the dearness of life and the taxes. *Oui, Monsieur le Comte est gentil, mais il a des idées, quoi?*'

Gargantua talked warily of the count's ideas as though they were dangerous, almost disreputable, possessions.

Trent waited patiently for Gargantua to unfold his story. He was clearly not a man to be hurried.

'*Enfin*, he diminished the rent by ten per cent, and in return I called the hotel "The Little Universe and the Chimera". *Ça lui faisait plaisir. Voilà.*'

He evidently considered the problem to be adequately explained.

'But,' asked Trent, 'did he not say why he had chosen so strange an appellation?'

Gargantua shrugged his shoulders. '*Monsieur le Comte a des idées*,' he repeated, as though that explained everything. 'He had a fancy to eat in a hotel that was called the Hotel of the

Little Universe. For, mark you, he often eats at that very table in the corner. It was something to do with a book he had written. Yes, Monsieur le Comte is not proud, though he has written books and one can see his name in the newspapers . . . *Hélas!*'

Gargantua shook his head and sighed heavily.

Madame Louise clucked sharply, like a hen, from behind the *caisse*, and laid her fingers on her lips, frowning heavily.

Her husband pulled himself together. 'Yes, the Comte d'Astalys is well known as a savant, a *psycho . . . psychosophe . . .* What is it, Louise?'

'*Psychologue*,' Louise said with pursed lips, 'but it would be well for us to mind our own business. It is not for us to inquire into the ideas of Monsieur le Comte.'

'No indeed,' said Gargantua. 'Least of all after the misfortune . . .'

Louise cut him short with a serpentine hiss. 'Alphonse, will you stop chattering and look after your customers? There is Monsieur Gautier waiting for you to receive him, and no one to take his hat and coat.'

Gargantua rose, and Trent had perforce to possess his soul in patience. He was evidently on the track of some obscure affair—perhaps some scandal—about which these two good folk were, for their own reasons, unwilling to talk; and in this might lie the key to the secret of Fairman's visit to the Impasse de la Chimère.

The newcomer, Monsieur Gautier, a lean stooping man with a short beard and big spectacles over bloodshot eyes, the violet ribbon of the academic palms in his buttonhole, sat down on the *banquette* at the table next to Trent's. He was, it appeared, a neighbouring bookseller, therefore a man of learning, and peculiarly gifted, as it occurred suddenly to Gargantua, to explain to this inquisitive foreigner the count's 'ideas' about the name of the hotel. So Trent and Monsieur Gautier were made acquainted with each other; they shook hands, and the bookseller was persuaded to have an *apéritif* with the visitor, who in his turn accepted a cigarette from the new friend whom Gargantua addressed as *Hégésippe*.

Then Monsieur Gautier, after sipping his Amer Picon—that formidable brown drink of which, according to legend, a single undiluted drop will burn a neat round hole in a shirt cuff and on which the average Frenchman thrives nevertheless—tried to expound to Trent the count's ideas of the Little Universe.

'The Comte d'Astalys, whose family has owned the Maison de la Chimère and the houses of the Impasse for many generations—'

'That includes the Pavillon de l'Ecstase?' asked Trent.

A curious expression passed over the bookseller's face, and he raised his eyebrows fractionally.

'Yes, but it used to be known as the Pavillon de la Chimère,' he said shortly; and went on, as if in haste to pass over an awkward subject. 'The Astalys family has always been famous for its love of curious learning. It was said the Count Balthazar, the alchemist and magician, first added the Chimera to their coat of arms. He made a great fortune, ascribed by less lucky people to the black art and to unholy intimacy with the devil, and built the Maison de la Chimère. The present count has followed the family tradition in his search for knowledge. The nature of consciousness has been his special interest. He studied hypnotism, and experimented with narcotic drugs.'

Monsieur Gautier quite frankly disapproved of such researches. In his opinion the less a man knew about artificial paradises the better. He admitted, however, that the knowledge acquired by the count had proved of practical utility, since it had given him a high position in the poison-gas department of G.Q.G. during the war. Later the count had been fascinated by the new-born science of psychology, and had published certain monographs and treatises—*bouquins*, Monsieur Gautier called them—which had won for him a considerable reputation among experts.

'*Je ne suis pas psychologue pour deux sous*,' said the bookseller, emphasizing the remark with a wave of his long artistic hands, 'I am of the old school, the generation which saw 1870. For me, this life, my country, *notre belle France,* are the only realities, and after death nothing. But M. le Comte has ideas. His researches have led him into strange paths, and sometimes he does me the honour to argue with me in my shop, when we turn over the pages of the latest books. Once he wrote a little book which he called *L'Univers Particulier*, and it was thence that he took the name of the Little Universe, that private world which each one of us inhabits, and from which he can never escape.'

'Now I understand,' Trent exclaimed. 'I have read it. It was translated into English under the title of *The Private Universe*.'

A dim recollection of that book had been in the background of his mind ever since he had seen the curious name of the hotel. He had thought it notable, in particular, for the charm of its author's personality, which had found a haunting expression even through the dark glass of translation. The bookseller's evident affection and respect for one with whose ideas he profoundly disagreed made it natural that the count should be just such a man. The book had been published by one of those firms that specialize in works dealing with magic, astrology and the occult in general. Not that there had been anything occult or magical in *The Private Universe*. It was no more than a development of Berkeley and Kant, maintaining that things in themselves we can never know, so that a man lives in a private universe of his own, of which he alone is the centre, though he may hold much of it in common with his fellows—the purpose of existence, then, must be the development of consciousness. The main part of the book was concerned with a series of experiments with narcotics and excitants which have the power of modifying consciousness either for good or ill, transforming the private universe into a hell of nightmares, or enriching and extending its content beyond this three-dimensional existence.

'But,' said Trent, 'the author's name . . . I have forgotten, but surely it was not d'Astalys?'

'The count has never written under his own name. His pseudonym is Pierre Deffaux. It was a strange book, and to my mind a dangerous book. As I said, *je n'aime pas les paradis artificiels.* Alas! events have proved me right.'

'I have not read the count's book,' said Gargantua suddenly and unnecessarily, just as Trent was about to ask the meaning of the bookseller's last words. 'I read only the *Petit Parisien.*'

M. Gautier shook his head with a gentle smile and went on. 'For the count, dreams were as real as life, and the idea has served him ill.'

He stopped abruptly. Once again the fringe of a dangerous subject had been reached.

Trent, to encourage him, repeated in a low voice the lines:

> *Le seul rêve intéresse;*
> *Vivre sans rêve, qu'est-ce?*
> *Moi, j'aime la Princesse*
> *Lointaine.'*

'It was no far-away princess,' said M. Gautier sadly. 'In fact, Monsieur'—and then again Trent was tantalized by an interruption. A tubby little man with a close-clipped beard and extraordinarily bright beady eyes bounced into the café with a boisterous '*Bonjour* Madame Louise; *bonjour, le Joufflu; bonjour, la compagnie.*' He was evidently a chartered buffoon, for he made a great ceremony of kissing the hand of Madame, whose statuesque serenity was for an instant broken by a smile. The newcomer was hailed affectionately as Bibi by Le Joufflu and M. Gautier, and after the indispensable formality of handshaking all round had been accomplished, he was presented to Trent as Monsieur William Rond-de-Cuir.

Trent, as he shook Bibi's hand, thought his ears must have played him false. William, camouflaged as Viyiamm, is not uncommon among the French in preference to Guillaume; but Rond-de-Cuir was a most unlikely surname, being a contemptuous sobriquet for a quill-driver or clerk, derived from the circular leather cushion on which in France he is wont to sit. Bibi saw the puzzlement on Trent's face, and produced from his pocket-book with a flourish of modest self-satisfaction an enormous card, bearing the inscription:

WILLIAM ROND-DE-CUIR.
(G. Dumanet.)
Rédacteur à la Gazette de la Manche.
Echotier et Courrieriste.

Bibi leaned across the table, and with a fat stumpy forefinger, stained with ink and tobacco, directed Trent's attention to 'William.'

'Viyiamm,' he said, 'Engleesh. It is like that—William Rond-de-Cuir—that I sign my *echoes* in the *Gazette de la Manche*; but to all the world in the Café of the Little Universe I am Bibi, just Bibi *tout court*.'

Trent, as in honour bound, brought out in exchange the miserable little slip of pasteboard which serves an Englishman as visiting card. He was duly impressed by the importance of Bibi's description. As '*échotier*,' he would be responsible for the miscellaneous notes that brightened the front page of his paper. No doubt they would be humorous over such a signature, and Bibi clearly tried to live up to his job. For payment he would have the right to insert a number of blatant advertisements, scarcely disguised in the form of news, and would make what he could out of the advertisers. As '*courriériste*' he probably produced a Paris letter, extracted and more or less cunningly worked up from the Paris papers. As *rédacteur* he would certainly be alive to the slightest breath of scandal in his town, and he was therefore just the man Trent needed.

Trent, however, found himself forgotten. Bibi challenged the bookseller to a game of '*trictrac*,' otherwise backgammon. This was an amusement which Trent had attempted only in his boyhood, and then with a minimum of enthusiasm; but in the Café of the Little Universe, the only athletic sport that Douglas Jerrold ever mastered was taken as seriously as cricket or football. Every evening—so Le Joufflu informed Trent in an undertone—Bibi and Hégésippe duelled desperately for the price of their drinks.

A waiter, appearing suddenly in a condition which suggested that he had just risen from bed after sleeping in his dress clothes, produced the necessary apparatus. The antagonists plunged into their combat. For the moment it evidently would be mere waste of time to talk to either of the players; so Trent tried a new opening with Le Joufflu, who was watching the game with the eye of an *aficionado* at a bullfight.

'Monsieur Legros,' he said, 'did you see one of my compatriots here the other day in the early morning—a rather thin, dark-haired fellow, about my own age? I believe he took some coffee here. He was ill, poor chap, and—'

Trent stopped. This time, it was only too clear, he had really put the cat among the pigeons. Le Joufflu blew his nose violently, and gulped as if he had swallowed an emetic. M. Gautier, who had overheard the fateful question, kept on shaking the dice box as if eventually it might provide an answer. Bibi screwed round his head like a bird, so that his shiny little eyes might gimlet into Trent's, and inquired casually: 'Is Monsieur of the police—of the English police, *bien entendu?*'

'*Mais non, jamais de la vie.*'

'Then perhaps Monsieur is of the press?'

'Well,' Trent said cautiously, 'I have not the honour of being *échotier* and *courriériste*, like M. Rond-de-Cuir.' He bowed ceremoniously. 'But it is true that I have written for the London papers—for the *Record* and the *Sun.*'

Bibi beamed, and jumped up to shake hands with Trent all over again. '*Mon cher confrère*, I understand perfectly. I ought to have recognized your name. We in Dieppe know well your London newspapers. Believe me, I am entirely at your disposal for all the information you may need, and I am sure that I can count on your discretion—*le secret professionel, quoi?*'

Trent replied that Bibi could rely on his honour and secrecy.

'*Mon cher confrère*, I am sure of it . . . but excuse me an instant while I restore the confidence of my fat friend here.'

He took Le Joufflu by the arm and led him off to the *caisse*, where an animated conversation *sotto voce* began between the two men and Louise. M. Gautier was left gazing at the abandoned backgammon board, in obvious fear that Trent would ask him some unanswerable question. However, he was not left long alone and in doubt. Madame Louise, who seemed to regard him as a wiser counsellor than the volatile Bibi, beckoned to him imperiously, and he joined the others. The muttered conversation went on, to be wound up by Bibi in a loud voice: '*C'est convenu. Faut pas s'en faire. Je m'en occupe. Comptez sur moi.*'

Bibi and Hégésippe returned to their backgammon. Other *habitués* began to come into the café, and there was a general orgy of handshaking, greetings and introductions. Trent began to think that the stars in their courses were fighting against him, and despaired of ever obtaining the information that Bibi had promised him.

Suddenly Bibi bent forward and whispered in his ear, '*Mon cher confrère*, do not disquiet yourself. You can depend on me, but you will understand that my friends are alarmed—the police, you know—and the affair is already *classé*. I have promised that we will not discuss it under this roof, so that they will be responsible for nothing. *On ne veut pas d'histoires.*'

What Bibi could mean by saying that the affair was already pigeonholed passed Trent's understanding; but it was clear that the little man wanted to be helpful.

'Monsieur Bibi . . .'

'Not Monsieur Bibi to a *confrère*—Bibi *tout court*.'

'All right,' Trent said laughing, 'Bibi; but have you not the same reason as they have to avoid *histoires?*'

'Me, my *confrère*,' Bibi said with a sublime gesture, 'I am a journalist, and I fear no one.'

'Then, my dear colleague, I invite you to do me the honour of dining with me tonight, and since we cannot dine here, I ask you to choose the best place in the town.'

CHAPTER XII

THE COUNT EXPLAINS

AN hour later Trent found himself sitting opposite a Bibi all smiles and satisfaction, his stout chest napkin-swathed from collar downwards. The restaurant was unpretentious, but the little journalist guaranteed both cuisine and cellar to be worthy of all respect.

Any mention of the affair that had brought them together was tactfully avoided by Trent until his guest had reached a second glass of Meursault 1906 with the *moules marinières*. Bibi smacked his lips, murmuring that this was real wine, with something to bite on. It was not often that he tasted such nectar.

'And now,' Trent said, 'will you explain to me, my dear friend, why we have to dine here like two conspirators? What is this terrible secret that you dare not even whisper to me under the roof of the Hotel of the Little Universe? What on earth could you say to me or I say to you that would bring disaster on the heads of your friends Le Joufflu, Madame Louise, and apparently M. Gautier as well?'

'But surely you understand,' Bibi exclaimed in a tone which suggested that he had somewhat overrated Trent's intelligence. 'There is the tobacco shop of Madame Louise's niece. There is Gautier's desire for the violet rosette. Even Le Joufflu has hopes of the *poireau* (leek), as he won the *soufflé* prize in the last *Concours de la Cuisine* at the Casino, and the deputy has promised him a *coup de piston*. Anyhow none of them want to have *histoires* concerning M. le Comte.'

'Name of a name!' Trent exploded, 'what have I to do with the tobacco shop of Madame Louise's niece? How could I prevent M. Gautier's promotion to officer *d'Académie*? How could I stand between Le Joufflu and the green and yellow ribbon? Why should anyone have a row with the count because of me? Have I stumbled into the middle of a secret of State?'

Bibi was obviously dismayed at the extent of Trent's ignorance. He took another sip of his Meursault, with brow wrinkled in thought, before he replied by another question.

'*Mon cher confrère*, will you be so obliging as to tell me quite frankly why you came to the Impasse de la Chimère?'

'Very willingly,' Trent said. 'In fact, I have tried already to tell your friend Le Joufflu, who refused to hear. Listen then. A few days ago a friend of mine, a certain Dr Fairman, came over to Dieppe by the night-boat. For some mysterious reason he visited the Impasse de la Chimère, and returned by the next steamer. On the way back he tried to jump overboard, and was arrested on a charge of attempting suicide.'

'Ah yes!' Bibi said. 'Over there you arrest people for trying to suicide themselves. Pity you cannot punish them when their crime is successful. *Ça, c'est bien anglais.*'

'That is true; but unfortunately there is another charge hanging over my friend—a charge of murder, the murder of a certain millionaire called Randolph. So far, you understand, he has not been accused of this crime; but there are some mysterious features about the affair which he has not explained, and declares that he will not explain. One of them is this short visit to Dieppe. Now, your police here say that he was seen hanging about the Impasse de la Chimère during the time between the two boats. I have come here to see whether I could not find some clue to the truth which Fairman persists in holding back.'

'Yes,' Bibi said, 'I have heard of the Randolph murder, of course. As for your friend's visit to the Impasse, certainly the police were making inquiries there after he left, and making everybody anxious. But it is equally certain, in my opinion, that they had a pretty good idea of why he came there. That is why Madame Louise and her husband did not want me to tell you anything. Surely, my friend, you yourself must have imagined that your Dr Fairman's visit might have some connection with the affair of the Pavillon de l'Ecstase and the scandal of the Fatal Woman.'

Bibi had dropped his voice impressively, though there was not a soul within earshot; for the restaurant was empty and the waiter was occupying himself with the Romanée St Vivant 1904 which was to follow the Meursault.

'I assure you,' Trent said earnestly, 'I have never in my life heard a whisper even of the Pavillon de l'Ecstase or of the scandal of the Fatal Woman.'

Bibi dropped his knife and fork, raised his hands and let them fall in a gesture of hopeless amazement.

'*Ça m'épate!* I know the affair was hushed up and shelved with what might seem indecent haste; but I thought the great press of London was so well informed that nothing was concealed from it.'

Trent feared he might be shattering one of Bibi's idols, but he was compelled to confess that, so far as he knew, not one word had been published in England about the matters so thrillingly described.

Bibi would not allow his disappointment at the shortcomings of the London press to interfere with his enjoyment of this heaven-sent dinner. The *poulet en casserole* was a dream, and as for the Romanée St Vivant, of which the first glass had been poured, he kissed his fingers at it in an ecstasy of appreciation.

'The good God,' he said piously, 'might no doubt have made a better wine, if He had so desired, but I very much doubt if He did. Fancy craving after an artificial paradise, when the natural juice of the grape is there to gladden the heart of man.

'I gather, *mon cher confrère*,' he went on after an interval of blissful silence, 'that it is your mission to pursue your own private inquiries about your Dr Fairman's object in coming to Dieppe. It is not your intention to write sensational articles about an unfortunate affair that has been shelved and suppressed?'

'You are right. My only purpose on this occasion is to discover what my unhappy friend was doing in Dieppe, and I give you my word of honour that I will not write a single word about this intriguing affair.'

'*Tant mieux*,' said Bibi. He breathed the sigh of the replete. 'It would not do to reopen this scabrous case. It might be fatal to the government at a moment of crisis, and it would certainly be detrimental to the hopes of my good friends, to which I have already alluded.'

He took another sip of his Burgundy, and cast aside the flippant waggishness which was the make-up of William Rond-de-Cuir. He leant forward across the table and started to tell his story.

'Count d'Astalys as a young man was very serious. He had great talent and devoted himself to his studies. His name first became known through his researches into the effects of *protoxide d'azote* on consciousness.'

'Stop,' said Trent. 'What is *protoxide d'azote?*'

'I'm not a chemist like the count, but I happen to know that it is the gas dentists use to make their patients happy when their teeth are being drawn—*gaz hilarant,* in fact.'

'Ah! laughing gas, we call it. Yes, I believe it is nitrous oxide, or something of the kind. I forgot that *azote* means nitrogen.'

'*Peut-être bien*,' Bibi said vaguely. 'I only know about it because the dentist once gave me gas, and I met the count when I was still quite green in the face and felt queer. He gave me something to restore me, and told me that long ago, when it was first discovered, people used to give laughing-gas parties for their guests to take a whiff of it, and enjoy the most exquisite sensations. To begin with, it seemed quite innocent. People did not remember their sensations. Then some savant found out that it was *très excitant, quoi?*'

Trent did not need Bibi's wink to explain the rather special significance of the '*excitant*,' which has betrayed not a few blameless English gentlewomen into shocking respectable French families.

'And so, it appears, those parties came to a sudden end. But all that, of course, did not prevent the count from going on with his experiments. In the war he was called to G.Q.G. after the first German gas attack, and was one of the chiefs of the poison gas department. After the war he returned to his experiments. He is not only a savant but also a philosopher, and Henri Poincaré and Bergson have both stayed at the Maison de la Chimère.'

'Your count seems a versatile fellow.'

'Then unhappily he became interested in that new science they call psychology. *Ça l'a détraqué.* I do not know myself what this psychology is, but it seems to be a *machin Boche* with its Freuds and its Jungs.'

'Not so Boche as that,' Trent protested. 'Freud is an Austrian and Jung a Swiss.'

'What differences does that make? Anyhow, psychology was the count's ruin. He fell in love.'

'What on earth had psychology to do with his falling in love?'

'All his life he had been *tellement sage et sérieux*. Up to then he had never *jété sa gourme*—not a woman in his life.'

'To my mind,' observed Trent, 'our English phrase about sowing wild oats is more picturesque than your French idiom, which I gather refers to an equine disease, or the rash of an infectious illness. Anyhow, what is the connection between his psychology and his love?'

'He fell in love with the Fatal Woman, the woman of the affair of the Pavillon de l'Ecstase, Marise Sylvain, the daughter of Raymond Sylvain the psychologist. He would never have met her but for his acquaintance with Sylvain—there is your connection! The count was forty-five, very gentle, studious and serious. She was twenty-two, *très rusée*, hard and immoral. He brought her back to the great dull Maison de la Chimère, and she was bored. Everyone in Dieppe knew it; for she was seen everywhere with her young men from Paris, and her bathing-dresses were the scandal of the place. The count went back to his experiments, but he was no longer rich. He had spent a fortune on Marise.'

'It is not an uncommon story.'

'No, the count had married a Parisienne, and had to take the consequences.'

Like other provincial bourgeois, Bibi regarded the frivolous women of the capital with a coveting hatred.

'Worse followed. There was no divorce. The count lived with his chemicals and books in the Maison de la Chimère. They say he still loved her. The countess spent most of her time in Paris, and when she came to Dieppe, she brought with her a band of Parisians who *faisaient la noce* in the Pavillon de la Chimère. It was she who gave this name to the Pavillon de la Chimère. Then she turned to politics and politicians. She made the conquest of . . .'

Bibi bent forward and whispered to Trent the name of a very well known personage who was still a member of the Cabinet.

'By this time she and the count were riddled with debts. All the gay parties had to be paid for. Then she had the idea of dealing in *les paradis artificiels*, in the strange drugs which her husband discovered and composed. Mind you, it was not a traffic in ordinary dope—cocaine, morphia, hashish and so on. They were drugs of which the law knew nothing, drugs that played mysterious tricks with the brain, and sometimes in the orgy led through ecstasy and transport to death.'

Trent murmured to himself a favourite passage of *The Odyssey*.

'Straightway she cast into the wine they were drinking a drug that stayed all pain and wrath and brought forgetfulness of every evil. Whoso should drink it down, not all that day would he let a tear drop down his cheeks, no, not though his father and mother should lie dead before him, or though before his face men should put to the sword his brother or the son of his soul and his eyes should behold it.'

Carried away by the swing of the Homeric hexameter, Trent rolled out the Greek lines as though he expected Bibi to understand them. Bibi, prepared for any madness from an Englishman, listened and looked at his host inquiringly.

'Golden Helen,' Trent explained, 'poured out for Telemachus a draught of Nepenthe and Forgetfulness. She was the first to dispense the artificial paradise.'

'Oh, I know that,' Bibi said surprisingly. '*The Odyssey* is one of my favourite books.'

'The deuce it is! Do you read it in Greek?'

'Alas, no!' said Bibi, 'but I read it in *Provençal*.'

Then to take his revenge he began to declaim at Trent.

'Alor, Elano, chato de Jupitèr, aguè uno autro pensado e tout d'un tèms vuejè dins lou vin que bevien lou trassegun que douno la demembrànço di mau. Aquèu qu'aurié begu d'aquèu boucoun pourrié pas toumba 'no lagremo de tout un jour, emai fuguèsson mort si paire e maire, emai davans éu fuguèsson mata pèr lou fèrri soun fraire o soun fiéu bèn ama, e quand meme de sis iue vesènt lou veirié.'

Bibi looked at Trent with a twinkle in his bright eyes, and an air of satisfaction suggestive of the schoolboy who has got successfully through his repetition, and feels that he is on even terms with his master.

'It was something like that, I know. I never saw Marise d'Astalys without thinking of Golden Helen, so lovely and so fatal. Charloun's translation of *The Odyssey* has been one of my bedside books ever since I can remember. You see my mother is of the Camargue, and when she married my father and came to the North, she taught me her language, and made me talk it

with her. But come! *mon cher confrère*, we are talking not of
Helen, but of Marise d'Astalys, who trafficked with her beauty
and strange drugs in this twentieth century.'

'Surely,' Trent said, 'the count was not involved in this traffic.'

'No, he lived in a world of dreams. He shut his eyes to his
wife's lovers. He was too gentle to deal with such a woman.
She went her way, while he worked in the Maison de la Chimère
with his servant Robert, trying to forget. It came out afterwards
that Robert, whom he trusted, stole the drugs and passed them
on to Lucette, the countess' maid, a *Parisienne* and a bad one,
too.'

Bibi paused for a time to attend to his dinner. Then he took
up his parable again.

'In Dieppe people gossiped more and more, but it was
some time before the scandal became public. First there were
some deplorable cases in Paris among the countess' acquaintances, cases that puzzled both the doctors and the police.
One of her lovers—he was said to have ruined himself for
her—went mad, actually and permanently mad, and the
doctors could find nothing to account for his condition. Other
rich young men who had made fools of themselves—*des fils
à papa, quoi?*—became mentally unhinged, and died equally
mysteriously.

'So it happened that the police were already keeping an eye
on the d'Astalys, when the scandal of the Pavillon de l'Ecstase
broke out. She was at the Pavillon with the minister whom I
have already named, several deputies, and heaven knows what
women. They were to inhale some new gas which was to
produce raptures beyond description. So there was another
orgy.

'At four o'clock in the morning a policeman on duty outside
the Impasse de la Chimère—his name is Jules Duphot—had a
vision. He saw dancing over the cobbles, singing as she went,
a very pretty girl clothed in nothing but a pair of slippers. Jules
could not believe his eyes, though I suspect he tried to. Then

he threw his cloak over the shameless hussy and marched her off to the *poste*.

'The lady turned out to be Madame Cloclo, *danseuse nue* of the Casino de Paris, so she was habituated to the situation, but when she came to the police station she began to laugh, and she laughed and she laughed as though she were being tickled until she fainted from exhaustion. They had to take her off to the hospital. And that was not the worst.

'About the same disreputable hour, some frightened servant called Dr Lambert by telephone to the Pavillon de l'Ecstase. He found a terrible state of affairs. The minister and the countess were lying unconscious on a divan; a deputy was groaning in agony on the floor, and a half-a-dozen more men and women were in the same state. The doctor called the police. They started by arresting everyone, but by that time the minister had come to. There were, as I have said, several deputies and another minister's wife concerned as well.

'Now this happened at an unfortunate moment. It was one of those periods when everyone feels that the Republic itself is in danger. This scandal therefore had to be hushed up at any cost—one more straw, and the régime was *fichu*. Only a few paragraphs appeared in the press, and in them the truth was veiled by innuendo. As for us here in Dieppe, no one desired to do the count a bad turn, but Dr Lambert told his wife what he had seen at the Pavillon de l'Ecstase; and that was very foolish. Just imagine for yourself the stories that began to fly about the town; for Madame Lambert is *bavarde*. However, at last the gossip died down. The countess disappeared, and they say she is now in Africa with a *marchand de comestibles*.'

Trent had listened to this savoury chapter of political history with keen attention. 'I am afraid,' he now said, 'your story rather complicates than simplifies my problem. It does not in the least explain why Fairman should have dashed off to the Place de la Chimère. A serious, sober-minded man of science such as he is would be the last person in the world to take part in a drug-orgy or wallow in an artificial paradise.'

'There I fear I cannot help you. I do not know your friend. Was he perhaps one of the countess's lovers?'

'Assuredly not. He was and is the victim of an unhappy love affair in England.'

Bibi shrugged his shoulders. 'Well, you understand, after what I have said, that the minister involved in the scandal would be favourably disposed towards any of us here who were by way of knowing the facts, and were willing to assist in keeping them dark. His influence would be at their disposal in any little matter of obtaining that which governments have to bestow. But on the other hand, what would have happened to those modest ambitions I mentioned to you, which mean so much to my good friends, if the scandal had been revived through indiscreet words let fall by any of them? And then, out of the blue, appears your friend Fairman. When Le Joufflu looked out of his window in the morning, he saw him wandering about like a ghost. He came to the inn and ordered coffee, and then he began to ask questions about where the Comte d'Astalys was to be found.'

As Bibi said the words, Trent struck the table with his open hand. 'Good!' he exclaimed. 'Then that point is definitely settled at least. Fairman came here to find the Comte d'Astalys. He knew him, or he knew about him. You are quite sure that he mentioned d'Astalys's name?'

Bibi regarded him open-eyed. 'But naturally, certainly! Was it not his mentioning that name that caused Le Joufflu, amiable as he is, to treat your friend with so little sympathy? I have heard all about it from his own lips. He told Dr Fairman, not too politely, that the château was shut up, and that he had no idea where the family had gone. As a matter of fact, the count had gone to Paris some time before, and the countess had disappeared, of course, with her *marchand de comestibles*. It took more than coffee to restore your Englishman, but after a cognac or two, he tottered away. Then the trouble began again.

The police arrived later in the day. They questioned everyone in the neighbourhood about the movements of the mysterious stranger; they took notes of what he had said to Le Joufflu, and what Le Joufflu had replied. It looked as if the scandal was being disinterred. However, nothing more happened that day, or the next day. Then, when we are beginning to feel at our ease again, you suddenly appear on the scene and put the wind up us again.'

Trent, summoning the waiter, gave another order, then turned to his guest with an apologetic smile. 'I understand now why my curiosity was so unwelcome. I am still, however, as far away as ever from a solution to my difficulty. It is established now that my friend came here with the object of seeing the Count d'Astalys; but why? If they know each other, the count himself might perhaps help me. Is he still in Paris?'

'No, I believe he came back to the Maison de la Chimère this morning. But as you can imagine, he does not receive visitors.'

'I must get hold of him somehow. He is my only hope.'

Bibi, flushed and important, was now engaged in smelling with manifest satisfaction a glass of old cognac, and he seemed to gain inspiration from its bouquet.

'We of the press,' he remarked, 'are not accustomed to be balked of our interviews, and professional solidarity demands that I should help you. I have an idea. The count, when he is in Dieppe, strolls every morning along the Grande Rue before lunch. All through the scandal he kept up that habit, and never seemed to notice that people in the street looked at him curiously. He drops in at Gautier's shop to look at his books and talk. They have great arguments, he and Hégésippe. Now tomorrow morning I will take you to Gautier's shop, and if the count is there, you will introduce yourself to him. Of course you will know nothing of what I have told you tonight, but are only occupied with the case of your compatriot. Your tact will do the rest.'

Trent jumped at the offer, and the rest of the evening was spent in less serious conversation inspired by an excellent dinner.

That night Trent, in his *pot-pourri*-scented bedroom, pleasantly haunted by the ghosts of centuries, tried to set his thoughts in order. He sat by the open window, looking out on the Pavillon de l'Ecstase, which wore an ethereal and less desolate appearance in the moonlight. It had been built for pleasure, but for a delight that was fastidious and delicate. Drugs and madness—in a way the scandal of the Pavillon de l'Ecstase was commonplace enough; but it was typical of France that it should have been mixed up with politics, and that private vice and folly such as every country knows should have become a question of state.

And when all the sordid tale was told, the matter of Randolph's death and the circumstances surrounding it remained as obscure as ever. Well, perhaps Count d'Astalys might be able to throw some light on it. Trent got into bed and slept.

There was an atmosphere of peace in the Librairie Gautier. The books of today inhabited the outer precincts of the temple; the latest books from Paris, waiting there to have their pages turned without consideration of purchase. Gautier himself passed lovingly from one to the other with the fastidious taste of the connoisseur, happy to discuss them with any visitor capable of appreciating their merits and shortcomings.

Thither Bibi led Trent on the morning of the following day. Hégésippe was not pleased to see them, though it was as impossible for him to be discourteous in his own shop as for an Arab chief to forget the law of hospitality. He feared for his coveted violet rosette, for it seemed only too possible that this inconvenient foreigner might rake up the scandal that had been so carefully buried. Yet his wariness vanished like frost under the sun when he found that Trent had an eye for a beautiful book.

'Il pleure dans mon cœur,
Comme il pleut sur la ville,'

Trent read from an edition of Verlaine that lay on the counter. 'And they say that there is no lyric poetry in French! What a joy it is to read such words on a perfect page!'

The bookseller, with his gentle features transfigured by the love of his life—his expression reminded Trent of the White Knight—led him away to see edition after edition that ranged from a startling *Aphrodite* of Pierre Louys to a dignified, yet humorous and confidential Montaigne. Hégésippe's quiet enthusiasm had so far captivated Trent that he started when Bibi touched him on the shoulder and murmured in his ear: '*Voilà Monsieur le Comte: je me sauve.*' Bibi shook Trent's hand and shot off; saluting a newcomer, as he went, with a flourish of his hat and *'Bonjour, Monsieur le Comte.'*

Against the light Trent perceived the outline of a very tall stooping figure. The bookseller darted towards the entrance, muttering phrases of welcome. They came forward together, and there was a moment of awkward silence; for Gautier showed no intention of presenting his English visitor. Trent seized the bull by the horns.

'Monsieur le Comte,' he said, 'allow me to introduce myself.' He held out his card. 'I believe you may be able to tell me something that is of vital importance to a friend of mine, who is, I have reason to believe, a friend of yours, Dr Bryan Fairman. It may be a matter of life and death.'

The count had drawn back at first with an involuntary movement of annoyance, but at the name of Fairman his manner changed. Taking Trent's card, he stretched out his hand to him and said, 'I am at your disposal, Monsieur. The friends of Fairman are my friends. Let me show you a place where we can speak privately.'

He led the way to a windowed recess at the back of the shop. The count now stood so that the light fell upon his face.

Trent, as a painter of human subjects, was fascinated by the lustrous eyes, set deep under shaggy brows above an eagle nose and a long ragged white moustache. They were greyish-green eyes, the pupil neatly bordered with a dark band, and gave an extraordinary impression of gazing not outwards but inwards. At Trent's first words there had been a hint of fear, or at least uneasiness, in their regard, as though the soul behind them had peeped out at the external world and disliked the prospect; but almost at once their serenity returned.

'You may possibly have heard,' Trent said, 'of the murder of Mr Randolph, a well-known English philanthropist, a few days ago in London. Dr Fairman appears to have been in some way connected with that crime; there is even some danger of his being accused as guilty of it.'

Count d'Astalys held up his hands. 'Fairman a murderer! *C'est inconcevable!* No, Monsieur, I have heard nothing about it. I never read newspapers.'

'I too,' Trent said, 'could not believe that he was guilty of such a crime, and that is why I have come to ask your help, since I can get none from Fairman himself. It seems just possible that you may know something which will explain his extraordinary conduct.'

He proceeded to state briefly the facts of Fairman's involvement in the crime, though he made no mention of what he had learned in confidence from Inspector Bligh—that the police had Fairman's own confession in their hands. 'The night of the murder,' he went on, 'he came over to Dieppe. Next morning he was seen in the Impasse de la Chimère, and I have been informed that he was asking for you by name. Finding you to be not at home, he went back to England by the next boat, and on the way he was arrested when on the point of committing suicide by jumping overboard. He refused to give any explanation of his actions, or indeed to say a word of any sort; and at present he is too ill to be seen by his friends.'

The count shook his head sadly, and pressed his hands over his eyes. 'I am more deeply grieved than I can express,' he said, 'to hear what you tell me. But I fear I can be of very little help. I cannot imagine why he should have come to seek me out in these terrible circumstances. Believe me, Monsieur, I am much attached to our friend. For a year we occupied the same rooms when we were studying in Paris, and I learned to know him as well as one man can know another. I admired above all things his integrity and fearless logic. Anything I could do for him I would do, even though it cost me much; but I am obliged to confess myself at a loss.'

'Perhaps,' Trent hazarded, 'from your special knowledge of our friend's character you may be able to lay your hand on the spring of such unaccountable behaviour. I thought I knew him well, but you may know him better.'

'If it comes to that intangible thing, character,' the count said, 'all I can say is that I am morally certain he could never be an ordinary murderer; that is, he could never have killed for personal advantage or for passion. But—' he hesitated a moment—'it is not altogether impossible that if the cold, hard reason which he had made his god had ordained his own death or that of any other person, he might have carried out its behests, however unwillingly. I must tell you a little about the intellectual footing on which we stood. You know, of course, what sort of philosophy Fairman has always held.'

'I think I understand what you mean,' Trent said. 'Science without art or religion, intellect without emotion. It is a hard master. It is apt, also, to betray those who submit to it. Fairman discovered that emotion can make demands which cannot be rejected.'

The count smiled faintly. 'That does not surprise me. Upon this matter Fairman and I always differed, though we were the better friends for our differences. There is one truth, and countless reflections of it. Neither of us ever tried to impose his truth on the other. My philosophy has brought me trouble and to spare, but Fairman's common-sense and materialism seem to have landed him in scarcely less difficulty. Always from the beginning he was a pure scientist, holding that mind was a mere function of body, and believing that it was the visible external which conditioned the invisible within. He had to see and touch things before he could believe in their existence. He never swerved from his principle, and in all the remarkable work he did among the insane he regarded his patients as machines, though all that did not prevent him from being the kindest and most considerate of men.

'I, on the other hand, have always found it harder to believe in the reality of the seen than in that of the unseen. I have never felt sure of the solidity of external objects, but I have no doubts about the existence of my own thoughts and feelings. It was this opposition between our outlooks that made us such great friends and enabled us to do valuable work together . . .

'I need not speak of Fairman's career. You will know more of it than I do. My turn of mind, my truth, led me along a different path. All my interest lay in the inner world, and when I was tempted out of it I paid bitterly for the adventure. But I have never lost interest in my old friend, and at rare intervals we have exchanged letters—enough for me to perceive that he had changed in his opinions no more than myself. And there, Monsieur, you have all that I can tell you about Fairman's ideas and character. It appears to me, and I regret it much, to throw little light upon your enigma of conduct.'

Trent did not attempt to conceal his disappointment. 'I thank you, M. le Comte, for listening to my appeal,' he said. 'It was no more than a forlorn hope after all; but I could not help building upon it. Unhappily I am now thrown back upon a theory which suggested itself to me at the outset, or rather was suggested to me by the police themselves. I confess that I have fought against accepting it.'

'I understand you too well,' the count said, 'though I hesitated to say the word to a friend of my friend's. You believe he may have lost his reason. The possibility is only too apparent on the facts as you have stated them to me.'

'That is my anxiety,' Trent said. 'Well, there is no more for me to say or to do here. Very soon, I hope, I shall receive permission to visit Fairman, and I shall then be able to form a more definite idea of his state of mind. Once again, M. le Comte, many thanks; and good-by. I return to England by the boat which leaves in a few hours from now.'

CHAPTER XIII

FELIX POUBELLE 1884

IT was in a mood of keen disappointment and increased perplexity that Trent returned from Dieppe. Without realizing it fully, he had built much upon the hope of picking up there some clue to Bryan Fairman's personal involvement in the Randolph case. But neither in the reticence that prevailed at the Hôtel du Petit Univers, in the highly-seasoned gossip of William Rond-de-Cuir, nor in the philosophic frankness of the Comte d'Astalys had he found any help. What the count had had to say had merely added force to the simplest but most tragic explanation of the affair; and if Inspector Bligh, Trent himself at one time, and finally the count—with all his knowledge of Fairman's character, and attachment to him as a friend—had felt that the idea of Fairman's madness had to be entertained, the argument for that most unacceptable solution was undeniably a strong one.

Yet it was still clear to Trent, and perhaps to him alone—since the monstrous suggestion of the prints on the razor-blade was known to no other person—that there was too much simplicity about that solution. There was still the possibility that Fairman had acted as he had done with the purpose of shielding another person. This had been officially considered, and had been set aside for what seemed sound reasons; but Trent, for his part, did not feel so sure. Certainly, it did not account for all the facts; but why should it do so? Trent asked himself the question as one passionately interested in proving the innocence of his friend; a motive which could not be said to actuate Inspector Bligh and the great institution he represented.

There remained one curiosity about the evidence available

in the Randolph affair—not an outstanding challenge to detective ingenuity, by any means; yet still, a detail that from the first Trent had felt to need explaining. This was the champagne cork found among the contents of the dead man's pockets. One might imagine a dozen ways in which it might have found its way into that random collection; only they would not be plausible ways. One might think of it as a talisman or luck-bringer, kept for just the same reason as moved people like Mrs McOmish, or Verney the secretary, to cherish rusty nails found in the street. But Randolph had, emphatically, not been the sort of man to do that sort of thing. Was it, then, one of the many incongruous objects supposed to have the occult power of warding off lumbago, or catarrh, or epilepsy? Was it a memento of some crapulous orgy of the Association for Moral and Social Hygiene? Or a passport to secret conclaves of the Protestant Truth Society? None of these things seemed to have about them much intrinsic probability; but Trent could think of nothing more simple and satisfying.

Again, the brand on the cork constituted a small problem in itself. Without aspiring to any height of connoisseurship, Trent had always been interested in wine and the curious lore of it; he numbered some acknowledged experts among his friends; and he knew enough to realize, as soon as Mr Bligh had shown him the cork in question, that 'Felix Poubelle 1884' must be something decidedly out of the common at this time of day. Anything strange in this affair was worth looking into, he thought; and there was no difficulty about the first step at least. He would seek counsel from an expert whose knowledge of wines, and therefore of corks, was unrivalled. William Clerihew, the renowned and erudite wine-merchant of Fountain Court, was the obvious man.

The house of Clerihew Bros. and Co. inspected, purchased and offered rare and ancient wines with a reverent dignity which made precious stones seem commonplace by comparison. The shop was an oasis of peace in the noise and mercenary bustle of the West End. Its panelling and its ancient floors, which dived capriciously in any plane but the horizontal, the collection of quaint historic wine-bottles, and the unequalled excellence of the wines that were tasted within its precincts, made it a place apart. While the rest of London was demolishing the old and masking the beauties of the past under the unsightly dullness of modernity, Mr Clerihew had been quietly busy preserving the traditional simplicity of his premises, and rescuing from the overlay of later bad taste the peculiar charm of the original building.

There, next morning, in the tranquillity of a forgotten world, Trent played with a glass of fine dry sherry as he talked with his friend, who, as he told him, was growing with the passage of time more than ever like Vandyke's portrait of Jacobus van der Geest. Soon Trent turned the conversation to the subject of corks.

'Corks!' said William Clerihew with a prefatory cough. (He was not altogether indifferent to the sound of his own voice.) 'They are almost as interesting as wine itself. The life of the wine is the life of the cork. There is a fascination in the brave cork which has preserved the beauty of an ancient wine for half a century or more against the assaults of its countless enemies. If only we could discover one of the secrets of the cork, it would be worth a king's ransom. Why does a cork, carefully chosen and to all appearances worthy of its high destiny, every now and then turn traitor, and infect the wine under its charge with the taste and smell of corruption? Does the evil come from within the bottle or without, or does it lie dormant in the cork itself? Science has no answer. Thousands and thousands of pounds are wasted on corked wine, and thousands and thousands of pounds have been expended on researches to discover the microbe—if it is a microbe—but it eludes the microscope, the filter and every device known to chemistry.'

Clerihew was launched on a favourite subject. Trent began to suggest that it was not quite from that point of view that he was interested in corks; and instantly his friend's eloquence took another direction.

'Ah! you are thinking of the history of the cork, of course. So far as I know, the ancient Greeks did not use corks for their wines. On the other hand, the Romans used them sometimes as stoppers for their amphoræ—you know your Horace—perhaps for those small glass amphoræ of rare wines of which Petronius speaks. In the Dark Ages the cork was forgotten, like nearly everything else. For centuries wine was drunk from the wood, and the bottle started life as a glass jug to convey the wine from the wood to the table. Legend has it that Dom Perignon, a monk of Hautvillers in Champagne, discovered at the end of the seventeenth century the use of the cork as a stopper for wine-bottles, and by its virtue enriched the world with sparkling Champagne. It is more flattering, I think, to the learning of the worthy Benedictine to suppose that he remembered his Horace, and simply re-introduced the Roman use of the bark of the cork-oak.'

Clerihew paused for breath, and Trent seized the fleeting opportunity.

'It is, in point of fact, about a Champagne cork that I want to consult you.' He described with as much exactitude as possible the cork that had been found among the contents of Randolph's pockets.

'Clearly, an excellent cork,' the wine-merchant said. 'The graceful shape—the texture grown firm with years of perpetual pressure. As for the brand—' he paused, savouring his memories of a great vintage as lovingly as if they had been the wine itself.

'Felix Poubelle 1884, a beautiful wine, a wine to be remembered, a wine of great character and delicacy which even now, in its old age, is superb. It contained, I believe, an unusually high proportion of white grapes. You know how largely the black grapes enter into the composition of most Champagnes ... Of course it is very old now; but to my mind a great Champagne rises to its noblest heights when through the alchemy of time it has laid aside the thoughtless effervescence of youth, that suspicion of vulgarity ...'

A vague gesture completed the sentence, and Trent hastened to put the practical question which was the object of his visit.

'Are there, do you know, any restaurants in London where you can find a Felix Poubelle 1884 on the wine-list?'

Clerihew shook his head pensively.

'I have a few bottles myself, but you are not likely to find it on the list of any restaurant. Old Champagnes are among the rarest of wines. They are too expensive; a huge amount of capital lies idle while they are aging, and then only the bottles with the best corks survive. No; old Champagnes are no wines for the ordinary restaurant keeper. He would hardly put Felix Poubelle 1884 on his list—most customers would think it was far too old.' Again he shook his head; then added, 'But there are three, perhaps four, old-fashioned restaurants where you might find a stray bottle or two in the cellars.'

Trent's look of disappointment vanished. 'My dear Will!' he exclaimed. 'My oracle and prophet! Let me into the secret of those few and, I fear, costly places of refreshment.'

Clerihew mentioned the names of four restaurants; all small, all exclusive, and all outrageously dear.

'Hm! I thought as much,' Trent said. 'None of them is exactly the sort of place I pick when I have a trifling foolish banquet towards. They don't give bread with one fish-ball, as the song says. Well, William, you see my idea. Randolph, as I told you, seems to have had this cork in his pocket on the day he was murdered. I am interested, as the police are, in the question of who killed him. It seems to me just possible that some light may be thrown on that, if we can find out where that cork came from, and why he was carrying it about with him. He probably got it at lunch that day, because his man says he never knew him to have a cork in his possession before; and he did go out to lunch somewhere, though where is not known. Now if there was anybody with him at lunch, I should like to meet him, and hear what he may have to say about it, and what they discussed over the walnuts and the wine. Also, merely as a matter of curiosity, I should value any suggestion he might have to make as to why any person, being of sound mind, should walk off after his meal with a champagne cork.'

Clerihew considered a few moments. 'Yes; I suppose it might be worth following up. And as for the explanation you say you would value—I can give you one myself, for what it is worth. It is not worth much, I should say.'

'William! You are a wonder.' Trent raised his glass of sherry. 'Here's to the long life and prosperity of the Amalgamated Federation of Cork-Snatchers, coupled with the name of Mr Clerihew, who will now address the meeting on the present position and immediate aims of that ancient institution.'

A reminiscent smile hovered on Clerihew's lips. 'I put a champagne cork in my pocket one evening,' he said, 'and carried it away, for a special reason. The truth of it is that I had lost my temper. Perhaps Mr Randolph had that cork in his pocket because he too had lost his temper.' He smiled again as he offered this enlightening suggestion.

Trent struck the arm of his chair lightly. '*Of course!*' he exclaimed. 'Why didn't I think of that before? When you lose your temper, you put a cork in your pocket—a quaint and widespread custom, traceable ultimately to the nature-worship and marriage ritual of the Solomon Islanders, as mentioned in *The Golden Bough*. The cork may be used to bite on, so as to prevent the teeth from grinding; or it may be forced down your enemy's throat; or it may be burnt, so that you can black his face like a seaside nigger's. Yes; a cork is clearly the very thing for an angry man. Its possibilities are endless.'

'All right,' Clerihew said equably. 'I know what I'm talking about, and it is an explanation, though very likely it isn't the right one. You asked me to tell you, didn't you? Now can you tell me, first, whether Mr Randolph knew anything about wine? He had a cellar, I suppose, at that place of his in Yorkshire.'

'Yes,' Trent said, 'he had; and he looked after it carefully, too. He told me so himself, when I was staying there; and certainly what I had was good. He drank very little wine himself; but he told me—as he would, of course—that he believed in doing a thing well, if you did it at all. He got his wine from Hughes & Saunders.'

'Very good people,' Clerihew observed with amiable condescension. 'It is possible he may have heard from them what I am going to tell you now—though mind you, it isn't everybody, even in the trade, that knows it.' And the wine-merchant proceeded to impart that esoteric knowledge for which he had so carefully prepared the way.

Armed with this information, Trent set forth on the quest of Felix Poubelle 1884. His first visit was to that mysterious little place known as L'Ecrevisse Souffrante, hidden shyly in the basement of a large building near the markets. There he was received with *empressement* by the French head-waiter and his henchmen, who bustled about him; but their solicitude was ill-rewarded, for he refused to remove his coat until he had inspected the wine-list. Waiters fluttered about with the bill of fare; but as it was early for a London luncheon, some minutes passed before the *sommelier* could be brought up from even lower depths than the dining-room, presumably from his beloved cellars.

While waiting, Trent spoke more in sorrow than in anger to the head-waiter and his satellites.

'I should not have thought that a restaurant of such repute would have fallen into this senseless habit of expecting its guests to choose their food before they decide on their wine. Do people buy a frame and then pick out a picture to match it? This cart-before-the-horse idea is heart-breaking. I have come here especially in search of a certain wine—a Champagne in fact. If you have it, I shall order a meal planned to bring out its finest qualities. If not, I shall just say good-by.'

The subordinate waiters—Italians for the most part—were most sympathetic, because they had only the vaguest idea what Trent was talking about; but even they showed signs of relief when the wine-waiter, hastily adjusting his chain of office, appeared.

He had caught the word Champagne, and his resentment at being disturbed by a guest who lunched too early was mollified; for Champagne sounded like a good tip. He was grey-haired, with the white whiskers proper to his office; and he appeared to belong to that nameless tribe which talks all languages equally fluently and incorrectly, but has none of its own.

Trent put the wine-list aside after a brief inspection. 'These wines are no use to me,' he said. 'Have you no Champagnes such as your special customers might ask for—wines that are not on the list? Felix Poubelle 1884, for instance?'

'Excuse, Señor, ze vine of Champagna ees not goot ven eet ees alt. Dopo tventi anni eet perds eets gleam and becommt as you say in Engleesh plat.'

'I did not come here,' Trent said with severity, 'for a lecture on Champagne. I want a bottle of Felix Poubelle 1884, and if you have not got it I will go elsewhere.'

The wine-waiter was 'ver' sorry'; all the waiters were in the same condition. Trent departed from the Suffering Crayfish.

He was no more fortunate at the Huître aux Perles. The oyster might have pearls, but it had no Felix Poubelle 1884.

Thence he took a taxi to a restaurant known as Porter's. It was famous for its English cooking and its English waiters, but the official who presided over the wine was French. He almost wept on Trent's shoulder in the joy of finding a client who ordered his wine before his food.

'Ah!' he said, 'Monsieur will perhaps take Bourgogne.'

His face fell when Trent asserted his intention of drinking Champagne. He, as least, had no respect for customers who ordered that beverage. Trent noticed the change in the man's manner, and was the more authoritative in his examination of the wine-list.

Again there was no sign of Felix Poubelle 1884.

With reproachful sadness he shook his head. 'I expected better of you than this. I must have a really old Champagne. Indeed there is only one wine I fancy at the moment—Felix Poubelle 1884.'

A look of amazement passed over the waiter's face.

'Felix Poubelle 1884! By an extraordinary hazard, Monsieur, we have three bottles; but it has not been on the list for years.'

Before Trent could say another word, the *sommelier* had bustled off. Trent, feeling that he had reached his goal, sat down and ordered himself a meal fit to celebrate the occasion. In a minute or two the precious bottle was presented for inspection. Trent's reputation went up when, after assuring himself that the bottle was really cold, he said he would have it at cellar temperature.

'I suppose,' he remarked to the waiter, 'you don't often sell any Champagne as old as this.'

Again the waiter's eyebrows threatened to mingle with his hair. 'It is very curious, Monsieur, but I sold a bottle of this same wine only last week, although it was years since it had been asked for. Monsieur knows, it is easy to see, how remarkable this wine is, but there are few others who would think so—few, in effect, capable of judging it. For almost everyone it is too old; they require what you call the kick, *n'est-ce-pas?*' He snapped his fingers illustratively; then added with tolerant pity, 'They know no better.'

'Certainly there are not many of us acquainted with this wine at least,' Trent said, refraining from the admission that he had never tasted it in his life. 'It is even possible that your client of last week was an acquaintance of mine. What was he like?'

The wine-waiter's lips, eyebrows and shoulders co-operated ably to suggest a certain distaste. 'He was old—much more old than Monsieur, *d'un air bourru*, the eyes hard; if I dare say so, not very sympathetic. But he knew something about wine. He said to me that if he must drink Champagne he would have an old wine, and I mentioned this as the best.'

Trent looked at him reflectively. 'Yes; that must have been my man. You describe him to the life. And I think there was—was there not?—some slight unpleasantness on that occasion.'

The waiter busied himself in silence with the opening of the bottle. He handed Trent the cork—own brother, as he could see, to the one which Inspector Bligh had shown him. Then he said, '*Eh bien*, it is clear that Monsieur has heard all about that.'

'My only reason for coming here,' Trent said coolly, 'was that I knew the gentleman in question had had a bottle of this wine.'

The waiter nodded as he completed the filling of Trent's glass. 'Yes; it is true, there was a little incident. You see, your friend had taken a private room, and the service was in charge of an English waiter—the personnel is English here, as Monsieur probably knows—a little man who is quite ignorant on the subject of wine. I do not as a rule attend the private rooms myself. When the old gentleman spoke of Champagne, this waiter had the presumption to recommend a sparkling wine— Monsieur knows what I mean—not a Champagne, but a wine of fantasy.'

'I do indeed know what you mean—some cheap white wine with carbonic acid gas pumped into it to make it fizz.'

'*Parfaitement*, Monsieur. In this country there are people who drink such wine. It is less dear, of course. But your friend was much annoyed—and he was right—at the suggestion that he should drink Silver Foam, as it is called. *Et voilà toute l'histoire!*'

Trent was already occupied with the spoonful of caviar which had just been set before him. 'Not quite all the story, perhaps,' he suggested quietly. 'Was there not a question of a cork?'

The waiter looked away. 'I do not understand, Monsieur.'

'I am not sure of that. Listen; I am going to imagine for you what happened. This acquaintance of mine was annoyed, not only because the wine with the lyrical name was recommended to him—but because he knew why it was recommended. And you know also, naturally.'

The waiter's mobile face expressed a blank bewilderment.

'It is a bad custom,' Trent went on, 'but it is not, after all, the fault of the restaurants or their personnel. It was the Champagne firms who began it. Competition between them was so keen that one of them started the practice of paying a commission on each cork which a waiter could produce to the company's agent. Then they all had to do the same. Then—since we live in an age of business organization—a cork-exchange was formed for collecting the corks and disbursing the commissions. But a time came when all that defeated itself.'

Here the waiter permitted himself a restrained smile as his wandering eye met Trent's; but he remained silent.

'The firm which concocts the stuff called Silver Foam pays a higher bonus than is paid upon any true Champagne cork. That is why your English waiter dwelt upon the merits of that superb liquid. And if the client happened to know about this nefarious traffic, that is why he was enraged. That is why he sent, perhaps, for the *sommelier*, and obtained from him the excellent advice to try Felix Poubelle 1884. And that, finally, is why he put the cork in his pocket as soon as the culpable waiter had opened the bottle.'

The waiter cast aside his embarrassment and faced Trent with a candid brow. 'Certainly,' he said, 'Monsieur is well informed. It is not to be denied that this deplorable system exists, and that it may lead to *bêtises* sometimes. The gentleman pocketed the cork for that reason, no doubt. I am very sorry.'

'I am not so sorry,' Trent said, 'since it has led me to your establishment, where I hope to obtain certain information. I must explain that the gentleman of whom we have been speaking is dead, murdered. He was named Mr James Randolph, and as you may have read in the papers, he was killed on the night of Wednesday last—the day when he had luncheon here.'

'*Mon Dieu!*' the waiter exclaimed with starting eyes. He slapped his forehead. 'I saw his photograph in the papers, but I did not recall the face. I can see now that it was the same. *Mon Dieu!*'

'The police officer who is in charge of the case,' Trent went on quickly, 'is one of my friends, and I am giving him my assistance in the inquiry. I am trying to learn what I can about this luncheon, because it may have some importance—one cannot say. Now you can, if you will, tell me certain things—you can see that, in the circumstances, no harm will be done if you do so. In the first place, if Mr Randolph had a private room, presumably he did not lunch alone.'

The waiter hesitated and looked uncomfortable. 'Monsieur, you understand that in our profession it is necessary to be very discreet. But in the circumstances, as Monsieur says, I will speak frankly. One must assist the law, after all; and if there should be an official inquiry—'

'You can count upon that,' Trent assured him, 'if I should not be satisfied with what I can learn now.'

'Well then, Mr Randolph had, in fact, a lady with him.'

'A lady! That's interesting. Can you describe the lady for me?'

'Ah! That, as Monsieur says, is very interesting. If I do not deceive myself, it was a very well-known lady, a lady whose photograph everyone has seen in the papers, a lady whom I myself have seen on the stage more than once.'

Trent fell back in his seat. Here was another totally

unexpected and disabling blow. 'Do you mean that Mr Randolph was here with Miss Eunice Faviell?'

'I am sure of it, Monsieur.'

Trent, rallying his senses, rewarded the man generously and went on with a meal for which he now had little appetite, while he considered the new and apparently senseless turn thus given to the affair. If Eunice had been the old man's guest at this place, in conditions of privacy which pointed to some sort of intimate relations at least, what became of all the fuss made about his disagreeable advances to her? What sort of a figure was cut by the chivalrous character who had been called upon to protect her, and had embraced the task with such generous ardour—by Philip Trent, in fact? He was not by nature sensitive about his personal dignity, but the man has yet to be born who enjoys being made to look a fool without knowing why. He did not like it; and he liked still less that it should be done by a woman whom he had always believed to be incapable of deceit or secretiveness. The Eunice Faviell whom he had learned to know so well was impulsive, impatient, headstrong, emotionally uncontrolled, but he had never met with a character more open and straightforward.

Whatever might lie behind all this, his next step was decided for him by logic and inclination alike. He must see Eunice as soon as might be. Before leaving Porter's he had, through the good offices of the wine-waiter, a few words with the 'little Englishman' who had attended on Randolph and his guest. The man, his memory refreshed by half a crown, could only say that he too had recognized Miss Faviell; that she had appeared to be on ordinarily good terms with her host until the end of the meal, when she had hurried away by herself, and apparently in a very bad temper; and that what he had heard of the conversation between the two, while he was in the room, seemed to be about theatrical matters.

When Trent, at a neighbouring post office, rang up Eunice Faviell's flat in Ovington Street he was answered by her maid.

Miss Faviell was not at home. She had been away since Thursday afternoon last. She had refused to say more than that she was going out of town, and did not wish any letters to be forwarded.

CHAPTER XIV

GENIUS MUST LIVE

THIS was not the first time, to Trent's knowledge, that Eunice Faviell had gone away, cutting her communications with the world for a time. Her disappearances usually had to do with the study of a difficult part; and for all he knew, that might be the reason in this case. He hoped devoutly, at least, that it was so. Each new turn taken by the Randolph affair gave it an appearance more sinister as well as more incomprehensible.

He could be sure of one thing. If Eunice had really meant to vanish for the time being, she was fully capable of doing it so effectively that any attempt to get on her track was far from hopeful. She could, and on occasion did, make herself quite unrecognizable with a few touches to her appearance and a change of manner; and she had a singular flair, moreover, for places where it was most unlikely that anyone known to the world had ever been seen or heard of by the natives.

Yet Trent could not accept the possibility of being unable to get in touch with her. For him there could be no question of leaving unturned any stone that might conceal a grain of the truth about the Randolph murder. Eunice had certainly been among the last persons to see and speak with Randolph; and she had done so in circumstances that were more than strange. Trent would have felt it wholly unpardonable, in any ordinary case, to interfere with her desire for privacy: he did not feel so now.

As he walked slowly westwards through Leicester Square an idea came to him. It was not an agreeable one; but he could not let any personal preference sway him while such an inquiry as this was on foot. If Eunice had intended her place of retreat to be generally unknown, there was one person at least to whom it might have been disclosed. Trent determined to see if anything could be got out of one who headed the list of the few people that he cordially disliked; and he set out at once to find him.

He was fortunate at the first cast. The big smoking-room at the Cactus Club was well filled, but there was a little island of empty chairs by the window in one corner. In the midst of this emptiness sat Eugene Wetherill. His tongue and reputation would make a void round him in the most crowded rooms; nor did that trouble him at all. He found a pleasure in his unpopularity, which he accepted as the sincerest possible tribute from the groundlings to a superior spirit.

Genius is often strangely housed. Wetherill's success with women was counted by the gossips as a wonder of the world, for he was atrociously ugly. The coarse black hair had retreated far from his bulging forehead. The heavy, ill-shaped nose and the thick lips made an effect of grossness not redeemed by the clipped beard and moustache, with their hint of Elizabethan swagger. One of his frosty grey eyes had a repulsive inward cast; but there was no common fire—often even a touch of madness—in the glance that shot out from beneath the bushy, overhanging eyebrows. His voice was harsh and disagreeable. What beauty the man had was in his tall and well-built frame, kept by constant exercise in athletic condition.

As Trent, sighting his quarry, walked through the room, he was hailed by several acquaintances who offered him a seat on a chairarm or space on a sofa; but with a cheerful salute he made his way to the corner. Wetherill, who was studying a small notebook through the monocle that was a part of his pose, looked up as he approached and greeted him with surprising affability.

'Ah! Trent,' he said. 'The very man I wanted to see.'

Trent could not imagine why Wetherill should want to see him, unless it were for the simple pleasure of inflicting his society on a man who did not desire it. That was a feeling which Trent had never tried to conceal, and he had marked it often enough by a discourtesy which would have led most men to ignore his existence for the future. But their occasional meetings had always left him with an exasperating sense that no word of his could make the slightest dent on Wetherill's impenetrable armour of self-esteem. Incivility, irony, laughter itself were powerless against a prodigious vanity that offered them not the smallest loop-hole. The worst of it was that Wetherill in his way was a poetic genius; as playwright and prosaist he had at command a beauty of imagery and a power of word-magic that carried all before them. His critics might say that behind all that felicity in externals there was nothing but a rubble of demoded hedonism; they could not deny the glamour of the façade.

Trent stretched his long legs in an armchair beside Wetherill and took a cigarette-case from his pocket. 'The last time we met,' he said as he proffered the case, 'I was in too much of a hurry to have a drink with you. Will you have one with me now?'

Wetherill met his eye with a faint smile that told more plainly than any words his mistrust of this hospitality; then, with a rasping laugh, he took a cigarette and opened a line of conversation which, as instinct truly told him, would make short work of Trent's patience. 'To be a splendid sinner,' he said, 'a man should deny himself. The great lover must be an ascetic, having little to do with drink or nicotine. I never taste alcohol, unless it is to take possession now and then of the soul of a noble wine, that blushes like a virgin.'

'When I saw you last,' Trent said briefly, 'you were talking about having an absinthe cocktail.'

'As for tobacco,' Wetherill went on, precisely as if Trent had made no remark at all, 'the extent of my abstinence is never to smoke anything that I have paid for myself. I allow myself the dissipation of one of your cigarettes.'

'You may be a great sinner,' Trent admitted. 'I remember Saint Augustine insisted that he was one, so you are probably correct. Anyhow, you do your best, by all accounts, and which of us can do more? As for love—how much does a caterpillar know of the beauty of a rose?'

Wetherill grinned delightedly, displaying a row of great teeth as white as an animal's. 'An excellent line!' he exclaimed. 'You surpass yourself, dear friend. People often do when talking to me, I have observed.' He reopened his notebook. 'Do you mind if I write that down for my own use?—you can stand it me instead of a drink.' He scribbled with his pencil. 'My memory is the one thing about me that does not satisfy me. There! It is recorded—a really nasty remark. My compliments! Men,' he added reflectively, 'are always jealous of me; and no wonder. But pardon me, I haven't yet said why I wanted to see you. What do you know about this Randolph case? It interests me. The last time I saw you, in the lobby downstairs, was the very day after I had got a good, round, comfortable sum of money out of the old man.'

Trent looked hard at Wetherill, who met his gaze with complete equanimity.

'I remember you said something about having done a good stroke of business. And that time we met was the same evening that Randolph was murdered. How could you have got his cheque through in time?'

'There was no cheque, dear friend. Among the lessons life has taught me is the truth that, in some transactions, the actual money in the pocket is better than a cheque. A cheque takes time to be cleared. The drawer may be visited by a second thought, and stop the cheque. Or other things may happen. Once—it is a long time ago now—I won a quite acceptable sum, nearly £400 in English money, from a young countryman of ours in a pleasant little game of baccarat at Ostend. I took his cheque; I knew he was a rich man, and that he would not repudiate a debt of honour. What happened? He left the club that night driving his own car; he had had too much to drink; he dashed his brains out running into a lamp-post on the *digue*; the cheque was useless; and his executors refused to pay a gambling debt. No, dear friend; I took no cheque from Randolph. At my suggestion, we drove round to his bank, where he handed me the sum in notes; and within the hour I had paid them into my own account at Henson's. But this is wandering from our subject. Tell me, why did this fellow Fairman shoot the old man?'

Trent affected an astonishment that he was far from feeling. He had foreseen what turn gossip must inevitably take. 'Fairman shoot him! What do you mean? He has never been accused of it, as far as I know.'

Raising a long, well-tended hand, Wetherill shook his head reproachfully. 'Give me credit for a little intelligence, dear friend. I am sure—everyone is sure, for that matter—that though they are detaining Fairman on a charge of attempting suicide, they are really holding him for the murder. And you have your friends in the police, as we all know. I assume you are better informed than the rest of us. Why did he do it?'

'Well, if my opinion matters so much,' Trent said unpleasantly, 'I don't believe he did, whatever you think or the police think. Why are you so anxious to take his guilt for granted? I didn't know you had ever even met him.'

'I never saw him in my life; though of course I cannot help knowing that he fosters a hopeless passion for a certain friend of ours, which she is not in a position, alas! to return.' Wetherill polished his eyeglass, then placed it in his eye and gazed tranquilly at Trent as he went on, 'I could quite understand his murdering me; but why Randolph? I am really curious. So would Eunice be, I am sure; for she has a high regard for him.'

Trent felt the blood rising in his face; and Wetherill's smile showed that he had observed it. He mastered his feelings and asked quietly, 'Did you never see the old man again after you had got your money?'

'Never again, dear friend. It was not I who did the deed, if your thoughts are taking that direction. Curiously enough, though, I did threaten to kill him; I did so just before we parted. You see, after I had got the money, he saw fit to make himself very disagreeable to me; and as I was really quite seriously displeased by what he said—it was not a simple matter of deliberate rudeness, my dear Trent, such as I find merely amusing—I told him that one of these days I would shoot him like a dog. How these quaint old phrases leap to the lips when one is deeply moved! Yes, I told him that.' Wetherill, who had not failed to note the effect on Trent's temper of his assumption of Fairman's guilt, added lazily, 'I should have smiled, I think, if I could have foreseen that Fairman was going to shoot him for me.'

Trent disregarded the thrust. 'You are being very frank about it. That means, I suppose, that your own position is quite secure—I mean, that you can give a satisfactory account of the way you spent your time on the evening Randolph was murdered?'

Wetherill raised his hands. 'What language you pick up, dear friend, from that Scotland Yard set! "Give a satisfactory account . . ." Soon you will be telling me that I am not obliged to make any statement, but that anything I may say . . . and the rest of the jargon. You know, you would look rather well in a dark blue helmet, Trent; it would go with your eyes, and lend just that little needed touch of austerity to your expression. Well, I will tell you. I stayed a few minutes only at the club here after our meeting; then I returned to my rooms to work until daybreak. I was having a fearful struggle—indeed, it continues still—with the last act of my *Crucifixion of Aphrodite*. No,' Wetherill continued musingly, 'I did not kill Randolph; but if I had really felt that there lay any advantage for me in doing so, how perfect might I not have made the crime? The criminal, you will say, always makes a mistake—a senseless catchword, surely. It is those who are detected, and only they, who make mistakes. As well say that a meteor is always visible, although space is known to be swarming with lightless bodies. If with my imagination I can create a world of my own, could I not devise an insoluble criminal problem? But pardon me; this is soliloquy. My dear Trent, I have answered your questions; you have evaded my one question to you. I will put another, a grossly practical one. Do you happen to have heard anything about the terms of Randolph's will?'

Trent, who was far from being impressed by Wetherill's conversational fopperies, could not help being taken aback by the direct simplicity of this inquiry; nor could he guess what might lie behind it. He was disagreeably reminded, moreover, that the direct and simple question which he himself had come there to ask of Wetherill had not yet been put to him, and that his shameless allusion to his relations with Eunice Faviell had made it more than ever difficult to turn to him for that information. He answered, then, with equal plainness, 'I understand that he died intestate.'

'He did!' Wetherill sat up with the first manifestation of unaffected interest that he had yet given. 'Dear friend, are you sure of what you say?' He stared at Trent with an evidently genuine anxiety.

'There isn't any doubt about it. He was just about to make a will when he was killed, but he never did so. That is what his lawyers say. But what has it got to do with you, Wetherill? Did you hope that he admired you to the extent of putting you down for a substantial legacy? Or did you think you had wormed your way into his affections by threatening to shoot him?'

Wetherill, his eyes half closed in deep consideration, only waved a hand vaguely, and for a few moments was silent. At last he said, 'Forgive me, dear friend. I was obliged to arrange my ideas on hearing what you tell me. It is good news to me; not a disappointment by any means, but an unexpected piece of good fortune. On the strength of it, I have just made up my mind to a very serious step. I am going to marry Eunice; and you, if you will, shall be the first to congratulate her.'

Astonishment and disgust went near to overcoming Trent's resolve to keep his temper. He drew a deep breath, then said, 'I haven't the least idea what all this means.'

Wetherill, still thoughtful, fingered his moustache. 'No, I suppose you haven't,' he replied coolly. 'But when I say that, dear friend, don't imagine that I look upon you as a fool. On the contrary, you have the very uncommon talent of being able to defeat my utmost efforts to infuriate you. No: you could not know what all this means. But you can make your mind easy about the main thing. I really am going to marry Eunice.'

'I don't believe it,' Trent said bluntly. 'You are assuming too much. She has had nothing to do with you for some time, I know. All her friends believe she has done with you for good and all,' he added somewhat inexactly; then, looking Wetherill candidly in the eyes, 'How she could ever bring herself to associate with such a ruffian as you are is quite incomprehensible to me.'

Wetherill turned to polishing his eyeglass once more. 'Naturally,' he said. 'You do not understand women, dear friend. That is a commonplace remark, I know; the sort of thing one alderman might say to another alderman. But it is true of you, just as it would incontestably be true of the other alderman. Perhaps you are to be envied your ignorance; who can say? As for my being a ruffian—do you know, dear friend, I rather like your choice of an epithet? So many men, and so many women, have done their best to find searing names for me; but none of them ever hit upon anything at all apt and significant. Really, the subject is an interesting one. When I am likened to one of the lower animals, or to some inferior social type, by some dolt whose neck I could break with one hand, I naturally am not impressed; and I always have the feeling, too, that my denouncer is not satisfied with his own efforts. But I wander from the point. Forgive me again, dear friend; with you I become loquacious. You were speaking of Eunice having done with me. You misconceive the situation—deliberately, perhaps. It was I who had done with Eunice. Now, however, I intend to marry her—make her an honest woman, as the saying is. You cannot disapprove of that.'

'You think not?' Trent asked. 'I assure you, I have disapproved of much less revolting brutalities of yours. If I believed what you say was possible, I should not only disapprove of it; I should do my best to prevent it. But I don't believe it.'

Wetherill smilingly waved his doubts aside. 'Well, dear friend, you shall see, and you may do your best. This evening I shall write to her.' He eyed Trent through his glass with an air of gentle amusement. 'She shall receive my wholly honourable proposal at your own house.'

Trent was startled out of his self-command. 'What the devil do you mean by that?' he exclaimed, thrusting back his chair.

'Yes, at your house,' Wetherill drawled, flicking a trace of cigarette-ash from his sleeve. 'I had a letter from her this morning, dated from Didbury Manor House, which is your property, I think.'

Trent stared at him in silence as he took in this breath-taking statement. He knew enough of Wetherill's ways to understand that he was speaking the truth. He knew that his wife, now staying at the Manor House, was a devoted friend of Eunice Faviell. But he had heard nothing from her of this visit; and he felt, not for the first time, that he was getting the worst of an interview that was entirely of his own seeking. But at least the sole object of it was attained. Without asking, he had learned where Eunice was to be found.

'She was writing to me about—shall I say, a matter of business?' Wetherill went on, as if helpfully anxious to end an awkward pause in the conversation. 'A disagreeable letter, too, I confess. But that has happened before; I disregard it; her heart will triumph before long, as it always does. By the way, her letter was concerned with our lamented Randolph—so much I may tell you. That also, I see, takes you aback; it is a day of little surprises for you, dear friend. How very visibly you react to such emotions—quite like the French poet, who likened his heart, you remember, to a suspended lute. "*Aussitôt qu'on y touche, il résonne.*" You don't think, do you,' he went on musingly, 'that Eunice herself murdered that old man? You seem determined to believe that the obvious man didn't. She can be very pettish, as we both know. That way she has of flying out at you suddenly—it is among the first of her charms. You recollect how Faust felt when Margaret snapped his nose off at their first meeting.

> *Wie sie kurz angebunden war,*
> *Das ist nun zum Entzücken gar!*

There have been moments when she would have liked to kill me, I am sure.'

What Wetherill had said of Trent's difficulty in hiding his emotions was, as he knew, true enough. He had turned white, and felt chilled to the heart, as this suggestion was airily put forward. But it was in a tone of hard contempt that he said, 'If you are so fond of *Faust*, let me remind you of what he said to the Witch in her kitchen—"You talk like a chorus of a hundred thousand idiots." Nobody but an imbecile could imagine that Eunice Faviell had anything to do with Randolph's death; and I'll do you the justice to assume that you don't seriously think so yourself. For one thing, she had no reason whatever to desire his death.'

Wetherill put his fingertips together and leaned back in his chair, as if prepared for some intellectual diversion. 'Well, perhaps we should distinguish. To desire a person's death is one thing; to be glad to hear of a person's death is, no doubt, not quite the same. I happen to know that Eunice must have been glad to hear of Randolph's.'

'Why?' Trent felt, and sounded, explosive.

'Because, dear friend, his death made her a very rich woman.' Wetherill gazed pleasantly out of the window, as if the chimney-pots on the other side of Down Street made the loveliest of prospects.

Trent felt as if his senses were leaving him at this last mad turn of the conversation. He put a hand to his forehead, and asked weakly, 'Would you mind explaining?'

'Not in the least,' Wetherill said affably. 'It is not a secret—at least, it soon will cease to be. Eunice Faviell is old James Randolph's niece, the daughter of his only sister with whom he quarrelled who knows how many years ago? I have it on the best authority—Randolph's own. He told me on the occasion of our last meeting, the time when I lightened his plethoric purse as I have mentioned already. He said he had discovered that Eunice was his next-of-kin, and that by his will she would inherit the greater part of his fortune.'

Trent thrust his hands into his pockets and laughed long and heartily. 'Is this the last of your revelations?' he inquired. 'Not that it matters, really. I think I have lost the capacity to be surprised any more; my sense of the marvellous is completely worn out. Tell me that you have just been admitted to holy orders. Tell me that the president of the Jockey Club is a Chinaman. Tell me I've got a tail. Nothing can astonish me now. But there is one thing I should like to hear. I can still feel curiosity. If he had been keeping this fact about Eunice Faviell dark, what was it that led him to confide in you?'

Wetherill shook his head sadly. 'I fear he told me in order to make himself unpleasant to me. I mentioned to you that he had done so, I think.'

'Still,' Trent remarked, 'I can imagine simpler ways of hurting your feelings than telling you somebody else was his niece. And as for the money, I don't suppose you positively object to the idea of her having it.' He was talking somewhat at random, while he tried privately to read a meaning into this amazing news and what had gone before it.

Did Eunice know of this? If she knew, how long had she known? Did it account for the mysterious rendezvous at Porter's? Was it the decent explanation of the affectionate interest in her which the old man had shown, and which she, not knowing the truth, had treated as the objectionable advances of an elderly amorist? But as for Wetherill, if he had believed for a week past that Eunice was to be Randolph's heir, why had he waited so long after Randolph's death before making up his mind to marry Randolph's money? And why, again, why had Wetherill been told by Randolph, who could not have been expecting to die, and so make Eunice 'a rich woman,' for years to come?

Wetherill was prepared, however, to help him out of this last difficulty. His peculiar taste for publishing his own iniquities was strong in him.

'I will tell you,' he said after a brief pause, 'why Randolph chose to confide in me, as you express it. You may find it an interesting story. You see, the transaction between us was the selling to him of a book of mine, an unpublished work of which he had heard, no doubt, when making his inquiries about Eunice.'

A light broke over Trent's mind. 'I see,' he said slowly. 'You mean the book you wrote so as to blackmail Eunice. That savoury part of the story is pretty well known.'

'Very likely,' Wetherill said. 'But don't be misled into disparaging *The Broken Wing*, dear friend. It is a masterpiece, in some ways the finest piece of work I have ever done, a possession for ever. When Eunice had read it, she was good enough to pay me as much as she could to have it suppressed; but if she had given me a million, it would have been monstrous in me to deprive the world permanently of such a work of art.'

'But you took her money.'

'Dear friend, I had to have money. Genius must live, you will allow; and to live in any tolerable sense of the word, it must have luxury. In any case, it is bound by the rules of its own nature, and by no others. And it is thanks to me, remember, that Eunice's own genius has unfolded itself.'

'Your other reasons for taking her money don't surprise me at all,' Trent said. 'I have heard that sort of cackle pretty often, and sometimes from people who really were artists. But I can't pass that last one. Eunice Faviell was what she was, and is, long before she was unfortunate enough to meet you, or acted in any of your plays.'

Wetherill's dignity was unruffled. 'Eunice knows, if others affect not to know, what she owes to me. That is why she gave me all that she could scrape together. All the same, it was foolish of her, I allow, to wish to have *The Broken Wing* suppressed. By that romance I have given her immortality; not as she would have it, perhaps, but in the figures of a woman, a great artist, struggling pitifully against a destroying and remorseless love, and against the advance of the years. It is a study—'

Trent cut him short. 'I can't stand more than a certain amount of that sort of thing. We will take it as said, if you don't mind. The question is where Randolph came into the matter.'

'Why,' Wetherill explained with agreeable candour, 'he came in, most fortunately, just about the time when all the money from Eunice was spent. He had heard about the book. He sent for me, and offered to buy it from me. At the time I had no idea of his real motive, for Eunice's name was not mentioned by either of us. He named a quite considerable sum that he was ready to pay for the copyright. I named a larger one; we came to an agreement; and later in the day I returned to his house with the manuscript, and made over my rights to him in a document which he had ready. In my innocence I thought that he desired the credit of giving the work to the world on his own responsibility; and a lot of money in hand was of more importance to me just then than the prospect of royalties. You can understand that, I am sure.'

'Perfectly. But I am still waiting to hear why he told you about Eunice's relationship to him.'

'You shall hear, dear friend. When he had got the manuscript and the agreement, and when the money had been handed over to me, he informed me politely that he did not mean to publish the book, but to keep it for his own purposes. It was then that I allowed myself to lose my temper. I lashed him with words in a way that I very seldom do. He smiled, and appeared to be highly pleased. I threatened to kill him; he seemed even more delighted. Then he told me, as if it were the most natural thing in the world, that he had discovered Eunice Faviell to be his nearest living relative, and that most of his money would go to her at his death.

'I was surprised, as you may imagine, by this introduction of a name which neither of us had pronounced until that moment. I said, however, with perfect truth, that I was charmed to hear this news. How should I not be? I told myself that nothing could suit me better than to have Eunice for my own in the character of an heiress on such a scale, and with a millionaire to look to, in the meantime, for maintenance in conditions suitable to that character. I promised myself that I would take steps to bring us together again without delay.'

'Yes; I can quite see all that,' Trent said with ready sympathy. 'Quite a glimpse of paradise for you—sponging for the rest of your life on a woman with money who is an incurable fool about you.'

Wetherill held up a hand as if in gentle reproof. 'These are words,' he returned mildly. 'Do not forget, dear friend, what I said about the necessities of genius. Let me resume. He had informed me that Eunice was his next-of-kin and destined heiress. I was dwelling in imagination on the agreeable prospect so disclosed. And then what did that wicked old man—that prodigy of coarse and bat-eyed prejudice—proceed to say?'

'I wonder.'

'He said that he intended to put an end to all connection between Eunice and myself. He said this with plain and undisguised enjoyment, as if he were savouring some delightful essence. I was—I admit it—struck dumb with amazement and indignation; and he went on to make his meaning clear. He said that by the terms of his will Eunice would inherit nothing whatever, and that she would get nothing from him during his lifetime, unless she promised now to break off all relations with me immediately, and kept strictly to that undertaking for the future.'

Wetherill paused, as if to let all the baseness of this atrocity sink in.

'And from his way of putting it,' he went on, 'I was led to assume that his will was already made, and there was an end of my hopes. And so there would have been, if he had lived long enough to carry out his monstrous intentions. The black-hearted old scoundrel! After leading me up to the very height of Pisgah! Well, I have my share of philosophy. When I left him, I put the idea of Eunice completely out of my mind. After all, I had extracted from him a sum large enough to meet my wants for some considerable time, and I was by so much the better off. And now, today, dear friend, imagine my feelings—the sudden glow of renewed and established happiness—when you told me that Randolph had died intestate after all!' He spread his hands abroad with a superb gesture.

'I see! I see!' Trent exclaimed hilariously. 'That was why you sat up so abruptly when you heard the glad news. As you say, I can imagine your feelings. Eunice gets the lot, you grab Eunice, and love leads the rebel discords up the sacred mount. Lord! It's enough to make a cat laugh!' He exploded in a shout of mirth that caused many in the room to turn round inquisitively in their chairs.

'Your imitation of a cat is not a flattering one,' Wetherill said. He had turned suddenly pale, and his voice was a little unsteady. 'May I know what amuses you?'

Trent rose to his feet and turned to go. 'Why, you ass! Randolph's only son has turned up, complete with proofs of his identity. Eunice Faviell will never get a farthing.'

CHAPTER XV

EUNICE MAKES A CLEAN BREAST OF IT

TRENT had discovered the Cotswold country as a very young man, newly land-conscious, when it had appealed to him with an irresistible compulsion. There are some places which, seen for the first time, yet seem to strike a chord of recollection. 'I have been here before,' we think to ourselves, 'and this is one of my true homes.' It is no mystery for those philosophers who hold that all which we shall see, with all which we have seen and are seeing, exists already in an eternal now; that all those places are home to us which in the pattern of our life are twisting, in past, present and future, tendrils of remembrance round our heart-strings.

Trent, in his travels, had often chanced upon a house, a town or a stretch of country, unknown to him in terms of normal experience, which claimed him as its own with unerring certainty. As it had once been on a magic day in Tuscany, driving up to Montalcino, so with that counterscarp of the Cotswolds overlooking the vale of Evesham. So he had set his heart on a long, grey, stone-tiled house, flanked by shaped yews, which stood on a terrace cut in the brow of the steep hill, with woods and fields and villages stretching away below to the barrier of the Malvern Hills, and a glimpse of the Welsh mountains beyond.

Along the ridge of the hill ran a Roman road—Old Campden Lane, the people called it—lonely between the low stone walls that bounded the fields. So broad it was that a dozen four-horse chariots might have been driven abreast along it; and in summer it was thigh-deep with flowers and feathery grasses. The highest point was crowned by a cluster of tall beeches, a landmark known far and wide as Cromwell's Clump, from which, said legend, Cromwell had watched and directed a battle in the plain below, but Oliver was a modern interloper among the warlike spirits haunting the spot. For the beeches edged the rampart of a Roman camp; and that had been raised on the foundations of some far more ancient native stronghold.

What a man desires whole-heartedly enough, it is said, he will surely attain. Not long after Trent's marriage, the house that he coveted fell to his lot with the smoothness of destiny; for it fell vacant and was put up for sale at a time when he was prosperous enough to become its owner.

On the day following his interview with Eugene Wetherill, Trent drove swiftly across the bare wolds until the country broke away before him, and the road plunged headlong down past a wood of lofty trees. A sharp left-hand turn brought him into the drive of the Manor House, and he steered his car into the garage among the farm buildings.

As he closed the garage doors a small figure dashed down the few steps from the terrace before the house, and then, checking itself, paced gravely towards him. It was a small, round-eyed boy of about six years old, arrayed in a bead-bedizened red shirt and a bristling fillet of feathers, his cheeks and forehead barred with streaks of what Trent divined to be lipstick, his left hand grasping a wooden hatchet.

'How!' said this apparition, raising the right hand in a solemn gesture.

'I beg your pardon,' Trent said blankly.

'How!' the child repeated; adding by way of explanation, 'Stamping Bull great chief!'

'Oh ah! Yes, of course,' Trent answered, calling on his memories. He raised his own hand. 'How! The pale-face from the regions of the morning gives greeting to Stamping Bull and all his tribe.'

'That's better,' said the great chief, with an ear-embracing grin. 'Stamping Bull glad to see pale-face. Pale-face just in time for lunch—bear's paw, buffalo-hump. Stamping Bull heap hungry!'

'Can Stamping Bull tell me,' Trent asked, 'if the pale-face squaw is—er—among his people?'

'Laughing Tortoise in the wigwam,' replied the chief with dignity. ''Nother pale-face squaw too—name Spring Cabbage, came last week, heap lovely.' Here the noble savage changed the conversation abruptly. 'Stamping Bull heap cruel, love kill, love scalp!' he screeched, and rushed off up the steps brandishing his tomahawk, while Trent followed at a slower pace.

Another voice, the voice of Eunice Faviell, hailed him from the edge of the terrace. 'Philip,' she called, I'm here incognita and I don't know you. Go away.'

Trent looked up into the small, vivacious face, now twisted in the exaggeration of a scowl. 'Is this gratitude?' he asked. 'Is it justice? I fight a lady's battles for her, play Perseus to her Andromeda, and all the thanks I get is that she forbids me my own house, and tries to look like Medusa.'

'What do you mean, Phil?' There was a catch of anxiety in her voice now that did not sound like joking. 'Perseus—didn't he kill the dragon that was worrying Andromeda?'

'That's it—teasing her unmercifully. But you must not take my Perseus literally any more than your own Andromeda. After all, you were not chained to a rock with nothing on, waiting to be eaten—at least, if you were, your press agent has been neglecting his work. All I did was to draw the dragon's teeth, clip his claws, unbarb his tail, and domesticate him generally—and then he was quite unnecessarily slain. Dragons, you know, are never just killed; always slain. Just as Douglases are always doughty, and paynims are always false.'

'Don't talk nonsense, Phil; it isn't any good. I am frightened, I tell you.'

Eunice Faviell was a creature of instinct who, in life, fell as naturally into the parts ordained for her as into those she played in the theatre. She was far from belonging to the country by taste or habit, yet here she had the air of being country born and bred. The tweeds she wore, with a burning spot of orange at the throat, made her somewhat a part of the landscape; her thrilling voice was tuned to the peace of the hills and woods. For all the distress and disquiet that showed in her face, she looked younger than art could make her look in town. When Mabel Trent appeared, dragged forcibly out of the house by Stamping Bull to join them, her dark and regular beauty gave much more of the effect of metropolitan life than was suggested by the woman who seldom entered into any other frame of existence. Trent's eye rejoiced a moment in the picture made by the two vivid and contrasted personalities in their setting of the grey house behind, the dark green of the yews on either side; then he mounted the steps to be with them, and embraced his wife as one clinging to her for protection.

'Mabel,' he said, 'you at least will not drive me away as if I were a verminous leper loitering with intent to commit a felony. What is this person doing here? She has been telling me to get to hell out of this, or words to that effect, though anyone can see that I am dying of hunger and thirst. Stamping Bull: will you kindly tell the women in the wigwam that the pale-face would like a fire-water and soda, as he is feeling rather like a wounded buffalo, after his long journey over the trackless prairie.'

'Yes, Bull,' his mother said. 'Tell Maggie to bring it to your father out here.'

'Fire-water for my great white father,' repeated the chief; and dashed into the house with a yell.

'Why didn't you let me know you were coming, Phil?' Mabel Trent said. 'Luckily you are just in time for lunch; and you won't be starved, because Eunice has eaten hardly anything since she came. You need feeding, too; you are looking thinner.'

She traced two lines of inanition on his cheeks with a slim forefinger. 'You have been worrying, or overworking—'

'Or painting the town red,' Eunice suggested. 'Those are the lines of reckless dissipation, my girl, not the results of pining away because he is separated from you, as you are trying to suggest.'

'They're the same thing,' Trent explained. 'When I attempt from love's sickness to fly, the first thing I do is to hurl myself into an ocean of drink and debauchery, of course. And if it comes to why-didn't-yous, why didn't you warn me that you had an actress in the house?'

'Because she wouldn't let me. She rang up last week saying she wanted to get away from everybody and everything, and would I give her a roof over her head? So I said I should like nothing better; and when she came she made me vow I would say nothing about her being here, not even to you. So I thought if she was slightly mad, it would be safest to humour her; especially as it didn't matter in the slightest to you or anybody else.'

At this point a sturdy and smiling parlourmaid emerged with Trent's refreshment, announcing that luncheon would be served in a few minutes; and Eunice, remarking that it was time she became tactful, disappeared into the house.

Mabel looked after her with a troubled eye. 'You know, my dear, I'm afraid it's something serious. I've known Eunice most of my life, and I've never seen her in such a state as she was when she came down last Friday, looking worried and scared and worn out. I have done what I could for her, and she seems much better, but you can see for yourself there is something wrong. I haven't asked her what it is, but she would have told me by this time if she was going to. And it is rather alarming when she insists on nobody being told she is here, not even you. Perhaps it is a good thing you didn't say you were coming— she might have rushed off to avoid meeting you. I can't understand it. Do you think you can induce her to say anything?'

'I mean to have a good try,' Trent said. 'I've come here on purpose to do that. And I'm glad you did as she asked about not telling me. She has had a bad shock of some sort, evidently, and raising objections would have made her worse.'

'I knew you would say so. It's just what I felt myself.'

Trent saw to it, with the able assistance of his little son, that luncheon should not be a too serious affair.

'When I saw you last,' he said to his wife, 'our child was going through a stage of being an animal—any sort of animal, so long as it was fierce. He was a fierce chimpanzee when I saw you off in the train, and he had been a fierce antelope just before that. Now, I gather, he is a Choctaw.'

'Not Choctaw—Pottawattomie,' the chief corrected him with some asperity. 'Choctaw no good, heap chickenheart, eat snake. Ugh!'

'You can thank Eunice for all that,' Mabel said. 'As if he and his little friends were not savages enough already, she has taught him to be the complete redskin. She has dressed him, and painted him, and made him what he calls a bonnet of chick-en-feathers, and taught him an entirely new language—including strange names for everybody in the house. She is packed with information on the subject.'

'It is about the only thing I ever learnt properly at school,' Eunice said, 'and I always had a good memory.'

'We both went through it at school,' Mabel said. 'Only all of us wanted to be braves, of course, and as I was one of the smallest girls I had to be a squaw, and I didn't take so much interest, I suppose.'

'Your heart wasn't in it; you were born civilized. It all comes of having a French grandfather,' Eunice said. 'You have finished your coffee, Phil, haven't you? Do you mind if I borrow him for a time, Mabel? I want to talk to him about my troubles.'

As they made their way to a seat above the house looking out over the plain, Eunice said, 'I meant that; I do want to talk about my troubles. Now that you are here, and we have got into the old atmosphere, it seems idiotic that I should ever have thought of keeping them from you, or keeping out of your way. I really wasn't quite in my right senses last week; that's the only excuse. Let us just sit here and take in the peacefulness of it for a little; then you can start by asking me questions, if you don't mind.'

'Well, why did you disappear like this?' Trent said at length. 'You don't like people interesting themselves in your affairs as a rule—I seem to remember you hinted something of the sort to me in a note a week ago—but when you actually ask me to pry into them, I hope it is because I may be of some good. We are delighted to have you here on any terms—I needn't tell you that—but I can't cure myself of wanting to be helpful where you are concerned.'

'I know that,' she said, looking into the distance. 'You are not the inquisitive kind, and I don't believe you care a damn how I behave myself. Nor does Mabel; only she wouldn't call it a damn. I suppose that is really the reason why I am here—I don't mean her not swearing, but not caring. There is nobody else I should have dreamed of planting myself on like this—nobody except Judith, that is; and she is abroad.'

'That is almost the definition of any friendship that is worth while—that we don't care a damn how you behave yourself. Not that you have tested us very severely.'

'Well,' she said, 'I will tell you. I wanted to get away out of sight if I could. I was afraid. If only Judith had been in England, I should have gone to her, and she would have told me what to do. But there was Mabel.'

'There was me too,' Trent observed. 'In other words, there was I also; and in London—within your very grasp, as it were.'

'Yes, I know; but you were mixed up in the very thing I was trying to escape from. You see, it was when I saw about Randolph's death, and poor old Bryan trying to commit suicide, that I felt I couldn't face things any longer. I wanted to get away from the police.'

Trent coughed dubiously. 'That isn't very easy—certainly not for an amateur. If they want you, they probably won't be long in catching up with you. But why on earth should they?'

'But surely you can guess! I know Judith told you about my being pestered by letters from Randolph which I didn't understand—at least, I thought I did understand them, and I resented them much more than I do that sort of nuisance as a rule. I never answered them, and he still went on, begging me to see him, because he had something of the greatest importance to say, that it concerned my whole future—hinting that I should never know troubles and uncertainties again—it was all that sort of thing. And when a rich old man writes to a woman in my position in that sort of prose style, she knows well enough what to think. Or she thinks she does. And who wouldn't?'

'You are trying to tell me,' Trent suggested, 'that you got him wrong?'

'Well, you will see. I am going to make a clean breast of it. But what I was saying was that I told Judith, and Judith told you; and then she wrote that you were going to have a row with Randolph, and that you could put a stop to it. I didn't see how you could; and anyhow I objected to having that sort of thing about me passed round without my leave; and so, as usual, I went in off the deep end, and wrote you a perfectly beastly letter. At least, I meant it to be—I don't remember what I said.'

'Oh, it was. You succeeded admirably. I was raked from stem to stern. Poking my nose into what was none—'

'Don't be a cad, Phil. You know how sorry I am; don't rub it in. I always am sorry after making a pig of myself; but I was a very special pig to write like that to you. But that isn't the worst. You see, some time before that I had been writing to Bryan—one of those letters about nothing in particular that we exchange from time to time—and I said something, not seriously at all, about the old man bothering me with silly letters. It was all mixed up with a lot of other personal chatter, and I never thought about it again—until—until I heard the news about Randolph, and about Bryan too. People were saying he must have done it; I heard it everywhere. Can you imagine what I felt?'

Trent digested this information with a clouded brow; for he himself had written to Fairman about that same 'bothering.' He could indeed imagine how Eunice felt; imagine, too, how much worse she would feel if she could know that their friend had confessed to the murder. But that could be told to no one without breach of a confidence that he had always been very careful to respect. Even if it were otherwise, what would be the good of turning Eunice's fears to certainty?—for so she would inevitably take it.

'You understand, don't you?' she said miserably. 'If Bryan did it, it may have been all my fault. Of course I know it would be idiotic to go off and kill a person for a thing like that; but all the same, it is the sort of thing that would make Bryan perfectly furious, and I was an utter fool ever to have mentioned it to him. That is why I was frightened. That is why I dreaded the police asking me questions. Everything I could say would have been against him. Even if I said nothing, they might have found my letter—he may have kept it.'

'That's highly probable, I should say,' Trent admitted with a wry smile.

'But, Phil, do you believe he did it? Tell me what you really think, whatever it is.'

'All I can tell you is that I don't know what to think. That isn't just a way of speaking; I really don't. There are too many infernal complications about the case; things I can make nothing of. What I can say is that I am working on the line that Bryan is not guilty. But it is going to take me all my time to get him out of the mess, if I ever do.'

Eunice clapped her hands. 'What, have you turned detective again? And you hope to get him out of the mess? Bless you, my dear, you can't say fairer than that! If I know that you are working at the thing, and doing all you can for him, it makes me feel—oh, I can't tell you how much better!'

'Yes,' he said, 'I have relapsed. Meet Philip Trent, the celebrated werewolf, who has been a man for some years, and is now a sleuth-hound once more. But I didn't want to be. I was dragged into it.'

'You mean Bryan being suspected.'

'That was only one thing. Among the other things was the discovery that Miss Eunice Faviell was floating vaguely around the outskirts of the case. I found that out before you told me. In fact, that's why I am here.'

She stared at him.

'I am not asking whether you murdered Randolph yourself,' he reassured her, 'because something in your manner tells me that you would be rather put out if I suggested such a thing. But you have been very much annoyed with him. And you were, I gather, very much annoyed with him again only a few hours before he was found shot. And besides that, there is the little matter of wealth beyond the dreams of avarice. Didn't Randolph tell you that his death would make you inordinately rich, whether he made a will or not?'

'Good heavens!' Eunice gasped. 'Then you mean—but I never thought of that side at all! You mean they might get to suspecting *me*?'

'Not necessarily that; but putting you on the list of possibles. In fact, I rather think you are there already. The last time I saw the officer in charge of the case he was taking a sort of faint interest in you that I couldn't quite account for. I can see now, from other things he said, what was in his mind. I didn't know then about your being Randolph's niece, and having expectations from his death; but *he* knew, and the old badger didn't tell me. I am sure he knew.'

'And you have found it out for yourself.'

'No I haven't,' Trent said tartly. 'I never had the slightest notion of it, or of your being related to the old man. I was told all that yesterday—told by Eugene Wetherill, who knew a lot more about the whole thing than I did. For instance, he knew where you were, and was kind enough to tell me. I was quite interested to hear that.'

'Devil!' Eunice murmured, as if confiding a secret to the landscape. 'I mean you,' she added, glancing at Trent.

'Never mind about what species I belong to,' Trent said warmly. 'It is no joke to get nipped in the machinery in a case of this kind, and I didn't like the idea of its happening to you, especially when I had already got Bryan and—er—other people to bother about. So if there is nothing against it, could you clear up one little point for me?'

'Of course I will if I can,' she said. 'I told you I was going to make a clean breast of it, you know, and I haven't really begun yet. I don't feel so much like running away from the whole beastly business, now I know you are taking a hand. What is your one little point?'

'Perhaps it is hardly worth mentioning,' Trent said apologetically. 'It's this. After complaining bitterly about the way Randolph was persecuting you, and blasting the poor old chap's reputation, and generally behaving like Lucrece in the clutches of Tarquin—'

'I don't know what that means,' she said, 'but it sounds improper.'

'Well, anyhow, after kicking up all that fuss, how did it happen that you were having a cosy little tête-à-tête luncheon with him on the same day that he was murdered? You see, I am putting it in simple terms; the kind of terms it would be discussed in if the facts were to become generally known. Come on then, Eunice; how about it?'

She sighed whimsically. 'Yes; this affair has certainly got you going again. So you know about that, do you?—when it was, and where it was, and what I was wearing, and how late I was for it, and what flowers there were on the table, and what the waiter's first name was, and what we had to drink—'

Trent mentioned what they had had to drink.

She nodded; then said reflectively: 'When I was learning my job, acting in the sort of places you never saw in your life, the public were very fond of those plays in which heroes were heroes, and villains were villains, and comic men were comic, and people were always getting tied down on railway lines, or turned out in the snow with their babies, or melting the heart of the prison governor by saying "I am inno-scent!" What you have just said is the cue for me to clutch you by the wrist and whisper through my clenched teeth, "How much do you know?" I shan't do it, though, because I don't care how much you know. I want you to know the whole thing, so I may as well tell it from the start, though you evidently know a lot of it already.'

'You'll tell me the whole thing,' Trent emphasized.

'Cross me 'eart,' Eunice said vulgarly; and told her tale.

She had first met Randolph about a year before, at a vast hotel in Scotland, to which she had taken Miss Yates as her guest for a brief visit. He had appeared a short time after their arrival; they had fallen into conversation with him, and he had done his not very successful best to make himself agreeable. Eunice had been struck by the fact that he made no reference at all to her work in the theatre—'though every one knew who I was, of course,' she said simply. Once he had mentioned that a portrait of him was to be painted, and had asked her if there was any artist whom she believed in for that sort of work. He said she must often have had her own portrait painted; which was the nearest he ever went to making a complimentary speech. Eunice told him that the right man for him was Philip Trent. 'I tried,' she said, 'to give him the impression that you were a most extraordinary genius, whose work would be fought for by collectors for ages to come. I heard afterwards that you had landed the job; but I was too much of a lady to ask you for the usual ten per cent.' Soon afterwards they had left the hotel, and Eunice had seen no more of him.

It was soon after this that unpleasant things had begun to happen to her professionally. Something seemed to have happened to her prestige—'with the accent on the press.' An important group of papers did not hide their disappointment with her work in one new play; of another they had nothing good to say. Faintly malicious paragraphs in gossip columns reached her from the press-cutting bureau; it was hinted that her reputation was being somewhat severely strained.

'You don't know,' she said to Trent, 'what a difference that kind of thing makes to anyone who is before the public. It is like something poisonous in the air. I told myself it wasn't going to kill me; it couldn't really shake my position, even, so long as it wasn't widespread. I knew I was as good as I had ever been, and I knew the public knew it. But I hated it like sin all the same. And just when it was beginning to worry me, I found I had to provide a considerable sum of money. It wasn't anything to do with the theatre; simply a private affair. It was utterly unexpected and very painful, and there was no getting out of it—not if I was ever to hold up my head again. But it's no use talking to you about it, because you don't know, and I can't explain.'

Trent did, on the contrary, know very well, but he had no desire at all to discuss the matter of Wetherill's infamous book, and the blackmailing use he had made of it. If Eunice, in her innocence, believed that transaction to be a secret from all the world, so much the better. So he merely said, 'All right; go ahead. You were saying you had to find a sum of money.'

'It took everything I had,' she said, 'and as much as I could raise. That hit me pretty hard; but I got it done and over, and there was an American tour being fixed up for me that would have pulled things straight again. Then that fell through. I really began to feel as if the gods had got a grudge against me. Still, I have always been able to earn my living, and soon I was on my feet again with the name part in Northmour's play. It was just then that I began to receive those letters from Randolph that I was telling you about. I suppose the reason why they upset me so much was just because, from what I had seen of him, they seemed so utterly unnatural and out of character. I have met with a good many nasty old men in my time, and though I could imagine Randolph being a brute in all sorts of ways, I had simply never thought of him in that particular way—no more than I should of the Cobden Statue in Hampstead Road. So I got more and more wrought up, and first I let slip something about it to Bryan, like a chattering fool, and then I relieved my feelings by telling Judith all about it, and then—well, what happened then really did surprise me.'

'Do you mean that Randolph flung off the mask, and revealed that he was quite respectable after all?'

'Yes, if that's all that being respectable means. I got a letter from him saying he had hoped to make everything plain in a personal interview, but I must have misunderstood his earlier letters. He said that two years before he had commissioned a firm of inquiry agents to find out whether any relations of his were alive, because he felt it was time he made up his mind what was to happen to his money, or something like that. The agents had found no trace of his son; but they had got on the trail of his only sister Caroline, and they had established the fact that she was my mother, who died when I was nineteen. He gave a few details that showed there was no doubt about it. He said his sister had left home to marry an actor named Hunt. Well, I had always known that was my father's real name; and I had known there was some sort of row about the marriage, because my mother had never let slip a single word about any of her relations in my hearing, and she would never tell me what her maiden name had been. Neither would my father, even when he wasn't sober, which was pretty often.

'Randolph's letter mentioned the place where I was born, and gave the addresses where my parents had lived since then, and—oh! there was a lot more, but what it all came to was that I was certainly the old man's niece. And that wasn't at all a pleasant surprise, I can tell you. For one thing, I hated the idea of my parents' history being nosed out like that. You see, Phil, my father had some lovable qualities, and had a splendid appearance, and was quite a good actor with a reputation of his own in the provinces; but he had serious weaknesses, and he died soon after he was forty. After that my mother kept a boarding-house in Portsmouth, and she did well enough out of that to keep us decent, and send me to a good school. But she was what they call soured, I suppose. I never saw her look happy, and though she was never unkind to me, she was not exactly a doting parent. The long and the short of it is that I was an unhappy kid, and I have always thought about my early years as little as possible. Then here came somebody I hardly knew, and didn't much like, full of information about my parentage and childhood, and proving himself to be an uncle who I didn't even know existed.'

Trent, as he listened to Eunice's tale, reflected that there were not, perhaps, very many women supporting themselves in an arduous calling who would have been seriously displeased by the discovery of a millionaire uncle looking about him for someone to inherit his wealth. But Eunice, as he knew, had always been one of those who seem able to steer a more or less happy course through life without troubling themselves about money. Not that she was one of the Skimpole family of that tribe; for she was devoted to her art, was a tireless worker, and for years had enjoyed such success that she might have laid the foundations of a fortune by now if she had been so inclined. As it was, though she valued her independence as much as life itself, she had never done anything to secure it in the pecuniary sense. She was generous and careless in the extreme. Sometimes she would make the pleasing discovery that there was a respectable balance to her credit at the bank; sometimes she was deep enough in debt to have alarmed a less mercurial spirit. She trusted to luck and to her genius to make ends meet; and when they even overlapped, it was not for long.

'That was what his letter told me,' she said, 'and it ended by asking me to have lunch with him and talk things over on a certain day when he would be next in London—that was last Wednesday, of course; the last day of his life.' She raised her shoulders in a movement of distress, and for a moment her eyes closed.

'So that is the explanation of your meeting with him,' Trent said quietly. 'A good deal of what I have been hearing and finding out is fitting itself together now—not all of it, unfortunately, but a lot. Do you care to tell me what happened when you saw him?'

'I want to tell you,' she said. 'It was the worst part of the whole business. I wrote back to him at Brinton accepting his invitation. I didn't want to, but I didn't see how I could decently do anything else. After all, it was perfectly natural he should do what he had done; it was natural he should want to see me; and I had been doing him an injustice, though I still didn't blame myself at all for that. So I accepted; and on the day, I met him as you know. He was quite frank and pleasant at the start; talked about my mother a little, and told me I was much more like my father—which I knew better than he did—and said that in his old age his being alone in the world had begun to trouble him for the first time. Then he spoke of the time when we had met in Scotland, and he confessed that he had gone to that hotel knowing I was to be there, because he wanted to see what kind of a person I was.'

Trent nodded. 'I rather thought that might be so,' he observed. 'But you say that was about a year ago. I suppose he liked the look of you then—it's usual to like the look of you. Why, I wonder, was he such a devilish long time about taking action? I should have expected him to bring the family tree to your notice without delay, after satisfying himself that you were all his fancy painted you.'

Eunice's look hardened. 'Well, you didn't understand my uncle, that's all,' she said. 'Not many men would understand him, I should think—or I should hope. You will soon see why he took his time. After speaking of that time in Scotland, he went on to asking about my career. That gave me something to talk about, which I was glad of; and I told him how I had started, and how I had got on—a regular autobiography. He took it all in, but looking a little bit grim, I thought; and then he asked me how I had been doing lately. So I told him, quite frankly, it was the worst year I had had since I qualified as a star. Then he put questions, and I told about the way the Westlake papers had been crabbing me, and how my American tour had failed to materialize for some reason; and I said I had lost a lot of money, for me, in a private venture—by which I meant that unpleasant affair I mentioned to you without telling you what it was. Randolph wanted to know about that, and I told him I preferred not to discuss it.

'And then, Phil, I got the jolt that he had been saving up for me. He said to me something like this: "Well, my dear, you see you can't reckon on the stage as a means of support all your life. You have had a good innings, but it looks to me as if your reputation was beginning to decline, and unless you have saved money your future is uncertain, to say the least of it. But I am your near relative. I am a rich man. I wish to place you in the position in life you are entitled to, as my niece, and I propose to leave you the bulk of my estate by will. But there are conditions attached to this; and one of them is that you give up the stage, which I regard as an immoral and disreputable way of earning a living. I would rather see anyone I cared for dead at my feet than winning success in the theatre."'

Eunice, who had put the whole of her talent into this impersonation of the dour old man, and reproduced his very accents with startling effect, now shook back her clipped hair and turned a wide smile on Trent. 'How did that go with you?' she asked. 'It has made me feel much better, anyhow. I can't swear to the actual words, except "immoral and disreputable way of earning a living," and the "dead at my feet" gag; but I swear I got the general sense of it right. And perhaps you can imagine how it got me going! I was bursting! But I didn't let myself explode. I simply said I didn't want his money, that I had got on without it before and could get on without it for the future. I said I was used to looking out for myself, and was quite ready to take my chance, and that I preferred it anyhow.

'The next minute I was very glad I hadn't let my temper get the better of me, because he turned white with rage, and if it gets to being thoroughly unpleasant I always think it's a much better arrangement if the other party starts it. He told me that I was a fool, that everybody wanted money. He said, if I had had money I should never have taken to this vagabond existence—those were his very words, my dear. So I just looked at him—like this—as if he was a bad smell, but as if I supposed he couldn't help being a bad smell. That made him madder, of course. He said I might talk about taking my chance, but that I hadn't any chance, and he could see to it that I didn't get one. He said he didn't mind telling me that it was he who had worked it so as to make the Westlake papers give me the bird, and get my American tour messed up, but that that was only the start, just to show me what a rotten game the stage was, and if I wanted any more I could have plenty.'

'You are giving me, as you say, his very words,' Trent suggested.

'Of course not—don't be aggravating, Phil. I'm merely putting what he said into ordinary English. He said he did not withdraw the proposal he had made me, because he meant to have his way. He said he knew it wouldn't be long before I came to him with my pride humbled, and that then I should have to agree to another condition which he hadn't mentioned yet. At that I looked snootier still, and he looked as if he was going to have a fit. He said the other condition was that I should have to break off my association with Eugene Wetherill and any other blackguards I might be mixed up with. Well, when he went as far as that, I just got up and began to put on my cloak. Then he went on that I was much too unreserved in all my relations with men, according to the reports he had received; and he had the damned insolence to mention Bryan's name.'

'Oho! He mentioned Bryan, did he? That,' Trent said, 'sheds a bright light on another of the enigmas. I wondered what he could possibly have got against Bryan.'

'He would hate any man he came across who was half-way decent,' Eunice said viciously. 'Now here's the last thing. He said that before I went there was just one thing more for me to bear in mind. I won't tell you what that thing was, Phil, because it is a private matter. I hadn't the ghost of a notion he knew anything about it, and hearing him speak of it nearly knocked me out. I'll just say this much: he had bought—something—from Eugene, which he had had to pay a high price for, he said; and if I drove him to making use of it, he would do so. I'm sorry I can't make it plainer. And by the way, plain wasn't the word for the language I used to Eugene when I wrote to him about it a few days ago.'

'Well, all that doesn't matter,' Trent said. 'It was something Randolph was going to hold over you. He had a taste for that sort of thing, it appears.'

'If I had had anything to hold over him just then—something hard and heavy—there would have been an end of his tastes,' Eunice said. 'That last threat of his was the worst thing he had said yet. Just at that moment the waiter came into the room, and I grabbed up my bag and legged it without another word. God knows what I should have said if I had opened my mouth— probably I should have been like the girls in the novels, who hear themselves saying words they didn't even know they had ever heard. Well, there you are, Phil; that is the whole story.

Pretty, isn't it?' Eunice shut her eyes, stretched out her feet and dropped her arms limply, in the manner adopted by boxers in the intervals between rounds.

'And you heard nothing more from him?' Trent inquired, realising that his own breath was coming quicker under the effect of Eunice's torrent of impetuous speech.

'Not a peep—nor a line either, if you mean writing. There wasn't much time for anything, was there? When I left him, I was in such a fury I hadn't room for anything else; but when I had cooled off, I began to think about the prospect for me, and you can guess how I felt about it. When you know a man with a disposition like that is going to use all his power to smash you, it's no merry jest, believe me. I couldn't study my new part. I couldn't sleep. It was well on into the next day before I could pull myself together and get back my pluck. And then, as soon as I went out, I heard the news of Randolph having been shot. If that had been all, it would have been—well, I won't say an answer to prayer; like a reprieve when one's just going to be hanged, let's say. But what the papers had about Bryan simply shattered me, as I told you. The only thing I could think of was getting away right out of things, and trying to get my balance again.'

Trent took off his hat and fanned himself with it. 'You have made it so exciting,' he said, 'that I feel all hot and agitated. By the way, there's one thing I can tell you that comes into the story. You are not in any danger of inheriting the old man's money. His prodigal son has turned up, and as far as I can see, he will get every farthing of what is left when the Chancellor of the Exchequer has had his whack. So you, my dear, will be just where you were before the band began to play.'

'Praise the Lord for that!' Eunice said with fervour. 'It's all I ask.' She got up and stretched her arms abroad. 'Mabel and that innocent child of yours have done me more good than I thought possible; but having got that long, long story off my chest with you has really completed the good work, I believe—that, and knowing you are once more upon the war-path, as Stamping Bull would say. Now, what my vocal cords chiefly need is rest.' She took his arm. 'I won't say another word till I have got outside at least two cups of tea. Lead me to it.'

CHAPTER XVI

THE WHISPERED WORD

A LONG day's work in the studio had followed upon Trent's return from Didbury, and diverted his mind from the tormenting doubts that arose at every turn in the labyrinth of the Randolph case. He had dined late, and now, after an hour with a pipe and a volume of Boswell, he sat thinking of the next move to be made in his adopted task of running down the truth that eluded him so persistently. There was little question, in fact, what that move should be. He had heard that morning that leave for him to visit Bryan Fairman in the prison infirmary at Newhaven had been granted, that Fairman wished to see him, and would probably be fit for the interview in two days' time. If his friend meant now at last to clear up the mystification brought about by his crazy-seeming avowal of guilt and subsequent dogged silence, it was idle to go on with guess-work in the meantime. The best to be done was to consider the points on which Fairman, it might be hoped, would shed some light.

It was still in the studio, the centre of his private life, that Trent was turning over these things in his mind. Outside, he knew, the weather was heavy and windless; and he was roused at length to consciousness of the fact that some slight noise, hard to account for in such conditions, had for some time been coming from the direction of the French window opening upon the garden.

He listened now with attention. This was a gentle tapping on the window-glass—a few light taps; then an interval of a quarter of a minute or more; then a few light taps again. No dog or cat could produce such sounds. A twig moved by the breeze might do it; but there was no branch close to the window, nor any breeze to stir it if there had been. Heavy rain had fallen earlier in the evening, and Trent thought of the possibility of water dripping from some gutter or cornice. But the tapping, almost certainly, had been upon the surface of the window.

The noise made itself heard again; and Trent went to the window quickly, twitched the curtains aside, unfastened and threw open the glass doors. The night was moonless, and no gleam penetrated from the lamp-lit road on the far side of the house. Outside the path of radiance shed from the open window, it was too dark in the garden even to distinguish the outline of trees against the sky. The air was heavy with the smell of wet soil. There was little fault to be found, Trent thought, with the night as a night. There was as much of nature's healing gift of darkness as could fairly be expected within the limits of St Marylebone, and the life of the earth was to be felt stirring in the warm dampness. Only there had been that noise.

Trent, loving, as ever, the mere sound of the words, began murmuring to himself:

Deep into that darkness peering, long I stood there wondering, fearing,
Doubting, dreaming dreams no mortal ever dared to dream before;
But the silence was unbroken, and the stillness gave no token,
And the only word there spoken was the whispered word . . .

'Guv'nor!'
The whispered word came from the black shadows under the wall to the right.

'Guv'nor,' the husky voice repeated. 'Can I 'ave a word with you . . . for Gord's sake?'

There was a pleading urgency in the whisper. Trent, deciding that he was really awake, and ready always to welcome and fall in with the unusual, answered quietly, 'Who's that?'

'Are you alone, sir?'

The question was asked in a slightly improved accent; and Trent, now vaguely conscious of having heard the voice before, answered 'Yes.'

'You aren't one to give an unfortunate man away, sir, I'm sure.'

'You'll have to leave that to me,' Trent said. 'You have no business to be here, you know. Who are you, and what's it all about?'

There was a rustle from the hidden bushes, and a small man came hesitantly into the lighted space on the lawn. He was dressed in a chauffeur's uniform. As he stepped forward he removed his peaked cap, and for a moment his furtive eye met Trent's.

There was a brief silence. 'I know you, of course,' Trent then said. 'You are Raught, the late Mr Randolph's manservant; you attended to me when I was staying at Brinton. I can't think why you should want to have a word with me, but if it's important I've no objection. The police haven't brought any charge against you, I believe, but they are looking for you—I suppose you know that.'

'I do indeed, sir,' Raught said. 'That's the only reason for my calling on you in this—this irregular sort of way, sir, which I hope you'll have the kindness to overlook it. I didn't dare risk standing in the light at the door, nor being seen by anybody in the house except yourself. I dodged in by the passage beside the house, sir, when there was nobody about in the road, and tapped on the window where I could see you between the curtains. If you please, sir, might I ask you a question or two? It's vital to me, or I wouldn't have thought of troubling you.' Raught, squeezing his cap in his hands, again turned his roving glance to Trent's face.

'Why should you suppose,' Trent said, 'that I am able to

answer questions that are vital to you? That is what I don't understand.'

Raught nodded. 'Course you wouldn't, sir. Well, I made up my mind before I came here that I should have to tell you all about it. Here's the first thing, sir—I know you have been visiting the house in Newbury Place, and I know the inspector in charge of the case was there at the same time. You were there for over an hour, sir. You must have been talking over the case; and if you did, you probably heard what I want to know about, sir. I'm not asking you to do anything wrong, sir; only to do a man a kindness who has had cruel bad luck, and has been treated hard for years on end, sir.'

Trent, in his little personal experience of Raught, had found nothing likeable about the man, but what he had lately learned made him pretty sure that there was truth in these last words. The appeal was one of a sort hard for him to resist; moreover, the wish to find out what lay behind all this was insuppressible.

'Let my heart be still a moment, and this mystery explore,' he said. 'Do you know, Raught, it's astonishing how you fit into the scheme of that fine poem that I was recalling just now, when you suddenly addressed me out of the shadows as "Guv'nor"— that one word, as if your soul in that one word you did outpour. You are even a little like a raven—more than you are like a bird of paradise, anyhow. And you thrill me, fill me with fantastic terrors never felt before. Come inside and explain them.'

'Thank you kindly, sir.' Raught stepped over the threshold and, glancing apprehensively at the door, took up a position by the table.

'I can't offer you a bust of Pallas to perch on,' Trent said apologetically, 'but there's one on the shelf there of George Robey which I did myself, and my friends tell me it's not a bad likeness. If you don't care about it, sit anywhere you like. You need not worry about anyone coming in to interrupt us at this hour. My family is ninety miles away, roughly, and the house-keeper who is looking after me is probably asleep and dreaming of Paisley. If she should happen to look in on us, I shall tell her I am thinking of engaging you as a model for my picture of Apollo being cast out of Olympus.'

Raught, who had seated himself uneasily on the edge of the model-throne, half rose at this suggestion.

'No, no; stay where you are. I'll make it Ulysses relating the story of his woes to Alcinous. I'll be Alcinous; and to start with, I think, I should like to hear how you come to know so much about my recent movements.'

Raught licked his lips and passed a hand over his cheeks and chin. 'Well, sir, it's a little bit awkward in a way. I mean, it isn't only myself that is concerned in that part of the story. You would always act honourable, sir, I'm sure.'

'I hope so, Raught.'

'The fact is, sir, during our visits to London last year and since, I formed the acquaintance of the cook at No. 46, Bullingdon Street; Sir Hector Findhorn's place, that is. She is a widow, Mrs Leather by name, and an attachment sprung up, as they say, between me and her. We used to go to the pictures and that, when I had my time off, and she had altered hers to be the same as mine. Besides that, we could see something of each other at odd times easy enough, the two houses being so close. You see, sir, No. 46 is just at the corner of Newbury Place, and the windows at the back—on the upper floors, that is—look right out over it; I mean, over Mr Randolph's and the other four houses in the row. I am telling you this, sir, because you will see why when I come to it.'

'I am beginning to see something already, I believe,' Trent said. 'The Randolph house was under observation when I went there—is that it?'

'Yes, sir—asking your pardon for the liberty. I am telling you the whole thing, like I said. It was me that saw you, when I was watching from one of the top back rooms at No. 46.'

Trent gazed at the man in delighted astonishment. 'When you were watching? Do you mean to say that on the morning after you disappeared from Mr Randolph's place, giving the police the slip, you were hiding in that house at the corner, almost under their noses?'

'Yes, sir. You see, sir, Sir Hector Findhorn and his family have gone abroad for some months, and they left the house to be took care of by Mrs Leather, like they have done often before, her being a thoroughly reliable person and used to looking after herself. When we came down from Yorkshire this time, I asked Mrs Leather to go out with me on the Wednesday evening, but she was not feeling well enough for it, her digestion being out of order, which she suffers from at times. So I phoned up my sister, Mrs Livings, and arranged to have a bit of dinner with her and her husband, and see a show; and that was what we did, and so I told the police when they wanted to know about where I was on the evening of the murder. Only there was one thing I didn't mention, sir.'

Trent had a lively recollection of the reserve with which Mr Bligh had repeated Raught's account of his doings. 'Perhaps,' he suggested, lighting a cigarette, 'they wouldn't be surprised to hear that.'

'You're right, sir,' Raught declared with feeling. 'Treating a man like dirt, and trying to make him give himself away, the way they do. The only thing I kept back was something that wasn't of no consequence whatever, but they were certain to be nasty about it. What I mean is, after I left the house for the evening, a little before 6:30 it was, I went first to make a call on Mrs Leather, to see how she was getting on; and there I stayed with her till it was time for me to be on my way, in her room that's on the top floor, looking out over Newbury Place, like I told you.'

At this point Trent, who had been observing the man with close attention, caught a stealthy glance suddenly directed at his face. Raught, plainly disconcerted at catching his attentive eye, continued hurriedly.

'After that I went on to meet the Livingses in Soho, stopping for a drink at a couple of places on the way; and I told the inspector that and everything else that happened, perfectly truthful, right up to the time of me coming home and finding the body and sending for the police. I am giving you all this perfectly straight, sir, which I hope you don't doubt it.'

'Well, I do rather,' Trent said gently, 'if you really insist on knowing. It is just an idea of mine and I may be wrong; but isn't there some other little thing that you are, as you say, keeping back—something, perhaps, that happened during that short time you were with Mrs Leather. Your manner just now gave me that impression.'

The colour came into Raught's pale face, and he looked sulky. 'You're taking me up wrong, sir. There *was* something happened then, like you say, and I was going to speak of it, I was truly. But it hadn't anything to do with my own story, and the reason for me asking you to help me with a bit of information. I wanted you to get it straight, first of all, how I come to be keeping out of the way at No. 46.'

'All right, tell it that way,' Trent agreed. 'It's your constructive scheme, not mine. But you did give such an excellent imitation of a man wondering whether to come quite clean or not, that for a moment I was quite deceived.'

Raught's air of resentment was not completely banished by this ingratiating speech, but he took up his tale.

'You see, sir, when I found Mr Randolph lying there dead it gave me such a shock as I never had before. I was too much flurried to think, and I took it for granted, like, that he had been murdered—it all looked that way, somehow. And I knew, sir, that if he had been murdered it might be very awkward for me. I don't only mean that I should be one of the parties under suspicion from the start, before any inquiries being made. There was something besides that.'

'Do you mean,' Trent asked, 'that you wouldn't be able to account quite fully for the way you had spent your time unless you explained about your visit to Mrs Leather, and that that would put Mrs Leather in a very unpleasant position, and that even then Mrs Leather might not be very useful as an entirely unsupported witness to an alibi for you. In the circumstances, of course, she might not—one sees that. Very awkward, as you say. You two were falcons taken in a snare, condemned to do the flitting of the bat.'

'No, sir, that wasn't the awkwardness I meant. All the same, it is true I never told them about my having been at No. 46 that evening, nor anything about me and Mrs Leather. Where was the good, if my telling about it wasn't going to put me in a safe position? And besides, sir—I don't deceive you—I did have the idea that No. 46 would be a useful place for me—in case I *should* want to get away and lie low for a bit. I knew I could always go there, so long as the family was away.'

'Yes, I see,' Trent said. 'You kept that card up your sleeve. And then, on the night after the night of the murder, you played it.'

'Yes, sir. I only had to get out of my room-window and over the wall at the end of the yard, into the alley that runs behind there. Then I walked down to Bullingdon Street and round to No. 46, and there I went down the basement steps and pushed the bell at the servants' entrance three times, like I always did. Mrs Leather got up and let me in, and there I have been ever since, sir, not having ventured out until tonight. She lent me their chauffeur's second-best uniform, what he left behind in his room. It alters my appearance a bit, especially the cap.'

Trent laughed. 'It all seems so simple. Good generalship always does. But—forgive my curiosity—why did you decide to do that, after staying at home when you had found the body, and informing the police, like a good citizen?'

Once more Raught smoothed his chin and cheeks with a nervous hand. 'Why there, sir, we come to the point; I mean the reason for me calling on you tonight. You see, when I told you that Mr Randolph being murdered made it very awkward for me, I wasn't thinking of Mrs Leather and her relations with me being brought into it. There was something much more serious, I am sorry to say.'

Trent pitched his cigarette into the fire. 'I know there was. Now you have come to it, Raught, I'll tell you—I heard all about it from Inspector Bligh.'

'You did, sir?' Raught scrambled to his feet and stood trembling. 'About the—the job at the Maidstone bank?'

'They have got your signed statement. It was forwarded to the police by Mr Randolph's solicitors. They received it on the morning after your disappearance.'

With a weary sigh Raught sat down again, his head bowed and his hands clasped between his knees. So he remained for a few moments; then, raising his eyes and staring straight before him, he poured out upon the memory of his late employer a muttered stream of curses and foul language that surpassed everything in Trent's fairly wide anathematical experience.

At length Raught was silent, and Trent went to the sideboard at the far end of the studio. 'Have a drink,' he said. 'It might do your mouth good. I won't say I know how you feel, because I've never even wanted to be as eloquent as that, but if I ever had I couldn't have done anything approaching it.' He handed a tumbler to Raught, who accepted it thankfully. 'Cigarette, too? That's better. There's a lot of nonsense talked about swearing by people who don't really understand the subject, don't you think? I mean, you may often read about some expert keeping it up for minutes on end without repeating himself. Now you certainly did wonders, but I should say it wasn't more than thirty seconds before you ran dry, and even then you used the same word nine times.'

Raught restored himself with a deep draught, and put down the tumbler beside him. 'I'm very much obliged to you, sir, for this, and for not minding me forgetting myself. It is a good thing to know the worst, they say, but it did knock me out for the moment. Now you know, sir, the question I wanted to ask of you, and you have answered it before me asking it. I wanted to know if that bank job was hanging over me still; that and the confession I was forced to sign. If you could have told me nothing was known about it, I should have gone away from here a happier man than what I have been for many a day—or for years if it comes to that. I did hope it might have been mislaid or destroyed, or that it was among the missing papers took out of the safe. Well, I might have known the old . . . might have known Mr Randolph better.

'You see what I meant, sir, when I said the murder might make it very awkward for me. If that paper I signed was to fall into the hands of the police, it would fix suspicion on me quite definite as a dangerous character, with a grudge against the old man for making me sign it. And they would be sure to think I had gone to the safe hoping to find the confession there, and that I had somehow made away with the lot of them when I didn't find it. And as you say yourself, sir, I hadn't got an alibi that would hold water. So I made up my mind the one thing I could do to make things worse would be to run off and try to disappear after finding the body. And I thought if I informed the police at once and told them a straight story it would look best for me, and I should maybe get off with a prosecution for that old job at Maidstone.'

Trent nodded appreciatively. 'You put that very well. And you know, it's remarkable what mind-readers the police are—that is exactly what Chief Inspector Bligh thought you thought.'

'Blast him!' Raught said savagely.

'And he thought that when you found next day that you were not being seriously suspected, and that another person had been arrested, you decided to have a try at disappearing, and to risk whether your confession of the Maidstone job turned up or not, because your running off would make no difference in the case of a crime that you had confessed to.'

Raught scowled bitterly. 'Well, he got me right. And there's just where it is, sir. You see what it means to me, their having got that statement of mine. It means that even if they don't get their hands on me I shall have to go on hiding and dodging, and trying to change my appearance; and wherever I may get to, no chance of any sort of job but the lowest of the low, being without a character. That's what I have got to face, sir. Well, there it is.' He got to his feet slowly.

'I am sorry for you,' Trent said in all sincerity. 'I am sorry for everyone who has put himself within reach of the criminal law; in fact, I have been sorry before now for men who had a good deal more against them than you seem to have, and who had had a more bearable time of it than you.'

'Well, sir,' Raught said, 'you didn't make the law—I know that; and me going wrong at the start wasn't none of your doing. You have treated me decent, too, like I thought you would; more decent than many a man would have done. Now, sir, there's one thing more.'

'You mean the thing that happened while you were looking in on Mrs Leather. It must be something worth mentioning, I suppose.'

'You can tell that, sir, when you hear it. All I ask is, if you do anything about it, you won't bring me in. I have put myself in your hands, sir, trusting to you to act honourable.'

'All right.'

'Well, sir, it was like this. When I went to see Mrs Leather, immediately after leaving Mr Randolph's, I stayed a little over half an hour. We heard it strike seven at St Chad's, and a few minutes after that I said to her I would have to go. We were in that top room, like I told you. It was dark outside, of course, and as I got up to leave I happened to glance down through the window, and I saw somebody at the door of No. 5. It was a gentleman just going in the door. I only saw him for a moment, sir, against the light coming from inside the passage; then the door shut, and that was all I saw. But that I did see, sir, as plain as what I see you now. I didn't think nothing about it then, because I knew Mr Randolph would sometimes have people to see him when I was not on the premises. I just went downstairs and out by the basement entrance in Bullingdon Street. And that's all about it, sir.'

As he listened to this brief recital, Trent felt the excitement of his quest thrilling every nerve and muscle, and it was with an effort that he spoke now in his usual tone.

'That was at a few minutes past seven. And you say it was a gentleman you saw. Why do you call him a gentleman? Because of the way he was dressed?'

'Yes, sir; partly that, and partly the way he carried himself. He looked—well, I don't know, sir. He looked class, as they say.'

'I know what you mean; but damn it! you say you only saw him for a moment. And if he was just going in at the door, he would have had his back to you, I suppose. Could you see him by some light from the street as well as the light from inside?'

'There's the lamp at the entrance to Newbury Place, the far end of it, sir. But I couldn't hardly have told what he looked like at all, not by that. I just saw the outline of him, quite plain, in the open doorway, as he stepped in. He was in evening dress, sir, with a top hat and dark overcoat, and I could see the top of a white muffler above his coat.'

'And nothing of his face at all, then?'

'No, sir.'

'Well, what else did you notice about him? Was he tall and thin, or short and fat? Was he knock-kneed, or humpbacked, or bat-eared, or anything else that would give a touch of character to his rear elevation?'

'Not short, sir, I should say. That's about all I *can* say, seeing him only for a second.'

'Hm! Portrait of a gentleman. Unmeasured in height, undistinguished in form, his breath it was lightning, his voice it was storm. As for his hair and complexion, he may have been a nigger for all we know. If one could have that little face of his painted upon a background of pale gold, such as the Tuscan's early art prefers, how much trouble it would save. By the way, what about Mr Randolph? Did you see anything of him on this occasion?'

'No, sir; but anyone letting a person in by that door could easy not be seen. The entrance is that narrow, you remember, sir, he would have to stand back against the wall, almost behind the door, to let a visitor pass in. I've done it so often, sir; I know.'

For a few moments Trent digested this information in silence; then asked, 'Was this man carrying a bag?'

'That I'm sure he wasn't, sir. Anything of any size, if he was carrying it, I should have seen, with him standing out against the light that way. I should say he hadn't anything in his hands at all, sir.'

'Three ringing cheers!' Trent exclaimed. 'This gets better and better. Evening dress, not short, no face and no bag! In a few deft strokes we have the man before us. Anything else you can remember? What about his tall hat, for instance? Was it a shiny one, or was it one of the collapsible sort?'

'That I couldn't say, sir. All I saw of him was just a glimpse, like, before the door shut.'

Trent considered again. 'The door shut. It would, of course. But not of its own accord, surely. Did the gentleman shut it, or did somebody else?'

'I couldn't see that, sir; it all happened so quick. But you remind me of one thing, sir—the door was shut very quiet.'

'Then did it shut with a slam, as a rule?'

'Well, sir, anyone letting himself out would have to slam it—it shuts a bit hard that way. But from inside you could shut it quite quiet if you liked. And speaking of being quiet, sir; that reminds me of something else, which I remember I passed a remark about it to Mrs Leather at the time. We had the window open at the top, the room being very warm from the stove; and we thought it was funny that neither of us had heard this gentleman's footsteps going up to No. 5. Being so close, we should be able to hear anyone walking on the flagstones in Newbury Place, without it was a cat or dog.'

Raught took up his cap, and moved to the open window. 'I won't keep you up any longer, sir. It's time I was on my way.'

'You have certainly given me enough to think about,' Trent said. 'By the way, Raught, before you go, I should like to know one thing. Perhaps you are the only person who can tell me, as you were the late Mr Randolph's valet.'

'What's that, sir?'

'Had he always used the same make of safety razor?'

'No, sir. Most of the time I was with him he used an Oswego razor, an old one with the plating rather worn. Then he took to using a Bok, a more up-to-date make, sir.'

'And that was not very long ago?'

'Only a few weeks, sir. How did you know?'

'I didn't know; I only hoped.' Trent laughed shortly and unpleasantly. 'A safety razor can be a dangerous thing. Speaking of that, Raught, I think you said the police would have you listed now as a dangerous character. Are you a dangerous character?'

For the first time Raught looked him directly in the face, and his expression hardened. 'I might be, for them as interferes with me. I don't mean to be took, not if I can help it. As for you, sir, you have treated me right, and I thank you. Good-night, sir.'

He went out into the shadows.

CHAPTER XVII

FINE BODY OF MEN

RAUGHT, as he made his way homewards to his place of refuge at the corner of Newbury Place, was in a dangerous temper. Always an unstable character, he had lived of late through days of desperate anxiety, a crushing culmination to the years of ceaseless chafing and smothered hatred in Randolph's service. With lack of occupation, self-pity had wholly taken possession of him, encouraged as it was by the affection of the woman who had befriended him. He knew now that what he had dreaded had happened in fact; that the old man's malevolence, even after death, had denounced him for the Maidstone crime of long ago. As he went through the half darkness of the lamp-lit streets, deserted almost entirely at this hour, he brooded over his hard luck. What chance had he ever been given? Raught, for that matter, like many another in cases like his, was far from grasping fully how bad his luck had been, how little the chance that life had offered. Neglect and harshness had marked him in infancy; there had been nothing at any time to tell against the effect of them. But in all of the past that he remembered and could understand there had been more than enough to be stored up as matter for savage resentment, for the soul-sick criminal's conviction that he owes the world no more than such repayment as he can make in its own coin.

The small figure, for all its scowling brow, moved with an assumed jauntiness of carriage. Raught knew well enough that he must not have the appearance of a hunted man; he was living up as he best could to the chauffeur's uniform that clothed him. He was a skilled man in a good job, a man with a character and prospects; he was nobody's football. It was well done, and the one or two policemen whom he passed had no more than a glance for him.

Even less reason, it seemed, was there to look for any trouble from the solitary person to be seen as Raught turned up the long westward side of Purbeck Square. The tall man who was approaching him from the other end of the line of solid Georgian houses was, to any experienced eye, a slightly intoxicated gentleman. His clothes and bearing, the just perceptible deviation from the straight line in his walk, the occasional pause to gaze attentively at nothing in particular, could easily be made out in the lamplight. They told their own story; and it was one with which Raught had no fault to find. He was less afraid of gentlemen than of most other kinds of men; for instinct told him that, however detestable a gentleman's personal character might be, he was usually not inclined to be censorious or even inquisitive about the conduct of his fellow-creatures. As for the condition in which this particular gentleman was, Raught made the natural assumption that, in what was evidently an early stage of it, tipsiness would conduce to an amiability that was even more to be approved than indifference.

But in this assumption Raught was ill-advised. There are some natures which are too complex to conform to any recognized standard of behaviour; which are, in other words, unpleasant natures. This was eminently true of the person whom Raught was now able to recognize as they approached each other, both coming under the white beams of a street lamp. It was Eugene Wetherill, on his way home from a private place of resort where gambling was the principal attraction, and champagne figured as a popular sub-motive. Wetherill had done, for once in a way, pretty well at both sources of entertainment. He was in merry mood; and it was among his peculiarities, when in that mood, to be disposed to make himself a nuisance. He was far from being fighting drunk—a state in which he sometimes was, and in which he was never less than a violent and dangerous brute; but he was feeling mischievous.

The recognition was mutual. On the two recent occasions when Wetherill had been admitted by Raught to the little establishment in Newbury Place, each had so far fallen in with prevalent public feeling as to dislike the other at sight. The second time, when Raught had dropped the visitor's hat in taking it from him, Wetherill had cursed him peevishly, and had been silently cursed in return in language much less printable. Now, as Raught was about to pass him by with a studiously blank expression, Wetherill suddenly shot out an arm and gripped the little man's shoulder.

'Well, well! See who's here!' he crowed. 'Murdered millionaire's damned ugly-looking devil of a manservant, disappeared in highly s'picious cir'mstances. Where you going to, my pretty maid? You know you're wanted by police? Damn queer taste to want you I must say; but police always had rotten taste—famous for it. Fine body of men, admiration and envy of civilized world, but as for their taste—simply 'plorable, no other word for it! Mind you, goes to my heart to say this, but fact must be faced—simply 'plorable.'

Raught tried vainly to shake off the vigorous grasp. 'You leave me alone,' he growled. 'Let go of my shoulder, blast you! I don't know you, and I don't know what you're talking about.'

'Says he doesn't know me,' Wetherill lamented, shaking his head in sorrowful reproof. 'Cutting me in the street, openly and ost'ashously. Modelling yourself on Beau Brummel—I know you! Tell your 'stinguished friends at White's—met that damn feller Wetherill—I looked all round him, and there was an end of him. Stuck up, that's what you are—just because you disappear in highly s'picious cir'mstances, and wanted by police. All right—not going to force my society on anybody.' He suddenly raised his voice to a loud shout. 'Police can have you . . . Police!'

'You let me go, or you'll be sorry,' Raught muttered, pouring out a stream of obscenity as he struggled to wrench himself free. The man was now blind with rage and quite reckless.

'Police!' roared Wetherill again.

'Have it then!' Raught darted his right hand to a breast pocket, and thrust the nose of an automatic against his tormentor's epigastrium. There was a dull report, and Wetherill, with a deep cough, dropped to the pavement and lay still.

Instantly a whistle was blown from the end of the square, at the corner from which Raught had come.

'Go on! Blow your—flute!' Raught screamed. He kicked the body viciously. 'You won't bring *him* back!' He fired a wild shot towards the uniformed figure that was now to be seen coming up at a run, and took to his heels in the opposite direction.

Half-way down Lapworth Street, turning at a right angle out of Purbeck Square, the black cat in residence at No. 38 was sitting upon the steps, submitting with dignified condescension to being tickled behind the ears by Constable Mavor. Such attention to any small animal was automatic with that officer. What was really occupying his mind at the moment was his chance of being included in the divisional first eleven at the opening of the season. The time had come for it, he thought; he had given his proofs. If they had any sense they ought to play him for his bowling alone, good enough as he was all round; and this, as he was happily conscious, was not merely his own idea, but an opinion widely held even among his seniors.

But Constable Mavor had another and yet more serious interest in life—the desire for advancement in his career. It was never far from his thoughts. He had devoted his capable and alert intelligence to those studies of police technique and the operation of the law which were a part of the routine of the force; and he had notions of his own. When his chance came, he would, he believed, be fully prepared for it.

All this side of Mavor's nature was startled into tense activity by a distant shout, 'Police!' from round the corner in Purbeck Square. The black cat, from whose ears his hand had been withdrawn as abruptly as if they were red-hot, stared after him with cool disdain as he departed at a brisk, athletic trot, pulling out his watch and noting the time as he went. Mavor was ready for business.

There was another shout, and then a sound that opened Mavor's eyes more wide, and brought a new light into them. It was that flat report for which American experts in homicide have coined the expressive word 'Ker-bap!'; and it was followed immediately by the deep buzzing chord of a police whistle. As Mavor quickened his pace, he pressed his helmet firmly down on his head, shifted the strap slightly on his chin to get the maximum tension, and drew his baton.

Another shot sounded; and then round the corner from the square, now some twenty yards away, a small man came pelting straight towards him. As the fugitive raised his hand with a menacing yell, Mavor could see the glint of lamplight on the automatic. Instantly he ducked his head, 'covering up' with his helmet and arms, and charged like a bull at a gate. A moment before the impact, there came a shattering pang in his left shoulder and the clap of the pistol deafened him; then Raught was down, fighting like a maniac to throw off the weight of Mavor's thirteen stone, and to free the right arm to whose wrist Mavor was clinging with the only hand he now could use.

All was over in the space of a few seconds. Before the first policeman could reach the scene of the wild-cat scramble, and while windows and doors were being flung open all the length of the street, the rising tumult of shouts and screams was cloven by a fourth report.

Helmetless, breathless, white from the pain of his broken bone, and with blood running into his eyes from a cut on the forehead, Constable Mavor rose on his knees and looked down at the ugly sight before him.

'—the—!' he panted, while his right hand pressed his wounded shoulder. 'He's done himself in after all!'

CHAPTER XVIII

INFORMATION RECEIVED

WHEN Raught had taken his leave after the secret interview in Trent's studio, it was already midnight; and for more than an hour afterwards Trent had sat smoking and gazing into the fire as his mind played vehemently with the new train of ideas called into being by the story to which he had listened. The fire was nearly cold when he knocked out the last pipe and went to his bedroom. Sleep, when it came at last, was broken and unrefreshing; but a clear view and a testing purpose had already begun to shape themselves after so much fumbling in the dark.

It was late in the following morning when, at work in his studio, he was called to the telephone and heard, to his surprise, the clear voice of Verney inquiring for him.

'I rang you up,' Verney said, 'about something I am sure you would like to hear, and besides that, you are the only person I can think of who might be able to do something about it. It's about Dr Fairman. I know you are a friend of his. It is a rather long story for telling over the phone. Can I see you about it sometime today?'

'Yes, of course.' Trent thought swiftly a few moments. 'I think you told me you spend most of your time at the Randolph Institute. If you are going to be there this evening, how would it suit you if I were to call there somewhere about six o'clock. I've never seen the place, you know, and I should like to if I may. I can't make it earlier, because I shall be working here as long as the light lasts.'

'That will be just the thing,' Verney said heartily. 'It is just about then that we begin to get busy, and you will get some idea of what the Institute means to this part of the world. You know where it is—Marigold Street; anyone in the neighbour-hood can tell you the way. I shall be about the place, and shall be delighted to see you.'

'Right. I'll be there.'

It was a few minutes past six that evening that Trent, driving his car, invaded the territory of the Randolph Institute. He pulled up and asked his way of an aged loafer who was buttressing the wall of a public house. The man painstakingly removed a battered pipe from his mouth, spat ritually, and made a jab with his thumb over his right shoulder.

'First to the right, second to the left. You'll see the lights, and hear them damned boys a-playing ball.'

He replaced his pipe and turned again to his Atlantean task with a finality that dried up any further inquiries on the tongue of Trent, who felt curious to know how any boys, whatever their spiritual state, could be playing ball in those narrow and crowded streets.

The answer came to him as soon as he had reached the second to the left. There was a blaze of light from the top of a high building. Its flat roof was covered by a vast wire cage, brilliantly illuminated, and the thuds of footballs, kicked violently against walls, mingled with short bursts of applause, told that several games of 'fug soccer' were proceeding at once in the upper air of London.

The entrance of the building was as easily to be seen. A powerful arc-lamp cast a pool of light round a large doorway, by which four or five youths were at the moment passing in. Trent left his car by the kerb and followed them into a tile-paved lobby from which half a dozen doors opened, with a stairway ascending from the opposite end. Addressing himself to a wiry-looking youth who was regarding him inquisitively, Trent asked if he knew where Verney could be found.

'Upstairs, I expect,' was the answer. 'I'll find him for you if you wait here. Any name?'

Trent confessed to having a name, and mentioned what it was. The helpful youth fled up the stairs and left the visitor standing in the centre of the lobby, savouring the faint aroma of the place, which seemed to be compounded of soft-soap, coconut-fibre, leather and other elements less readily identifiable—a not displeasing, indeed a confidence-inspiring smell, as Trent thought.

At one side of the lobby, some distance from him, a wall lamp shed its beams upon a green baize board, and before it a small group of youths stood examining notices displayed.

'Somebody left his ticker lying about,' one of them announced. 'Found in the upstairs changing-room, it says here. Any claimants?'

'Does it say a platinum bracelet wrist-watch, jewelled in forty-nine holes?' another asked with affected anxiety. 'I couldn't think what I'd done with it. I was up there last night.'

'Funny ass!' the first youth remarked dispassionately. 'It can't be much good, anyway, or you'd have pinched it. Hullo! Here's Ginger. Why ain't you murdering mice at South Kensington, Ginger, this fine evening? Lost your interest in science? Or has the supply of poor dumb animals run out?'

'I wish some of you could be dumb animals for a change,' rejoined a tall youth with rebellious red hair and spectacles, who had just joined the group. 'Lord knows I can't afford to waste time, with my biology final coming on in a fortnight, but it's the library committee this evening.'

'Liar!' another youth said. 'The library committee's tomorrow, like it always has been.'

'My God!' the spectacled one exclaimed. 'I thought today was Friday.' He swore fervently, and there was a burst of hearty merriment from his sympathizing friends.

'You'll forget your name's Ginger next,' one of them said.

'You ain't a professor yet, you know, Ginger,' another said. 'When you are, it will be all right to do that absent-minded stuff—like the old bloke who buttered his newspaper and read his toast.'

'Ginger's drunk, I believe,' another said.

'Drunk with the blood of poor dumb animals,' amended the youth who had already raised this humanitarian point.

'All right; you can laugh!' the young man called Ginger grumbled. He grinned drily himself; and Trent, listening unobtrusively to the conversation, could realize something of the amiability in Ginger which his companions were recognizing in their peculiar way. 'Talk about me being absent-minded!' he pursued, scratching his nose with a large notebook, 'A pithed frog has got more mind that you have among the lot of you. And look here! If this is Thursday, why isn't young Peters out in the streets in his underwear, doing his seven and a half miles with the rest of the circus, instead of playing upsy-daisy all by himself?'

'Hark at him!' said young Peters, who, dressed in shorts and a sweater, and with one leg held out straight in front of him, was going repeatedly and rapidly through the motions of sitting on an imaginary stool and rising from it. 'Wednesday's the day for the grind now, you old fathead, and has been for the last month,' he went on, without a pause in his invigorating exercise. 'Getting out of touch—that's what you are, Ginger. You ought to give the rabbits a rest oftener than what you do, and come here and give us something to laugh at.' He changed to the other leg.

'Your wind seems to be all right, that's one thing,' Ginger observed. 'If you're as good at sucking as you are at blowing, I might get you a job as an air-pump in the physics lab.' Here the conversation was broken off as Verney appeared running down the stairway from the upper regions, and was greeted cordially by all the group.

'I hope you haven't been waiting long,' he said to Trent. 'Hullo, Ginger! We don't often see you here nowadays. Trent, let me make you acquainted with Ginger Stimpson, the best goalkeeper we have ever had—now a man of science. Come along, we'll go up to my office—it's on the first floor.' He led the way up the lino-covered stairs to a big reading-room, having at one end of it a bar-like counter presided over by an elderly woman engaged in darning a sock. Here a number of youths were sitting round the long table occupied with papers and magazines, and enjoying refreshments among which cocoa had a popular place. From overhead came faintly the noise of ping-pong, mingled with stampings and thuddings that told of some more robust forms of exercise—boxing and gymnastics, as Trent could guess.

Verney opened a door half-way down the reading-room, disclosing a small room of strictly utilitarian aspect, with a roll-top desk, a plain table and a filing-cabinet of green-painted metal for its principal furniture. As they entered, a tall and lean old man with a neat white beard and gold-rimmed spectacles rose alertly from the table, where he had been busy with a ruler and a fountain pen.

'This is Mr Bowes, who is kind enough to take a lot of the work of this place off my shoulders,' Verney said. 'This is the friend I told you about, Bowes—Mr Trent.'

The expression of Mr Bowes's pink face was open and generous. 'Pleased to meet you,' he said, shaking hands vigorously. 'It was you who were to have done a portrait of the governor for us, I believe. A terrible business that, sir—terrible. I was out of town when it happened, and heard nothing about it until I saw the headlines in the paper. I never had such a shock. I came back to London at once—not that I could do anything or be of any use; but you know how it is. I take a great interest in the Randolph Institute, and I wanted to hear what was likely to happen about that, and to talk the thing over with our friend Verney. I did hope that the inquest would throw some light on the mystery of the murder; but it was adjourned—I suppose you saw that—as soon as they had taken the doctor's evidence, which didn't tell you any more than was in the papers at first.'

'It is what usually happens,' Trent said, 'when the police are still busy with their inquiries.'

'So I am told,' Mr Bowes said. 'Well, we don't know what it is going to mean for us here, if it is true that Randolph left no will, as Verney believes. But the Lord will provide; that is what I always say. Anyhow, we carry on, sir, even in the shadow of death. I am busy with the scheme for the boxing tournament, Verney; it ought to have been ready sooner. You were quite right about my needing a holiday, my dear boy; I am feeling twice the man I was; but it has got me a little behindhand with some of the jobs. I will get on with it in the library, and stick it up before I go. I know you two have something private to talk about.'

'Thanks very much, Bowes,' Verney said, as the old gentleman gathered his papers together and went out. 'That is one of the Institute's best friends,' Verney went on. 'A wealthy man, retired from business, and unmarried, who devotes himself to church work and practical philanthropy. He has been kindness itself to me personally, too. Bowes is a man with few friends, in spite of his having a heart of gold, and I think this is about the only social life he has. He spends half his time here, and I don't know what I should do without him.' He motioned Trent to the bentwood arm-chair just vacated by Mr Bowes, and, gently expelling a curled-up black kitten from the one which stood before the desk, took it himself.

'You are a cat-lover?' hazarded Trent as he seated himself.

'Not in a general way,' Verney said. 'I haven't got a horror of cats, as some people are said to have; but I would rather have their room than their company if I had any choice in the matter. It makes all the difference, though, when a black kitten walks into your room and makes itself at home, as this one did about a week ago. Some good luck is what I need just now, by way of a change.' He handed over a box of cigarettes. 'Please help yourself, and excuse me if I don't join you. That one I had at your place was my only smoke in two years or thereabouts, and in any case I should never smoke here. It's a habit that doesn't do boys any good—they always overdo it. I know I used to.'

'You are quite right.' Trent took and lighted a cigarette. 'If any of them see me at it, you can always tell them I am a broken-down debauchee with one foot in the grave, and that it all began with smoking.'

Verney smiled grimly. 'You don't look the part, I'm afraid. Well, I suppose I need not worry about such things now—perhaps that is what you're thinking too. I shall very likely not be here much longer. Just how long I don't know. There are a few friends of the Institute, men of means, who have got together and guaranteed the expenses for some time ahead. Dear old Bowes was the leading spirit in that. It is generally believed that some person or persons will turn up claiming to be next-of-kin—may have turned up already, for all I know; and we hope that whoever does ultimately inherit Randolph's money will decide to keep the place going. But the future is absolutely uncertain. We can but wait and see.

'And now about your friend, Dr Fairman. The position really is amazing. To begin with, we know he was arrested on the day after the murder and charged with attempting suicide; and as the newspapers have published the fact that he had lost his job at the Randolph Hospital, it is generally assumed that he is suspected of the murder as well. Now that is simply incredible to me. I don't know him intimately, and you do; but I have had a good deal to do with him when I was attending to the Randolph Hospital's affairs, and I cannot believe this. I should put him down as a man of principle and rather unusually strong character, the last in the world to have any hand in such a crime. Why he was discharged from his position at the hospital I haven't the least idea, but if the suggestion is that it made a murderer of a man like Fairman, I should say it was absolute nonsense.'

'I agree with you entirely,' Trent said. 'For my part, I am quite convinced that he is innocent. Perhaps you have heard, too, that he has had a bad break-down, and is in the prison infirmary.'

'No, I hadn't heard that. I am very sorry to hear it now. We shall learn a lot more, no doubt, when he is well enough to be taken into court.' Verney paused, as if inviting more information from one evidently better posted than himself; but Trent decided to leave the subject of Fairman's proceedings there. At all times he had been scrupulously careful to avoid the least breach of confidence in his friendly relations with Mr Bligh and other officers of the law. Fairman's confession, he knew, was still a well-kept official secret, and that was equally true of other details of the crime beyond the bare statement which had been given out at the outset.

'Well, it will take a lot to persuade me that he did it,' Verney said at length. 'However, that is not the point I wanted to tell you about. It's this. Two days after Randolph was murdered, and before anyone knew that Fairman was the man who had been arrested, I had a letter from Dr Dallow, who is the medical superintendent of the hospital. He knew me, of course, as the old man's personal representative in dealing with the hospital's business; and he began by saying how deeply shocked he and all the staff had been when they heard of the crime. Then he went on to say something that didn't surprise me, because I knew it had been in the wind for some time. He said he had been given to understand that if the position of the hospital should ever become difficult for any reason—I suppose he meant Randolph's dying, and some trouble arising about his estate—the West Riding County Council were prepared to take over the entire responsibility of the hospital just as it stood, including himself and the rest of the staff, and run it themselves as a part of their own mental service, if that could be arranged.'

'I see,' Trent said thoughtfully. 'The county had been getting the advantage of a perfectly good institution for nothing, and the council had no objection to taking it over as a going concern. I dare say it is doing indispensable work.'

'So it is, and of a very special kind—this is the point. Well, that is what Dallow had been told, and what I had heard unofficially myself. But what he went on to say did surprise me. He asked if I was in touch with Dr Fairman, or knew where he could be found. When he wrote this, remember, he didn't know that Fairman had been arrested. He said that Fairman's leaving the staff had been due to a most regrettable misunderstanding, which he was only too anxious to set right without delay if it was possible. Fairman had been doing invaluable work, he said, and if he could be prevailed upon to come back upon the old footing everybody would be delighted, and no one more so than mine very truly Maxwell Dallow. That was his letter. I must say I was astonished. Wouldn't you have been?'

'I should. I am,' Trent said. 'One can't help wondering what lies behind it. You don't deprive yourself of the services of a man like Bryan Fairman without having very good reasons indeed. If there had been a misunderstanding, I should say that yours very truly, Maxwell Dallow, ought to be bally well ashamed of himself.'

He paused, reflecting that that probably was Dr Dallow's own feeling, if the joint surmises of Mr Bligh and himself were at all well-founded. To have done an act of injustice in submission to a threat could not be agreeable to any man's self-esteem. If Randolph's sudden death had meant, for Dallow, liberation from a secret yoke, and if he had at once set about trying to undo what had been forced upon him, there was at least some merit in that; for to restore Fairman would be to humiliate himself.

'If Dallow really means that—' he began.

'Oh, he means it,' Verney said. 'His letter could leave no one in any doubt about that. I have quoted it from memory, but I have got it at my rooms, and you can see it if you like; so can Fairman. And it is right enough, too, about the future position of the hospital. The council intend to save it, if it needs saving; the medical officer has told me that, privately but quite definitely, more than once, and Dallow probably got it from the chairman, Sir Norman Connors, who is an old friend of his. No; if Fairman gets out of this trouble he is in now, without any reflection on his character, it looks as if it will be open to him to go back to the job if he chooses. Dallow is evidently ready to eat humble pie if required. But I shouldn't think Fairman is the sort of ass to demand written apologies and all the rest of it. The work he was doing on the invasion of the brain by toxins was all he seemed to care about, and if he is able to get back to it with all the honours, I should think he would.'

'So should I,' Trent said. 'I will see that he hears all this as soon as may be. Getting him out of the hole he is in at present may not be so easy, but I have hopes of that too.'

'How on earth he got into it is what puzzles me. The whole thing looks—' Here Verney checked himself, and began playing with a pen on the desk.

'You were going to say,' Trent suggested.

'Why, I was going to say'—Verney spoke reluctantly—'it looked perfectly mad. That is just a phrase, of course; but it does happen to fit in with a possibility that has occurred to me. Isn't it conceivable that Fairman may have gone out of his mind, and that he did, after all, murder Randolph when he was not responsible for his actions? Much as I hate the idea, I cannot help thinking there may be something in it; and what you told me just now about his having had some sort of a collapse seems rather to bear it out.'

Trent rose to his feet. 'Yes; as you say, it is conceivable. In fact, I don't mind saying that I conceived it myself at quite an early stage of the affair. Probably a lot of people have done the same. Still, it is not much use speculating about that, is it? We shall get at the facts in due course. And now, before I go, I must congratulate you on the work you are doing in this place. It must have simply changed the face of life for most of these young fellows, I should think.'

A shade came over Verney's face. 'The man who deserves to be congratulated is the man who made it possible,' he said, 'and James Randolph is gone beyond the reach of our goodwill.'

Trent drummed lightly with his fingers on the window-pane. 'You know, Verney,' he said, looking out on the dismal street below, 'this business is telling on you too much. One can see it in your face. It must have been ghastly for you, of course, but you mustn't let it get you down. Look here'—he turned to face the other—'I have a suggestion to make. I remember you saying you enjoyed a round of golf from time to time; in fact, you spoke of it like a true devotee. If you really do feel that way about the game, I believe a little of it is just the treatment for you. How about a match with me at Molesworth one after-noon—next Monday, say? I could drive you down, and we could have lunch at the club.'

Verney's eyes had lighted up unmistakably at the proposal. 'I can't think,' he said, 'of anything I should like better. I know Molesworth of old, though it is long since I played there.' He caught Trent's inquiring eye, and added a little awkwardly, 'I used to be a good deal better off than I am now, you see; I have played on a good many famous courses, and I know what good golf is. Molesworth! I should say the fifth at Molesworth is one of the finest holes I know. It is like a combination of the Gadger's Hough at Strathinver with the seventeenth at Kempshill. There's the double-twisted stream that you want to carry with your second, and then there's the narrow green with the road bunker in the face of it, and all sorts of horrors behind it.'

Trent laughed aloud. 'I can see I have bitten off rather more than I can chew. What handicap do you confess to?'

'Five.'

'Then I shall want—let's see—three strokes. And Monday afternoon will suit you?'

'Yes; but,' Verney said, 'I can't go down there to lunch, I'm sorry to say. The morning will be a pretty busy one, and I expect I shall not be able to get away before two o'clock. How would it do if I run down in my own ancient car, and join you there as early as I can? I should get some food from the canteen here while I'm working—I often do.'

'No, no,' Trent said. 'We will go together. I'll have lunch early, and call for you here about two. That right? Very well then; I'll be on my way.'

Trent, as he descended the stairway to the now deserted lobby, was busy with thoughts. His glance fell on the green notice-board, and he went to inspect it more closely. There was a schedule of weekly committee meetings. There were intimations of articles lost and articles found. There was a list of the fixtures of the Institute's Soccer team. There was a plan of the route of the Athletic Club's weekly long-distance run—a beautifully neat piece of work, with the names of streets and landmarks done in red ink; the work, Trent felt sure, as he studied it, of the excellent Mr Bowes. There were some advertisements of Saturday motor-coach tours, with the football ground of a famous club as the objective in each case. There were two announcements from places of worship in the neighbourhood, giving the subjects with which their respective pastors proposed to deal in addressing their congregations during the present and the following months; and Trent noted with interest that while the one list led off sternly with the question 'What Do We Mean by a Sacrament?' the other began by asking, with tenderly reproachful irony, 'Only a Bob Each Way?' The draw for the boxing tournament had not yet made its appearance.

When he left the building, Trent found another and a larger car standing at the roadside, and a pleasant-faced chauffeur, with hands behind him, closely examining his own.

'Nice little car, sir,' the man said, as Trent made to open the door.

'You know this make?' Trent asked. 'You are a better judge than I am.'

'I had one, an older model, to look after two years ago,' the chauffeur said, evidently relieved at the prospect of a little conversation. 'There's no better value in the trade, to my way of thinking. If they have a fault—' Here the chauffeur became immersed in technicalities, until Trent, expressing his substantial agreement on the points raised, offered him a cigarette.

'You don't know if my boss is ready to go—Mr Bowes, that is?' the man asked. 'Thank you, sir; I'll risk it.'

'You know Mr Verney, I expect, if you are here often,' Trent said as he lighted the chauffeur's cigarette and his own. 'What sort of a car has he got?'

'A Ludford Comet,' the chauffeur said. 'She's old, but she's a nice-looking bus still, and got plenty of work in her, makes very little noise if she ain't shoved, good acceleration—' The catalogue of details ended with, 'Mr Verney told me what he gave for her, second hand, and I told him he had a bargain.'

'You seem to know all about the car.'

'I did ought to,' the chauffeur said. 'I have been looking after it for more than a year. It's kept in our garage, where there is space for two big cars, and Mr Bowes has only got the one. Mr Verney has regularly got on the right side of the boss, both of them being as keen as what they are about this here place. I don't say they ain't right to be, mind you. I only wish I'd had any of them advantages in Bermondsey, when I was a young chap. When Mr Verney got his car, the boss insisted on his keeping it at our place, and he didn't say no, which you might say it would be wicked waste if he had done, the space being going begging, and him living quite near at hand in Purvis Crescent. Besides, it's a pleasure to do anything for a gentleman like him.'

'Where does Mr Bowes live, then?' Trent asked. 'It's a queer thing about this part of London, that a well-to-do district joins on to a district like this so suddenly as it does.'

'That's right, it does,' the chauffeur said. 'Our place, which Silkwood is the name of the house, is less than a minute's run up the main road, corner of Pilbeam Road. Mr Bowes comes here nearly every day of his life, all but a fortnight in Torquay now and again.'

'You have been there lately, haven't you?' Trent asked. 'I

don't know it myself, but I know a lot of people make a habit of going there.'

'We only came back a week ago,' the chauffeur said. 'No, it ain't so bad. Give me Margate for a blow of sea air; Torquay makes me feel like I was in Kew Gardens of a Whit Monday. But anything for a change, I say. You can't help liking the boss, but the life here *is* a bit one-sided. Might as well be a goldfish in a bowl, almost. He couldn't take more interest in these lads, not if they were all his own sons. If we don't come here, we go to a football or cricket match when the Randolph team is playing; or if it's the day for one of these here steeplechases through London that Mr Verney is so keen about, the boss will sit at his window at home and watch them a-trotting past. There'd be a bit more variety, if I had my way. But there! It's a good job, and you can't have everything, can you?'

'It doesn't seem to have damaged your health or happiness, anyway,' Trent said as he took his seat in his own car, and started the engine.

'Yes, I'm still up and about,' the chauffeur grinned. 'Good-night, sir.'

As the chauffeur had estimated, it was less than a minute later that Trent checked his car and drove slowly past the house Silkwood. This pleasing, even poetic, name turned out to be attached to a large, glum-looking, early-Victorian double-fronted mansion, its frowning portico approached by a flight of stone steps, and a cockatoo in a gilded cage gravely surveying the busy traffic of the Willesley Road from one of the front windows. In an earlier day, it could be guessed, Silkwood had afforded accommodation for a large family and a commensurate domestic establishment. The fact that it was now the residence of one unmarried old gentleman of a retiring nature was, Trent thought, among those facts with which the foreign student of English character and customs is doomed to wrestle in vain.

The entrance to the garage was round the corner in Pilbeam

Road, a smaller and much more quiet thoroughfare, with the wall of a row of tennis courts running along its opposite side. Turning into this backwater of the traffic stream, Trent stopped his car and made a brief reconnaissance. The garage, converted from its use as coach-house and stable for some Thackerayan business magnate, was entered by a high wooden double door; and one leaf of this being at the moment left open, it could be seen that it gave inwards upon a small paved yard. At the other end of the yard was the garage itself, also open-doored, clean, dry and, as the chauffeur had said, spacious enough.

In the farther corner of it stood a car—a smaller car than Mr Bowes's—a car that Trent sincerely wished could be endowed with the power of speech divinely conferred on Balaam's donkey, or the horse of Patroclus.

But if the car was dumb, the garage and its situation had plenty to say for themselves; fully as much, indeed, as Trent had dared to hope.

When Trent pulled up, a little later, before the vast red pile of the Woburn Hotel, it was nearly half-past seven. He was told at the reception office that no one of the name of Randolph was staying in the place; but when, recollecting himself, he inquired for Mr J. B. Waters, of Salisbury, he found that he was fortunate. Mr Waters was still staying at the hotel; he had, as it chanced, come in some ten minutes before, and was probably in his room.

James Randolph, when he came down with Trent's card in his hand, did not appear displeased with life, but he owned to being a little tired of his own company, and immediately suggested that anything Trent wished to talk to him about could be more comfortably discussed over a drink in the lounge. 'It was lucky,' he remarked when he had given his order to the waiter, 'you thought of asking for me by the name of Waters. I have used it for so many years now that it's hard for me to remember what my right name is; but even if I had done, I should not have put up here as James Randolph. The news would have been all over the place in a minute, and I shouldn't have had any peace till the papers had got the whole story. I don't want to be bothered more than I can help, and it will all come out soon enough, when my application comes before the Court. I suppose I can speak to you in confidence, Mr Trent, as the inspector said. You are here about something connected with the police inquiries, I take it.'

'Connected with them—yes,' Trent said. 'I am busy on a line of inquiry which I don't believe the police have been giving attention to. But it has got to the point now where I am going to put all my results, such as they are, before Inspector Bligh. In fact, my intention is to put it in writing and post it to him tonight; only I wanted to see you first if I could find you.'

Randolph looked at him warily. 'I'll be hanged if I see where I come in,' he observed.

'You don't come in if you would rather not; but if you decline, Mr Randolph, it is going to make it much more difficult to prove what I believe to be the truth about your father's death. I have a plan in my head which I should like to lay before you. It depends entirely on your co-operation.'

'You can have that, and welcome,' Randolph said; adding cautiously, 'That's to say, if the plan seems to me as good as it seems to you. It's not my way to go into anything blindfold, you know; but I suppose you wouldn't suggest that.'

'No, of course not,' Trent said. 'My idea is to put all my cards on the table, Mr Randolph, and to tell you, first, everything I have discovered, and next, the method we can try for getting proof of what I am convinced is the truth. Then, if you think I am wrong, or if you don't like my proposal, you have only to say so.'

'Well, you can't say fairer than that,' Randolph admitted. 'I'm not the sort of chap that can't say no, if he feels that way. Tell you what, Mr Trent; this looks like being a yarn that will take some time, and besides that, we might as well be quite sure we are not overheard. How about having a bit of dinner with me here—it's none too early for me, I can tell you—and afterwards we can go into the matter in my room? I have driven up to Cambridge and back today, to look into a business there which I have some idea of taking over, and I am as sharp-set as I ever expect to be in my life. I hope you're the same. What do you say?'

Trent, who felt himself confirmed in his first instinctive liking for Randolph's very direct and unornamented personality, said yes, and said it with cordiality. They found a table for themselves in the large, fully-populated dining-room. Trent had never yet tested the reputation the hotel possessed, in a quiet way, for cookery of the more substantial sort; and he now found it to be very well deserved. James Randolph declared his conviction that, when you were hungry, there was nothing to touch the right kind of beefsteak done in the right way; and he mentioned the details of rightness with an assurance that told of careful thought as well as experience. He spoke highly too of boiled cabbage with a dash of vinegar. Trent, who since his schooldays had indulged a prejudice against precisely these two articles of diet, declared in favour of saddle of mutton; but he joined his host with enthusiasm in drinking what Randolph described as the best beer he had ever found in London.

'This beer reminds me,' Trent said, 'of all that the poets have ever said about beer. It is more than you might think, Mr Randolph. You may not care about poetry; I like it myself. This stuff makes me think of what one of them calls it—"that mild, luxurious, and artful beverage, beer."'

'It isn't only the beer; it's the way it's looked after,' Randolph answered thoughtfully. 'As for poetry, you are quite right, it isn't much in my line; but any poet that understands beer is a poet I can understand—anyhow, when he's on that subject. I am going to be a rich man now, by what I can see of it; but I don't reckon I shall ever give up beer till it gives up me. Some chaps have to knock it off, you know, in their old age; I only hope I shan't be one of them.'

'When you say you are going to be a rich man,' Trent hazarded, 'you mean that there isn't any difficulty about your claim to your father's estate.'

'Nought to speak of,' Randolph answered. 'Muirhead & Soames say they have ought to have old Mrs Waters's evidence about my identity, and she is laid up with a sprained ankle, so they can't get it till she is able to travel. But they treat me as if it was all settled. They know there isn't a will, you see. The old man made it quite plain to them, before his death, that there wasn't one, and never had been one, and that he was for the first time in his life thinking about making one. In fact, he even told them the name of the person who would probably come in for most of the money. It would surprise you to hear who it was, if I was at liberty to tell you.'

'I don't think it would, really,' Trent said. 'You see, your father told her himself, just before his death.'

'Did he, by gum?' exclaimed Randolph.

'Yes; and she told me, only two days ago. I know her very well. In fact, I thought it was right for me, as a friend, to advise her that she had nothing to expect as a result of your father's death, because the idea of her being his nearest living relative was not correct.'

James Randolph shot a queer glance at his guest, the while he helped himself prodigally to toasted cheese. 'So that was your advice to her,' he remarked after a slight pause. 'Well, we were going to keep private matters for our talk upstairs, now I come to think of it.' He turned the conversation back to the subject of food, mentioning the curious substances that many people nowadays preferred to eat. One of his best mechanics, he said, a man who earned good money, insisted on having a pound of tinned salmon for his evening meal every day of his life.

Trent wanted to know if this epicure had ever tried the fresh variety of salmon. 'He told me,' Randolph said, 'he had tried it now and again, but it hadn't got any taste, and it was waste of money to have it, costing so much more, not to mention the Worcester sauce it needed to make it eatable at all. Then there is another fellow I know who never has but one meal a day, which he takes at lunch-time. There might be some sense in that, perhaps, if it had been something like what we have been having this evening; but all he ever has is porridge and apples and nuts.'

'What does he do for a living?' Trent inquired.

'It's nought that requires much hard labour, you may depend,' Randolph said. 'He is a quantity-surveyor, if you know what that is.'

'I don't,' Trent admitted. 'But I remember reading of another famous one-meal-a-day man who might be said to have surveyed quantities, in a sense—Dr Fordyce, a professor of chemistry, who lived in days when people dined at four o'clock. You never heard of him? For more than twenty years he always had his one meal at the same chophouse in the City, beginning with half a chicken and a gill of brandy, then a pound and half of grilled rumpsteak with a quart of strong beer, and finally a bottle of port. Afterwards he used to stroll down to Essex Street and lecture to his chemistry class.'

'I should think the chemistry of his inside would have made a lecture worth hearing,' Randolph observed. 'And now, Mr Trent, if you feel like a bottle of port on top of your beer, say the word—though you must excuse me from joining you. No? Then let us go upstairs and make ourselves comfortable while you tell me about this business of yours.' He led the way to the lift, and thence to a large bedroom on the third floor.

They sat facing each other in the two arm-chairs after Randolph had produced a box of cigars. 'Before you start,' he said, 'there's something I should like to tell you, as you say you are a friend of Miss Faviell's. It's this way. When I heard from the lawyers about all the mess and trouble that was going to result from the old man not having put his affairs in order, I made up my mind that if the money came to me I should do what he ought to have done. Don't think I mean sharing it all out among other people—no fear! I can use a big fortune myself; I have got my business ideas, and I mean to try them out. But it's these hospitals and charities and that, which he founded himself, and called by his name, and used to finance entirely out of his own pocket, from hand to mouth, as you might say. My notion is to make a sufficient settlement on each of them, so as they will know where they are.'

Trent began to say what he thought of this intention, but Randolph cut him short impatiently. 'That's nought to make a fuss about. They have got a claim, which any chap that wasn't a hog would be bound to respect. Besides, they stand in my name, like. As for the others—the charities that had my father on the list of their supporters—they will have to take their luck. I don't consider myself bound to anything, as far as they go; I haven't even inquired what they are. What I contribute to charity will be off my own bat, whoever it goes to. But there is one other thing. It is quite certain that the old man meant to do your friend Miss Faviell a bit of good; and now I have stepped into her place.' Here Randolph showed some signs of embarrassment, and the trace of Yorkshire in his speech became something more apparent. 'Now this is the point, Mr Trent. I hear from you—I didn't know it before—that she was informed by the old man of his intention to leave her the residue of his estate, which would have been a lot of money. Now she is a near relation; she had been led to expect something; and I think my father's intentions ought not to be disregarded altogether. When things are all settled up, I should wish her to accept something substantial, which she could regard in the light of a legacy—and there you have it.' Randolph leant back in his chair, drew long at his cigar, and gazed through half-closed eyes at Trent.

'It is most generous of you to think of such a thing,' Trent said.

'It's nowt o' t'sort,' Randolph said atavistically and abruptly. 'What I mean is, Mr Trent, it's her having been told about it that makes the difference to me. It she hadn't been, I shouldn't have thought of it, I dare say. It's my own credit I am thinking about.'

'Put it how you like,' Trent said laughing. 'It's quite possible she would refuse to accept anything, from what I know of her. She can support herself well enough—and if she did accept anything,' he added a little bitterly, 'it wouldn't stay in her possession long, probably.' He was thinking of the insatiable Wetherill; for the news of the death of that ornament of English letters had not yet reached him.

'If you mean that she is a brass-finisher, she is not the only one of her sex, by what I hear,' Randolph remarked. 'Anyhow, that's her business. Well, keep all this to yourself, Mr Trent, if you please. I only mentioned it to you in the hope of hearing what I have just heard—I mean, what sort of a position she is in. We'll see what she says about my notion when the time comes. And now, what was it that you were wanting to put before me?'

Trent put it before him.

James Randolph listened with close attention, his face grown set and harsh. Now and then he shot out a question, but he made no comment.

'There!' Trent said in conclusion. 'That's my case, as the lawyers say. What do you think about it?'

Randolph's answer was brief and blasphemous, but it made very clear his conviction that Trent's case was a sound one. He rose to his feet, squared his shoulders, and thrust his hands deep into his pockets. 'Now, Mr Trent,' he said, 'let's hear what you propose. There's nought much I wouldn't do, after what you've told me; so fire away.'

As Trent set forth his scheme, Randolph's features relaxed into a grim smile. 'It's a rum notion, sure enough,' he said at last, 'but it might come off, and it's well worth trying, if what you say about me is correct. Come to think of it, Inspector

Bligh said the same, that day I turned up at Newbury Place; and he put it pretty strong, too. All right; you can count me in. It's not as if you had given me much to do—what they call a walking-on part, and short at that. It's lucky it is, because I'm no actor.'

'You haven't got to act at all,' Trent assured him. 'You have only got to be yourself. Now about the arrangements. Tomorrow is Saturday, and I have to see Dr Fairman—in the prison infirmary, you know, as I told you. But we have got to look over the scene of action and get it all properly planned out; so on Sunday morning, if it's convenient, we can do that. Then on the Monday morning we can see about getting your own little adornments; and then—'

'And then the balloon will go up,' James Randolph said, with a frosty gleam in his hard blue eye. 'All right, lad; that suits me.'

CHAPTER XIX

RESURRECTION

In a small room opening out of a ward in the Newhaven prison infirmary Trent sat facing Bryan Fairman, who lay back, enveloped in a dressing-gown, in a somewhat timeworn arm-chair. Trent had last seen his friend, and then for a few moments only, on the evening when he had so narrowly escaped missing the boat-train at Victoria. Fairman had then looked wildly excited as well as white and drawn with illness—in both respects unlike the austerely composed and vigorous personality known to Trent since student days in Paris. Today he appeared depressed and languid; his movements were listless and his voice, as he greeted his visitor, was apathetic. At the first glimpse of him Trent's mind was made up as to the best means of broaching his business.

'Look here, Bryan,' he said lightly. 'Before we speak of anything else, I want to give you a piece of news about yourself; good news too—at least I hope you'll think so.'

Fairman's brow contracted slightly. 'Good news about me would be a nice change. I can't guess what you mean.'

'Don't try,' Trent advised him. 'You wouldn't succeed. The news is that old Dallow has repented in sackcloth and ashes. He says that it was all a mistake, and that he is sorry he made such a fool of himself, or words to that effect. He says that if you can get out of this jam you are in now, and go back to your job, and forget that there was ever any sundering of your loves, he will be devilish glad to see you again.'

The effect upon Fairman of these words was instant and transforming. His eyes opened and lit up, his cheeks flushed, his expression lost all its rigidity, a deep inspiration raised his chest and threw back his drooping shoulders. He sat up in his chair, his hands grasping the arms of it, and looked at his friend with all the well-remembered keenness. His voice had a new strength in it as he said, 'I know you too well, Phil, to think you would tell me a thing like this unless you were sure of it. You understand what it means to me. Will you give me the details?'

Although Trent had counted upon something of the kind, the extent of the change in Fairman astonished him. Wasting no words on that, however, he proceeded at once to give, as fully as he could, the sense of what Verney had told him at their last interview. Fairman listened eagerly, and when the story was told he lay back in his chair and again drew a long breath.

'Good Lord!' he said, pressing his hands to his ribs. 'This ought to wake up my metabolism properly, Phil. I believe I shall really be able to look lunch in the face for the first time in weeks. Now I will tell you something. There is another side to this business about Dallow, and you shall hear it presently; but first, what am I to do about escaping from what you so poetically call the jam I'm in? To begin with, there is a lot for you to explain—'

'For *me* to explain?' Trent exclaimed.

'Yes, you. I feel interested at last, thank God! What you tell me has put a new heart in me.'

'Stimulated the activity of the cardiac functions, I suppose you mean,' Trent said reproachfully. 'And you accuse *me* of using lyrical expressions. A new heart! Why, you ought to be kicked out of the Royal College of Surgeons, his Majesty having no further use for your services. Well, I will explain as much as you like when I know what needs explaining.'

Fairman smiled a tight-lipped smile. 'That's all right. First of all, then, I wish you would answer one or two plain questions. Had you anything to do with the murder of Randolph—anything at all, even indirectly?'

'Absolutely nothing whatever, Bryan. Will that do for you? But what put this notion in your head? Not thrice your branching limes have blown since I beheld that person dead; but why the devil should you imagine I had anything to do with it? Never shake thy gory locks at me, old man; thou canst not say I did it. I mean, can you? Or do you? Or did you?'

'I can't say you did it,' Fairman answered gravely. 'I know you didn't do it, if you tell me so. But you remember you wrote to me about Randolph making himself a nuisance to Eunice Faviell, and said you were going to see him, and you knew how to put a stop to it. When I saw him lying dead that came back to me. Still, if I had been in my proper senses at the time I shouldn't have imagined you had actually shot him. But the important question is, Phil, does anyone else think you did it?'

Trent stared at him for some seconds. 'Do you remember,' he inquired at length, 'what the Frenchman said when St Peter told him he could enter into heaven? He said, "*Je vous entends la bouche bée.*" That is how I feel now. Does anybody think I did it? Who do you mean?'

'I mean the police,' Fairman said quietly.

Again Trent stared at him, and his face flushed. 'Oh! the police,' he said slowly. 'Does this mean, Bryan, that you know something that—but no; that's impossible, of course. Still, you must have had some sort of reason for imagining that I might be suspected?'

'That you might be—yes, I had. And it seemed a good reason to me.'

'Well, it didn't work, that's all,' Trent said. 'And I will tell you why. I did call on Randolph that evening, at six; but I was let in by his manservant, Raught, and let out again by him about a quarter-past. I told the police so myself, without waiting to be asked; and Raught told them the same, before I saw them. Another point is that the surgeon put the earliest time that Randolph could have been shot as seven o'clock, whereas by

6:30 I was in the Cactus Club with Major Robert Sellick Patmore, D.S.O. He didn't get rid of me until it was time for me to drive to Victoria, where I ostentatiously bought some flowers, saw someone off by the 8:20, and watched you just failing to miss it. Ten minutes later I was helping to start the Oastlers' housewarming party in Bloomfield Terrace, and stayed there until midnight. So there you are. Philip Trent, the well-known prison-visitor, left the Court without a stain on his character, amid deafening cheers which the magistrate made no attempt to suppress.'

'My reason was a good one, all the same,' Fairman said. 'You'll say so when I tell you what it was. But if you are not suspected, there is one other question. Is someone else—someone we both know?'

'You are making my brain reel,' Trent complained. 'I wish you wouldn't; I hate the feeling. No, and no, and no; in other words, the answer is in the negative. As far as I can say, the only person who has been suspected up to now, my dear friend, is your mysterious self—also for a very good reason, written in your own hand, and posted to Scotland Yard.'

'Ah!' Fairman said. 'So you know about that. It is part of the story, of course.'

'I guessed that it might be.'

'Well,' Fairman said, 'now the ground is cleared of all that, I will tell the story, and you can let me know what you make of it.

'It begins on the morning of the day Randolph was shot, when I got a note from Dallow—my chief, you know—telling me, without any beating about the bush, that he was not satisfied with my work and that I was discharged with a half-year's salary. Of course, you don't know Dallow. I wasn't astounded so much at his putting it like that, curtly and without preliminary. Dallow is like that. If he had caught any of the staff doing something discreditable, or if he was satisfied a man was slacking on the job, he would sack him in just that way. What did amaze me was his treating me in that style. It wasn't only that I knew there was absolutely nothing against me—he had often said nice things about my work, in fact, and I knew it was sound work myself. But Dallow, you see, has always been a scrupulously fair man, and a good fellow generally in his dry way—though for all I personally cared he could have been what sort of man he liked so long as he was the very great alienist that he undoubtedly is.

'So I was completely taken aback at hearing this from him. Still, I assumed there had been some mistake, which could easily be cleared up in a personal interview. But not a bit of it. When I saw him, he simply stuck to it that I had got to go, and that there was no more to be said; and when I realized that there wasn't, in fact, any more to be said, I simply went to pieces. As you know, Phil, I was in no condition at that time for standing a shock. I had had 'flu badly on top of months of overwork, and I had known well enough I was due for a serious break-down if I couldn't get away for a rest. Dallow himself had told me I would have to, only the week before, and had urged me to knock off. I would have done it, if I hadn't been at the critical stage of a controlled experiment—the sort of thing you can't wash out and start all over again.

'I don't remember much of what I said to Dallow when it became clear that it was a settled thing, and I had got to go; but I know it was not polite. Then I went back to my quarters and—you are the only man I would tell this to, Phil—I shed tears for the first time since I was a little boy. You don't know what acute nervous fatigue is. It is bad enough when you haven't really got anything to worry about; when you are merely at the end of your strength. Even in that condition you can get the feeling, a purely causeless feeling, that life is not only not worth living, but unbearable. It's the state in which many a man has done away with himself without any ostensible reason whatever. But when you get, on the top of that, the abrupt removal of the only thing that was keeping you more or less balanced—well, that is the end. Or so it seems to you. When I left Dallow I felt that it was impossible to go on living; and at the same time I felt, with the last relics of sense I had left, a horror of the idea of suicide—of the painful and repulsive sort of circumstances that go with suicide.

'But it's no use, I know, trying to explain to you what my sensations were. They were completely morbid, and if you haven't had them yourself you can't possibly understand. I will just go on to tell you what came into my mind as I sat there having the horrors. I thought of my old friend Raoul d'Astalys, that I used to share rooms with when we were both students at the Salpêtrière. I don't think you met him.'

Trent, who knew the time allowed to him for his visit to Fairman to be limited, had already decided to waste none of it in describing his fruitless journey to Dieppe. He therefore said, 'I have met him, though. The Comte d'Astalys—a tall fellow with large, melancholy eyes.'

'That's the man. He was not the ordinary student by any means. I don't believe anyone else knew as much as I did about the work he was doing, and especially about his study of eutha-nasia. He had the idea, you see, that a time was coming when getting rid of life by agreeable means would be a legally recognized thing; not a crime at all, but a part of the regular apparatus of civilization. Now I knew that d'Astalys had kept up his researches. The last time I had been in touch with him, a few years ago, he had read a paper on Eastern methods of analgesia, at the *Académie de Médecine*, that started a big discussion. I had written to him then, and he had replied from an address in Dieppe—he said in his letter it was a house that had belonged to his family for generations, but was now officially known by the good republican name of 7A, *Impasse de la Chimère*. I gathered that he was not very deeply attached to the Republic. The *Impasse de la Chimère*! That is,' Fairman said with conviction, 'a God-forsaken spot if there ever was one.'

'Is it?' Trent inquired innocently.

'Yes—but never mind that. I was going to say that, some time after getting his letter, I happened to hear some vague gossip about a scandal in which d'Astalys was mixed up; something that had been kept very dark by the authorities. I heard it from a French doctor who had come over to see what we were doing at the hospital. It was a story about orgies of drug addicts being held at a place in Dieppe with the queer name of the *Pavillon de l'Ecstase*, which belonged to d'Astalys. I didn't really believe, when I heard it, that d'Astalys would ever have had anything to do with that sort of thing; but when the blow fell on me as I have told you, it was enough for me that there was even a chance of d'Astalys having become an unscrupulous character. I knew he approved of euthanasia in principle, and I hoped now that he would not mind breaking the law. I resolved then and there that I would look him up, and get out of him some means of putting myself away comfortably and happily, and so as to look as if I hadn't done it on purpose. I felt sure he could do that, and I hoped he would do it, if I undertook to keep him out of it. But I didn't really think about any snags there might be; I just wanted to get going, to be doing something, and I routed out my passport and began packing a bag at once.

'It was while I was doing so that I had another idea. It struck me suddenly that this sacking me was almost certainly not Dallow's work at all, but Randolph's. More than once he had made it pretty clear that he had taken a dislike to me; I couldn't imagine why, and I didn't bother, because it never occurred to me he would go the length of ruining my life just for a whim. But now, the more I considered it the more sure I became that this must be the explanation, whatever Dallow's reason might have been for lending himself to such an outrage.

'I went down at once to the telephone and got through to Brinton Lodge. They told me Randolph was in London, and gave me the address. I thought, all the better; I'm going through

London anyhow. I determined to see if I could find him, and make an appeal to him—I didn't care what I did if only I could get back to my work. I say, Phil, I'd like a cigarette if you've got one. They'll let me smoke in here.'

Trent gave him what he wanted, standing over him while he gratefully drew the smoke into his lungs. 'Poor old Bryan!' he said, laying a hand on the other's shoulder. 'What an awful time you have been through! I suppose it's all right for you to go on yarning away like this. As a doctor, I mean, you know what suits you.'

'Do me good!' Fairman said. 'I have had a long rest; and if I know anything about psychology, letting loose all this that I've had bottled up inside me is the very thing for my complaint. Besides, what I have heard from you this morning has undone the worst of the knots I was tied up in. You don't know!' He reached up and pressed for a moment the hand on his shoulder as he resumed his tale.

After obtaining Randolph's address (he said) he took the next train to London, arriving there with nearly an hour to pass before the departure of the boat-train from Victoria. From Euston he took a cab to Newbury Place. He was feeling exhausted and ill, but he was determined to go on with the program he had vaguely mapped out for himself. He rang once; then, hearing no sound in the little house, rang again. Still nobody came, and he stepped out from the doorway to look at the upper floor. He could see that there was a light in the upper front room. The window was thickly curtained, but there was a thin pencil of light where the curtains had not been drawn together completely. While ringing a third time, he happened to place his hand on the door, and found to his surprise that it was not latched.

He pushed it open, stepped into the lighted passage, and called out asking if anyone was at home. There was no answer; and Fairman, who in his state of mental disturbance cared for nothing but his purpose of coming face to face with Randolph, put down his bag and began hastily to search the place. The rooms on the ground floor were in darkness, and he proceeded to mount the stairs. Turning to the left, he came to the open door of a brightly lighted room, and the first glance within showed him the dead body of the man he sought lying where he had fallen.

Fairman hurried into the bedroom. As a doctor, he needed no more than a moment's examination to make sure that Randolph was past all help, and he left the body undisturbed. The shock of surprise had for the moment a steadying effect, and the plain fact that murder had been done produced its natural reaction of horrified interest. His attention was attracted at once by a litter of papers, wrappings and string on the floor before the open safe, and he went over to look more closely at what lay scattered there.

At this point in his story Fairman was checked by an exclamation from Trent.

'Papers! Do you mean written papers, Bryan—written or printed; not only brown-paper wrappings?'

'Yes; a number of small packets of papers—seven of them, to be precise—I counted afterwards. Each packet was secured with an elastic band. I could see at once that the outside sheet of each packet was headed by a name in large letters, with lines of close, neat writing underneath it. There was also a thick budget of manuscript in a parchment cover.'

'Documents! This is getting interesting, Bryan; because the police—I happen to know this—didn't find anything of that sort.'

'No,' Fairman said. 'Like you, I happen to know they didn't find anything of that sort; because nothing of that sort happened to be there when they looked. I will tell you how it was.'

Fairman had bent down to look more closely at the papers on the floor (he said) and immediately his eye was caught by a name on one of the packets. It was the name DALLOW.

Fairman took the packet in his hand. It was thin and light, consisting apparently of a few letters on ordinary note-paper—as was the case, he found afterwards, with most of the packets. He looked then at the writing on the covering sheet, which was in Randolph's characteristic hand; and as soon as he had read the first paragraph he understood very well the nature of the compulsion under which Dr Dallow had been brought to act as he had done that morning.

'I am not going to tell you what it was,' Fairman said. 'You wouldn't, Phil, if you were in my place. All I need say is that it was something which meant utter ruin for Dallow if ever it was disclosed. I might add, too, that it was something he had done, very probably, out of kindness of heart. It's only fair to him to say so.

'Well, there I stood for a minute or two, taking in this discovery. It didn't make me feel any happier; it made no difference to my position, that I could see. Randolph had done his worst for me. Someone else that he had had under his thumb, I imagine, had paid him back with a bullet, and had gone off with the papers relating to himself. But as for me, I was no better off; and the wave of unbearable depression came over me again as I stood there. I was sweating at the palms, my ears were singing, and my feet felt as if I was shod with cotton wool. One thing occurred to me to do. I looked rapidly over the notes written on the other packets. They were quite evidently all of the same character. Although none of the names was known to me, I decided to do those unfortunates the kindness of destroying the evidence of their indiscretions in the past; and I stowed away the lot of them, including Dallow's, in my coat pockets.

'And then, Phil, I looked at the first page of the bundle of manuscript. Can you imagine what I found it to be? You can't, of course; yet it was the text of a book you have told me about more than once. It was that thing of Wetherill's.'

'What!' Trent exclaimed. 'Do you mean *The Broken Wing*? And he had it in that safe—of course, that is just where it would be. And what happened to that, Bryan? Did you take it? The police didn't find it.'

Fairman nodded with a lowering face. 'I took it—yes. Stole it, if you like, for that at least was Randolph's legitimate property, I suppose, though how he came by it I cannot think. Or perhaps he had borrowed it from the repulsive brute who wrote it. I didn't care. I only knew I wasn't going to leave that infamous thing lying about for anyone else to see. So I put it under my arm and carried it off; and at the present moment it is at the bottom of the Channel, tied up in a bundle along with the other papers.'

'Good!' Trent said with keen satisfaction. 'And what then, Bryan?'

'Why then, handling those packets of letters, as most of them were, I was reminded of something. I thought I would send a farewell note to yourself, Phil, as my best friend, saying a few of the things that one leaves unspoken as a rule, before I took the final step. I meant to write it in the boat-train. I had pen and pencil on me, stamps in my note-case; but I had no paper. There was none to be seen in the bedroom, and I hurried downstairs thinking I would forage for some in the living-room before I left the place.'

Fairman had entered the front room on the ground floor, and switched on the lights. He saw the writing-table at once, and upon it the open-fronted cabinet with its ample choice of what he was seeking. He helped himself to a number of sheets of blank paper and some envelopes; and as he was doing so, his eye was caught by the names written on the visible leaf of the engagement-block that stood on the top of the cabinet. He gazed in bewilderment at the neatly pencilled record that would speak so plainly to those looking for light on the matter of Randolph's death.

'1:15, Eunice, Porter's,' he read. '6, Trent.' And at the bottom of the page, '7:45, Tabarders', followed by a printed sentence from one of the *Epistles*.

The name of Eunice in this context was quite unmeaning to Fairman. The mere name was a stab to his sensibilities;

and for an instant he wondered hazily how this note of an appointment with Randolph could be reconciled with what he had heard of her resentment at the old man's attempts to win her favour. But, what fixed his attention was the name of his friend, put down for a visit that had preceded by little more than an hour his own unappointed appearance on the scene of a fatal crime.

'You can see for yourself, Phil,' Fairman said, 'how it might look to anyone in a state of mental incoherence. Muzzy as I was, I simply wasn't capable of thinking straight. The nearest I could get to putting my ideas together was something like this: "Here is Randolph shot dead—Phil was here with Randolph only a short time ago—Phil came here intending to have a row with Randolph—Phil may be suspected, whether he did it or not." And at that point, you see, I had my brilliant inspiration.'

Trent looked fixedly at his friend. 'Yes,' he said slowly. 'I begin to see.'

'If I was going to make an end of myself, as I very certainly meant to do in any case, here was the chance of doing it to some purpose. You have saved my life, which is the sort of thing a man doesn't forget—'

'A man might try,' Trent said impatiently. 'Anyone who happens to be a good swimmer is not a hero because he rescues someone who isn't; if he didn't, he ought to be drowned himself. I would have done the same for anybody; you know that.'

Fairman laughed gently. 'Yes, I know that. But it happened to be me, through no fault of yours, and it is one of those little trifles that stick in one's memory, as I was saying. And so, when I saw your name written there, inviting the attention of anyone looking into the matter of Randolph's murder, my mind was made up in a moment. Then I just did the first things that came into my head. I tore off the leaf from the block and stuck it in my pocket. I went out into the passage and ripped the label with my name on it off the bag, and chucked it into a corner. Then, just as I was going, I thought about fingerprints; so I went upstairs again to the bedroom, where I had noticed the water-bottle and glass, and took a drink.

'After that I cleared out as quick as I could, and hailed a taxi in Bullingdon Street. I had been much longer at Randolph's than I had ever anticipated, and I had only just time to book a passage and catch the train—as you saw. That was another little jolt for me.' Fairman closed his eyes with a reminiscent smile. 'There you were, as cool as Christmas, and evidently with not the least idea of fleeing the country—in fact, looking a little bit bored, I thought—and there was I, flustered and feverish and right at the end of my tether, feeling far worse than I should have done if I had shot the old man myself.'

After this brief glimpse of his friend, Fairman said, he had taken his seat at the table in the Pullman and begun to consider what he should do. He had already settled it with himself that he would leave behind him a letter to the police stating that he was guilty of the murder of Randolph. Deciding on the form of the letter was not so easy. He began and then abandoned first one, then another; in the end he came to see that the more of detail he put into the story, the more chance there was of its being discredited by some small, unrealized error. The final letter satisfied him as being the barest possible form that could be given to his false confession; and he had posted it at the station office at Newhaven.

One disconcerting thing had happened during the change from the train to the steamer at Newhaven. Without his perceiving it, the leaf torn from Randolph's engagement-block had dropped from among his papers to the floor of the carriage; and it had been picked up by an old lady, who afterwards tried to restore it to him. Confused at first, he had quickly reflected that there was nothing on the leaf that could tell a story, and had simply denied all knowledge of it. In mid-Channel he had watched his opportunity to go to the side of the vessel, unseen, and drop overboard the parcel he had made of the documents taken from Randolph's bedroom.

Arriving at Dieppe about two in the morning, he took a room at a hotel, and passed a few hours in drug-induced, yet broken, sleep. He then rose, and asked to be directed to the *Impasse de la Chimère*. After several times renewing his inquiries, he came at length to that remote neighbourhood. There was no mistaking the house when he came to it—a typical *château*—but it was, to all appearance, deserted. Repeatedly he rang the bell at the somewhat dilapidated outer gateway without result, and no sign of habitation was to be seen about the house itself. The smaller house whose grounds adjoined those of the d'Astalys mansion, and which bore the name of which he had heard—*Pavillon de l'Ecstase*—was silent and deserted too.

Worn out and distraught as he was, Fairman had not failed to notice that he was being curiously observed from the windows of the large, old-fashioned inn that occupied the end of the *Impasse*. This was evidently the place to yield information about the whereabouts of the people of the big house; and thither Fairman now betook himself, ordering coffee and brandy to be served to him in the room looking out on the quiet street. But he found there was nothing to be learned at the *Hôtel du Petit Univers*. The huge man who kept the place avoided his eye when questioned, and mumbled that he had enough to occupy him without keeping watch on the comings and goings of his neighbours—if the comte was not at home, that was none of his, the innkeeper's business; nor did he know of any other address at which the *comte* might be found.

After such a reception, Fairman had not energy enough for any further pursuit of his attempt to regain touch with the Comte d'Astalys. Weary, sick, and engulfed in the blackest despair of the soul, he had dragged his footsteps back to the harbour and booked a passage by the one o'clock boat back to Newhaven. 'It was,' he said to Trent, 'the only thing I could think of. I meant to destroy myself; and by that time I was too far gone to think of anything the least little bit out of the way. Do you know what I mean? I mean that I had crossed over by sea, and naturally I had thought about drowning when I looked into the water, and when I threw those papers overboard; and now, after failing in the crazy business I had set out on, I came back to that, and never thought of anything else.

'And what happened afterwards I expect you know. I did try to jump overboard, when I thought nobody was paying the slightest attention to me; and the first move I made, a large and powerful man, whom I had been watching scratching his head over a crossword puzzle, was on me like a cat on a mouse. If I hadn't been such a wreck as I was,' Fairman added regretfully, 'I would have given him a lesson against interfering with other people's private business.'

'You didn't do so badly, at that,' Trent assured him. 'I am told that Sergeant Hewitt's appearance has been simply ruined for the time being.'

'Oh, well!' Fairman said. 'If I did anything of that sort, I'm sorry. I didn't really mean what I said about giving him a lesson—it's the sort of thing one says without thinking. Of course I soon found that he was a police officer, doing his infernal duty; but at the time when he tackled me, I would have torn his heart out with all the pleasure in the world.'

'Never mind,' Trent said. 'I don't suppose Sergeant Hewitt minds. The sort of marks you gave him don't last long, and the sort he has got added to his record for pinching you will do him plenty of good. And so you were run in as a suicide; and then, according to what I hear, you crumbled into ruins. Now, look here, Bryan; we have got to think about the best way of getting you let loose again. The only thing for you to do if you will take my advice, is that whenever anybody asks you, you give the whole story, without any reservation whatever— including your reason for stacking it all up against yourself.'

'All right,' Fairman said. 'I was thinking I would do that in any case. If you are out of it, there's no point in keeping my mouth shut any longer. But they won't believe me. There is a good enough case against me.'

'Though you say it as shouldn't, eh? Well, never mind about that; it may not be as good as you think. You haven't been tried for murder yet, you know, and if you ever are, it may not be in the precise form that you expect. You know what they are holding you for at present, of course.'

'Of course. Suicide.'

'So I thought; but I am told that the official way of putting it is rather more ornamental. A captious critic might even call it laboured. The way the law looks at it is that when you tried to jump overboard, you did it with intent then feloniously, wilfully, and of your malice of aforethought, to kill and murder yourself. It is possible that that is the only murder charge you will have to meet, and I don't think it should worry you. When you are taken to court again, which will be quite soon, the evidence as to your state of health, both before and after the rash act that didn't come off, should be quite enough. What will happen—so I am told—is that if you consent to be dealt with summarily, you will be bound over to come up for judgment when called upon; which will be never, if you behave yourself. And now I must leave you, Bryan, before they throw me out. The next time I see you, I hope and believe, you will be at liberty again—at liberty to dine with me, in the first place.'

Trent got up to go, then checked himself. 'Oh, I forgot one thing,' he said. 'You have heard me mention my aunt, Miss Yates, haven't you? I had a letter from her this morning, to say she is returning soon from Rome, where she has been making a short stay with friends. She describes an odd experience she had on the way there, between London and Dieppe.'

Fairman looked a little mystified. 'Well?' he said.

'She enclosed a little document which she thought would interest me. I thought it would interest you.' He drew from his letter-case a slip of thin paper, which he handed to his friend—a printed leaf, with a few words of handwriting upon it as follows:

APRIL 12.

1.15 Eunice — Porter's
6   Trent
7.45 Tabarders'

"Henceforth there is laid up for me a crown of righteousness,
which the Lord, the righteous judge, shall give me at that day."
—2 Tim., iv. 8.

At Scotland Yard a few hours later, Inspector Bligh succeeded,
after several attempts, in getting speech by telephone with Trent
at his house. His words were brief and guarded. 'I've got your
letter,' he said, 'and I believe you have got hold of the right end
of the stick. As for what you propose, I'm willing to try it. But
we can't talk about these things over the wire. How soon can
you see me here?'

'In about half an hour.'

'Right. Come along.'

'There's one thing,' Trent said, 'that I didn't mention in my
letter. You might think it over while I am on my way. Those
fingerprints on the razor-blade—you haven't traced them, have
you?'

'No.'

'I thought not. They were mine.' And Trent hung up the
receiver.

CHAPTER XX

A GOLF MATCH

It was a bright and lively April afternoon when Verney travelled in Trent's car to the scene of their pre-arranged golf match at Molesworth. The secretary was a different man indeed from the distressed and shaken being of the day after the murder of his employer; in better trim, too, than he had seemed to be when Trent had seen him at the Randolph Institute four days ago. The fresh, clean air, and the prospect of a little freedom from the bonds of duty, had put some colour in his firm, aquiline face. If it looked still a little drawn, and if in his clear blue eyes there was still something of a brooding expression that had not been there when Trent met with him first at Brinton Lodge three months before, he was certainly in better spirits as he talked of indifferent things, or discussed golf with that earnest gravity which Trent always found so impressive in the true votaries. He noted that Verney never said a word about his own game, or any successes that might have fallen to him; but Trent had never placed him among the numskulls of the fraternity.

Verney enlarged upon his happy memories of the course they were about to visit, the details of which he seemed to recall as readily as if it had been not years, but days, since he last played there. As the car cleared the remoter northern outskirts of London, he took off his cap, breathed deep, and came nearer than Trent had yet seen him to looking satisfied with the world we live in.

The prospect for the Institute, he said in answer to a discreet inquiry, was quite uncertain still; but he had received more than one offer which showed him that there were better opportunities than he had thought for one of his peculiar experience. The administration of charity seemed not to be an overcrowded profession; which was fortunate, he said simply, as he had come to care for nothing else.

'Not only fortunate, but natural,' Trent suggested, 'as there is no more than a bare living to be made by it as a paid job, I suppose. And it leads to nothing, does it?'

'Only to itself,' Verney said.

He began to talk of the work to which he had devoted himself; and Trent was an interested listener. Verney had inside knowledge of the working of almost every known kind of organized philanthropy, from the maintenance of Nonconformist pastors' retiring funds to the provision of lifeboats; and he showed himself to have a keen, if cold, eye for the absurdities occasionally to be met with when those concerned have least idea of being amusing. There was, he assured Trent, a small fund, recently created by will, for the annual provision of twelve pairs of knickerbockers for poor little boys in a certain parish; it being carefully laid down by the testator that the knickerbockers should be fastened below the knee, so as to avoid the repulsive impropriety of the garments known as shorts.

He mentioned also the case of an elderly benefactor who had, at great expense, presented a certain orphanage with an up-to-date gymnasium. This gentleman, being invited to perform the ceremony of opening the building, had been transported with rage on finding that no arrangement had been made for his being presented with a golden key in honour of the event; and this had had to be provided for him, by a committee struggling with money difficulties, under the threat of his removing his name from the list of the institution's supporters.

By this time they were nearing their destination; and Trent noted with relief, as they passed by the opening of a lane leading towards the course, that a small canary-coloured car was parked some distance down it.

'I never have a caddie—d'you mind?' Verney said in the

dressing-room, as they prepared themselves for the fray. 'I can't allow myself any luxuries, for one thing; and for another, the work I do among boys doesn't make me much in love with any employment of that kind.'

'I think you mentioned it before,' said Trent, who in fact had borne this principle of Verney's very clearly in mind. 'It makes no difference to me. I won't have one either. Shall we have anything on the game? Some people always like to. I am just as happy whether we do or not.'

'I'd rather not,' Verney said. 'If one's always carrying on a fight against betting among other people, I think one ought to avoid it oneself. It's a good enough game without that, if one's at all keen.'

It was close on three o'clock when they went to the first tee, and Verney, who was giving three strokes, opened the match. He swung with an easy perfection of style, and there was a sting in his drive that moved Trent's admiration. There were no other players near them, before or behind; for Trent had deliberately chosen the day of the week when the average attendance at the course was least. The conditions were in every way ideal; and both gave themselves up .to the pure pleasure of a keenly contested game. During the first half of the round the match was an even one, and the position as they quitted the ninth green was all square.

'A man I know,' Trent said as they walked towards the tenth tee, 'is fond of calling golf the silliest of games.'

'If he plays golf,' Verney said, 'it's excusable in a way. It's only a sort of swearing. It would probably mean that he was playing below his form, and couldn't make out what he was doing wrong. You get the extreme form of it in the man who chucks his clubs into the sea, and swears he will never touch one again, and then turns up at the first tee next morning with a new outfit. But if the man you mention doesn't play, I should think he was the silliest of your friends.'

'No,' Trent said, 'he is far from that. He has a very fine mind.

But he believes it is his duty to lash the age, modern life being made up entirely, in his view, of follies and corruptions. So when he sees nine out of ten of the people he knows doing any particular thing, he assumes it must be wrong or idiotic, and he feels he has to castigate it.'

'Well, golf will survive it, I daresay,' Verney said. 'If it has survived all the silly fuss that has been made about it by the golf-maniacs, it isn't likely to be hurt by the golfophobes. Especially as so many of them get unexpectedly converted, and drive everybody frantic by talking about their own performances. Anyhow, people who lash the age don't get too much attention paid to them, as a rule, do they?—even when what they say is perfectly right.'

'I wouldn't quite say that,' Trent answered, as he teed his ball. 'They get attention enough, I think—in fact, they are quite popular, and are expected to say the most amusing things. Like comic colonels when they get into bunkers.'

Trent was sincere in his compliments upon the brilliant three which gave Verney the lead at the eleventh hole. At the next, Trent drew level again, and on the thirteenth tee the honour was his.

This was an uphill beat, with a belt of thick wood flanking the fairway on the left side, and a high hedge on the right. Half-way up the slope could be seen white posts on either side, marking the direction of a public footpath which led straight across the fairway from a gate in the fence to an opening in the wood; and it was at this gate that Trent was glancing with the tail of his eye as he teed his ball.

'It's a funny thing about the number thirteen,' he remarked, 'that though the superstition about it is so strong, you never find a golf course without a thirteenth hole. It is often left out when houses are being given numbers, or almost anything else, except golf-holes. Perhaps they are immune because somebody has got to lose the hole anyhow, and that may count as the bad luck. All the same, lots of people don't like the thirteenth, simply because of the number.'

Verney heard this with a clouded brow. 'I know,' he said briefly; and Trent turned to grounding the club behind his ball.

'Hold hard!' Verney said, suddenly. 'You can't go yet. Someone's crossing the fairway. You might easily hit—' Here he broke off with a sharp catching of the breath, and the bag of clubs that he was holding fell to the ground with a clatter.

Trent, staring at him, then up the slope before them, was the picture of bewilderment and concern. 'Someone crossing!' he repeated blankly. 'You must be dreaming, my dear chap! Aren't you well?'

The question needed no answer; for Verney, supporting himself against a tree-trunk, was the colour of paper. His eyes still fixed ahead, he passed a hand across his bare forehead and seemed to breathe with difficulty. At length he turned a lamentable look upon Trent, and attempted to rally himself.

'No, not quite well,' he panted. 'Nothing really wrong, though.' He pressed a hand over his heart. 'I get taken—this way—sometimes. Fancying things—and feeling pretty sick. It soon passes off.'

Trent spoke words of sympathy. 'Well, it's a bad finish to a good game,' he ended, picking up his ball. 'You don't feel like going on, I'm sure.'

'I couldn't do it,' Verney declared with vehemence, his eyes still turned fearfully towards the distant opening in the wood. 'I can't go on, really—not up that hill. I dare not try. These attacks—they leave me in a devil of a state. I'm terribly sorry.' He wetted his handkerchief with water from the tee-box, and pressed it to his forehead. 'Do you mind if we walk back now?'

'It isn't far,' Trent said. 'I'll carry your clubs.' But this Verney would not allow. He grew more composed as they made their way towards the clubhouse, but he still looked shaken, and made brief and disjointed replies to Trent's efforts to make conversation. He refused a drink at the bar, though evidently not without an inward struggle; but he thankfully accepted a cup of coffee, and he seemed to be almost restored when he took his seat beside Trent for the run back to town.

A glance told Trent that the yellow car was gone from its halting-place in the lane near the course. It was five minutes later, as they passed a crossroads inn, that he had another glimpse of it drawn up beside the building. He saw with satisfaction that it was empty. The affair was going according to plan.

A long, straight stretch of houseless country road now opened before them, a few pedestrian figures dotting its length. A moment later there came a strangled exclamation of terror from the man at his side.

'He's there!' Verney gasped in a dreadful voice. 'He's there—again!'

'Where do you mean?' Trent asked in a carefully casual tone, as though resolved to discourage any outbreak of hysteria in his companion.

'On the footpath—right on ahead there—walking with his back to us. Good heaven! Can't you see?'

'I see two women,' Trent replied, grimly staring before him, 'with a dog on a lead.' And this was true.

'The old man—with his bag. We're going to pass him. I won't see his face!' Verney bent down and covered his eyes with his hands, shuddering violently.

Trent slackened the pace of the car, and said nothing while Verney gradually recovered himself. He sat crouched in his corner, a hand still shading his eyes, and never looking out of the car, right, left or ahead. When the yellow car presently overtook and passed them with a nerve-racking screech, he did not glance at it.

'I'm sorry,' he said at last in a low tone, 'for giving such a performance. I've never been as bad as this before—can't understand it.'

'You'll have to see a doctor at once, won't you?' Trent said conversationally. 'It isn't any use letting yourself get worked up about it; there can't be anything much that's wrong. Why, you were the picture of health an hour ago. You'll be ordered a rest, I expect, and in a short time you'll be as fit as the proverbial flea. But now, we shall be passing my place in a minute, and you must come in and have a restorative—anything you like, from tea to sal volatile, not to mention Christian drinks. You know,' he added seriously, 'you seemed to be a little more upset after that second—er—attack than you were after the first. I really think you need a bracer of some sort.' And Verney, with genuine gratitude, agreed to the suggestion.

The car came to rest before Trent's little house and studio in Grove End Road. 'Here we are,' he said, as he opened the front door and made way for Verney to enter. 'On the right is the door of my mean and virtually uninhabitable sitting-room, as Kai Lung would say. Inside it you will find a few character-less arm-chairs, a very commonplace fire, and waiting ready for us, a few drinks guaranteed to sting like an adder and bite like a serpent. For you, perhaps, a brandy and— Why, what the devil's wrong now, man?'

For Verney, entering the room first, had fallen back against Trent with a cry. 'There!' he gasped. 'It's there!'

'What d'you mean? Where? For the Lord's sake, get a hold on yourself, Verney,' Trent said roughly, and shook the trembling wretch by the shoulders. 'Tell yourself it isn't real, whatever it is. Tell yourself it's fancy. Go and shove your fist through it. There's no ghost there, Verney; it's just your imagination—no ghost at all. Nerves out of order, that's all that's the matter; or tummy gone wrong—like the chap in Kipling, don't you remember? When he saw what he thought he saw, it got up out of the chair and walked into the back room; but there was nothing there really.'

'That's what it's doing! That's what it's doing!' Verney sobbed, clutching his arm. 'Getting up from that chair at the writing-table—going into the other room—always with its back to me. There! It's shut the door—didn't you see? It's in there—in there, I tell you! My God! If it comes out, and I see the face— Let me go, damn you! Stand away from that door, get out of my way, or I'll kill you too! Let me out!' And he grappled furiously with Trent, whose broad shoulders were planted now against the door by which they had entered the room.

'Not till you tell me what you saw—who it was you saw,' Trent panted, his grip locked round the other's arms and body.

'James Randolph, you devil!' Verney screamed. 'Old James Randolph! Let me out!'

'James Randolph is dead, Verney. James Randolph was murdered. How could you see a dead man? Why should he come for you, Verney? Why should he come for you, Verney? Why should he—'

'Because I did it, because I killed him! Now will you let me go? Ah! You won't, because I tried to put it on to you— Yes, I did, I confess it, only let me go, for pity's sake, Trent. Have mercy! I'll tell everything, I'll give myself up for the murder, I'll do anything you ask, only let me— Oh God!' For he had caught a slight sound from the direction of the door leading to the studio. 'Look! The door's moving, it's opening!' And again he struggled madly to escape.

A horrible sound broke from Verney's lips as he felt a light touch on his shoulder. But the figure that met his starting eyes as he whirled round was no phantom. A tall, ungainly man with a basilisk eye stood there: and he said, 'Henry Malcolm Verney, I am a police officer, and I arrest you for the murder of James Randolph by shooting him on the twelfth of this month.'

Inspector Bligh then administered the usual caution.

CHAPTER XXI

AUNT JUDITH KNITS

CHIEF INSPECTOR BLIGH lowered himself by sections into an armchair in Trent's studio, on the evening of the day following that of Verney's arrest and removal. Bryan Fairman, who had been 'bound over' at Newhaven that morning, and Miss Yates, just returned from her visit to Rome, were already there. They had been Trent's guests at dinner; and the old lady's fingers were actively busy with some kind of knitting that seemed not to prevent her taking the keenest interest in all that passed.

'He went quietly enough,' Mr Bligh told them. 'In fact, he was pretty well prostrated by what he had been put through. But he had got enough hold on himself, by the time he was charged at Marlborough Street this morning, to refuse to say anything at all. He'll need to do a lot of thinking to get himself out of the fix he's in. He's the kind that will very likely try to short-circuit the case by doing himself a mischief; but they'll see after that at Brixton. As it is, we shall have everything in order very nicely for the adjourned inquest on Friday. You're a clever dog,' he added, turning a thoughtful eye on his host.

'If rather a dirty one, you mean,' Trent suggested, clasping his fingers behind his head. 'It's true, I didn't feel disposed to deal very gently with a man who had been plotting for weeks to get me hanged for a murder he did himself. Verney is a dangerous, treacherous beast, but there wasn't enough evidence for you to go on, as you said yourself, and I had to try and get what was wanted, simply in self-defence. To tell the truth, it worked out better than I ever hoped.'

'Same here,' said Mr Bligh succinctly; then he laughed a little. 'I wish you could have seen Bloom's face—that's my shorthand man—when Verney got as far as saying he would give himself up for the murder. I started for the door when we heard that, and Bloom cocked his eye at me, grinning, as much as to say, "Don't you wish we could put over these sort of games?"'

'And why can't you?' Miss Yates inquired.

'Because, ma'am,' the inspector explained stiffly, 'if a person in authority induces a suspected person to make a statement, it isn't evidence. That was why Bloom grinned. But there wasn't much grin about Mr Randolph,' he added reflectively. 'Why, when he came in to us through that door, what with the farmer's hat, and the little bag, and the set look on his face, he was so exactly like his father that it almost made me jump. He slung down the hat and bag, and he says to me, "If you need any assistance in taking him, Officer, I'm your man. If it was legal," he says, "I'd handle him myself, and be glad of the chance."'

'Well, you and he might have liked the job: I didn't,' Trent said, 'I simply wanted that engaging young fellow put in a safe place, where he couldn't get at me or anyone else he happened to take a dislike to. I shall be stiff for a week, I think. As for what the law will do to him now, it is no business of mine, but he will deserve it a lot more than many men do who have to face the same thing.'

Fairman confirmed this with a judicial nod. 'He ought to have been content with shooting Randolph,' he said severely.

'Just so; there ought to be moderation in all things,' Trent agreed.

Miss Yates, still knitting composedly, observed without looking up, 'I know very well what it is that Inspector Bligh has very nearly taken out of his pocket half a dozen times in the last five minutes. Philip knows I haven't the least objection, so will you all please smoke?'

Mr Bligh thankfully accepted this suggestion, and Fairman, being supplied with a long cigar, did likewise. Miss Yates's faintly-clicking needles now seemed to signal expectation in a code of their own, and Trent responded to it.

'I had been telling them all about the case before you came,' he said to the inspector, 'and I had just finished speaking of the visit paid to me by that poor devil Raught.'

'That dangerous criminal Raught, you mean,' Mr Bligh growled. 'When I think of that fellow lying up all that time under our very noses, where I could almost have put out my hand and touched him—'

'Now *I* think,' Miss Yates interposed, 'we ought not to talk of the poor wretch like that now he is dead—even if he did shoot a man nobody is likely to miss.'

'Never mind,' Trent soothed the disconcerted inspector. 'You'll get over it in time. As I was saying, I had been telling them all about how he came here, and all that he said, just as I told you last week—including the strange story of the man that he caught sight of going into No. 5 a little after seven o'clock on the night of the crime. And I was going to tell them how it was that that story put me, for the first time, definitely on the track of Verney.'

'You didn't tell me that,' the inspector observed.

'No; because it wasn't of any immediate importance just then. I told you the material points of the case that built itself up against Verney, once I began to take him seriously as a suspect. But I thought all of you might find it interesting to hear what it was that turned my nose in his direction, so to speak, because it shows how useful luck is in matters of this sort. Inspector Bligh would admit that, if he ever admitted anything. He would tell you that he would rather have a good fat slice of luck in any investigation than the most brilliant piece of sleuthing work.'

The inspector, apparently rapt in contemplation of the toe of his left boot, made no remark.

'In this case,' Trent resumed, 'it was just a chance recollection that came to me while listening to Raught; something that I hadn't remembered for years until then. It started from Raught's saying that the man he saw going into Randolph's place looked like what he called a gentleman. He explained that by saying that the man carried himself well, and was in evening dress, and was, he thought, not a short man. Now you remember that all he saw was the fellow's back-view, and that for only a few seconds; so I got him to revise his impressions, and he then added that the man was wearing an overcoat, a white scarf and a tall hat.'

'Well, naturally,' Fairman interjected. 'A coat and scarf and a tall hat—it's a sort of uniform when you're in evening dress. But I don't see how that could help you to spot the wearer. For all you could tell from Raught's account, it might have been one of hundreds who would be about at that hour of the evening in the West End.'

Trent waved him a cordial assent. 'O wild West End, thou breath of London's being, as the poet sings. As you say, there might have been hundreds of them. Put the figure higher if you like. Ten thousand times ten thousand, in sparkling raiment bright, may have been thronging up the slopes of Piccadilly or any neighbouring thoroughfare at the time. But I was thinking about the rather smaller number of people who were more or less mixed up in the Randolph affair, and I was wondering which of them this rear elevation described by Raught might have belonged to.'

'There seem to have been enough of them, at that,' Fairman observed grimly. 'And as for the description, the visitor might have been any of us in this room, as far as I can see.'

Miss Yates, still knitting, remarked tranquilly: 'It couldn't have been me.'

The sniff evoked by this frivolity was not quite suppressed by Fairman; but the sound of it was lost in Trent's immediate comment.

'There you are! That's the point, or one of the points. If you remember, Inspector, once in the dim damned days beyond recall there was some morbid idea—which you refrained from mentioning to me—about a lady being in the case. But the mysterious visitor wasn't a woman.'

Mr Bligh, challenged, eyed him with severity. 'So you say now,' he remarked. 'We all know who it was now. But how could you be sure *then* that what Raught saw wasn't a woman masquerading as a man?'

Trent laughed. 'Oh well! You can argue that. It *might* have been the Mayoress of Bruddersfield dressed up as the Ruritanian *Chargé d'Affaires*. But really the only woman who was in question at all was Eunice Faviell, wasn't it? We all know what she looks like. We all know that, however she was dressed, and from whatever angle she was regarded, she couldn't possibly suggest the idea of a gentleman. No gentleman would suggest such an idea. If she impersonated a man at all, she would look like something that—'

'Never mind that,' Miss Yates said firmly. 'You were going to say something objectionable, Philip, I know. You were sure that the man Raught saw must be a man; that's enough.'

Mr Bligh stirred in his chair a little impatiently. 'All right,' he said. 'I'll concede that. Let us get to the point. This interests me. Mr Trent says that Raught's tale put him definitely on the track of Verney. That means, I suppose, that he was able to convince himself that the tale ruled out everybody else but Verney.'

He looked at Trent, who contented himself with a polite inclination of the head.

'Then,' the inspector went on, 'I *should* like to know, certainly, why it ruled out everybody else, and especially why the devil— sorry!—it didn't rule out Verney, who at the time of the mysterious visit was supposed to be prancing about the streets with only just enough on to prevent him being arrested for indecency. I mean, that's what *you* supposed, just as other people did. Taking the story at its face value, we can admit that it ruled out Raught himself. And I'm willing to agree that it ruled out Miss Faviell. Well, who else was there mixed up in the affair who the visitor might have been? It might have been yourself, to begin with. It might have been Dr Fairman here. It might have been Wetherill, who you tell me had been threatening him. It might have been Randolph junior. And of course it might have been Verney, because we know it was.'

'Very well put,' Trent said. 'Only, by parity of reasoning, it couldn't have been me, because I know it wasn't. As for the others you mention: let us start with Randolph junior. Now I knew very well what he looked like; he looked just like his father; whereas the unknown man looked like Raught's idea of how a gentleman looks. Sir Walter Scott, I remember, put the same thing another way when describing the celebrated Claver'se; he said he had the air of one whose life had been spent among the noble and the gay. I told myself, then, that even from behind, and in a bad light, neither Randolph *père* nor Randolph *fils* would make exactly that impression on a casual observer.

'And I thought there was a good case for ruling out Wetherill. It was true that I had met him in the Cactus Club, not far from Randolph's place, shortly after the unknown man was seen by Raught; and it was true that when I met him Wetherill had on much the same sort of rig that Raught described. But there was one exception—the hat. Wetherill, when I saw him, was wearing a broad-brimmed, black, soft hat. He always did. It was a vital element in his personal make-up. I mean, Eugene Wetherill had been giving his impersonation of Eugene Wetherill all his life, and he always dressed the part very carefully. I felt certain he didn't own such a thing as a tall hat of any description; and so I didn't believe the visitor had been Wetherill.

'Then again, I didn't see much sense in the idea that it had been Fairman, because I had seen Fairman catch the boat-train at Victoria at 8:20; and at Victoria he was wearing a brown hat and brown overcoat, terminating in brown trouser-legs and brown shoes—quite a colour-scheme, really. Of course, I knew Fairman *had* been at Randolph's that evening; but it was some time after the man Raught saw. The time Fairman's train from Claypoole got to London settled that. But suppose, I thought,

Raught had been wrong about the time. Well, I still didn't see why Fairman should have called on Randolph in evening clothes; and even if he did, how or where could he have changed out of them rapidly enough to get to Victoria and catch the 8:20? That seemed to me an impossibly rapid transformation-scene.' Trent turned to Fairman. 'So you see why I thought, after hearing what Raught had to tell me, that the man he had caught sight of couldn't have been you.

'And then, quite suddenly, while I was giving that wretched fellow a cigarette and a drink—'

'Aiding and abetting,' Inspector Bligh remarked gloomily.

'Is that what they call a cigarette and a drink at Scotland Yard?' Trent inquired with interest. 'Well, I gave the poor devil what I could see he wanted. And just then, as I was saying, a notion suddenly came to me that was altogether new. While I was considering whether Fairman could have changed his clothes, the phrase "transformation-scene" had come into my mind, as I've just been telling you; and there it stuck, somewhere in the background. My thoughts kept catching sight of it again and again—and then, in a flash, I saw why.'

Trent paused; and Inspector Bligh, staring at him in a slightly dazed manner, observed, 'I'll be damned if I know what you're talking about.'

'So will I,' Miss Yates said, continuing to knit; and Mr Bligh stiffened for an instant in his chair.

Dr Fairman coughed instructively. 'What Trent means,' he said, 'is, to put it quite simply, that a certain concept had planted itself in his subconsciousness, where an association of ideas had taken place which abruptly emerged, quite spontaneously and unsought, in the sphere of consciousness.'

The inspector gazed grimly at the speaker for some moments. 'Oh! If that's all he means,' he said at last, 'why couldn't he say so? You *have* relieved my mind.' He turned to Trent. 'You had a brain-wave—is that it?—started somehow by the idea of a transformation-scene.'

'That's it,' Trent said. 'You see, I suddenly remembered Charles Hawtrey.'

His three hearers looked at each other dazedly.

'In *A Message from Mars*,' Trent hastened to explain. 'Didn't any of you ever see it?'

'I saw it,' Miss Yates said, now keenly interested. 'I went to it with the Pethertons—you remember them, Philip; their second daughter, Juliet, had very nearly married an Oriental of some sort just before that, and they were both in such spirits, I recollect, because the thing had been broken off. There was a man who came down to earth from Mars in the play, a kind of magician, who made all the furniture jump about when he got annoyed. And Hawtrey had the part of a useless rich man, very lazy and selfish. The Martian changed him into a homeless tramp, very ragged and without a shirt.'

Trent laughed. 'That was it—the transformation-scene. It couldn't be better described. And do you remember, Aunt Judith, how he was dressed before he was changed into a tramp?'

'Why, of course!' Miss Yates exclaimed. 'He was in evening dress, just going out to a dinner-party or somewhere.'

'You are quite clear about the evening dress, Aunt?'

Miss Yates considered. 'Dear me, yes! I can see him now. A very shiny top hat—'

'And a very patrician black overcoat,' Trent added quickly, 'and round his neck, inside the coat collar, a white muffler hiding everything up to his chin. That was all you saw of his evening dress. In fact, you didn't see it at all, except two ends of black trouser below the coat; his feet were hidden by some small obstacle or other—do you remember? You just knew he *must* be in evening dress, because of the uniform, as Bryan calls it.'

At this point Fairman ejaculated 'Ha!' Miss Yates, allowing her knitting to relapse into her lap, met her nephew's eye. 'Yes,' she said thoughtfully. 'I see now what you're driving at, Phil.' Inspector Bligh smiled a sphynx-like smile.

'And then,' Trent went on with animation, 'as he stood backed up against the scene, facing you, the hat, scarf and coat were all twitched off him together from behind; all done in the twinkling of an eye, wasn't it?—so that you could hardly see that they disappeared through an open-and-shut trap in the scene.'

'I didn't see how they disappeared at all,' Miss Yates said. 'They just went—and there he was, a ragged, shivering poor wretch.'

Again Trent took up the tale. 'And when he stepped forward, shivering and hugging himself against the cold, you could see the tattered ends of his trouser-legs and his aerated boots. There you are, then; that was the eye-opener for me. I saw it was, at any rate, on the cards that the somebody seen by Raught had been wearing the simplest and most effective of camouflage clothing. All that was needed was a pair of dress trousers—with braces ready adjusted, no doubt—an overcoat, muffler and hat.

'But though I saw that much, and also that it might lead to something, it didn't lead me at once to the idea of Verney. What I did began to wonder was whether the man might not have been Bryan after all, as an uncommonly quick change now seemed to be possible. He would have had to change only the trousers and shoes and hat, if the other clothes were simply being worn all the time under the camouflage. It could have been done in a taxi. Only where was the sense of it, even then? A taxi-man would certainly notice it, and remember it, if he took up a fare in one kind of clothes and set him down a few minutes later, at Victoria, in a totally different costume. Besides, if there was any humbug about the evening dress get-up, it was hard to account for that humbug except on the assumption that somebody, being about to shoot Randolph, was trying to cover his tracks in some way. And of course that was exactly what Bryan never attempted to do; quite the contrary. He simply did a public bunk, in addition to leaving his traces all about the place, and making a confession afterwards. That was what I told myself; and it was just then that another little point occurred to me.'

Mr Bligh, who had been listening so closely that he had forgotten to smoke, now sighed gently, and began abstractedly searching his pockets.

'He knows not where is that Promethean heat,' Trent murmured. 'Your matchbox is on the table at your elbow, Inspector, where you put it.'

'Ha! Thanks,' Mr Bligh grunted, and attended to his relighting.

'You two can be cold-blooded if you like,' Fairman exploded. 'I want to hear the rest.' Miss Yates knitted on in ostentatious patience.

'It wasn't me, please,' Trent said. 'It was him—letting his pipe go out just when I was coming to the part that will make your six eyes, like stars, start from their spheres. The new point that occurred to me was this. Raught had mentioned that it surprised him to see a man at the door of No. 5, because he had heard no footsteps, although the window that he peeped out of was open at the top—and Raught had sharp ears, too. Now, if that was so, the visitor must have been walking with most unnatural noiselessness; and the idea presented itself to me that he was perhaps wearing rubber-soled shoes.

'As soon as that notion came to me, things began to explode quite rapidly in my imagination. That is the way it works; the moment a match is really put to the train, off go the fireworks. It isn't at all logical or scientific, I suppose; but that is how it happens. The order of ideas was something like this: Rubber-soled shoes are not commonly worn in the streets of London during the evening hours; but they are worn at that time by Verney and his lads when leaping about the highways and byways. I have not hitherto considered Verney, just because he was supposed to be on the run at the time when the mystery-man appeared. It is known that he started and finished the run, because he did so in the presence of witnesses; but is it at all possible that he could have fallen out for some time while the run was in progress? If so, could he have got to Newbury Place and away from it in the interval?

'So there I was, fairly started on the proposition that Verney might be, after all, the man we were after. Then, as always does happen when you have got hold of the right idea at last, a lot of things began to fall into their places of their own accord. First, it occurred to me that rubber-soled shoes were not only suitable for roadway athletics, but would be just as useful for entering a house quietly—if one had a latch-key—and pussy-footing up the stairs without being heard by the occupier of the premises. It had been thought at first, you see, that the man who shot Randolph had had an appointment with him; that Randolph had been expecting him, and had opened the door to him himself—being alone in the place at the time. That was what he did sometimes do, according to what Raught told the police; but there was also the possibility that he had been taken quite by surprise, in the way I have described. And you see it was important for Verney that he should be taken by surprise. He didn't want to have the old man making any resistance, or yelling for help. There was no telling what might happen if he wasn't taken unawares.

'Then I realized that, as far as changing clothes went, Verney would not have had to change at all. What he was wearing for the run was simply the equivalent of the lightest of summer under-clothing, and he would have had merely to put on the camouflage over that, and, later on, peel it off again. He wouldn't take off his shoes at any point in the performance. They would be black shoes, you see; suitable for wearing with evening dress. By the way, Inspector, have you got them?'

Mr Bligh turned to the others with a curt nod. 'That was what he advised me to look for,' he said. 'A pair of black, rubber-soled gym-shoes. They were almost the first things I found when searching Verney's rooms this morning. I didn't find the weapon, though,' he added, addressing Trent. 'That would be too much to expect. It may be anywhere in the Home Counties, as he has had nearly a fortnight for putting it out of sight.'

'Well, it doesn't matter, fortunately,' Trent said. 'To go back to what I was saying: once I got started, there were a lot of things that came to me. Especially, some details from a conversation I had with Verney on the evening of the day after the murder, when he came to see me. His pretence was, of course, that he had not even known that Randolph was in London; that he had heard of Randolph's death for the first time that morning when Inspector Bligh had called on him in quest of information. Verney said to me then that the inspector had told him nothing beyond the bare fact of Randolph's having been murdered.'

'Naturally,' Mr Bligh put in. 'It wasn't for me to be giving anything away.'

'I know. It was for him to give himself away.'

'Which he didn't,' the inspector said. 'He handled the situation beautifully, I will say. Quite cool at first; curious to know what I wanted. Then his distress when he heard the news—why, it was a treat to watch him.'

Trent turned to Miss Yates. 'He isn't such a brute, really,' he assured her. 'He only means it would have been a treat if he had known Verney was the guilty man. That's the police idea of a bit of fun—watching the criminal tie himself in knots, thinking he's going to get away with it.' Mr Bligh's austere features relaxed into a grin. 'You see; that's when they smile a smile more dreadful than their own dreadful frown. But as I was saying—Verney told me he had learnt practically nothing from the inspector; and when the evening paper appeared, it gave merely the fact that Randolph had been shot through the heart, and had been found lying dead on the bedroom floor. And yet when Verney called on me, he was full of indignation about the cowardly atrocity of shooting a defenceless old man in the back. And that "in the back" really was a blunder. It puzzled me when I came to think about it, after he had gone. All the same, at that time the notion of Verney really knowing something about the crime seemed to me ridiculous; and I came to the conclusion, I regret to say, that Inspector Bligh had been a little more communicative than he need have been when putting Verney through it.'

Mr Bligh directed a withering stare at the speaker; and Miss Yates, still knitting, placidly inquired, 'Through what, Philip?'

'The mangle,' Trent explained. 'An apparatus used by the police for making people come clean. Of course I was wrong to come to that conclusion, and this case will always be a lesson to me to think only beautiful thoughts about officers of the law. If I had done so then, I might have got properly on to Verney sooner. But there were some other things in what he had said to me that seemed odd, though I took no more than a passing notice of them at the time. For instance, his professing not to have known the old man was in London on that day. Even I knew, from the way Randolph had talked while he was sitting to me, that he was particularly pleased with himself as an important figure in the Worshipful Company of Tabarders, and never missed their dinners on any account. It was strange, I had thought at the time, that Verney should not have known about that engagement.

'Then again, he had spoken repeatedly of the late Randolph as if he had been a totally unspotted saint upon earth—said he had a veneration for him, and that he didn't know of the old man having an enemy in the world. Now I didn't know much about Randolph then—less than I do now—but I did know enough to take him out of the class of prodigies of spiritual loveliness; and I didn't quite believe that Verney, after two years of him at close quarters, could genuinely take that view of him.

'One thing more I recalled about that talk I had with Verney on the day after the crime. He had said one or two things that sounded like fishing to find out whether I had or hadn't been at Randolph's place that Wednesday evening. I didn't rise to it, because I had gone there on purpose to give Randolph an unpleasant quarter of an hour; not to talk about doing a job for him, as Verney believed. My purpose was no business of Verney's, so I just left him guessing whether I had kept the

appointment or not. He couldn't ask me straight out, because
he was pretending not to know that Randolph had made any
appointment with me. It must have been maddening for Verney;
because my going there was necessary to his little plan. If I
had stayed away for any reason, I should probably be able to
prove an alibi if I was ever suspected at all. You see, he had
come round to call here in the confident expectation of finding
that I had already been scooped in by the iron talons of the
law. Then he saw me grinning out of the window as if nothing
at all had happened; and being already, no doubt, a bit edgy—
he must have been having a pretty anxious day—it made him
jump as if he had been shot. So he came in, to try and find
out how the land lay, and work off a lot of lies about how
broken up he was by Randolph's death. I thought at the time
that he was rather more shattered than was altogether natural
in a healthy young fellow in first-class condition. What was
really the matter with him was a very nasty jar on top of a
murderer's conscience.

'Verney isn't cut out for a murderer, really. He is a daring
man, and like a good gambler, he doesn't mind taking risks that
the average man would funk. But he has another of the gambler's
traits: he is devilish superstitious. I could tell that from several
things I had noticed in him; and when the time came, I played
on it without any hesitation.

'Well, I have told you what were the points that I recalled
from that conversation, while I was turning over the idea that
Verney might be the guilty man. And then, apart from all that,
I remembered one little reason I had already for thinking that
Verney might not be an absolutely flawless mirror of sincerity.'

Fairman raised his eyebrows. 'How was that?' he asked. 'Most
people, I believe, thought he was as guileless as an infant. I
only met him a few times, quite casually, when he came to
Claypoole on the business of the hospital; but he always struck
me as just the sort of person one could trust—open, and frank,
and a little severe; one might even say high-minded.'

Trent shook his head. 'That comes of being a psychological expert,' he remarked.

'Oh! I know I was wrong,' Fairman said testily. 'I never had him under observation, of course. And I know there is a class of pretenders who have the secret of making just that kind of impression. How was it you diagnosed his weakness?'

'I'll tell you. Verney has, you know, a rather unusual face—beaky and chinny and fine-drawn in structure, with that wide-eyed and my-spirit-beats-its-mortal-bars sort of look. Did it ever strike you, Bryan, that the least little contraction of the muscles—just a touch of the brush between the eyebrows and at the mouth-corners—would turn that expression into something rather more than severity?'

'Ha!' Fairman exclaimed. 'You mean cruelty—yes!'

'Ruthlessness,' Trent said, 'is rather the idea, I think. A cruel man has a positive taste for inflicting pain. Old James Randolph had that, I'm afraid; complicated with what he thought was religion—a depressing mixture. But a ruthless man will inflict pain for a purpose, and without necessarily getting any fun out of it. Now, I had seen Verney just once before I became acquainted with him. I mentioned it to you, Inspector; it was when I saw him playing roulette at Monte Carlo—and he didn't see me. I hadn't a notion who he might be, of course, but the look of him interested me. He had a seat at the table, and he was intent on the game.'

Miss Yates sighed gently. 'Sitting at the table,' she remarked to her needles, 'is *such* a bad sign.'

'Yes,' Trent said. 'But at least he didn't have a beastly little notebook, and jot down the results after every whirl. He knew he was playing a game of chance, and he didn't want it to be anything else. It was easy to see he was an old hand, and his gambling face, like many other people's, was not quite his vicarage tea-party expression. It attracted me as a portrait-painter. I thought that as a cross between Cardinal Manning and Lucretia Borgia—'

'My dear Phil!' Miss Yates interjected.

'That's to say, I thought it was a head that I was bound to recognize if I ever met it again. Then, a few years later, I did meet it again, wearing a rather more saintly expression, at Randolph's place at Brinton; and when I said, in the tentative sort of way we polite creatures have, that I believed I had seen it before at Monte, it answered, without the flicker of an eyelash, that it had never been anywhere near the place. So that's why Verney was filed away in my mind among those who might not, at a pinch, admit that they did it with their little hatchets.

'So there you are. I had Verney before me now as a man who was capable of telling a thumping lie without the least hesitation or trace of nervousness. A man with a taste for an amusement that often gets people into tight places, and doesn't fit in very well with the character of a fundamentally puritanical, if cheerful, social worker. A man who, when off his guard, could look more than a little sinister. A man who had seemed to me to know a trifle too much about the details of the Randolph crime, and not to know enough about Randolph's movements before the crime. And a man who could have been, so far as height and figure went, the mysterious visitor seen by Raught. In fact, before Raught left the studio that night I was turning over in my mind quite seriously the idea that Verney might be the murderer of James Randolph.

'Before I went to bed that night I had turned it over a lot more. Once I had him in mind, I saw that nothing could have been easier than for him to get hold of a razor-blade with my fingermarks on it—the thing which, as I told you, was so unaccountable to me that it nearly drove me silly. Like an ass, I never thought of its having been kept in cold storage weeks before it was planted; though in fact such marks will stay on metal for years if they aren't messed about, and I ought to have remembered it. He must have done it when I was staying at Brinton; probably during my second visit.

'What had happened, I guess, was that after my making that

indiscreet remark about seeing him at Monte, which Randolph heard, the old man must have done a little thinking on the subject. He may have decided to look into the accounts more carefully at the Institute and elsewhere; and if he did that, and found that there had been any funny business going on in that quarter—'

'Funny business!' Mr Bligh exclaimed. 'Why, what the auditors have found out already, since I arrested Verney, would be enough to get him two years. He had been helping himself for seventeen months, up to the middle of last January; after that the accounts are quite straight. Where the money went we don't know yet; but a man who is in the know can always get the kind of amusement that Verney liked in London. It was the usual thing, no doubt—he meant to put things straight again when his luck changed. It's very likely, too, that the people who ran the gaming-house got on to who he was, and threatened to inform on him to the old man, and get him prosecuted, if he didn't dig up more money. That sort of thing often happens.'

'That wouldn't matter to Verney,' Trent observed, 'if once the old man had found out for himself. The point is that he stopped stealing shortly after I had unconsciously given Randolph the tip. Randolph, as I say, must have investigated after that; and then the game was up for Verney. He would be just where Randolph liked to have people—under his thumb, where he could keep them; not for any sordid pecuniary motive, but just for the pure pleasure of making them squeak. Also, everything points to his having treated Verney as he treated Raught—made him sign a confession, which could be filed away for use when required. If Randolph did all that, Verney was not the sort of young man to accept the situation without any effort to change it; and if he meant to kill Randolph, he would naturally prefer that someone else should be suspected of the crime, as well as faking an alibi for himself. What more suitable object of suspicion than the interfering fool whose remark had so completely and disastrously upset the applecart?

'As for the blade, all he had to do was to visit my bedroom—while I was in my bath, say—find what blade I was equipped with, get a packet of them for himself, and then next day steal the one I had been using and fingering, and substitute another. Then—this is a point I got from Raught—he must have advised Randolph to give up his out-of-date razor, and to take to the razor and blade that I prefer, as countless multitudes of other shavers do—see advertisements. We know that Randolph did take advice from Verney about some things. For instance, from what Raught said, we know that it was Verney who persuaded him to get me to paint a replica of his portrait; whereas Verney pretended it was Randolph who had originated that very praiseworthy idea.

'Anyhow Randolph certainly did change his type of razor; and once he had done that, Verney's little bit of framework was all in readiness to go merry as a marriage bell. The man who murdered Randolph would, to all appearance, have proceeded to take the blade out of Randolph's razor to cut the strings of the packets, and then left it lying about with his fingerprints—mine—all over it.

'Then there was another thing that occurred to me while I was meditating in here after Raught had gone. I told you, Aunt Judith, how the engagement-block was found standing on the table in Randolph's sitting-room, with the leaf for the day torn off.'

'Yes,' Miss Yates said, smiling gently. 'The leaf which I picked up in the boat-train, and which Dr Fairman had never seen before when I suggested that he had dropped it.'

'Oh well! The leaf's adventures don't matter now,' Trent went on hurriedly, observant of Fairman's reddening face. 'All it did, when you enclosed it in your letter to me, was to clinch the fact that I was the only visitor Randolph was expecting at Newbury Place before his dinner engagement. The block was left in sight for the purpose of letting the police know that very important fact; and Bryan tore it off so as to prevent them knowing it. But who, I asked myself while thinking it over, could have left it in that position? Raught had declared, and there was no reason to doubt him, that it never was left out, but kept in a locked drawer. Who else would be likely to know of its existence, and where to find it, besides Raught? Only Verney, so it seemed to me; and so it seems still.'

Trent paused to light a cigarette; and Inspector Bligh observed meditatively, 'I've often heard of chaps who could talk the hind leg off a donkey.'

Miss Yates, shooting a glance at him between stitches, said precisely, 'That is all very well, Mr Bligh, but you have heard all this before, perhaps, and Dr Fairman and I have not. We find it most interesting.'

The inspector handsomely acknowledged the hit. 'You are quite right, ma'am,' he said. 'I was forgetting. Yes, I have not only heard it before, but I have filed a note of all these points which Mr Trent was good enough to draw up for me. It is in rather more official language, in some places; that's all.'

Bryan Fairman made a sound of slight impatience. 'None the better for being in that language, I should think,' he said. 'I know, if anybody does—all research workers know—how much is missed that really matters because reports have to be written in officialese. They have to be, because a lot of us can't take anything seriously unless you make it dull for them. But what Miss Yates and I would like to hear, Phil, is how Verney managed the carrying out of the crime. You have made it clear that he could change himself in half a minute from an athlete with hardly anything on to a diner-out in complete evening dress, and back again. But how did he do it at the same time that he was running round London with the boys, and where did he change, and how did he get to Newbury Place and get away again?'

Trent and the inspector regarded one another with some amusement. 'Exactly what I asked him,' Mr Bligh remarked, 'when he explained to me about the quick-change dodge.'

'And exactly what I asked myself,' Trent said. 'I could see, I thought, that it was possible, or perhaps easy, for him to dodge out of the procession at some point, and to rejoin it again later, without its being spotted. They run in little groups of twos and threes, you may have noticed if you have seen them at it; so as not to impede traffic, I suppose. And none of them has much energy to spare for keeping an eye on the others. Fairly easy, I should think, for one of them to fall out to tie a shoe-lace or something, at some favourable spot; and he could join in again later, when the run was nearly at an end, by falling in at the tail of one of the groups, without his absence ever having been noticed.'

'That's right,' the inspector said. 'It never was noticed. All the lads who were out that night have been interrogated. It can be proved that he started and it can be proved that he finished; but there isn't one of them who can say he had Verney in sight at any time except the beginning and the end. They never gave it a thought till they were asked.'

'Good! Of course, the place where he dropped out would have to be out of sight. So it was, as I shall tell you. But when he had done his disappearing act, Verney had to get to Randolph's, and spend some time there—ten minutes at the very least, I figured it out—and get away again; because though the line of the run goes not far from Newbury Place, it doesn't pass it.

'The only answer that I could think of was a car; and it would have to be a car that was standing all ready at some convenient place; and that place would be the place where Verney dropped out of the company.'

'How clever!' Miss Yates exclaimed.

'It's very good of you to say so, Aunt.'

'It was Verney I meant, my dear Phil. He thought of it first,' Miss Yates pointed out.

'That's true,' Trent admitted. 'In fact, now you put it that way, I'm dashed glad I wasn't the criminal and he the sleuth.

He would probably have had the salt on my tail much quicker than I got it on his. However—when I got to that point in my musings, the next thing obviously was to scout round for some information bearing on these matters; so when Verney rang up saying he wanted to see me about Bryan, I had the devilish cunning to say I would go round and see him at the Randolph Institute, where I hoped I might be able to pick up a thing or two. And so I jolly well did!

'I won't go into all the details about how I got at the facts, because that would be a long story. It was just by listening to some of the lads at the Institute chatting back and forth, and talking to one or two people who were there. But I came away with quite a bagful of useful knowledge. To begin with, I had had a careful look at the track of the weekly run, stuck up on the notice-board. I had also learnt that the evening for the run had recently been changed from the usual day to Wednesday, the day of the murder. I knew already that Verney possessed what he called an ancient car; and I found out now that it was a very good and reliable car, old as it was. Also, I learnt that he was allowed the free use of the garage attached to the house of a very nice old man, who was helping Verney to run the Institute. Also, that this garage was in a nice, quiet place, not far from the Institute, and just round a corner which was right on the track of the run. Also, that the nice old man had been persuaded by Verney to go away to Torquay for a rest and change, taking his own car and chauffeur with him; so that Verney had the garage all to himself on the night of the crime. And I think that was about all.'

'Enough too, I should think,' Mr Bligh grumbled. 'I wish I ever had such luck.'

'Perhaps you often have, and took it to be the result of dazzling detective genius,' Trent suggested amiably. 'You wouldn't think it to hear him now, Aunt Ju, but he was quite pleased when I told him all this a few days ago. It gives you the raw material of the crime, so to speak. Verney had the car waiting for him in the garage before they started on the run. In the car were the hat and the clothing and a loaded revolver, probably with a silencer on its nose. He dropped out and dodged in there, shut the garage door, slipped on the camou-flage—not forgetting a pair of gloves—then took out the car and was off and away to the West End, looking the complete swell. He left the car at the entrance to Newbury Place, stepped across to No. 5 in his rubber-soled shoes, opened the door quietly with his key, slipped upstairs, and very likely shot Randolph without the old man ever hearing or seeing him. Then he pocketed the revolver, took Randolph's keys from the table, opened the safe, and took out the packets. He could tell at once which was the Verney packet, as they were all docketed on the outside; so Bryan has told us. Probably he shoved that in his pocket straight away, unopened. Then he took the blade out of Randolph's razor and pocketed that; got out my blade that he had been saving up for me, and used that—very delicately, so as not to blur my fingermarks—to cut the strings of the remaining packets.'

'Why did he take the trouble to do that?' Fairman wanted to know.

'Because there had to be a reason for the blade being taken from the razor and left on the floor. So he just cut them all open and left them there, where Bryan found them and walked off with them.'

'Abominable!' Miss Yates remarked with emphasis. 'Other people's disagreeable secrets left lying about for the police to find!'

Mr Bligh grunted expressively. 'A fat lot he cared about that! Of course,' he added a little wistfully, 'they would have been very interesting.'

'But why,' Fairman persisted, 'did he use your blade for cutting the strings, when he had to take pains not to blur the marks? He could have used Randolph's blade for that, and made a quicker job of it, not having to be careful.'

'Verney is clever, as my aunt says. He knew that a very fine edge which has been used for sawing through a lot of string bears very plain traces of having been misused in that way. Even with the naked eye you can see them. The blade with my marks on had to bear those traces. Well, when that job was done, he took the keys again, went downstairs, got out the engagement-block from the drawer where he knew Randolph usually kept it when he was at Newbury Place, and stuck it up where it could be seen.'

'That wasn't so clever,' Mr Bligh observed. 'I should have found it soon enough without that; and its being left out like that wasn't quite natural. He ought to have realized that.'

'Yes; it was a slip,' Trent agreed. 'You wouldn't have done it yourself, Inspector. But Verney hadn't had your experience, you see. Now I come to think of it, it seems likely that all the really perfect crimes are committed by officers of the C.I.D. However, that was what he did; and then, I think, all he had to do was to make his exit and get back to his car. One thing he did was to leave the front door not quite shut, as Bryan found it later on. He didn't want to make any unnecessary noise, you see. To walk in an unhurried manner from the door to the spot just outside the archway, where I think he must have left his car, takes about ten seconds—I've timed it myself.'

'Why, Phil!' Miss Yates exclaimed. 'Ten seconds! That is no time at all!'

'A very generous allowance, I assure you,' Trent said. 'So many people think a second is the sort of time it takes to blink your eye. But a man can run a hundred yards in ten seconds— some men can, anyhow. And in America it has been proved that a good murderer can shoot up six people in one second.'

'Well, but suppose,' Fairman said, 'he had met somebody coming in by the archway as he went out. His face would have been seen and remembered.'

'Not if he had been blowing his nose at the moment, which he would have been, if he is the man I take him for. So now, Verney returned to his car, ran back to the garage in North London, put away the car, and then waited behind the garage doors until the first of the returning runners showed up. All he had to do then was to shed the outer clothing, and step out and attach himself to the tail of one of the little groups. It was all over!'

The brief but thoughtful silence which ensued was broken by Inspector Bligh. 'And a very nice bit of work too,' he remarked appreciatively, pressing down a new charge of tobacco in his pipe. 'It was more by accident than anything else that it came unstuck.'

'You mean the accident of my mind being engaged on the case,' Trent suggested. 'There is something in that, no doubt.'

'What I mean,' Mr Bligh answered with a shade of truculence, 'is the pure and simple accident of Raught having seen a man in what looked like evening dress going into the place at the time he did.' He lighted the refilled pipe.

'Which, you were about to say, provided a starting-point for the operations of my flame-like intelligence. Yes: true,' Trent said. 'The accompanying fact that the man seen was wearing silent shoes was no accident, of course. It was just because Verney was so jolly careful; and it gave him away, as happens so often in this vale of tears. There was another large-scale accident, though.'

'What was that, Phil?' Miss Yates inquired.

'I mean Raught not going out until some hours later than he usually did on his half-day off. Verney's idea was, you see, that the old man would be alone in the house when I called, and that I couldn't possibly prove that he was alive and well when I left. But its being such beastly weather kept Raught at No. 5, not only to let me into the place, instead of Randolph admitting me himself, but to see me off the premises afterwards. And as I had a solid mass of coagulated alibi for the rest of the night, that accident completely ruined the part of the plan that was intended for my benefit. And so, one thing leading to another, not even my old friend Inspector Bligh dreamed of connecting me with the crime, and I was left at large to go nearly off my head worrying about the case, and finally to get on the track—as I fully and freely admit, the fact being obvious—entirely by accident.'

'Well, if you come to accidents, Phil,' Fairman observed, 'the whole of this hideous business came of those few casual words you let drop to Verney, as you were telling us, when you first met him. Those words cost Randolph his life in the end. They will cost Verney his, I suppose. He certainly meant that they should cost you yours.'

'You might take it a step farther back,' Trent said, 'and make the trouble date from the day when the Prince of Monaco leased the gambling concession to M. Louis Blanc. It's an endless chain. Still, it can't be denied that what I said so carelessly at Brinton was a link in it. The awful power of a chance remark! But listen! I see the inspector pricking up his ears. What is that faint musical sound—as if some seraph hand, with touch of fire, were arranging glasses on a tray in the pantry? Inspector Bligh, the hour is nigh, the sun has left the lea.'

'Yes: some time ago,' said that officer, now amiably expectant. 'But I don't see what it has to do with me.'

'The nark, his lay who trilled all day, sits hushed—'

'*You* sit hushed,' suggested Inspector Bligh.

Also available

Trent's Last Case

E. C. Bentley

A powerful and ruthless American capitalist is found dead in the garden of his English country house. But why is he not wearing his false teeth? And why is his young widow so relieved at his death? Sent by his newspaper to investigate, journalist and amateur detective Philip Trent encounters a lot more than he bargained for.

Written as the result of a wager with *Father Brown* author G. K. Chesterton, *Trent's Last Case* was Edmund Bentley's attempt to write a novel that would ridicule the stale conventions of detective fiction. Unwittingly, he produced what Agatha Christie called 'one of the best detective stories ever written'. Its flesh-and-blood characters, easy humour and cunning solution became the prototype for an entire generation of crime writers, although few ever matched the genius of *Trent's Last Case*.

This Crime Club classic is introduced by Golden Age fiction expert and writer Dr John Curran, and also includes a unique afterword by Dorothy L. Sayers, who described it as 'the one detective story of the present century which I am certain will go down to posterity as a classic. It is a masterpiece.'

'One of the best detective stories ever written.'

AGATHA CHRISTIE

Also available

Trent Intervenes

E. C. Bentley

Private detective Philip Trent is an artist, a journalist and an urbane unraveller of highly problematical mysteries. Here the unshakable sleuth encounters crimes ranging from fraud and embezzlement to criminal assault and murder, yet they all succumb to his adept methods of detection.

Twenty-five years after E. C. Bentley's sensational *Trent's Last Case*, his publishers marked the anniversary with this collection of short stories, declaring: 'No apology is needed for the fact that Mr E. C. Bentley has decided it was not to be Trent's *last* case after all.' Here we have his character in a dozen exciting episodes, in which a cockatoo and a lipstick, an escape from Dartmoor, a knowledge of vintages and a prima donna's hairpins all play their varied but essential parts.

This Crime Club classic includes an introduction by the editor and critic Ben Ray Redman, whose column 'Old Wine in New Bottles' in the *New York Herald-Tribune* was devoted to reviewing classic reprints. Bentley's own retrospective, 'On Trent', plus the thirteenth and final Trent story, 'The Ministering Angel' (originally published after *Trent Intervenes*), are also included for the very first time.

'*Episodic and exciting . . . the twelve stories are far above the ruck.*'
S. S. VAN DINE

Also available

The Cask

Freeman Wills Crofts

The unloading of a consignment of French wine from the steamship *Bullfinch* is interrupted by a gruesome discovery in a broken cask leaking sawdust and gold sovereigns. But when the shipping clerk returns with the police, the cask and its macabre contents have gone. Following the clues to Paris, Inspector Burnley of Scotland Yard enlists the help of the genial French detective M. Lefarge to check motives and alibis in their hunt for evidence of a particularly fiendish murder.

Freeman Wills Crofts (1879–1957), the son of an army doctor who died before he was born, was raised in Northern Ireland and became a civil engineer. His first book, *The Cask*, was published in the summer of 1920, immediately establishing him as a new master of detective fiction. Scrupulously planting clues for the reader to find, he was continually praised for his flawless plotting, with Raymond Chandler describing him as 'the soundest builder of them all'.

This Crime Club classic is introduced by Freeman Wills Crofts himself in a unique preface from 1946 about *The Cask*'s origins.

'Detective stories by Freeman Wills Crofts are calculated to make the purist detection fan hug himself.'

DAILY TELEGRAPH

Also available

The Mystery of the Skeleton Key

Bernard Capes

A body is discovered after a shooting party in the grounds of a country house in Hampshire. The police are called in and a clever young detective, Sergeant Ridgway, begins to unravel a much more complicated and brutal case of murder than was first suspected. But has he met his match with Le Sage, a chess-playing Baron, who is convinced that the answers lie not in Hampshire but in Paris?

The Skeleton Key (1919) was the first detective novel published by Collins, ushering in the Golden Age, the Crime Club and 100 years of remarkable crime fiction that would follow. And after 20 years of writing in various genres, it was Bernard Capes' crowning achievement, as he died shortly after completing the book.

Introduced by Hugh Lamb, whose anthology *The Black Reaper* resurrected Capes' reputation as one of the best horror writers of his generation, the book also includes its original tribute to Capes by G. K. Chesterton, author of the Father Brown mysteries.

'It is a fair bet that one of Agatha Christie's most successful crime outings owed a lot to this riveting story. A thrilling read—who could ask for more?'
DAILY MAIL